Quincas Borba

Quincas Borba

— A Novel

Joaquim Maria Machado de Assis

Translated by
Margaret Jull Costa and Robin Patterson

Liveright Publishing Corporation
A Division of W. W. Norton & Company
Independent Publishers Since 1923

Copyright © 2024 by Margaret Jull Costa and Robin Patterson

All rights reserved
Printed in the United States of America
First published as a Liveright paperback 2025

For information about permission to reproduce selections from this book, write to Permissions, Liveright Publishing Corporation, a division of W. W. Norton & Company, Inc., 500 Fifth Avenue, New York, NY 10110

For information about special discounts for bulk purchases, please contact W. W. Norton Special Sales at specialsales@wwnorton.com or 800-233-4830

Manufacturing by Lake Book Manufacturing
Production manager: Anna Oler

ISBN 978-1-324-09670-2 pbk.

Liveright Publishing Corporation, 500 Fifth Avenue, New York, N.Y. 10110
www.wwnorton.com

W. W. Norton & Company Ltd., 15 Carlisle Street, London W1D 3BS

1 2 3 4 5 6 7 8 9 0

Introduction

AFTER A TEN-YEAR GAP following the publication of his previous novel, *Posthumous Memoirs of Brás Cubas*, Machado de Assis began publishing *Quincas Borba* in serial form in 1886, and then, after he had made some subtle but substantial changes, it was finally published in book form in 1891. Between these two dates momentous changes had taken place in Brazil: the abolition of slavery in 1888, promptly followed by Brazil's transformation from empire (a form of constitutional monarchy based loosely on the British parliamentary model combined with Napoleonic influences) to republic. Both of these changes had been long in the making and were intimately connected: abolition had been discussed for decades under increasing international pressure, with Emperor Pedro II tentatively advocating change but fearing the consequences for his own rule if he lost the support of slave owners. Events proved him right.

Against this febrile contemporary background, Machado de Assis chose to set *Quincas Borba* some twenty years earlier. Tellingly, the late 1860s through early 1870s was the period that marked the first steps toward abolition: there were various legislative proposals for limited emancipation from 1866 onward (echoed in the references to the Emperor's speech in Chapter XXI), with slave auctions being prohibited in 1869 (alluded to in Dona Maria Augusta's difficulty in "liquidating her assets" in Chapter LXVIII), and the emancipation of children born to enslaved parents after 1871 (the Law of the Free Womb, mentioned in Chapter CXCII). Machado refers to these events sparingly, and, at first blush, they seem incidental to the action of the novel. And yet politics is very much a theme, from Senhor Camacho's bombastic journalism and Teófilo's ministerial ambitions, to Rubião's own half-hearted attempts to enter politics combined with his imperial and Napoleonic fantasies. Perhaps to balance any whiff of nostalgia for these imaginings of imperial grandeur, in Chapter XLVII Machado takes us still further back in time to witness the gruesome public hanging of a Black man (implicitly a slave), comparing it to the cruelty of the Roman amphitheater seen through the eyes of an early Christian. As so often with Machado, himself the grandson of freed slaves, readers are left to draw their own conclusions.

In a similar vein, we find seemingly subdued references to the Paraguayan War (1864–70) and its protagonists. A contemporary Brazilian reader would not, of course, have needed to be told how horrifying that war was, pitting an expansionist Paraguay against the triple alliance of Brazil, Argentina, and Uruguay, and resulting in appalling loss of life. It remains to this day the bloodiest military conflict in Latin American history. The war also resulted in crippling war debts (alluded to in Chapters CXXIX and CLXXV), which weighed on the Brazilian economy for decades to come and were the other major factor in bringing the monarchy to its knees.

All of which goes some way to explaining why, in one of the very few contemporary reviews of the novel, the literary critic Tristão de Alencar Araripe Júnior wondered if the central character, Rubião, was in fact an allegorical representation of Brazil itself.

Machado rarely deals in straightforward allegory, but Rubião's full name, Pedro Rubião de Alvarenga, does seem to mimic that of the Emperor, Pedro de Alcântara, and the names of Machado's characters are always carefully chosen with just such allusions in mind. Among other main characters, Cristiano Falha's surname means "straw," and there is an amusing wordplay between philosophy ("*filosofia*" in Portuguese) and Rubião's love for Sofia.

As with all of Machado's work, the novel is largely set in Rio de Janeiro, the imperial capital, where Machado lived his whole life. When it comes to describing the city, Machado is primarily writing for its own inhabitants, the *cariocas*, and is correspondingly sparing with any detailed descriptions. For example, Chapter I begins with Rubião gazing out the window of his house in Botafogo: he mentions the water, a "small expanse of sea," and "the beach, the hills, and the sky." That's all. The view he is describing is, in fact, the picture-postcard view of Sugarloaf Mountain, perhaps the most breathtaking and iconic image of Rio, or of any city in the world. His readers would, of course, have instantly supplied the relevant mental image—it is perhaps a foretaste of Machado's expectation that his readers work with him to fill the tantalizing gaps in his narrative.

The names of streets and neighborhoods would also have given the book's original readers more information than they do to us today. Rua dos Inválidos and the adjacent Rua de Matacavalos, where Carlos Maria and his cousin Dona Fernanda live, were the streets where old money lived in large, sometimes crumbling, mansions. Flamengo and Botafogo, curling southward along the shoreline of Guanabara Bay and enjoying those spectacular views, were quiet suburbs being colonized by fashionable society and new money. Rua do Ouvidor and Rua dos Ourives were the commercial heart of the city, buzzing with shops, offices, cafés, and theaters.

Largo do Paço was the colonial-era main square, open to the sea on one side and bounded on the others by the seats of ecclesiastical and secular power—the cathedral, imperial chapel, and former viceroy's palace (although the Emperor had by that time moved to a larger, more comfortable palace just outside the city). On the other side of the city center, Saúde and then Gamboa, through which Rubião walks in Chapter LXXXVI, were the old port districts of docks, warehouses, congested housing, and grinding poverty—for once, Machado describes them in some detail, perhaps because most of his readers would rarely, if ever, venture there.

Machado himself, however, did; indeed, he was born and grew up on the slopes of the adjacent Morro do Livramento, fleetingly mentioned when Rubião stops at the English cemetery "with its old gravestones clambering up the hillside." Nineteenth century English traders tended to stay close to their ships and warehouses, and were discouraged from settling in more desirable parts of the city. Unusually in Machado's writing, there is an overtly nostalgic feel to the whole chapter, and for a moment one can be forgiven for wondering if this is Machado's own voice, revisiting his childhood haunts in the guise of Rubião retracing his steps. Or is this Machado simply playing tricks with us, inviting us to confuse the narrator, who claims to be the author and addresses his readers as such, with Machado himself?

The character Quincas Borba first appears in *Posthumous Memoirs of Brás Cubas* as an old school friend of Brás Cubas's, who has fallen on hard times and proclaims himself to be the inventor of a philosophy he calls Humanitism, by which Brás Cubas is briefly seduced. Ultimately, Quincas Borba goes mad. In the novel bearing his name (but in which, perhaps unsurprisingly for Machado, he is not the main character), the philosopher has since inherited a fortune and is slowly dying, being devotedly cared for by Rubião, the brother of the woman Quincas Borba had wished to marry, but who turned him down and subsequently died. Quincas Borba continues to haunt Rubião and the novel in the form of his dog—also named Quincas Borba. He is also responsible, unwittingly, for changing and, indeed, ruining Rubião's life.

Unlike *Posthumous Memoirs of Brás Cubas* (and Machado's later novel *Dom Casmurro*), Machado chooses to tell the story in the third person, giving us an omniscient narrator, who is often far from omniscient and far from reliable. While this perhaps allows for a greater degree of character development, because we are not seeing everyone and everything through the eyes of a very self-centered first-person narrator, it also means that Machado does not have to provide any answers. For example, there is the matter of the book's title. Why is the novel called *Quincas Borba*? As our narrator rightly says in the very final chapter:

> ... seeing me devote a separate chapter to the death of the dog, you might well ask if it is he or his defunct homonym who gives this book its title, and why one rather than the other—a question pregnant with still more questions that would lead us far and beyond.

And there he leaves us, pregnant with questions. Perhaps we should consider the nature of Quincas Borba's philosophy, Humanitism, which he sums up thus:

> "Imagine for a moment a field of potatoes and two starving tribes. There are only enough potatoes to feed one tribe, which would thereby gain sufficient strength to cross the

mountains and reach the other slope, where there is an abundance of potatoes. But if the two tribes divided the field of potatoes between them peacefully, there wouldn't be enough to nourish both tribes sufficiently, and they would all die of starvation. Peace, in this case, is destruction; war is preservation. One of the tribes exterminates the other and reaps the spoils. Hence the joy of victory, the hymns, acclamations, public recompense, and all the other effects of belligerent actions. If war was not thus, there would be no such response, for the practical reason that man only cherishes and commemorates what is pleasing or advantageous to him, and for the rational reason that no one extols an action that will potentially destroy them. To the vanquished, loathing or compassion; to the winner, the potatoes."

Many critics see this as Machado's ironic take on the prevailing philosophies or theories of the time: Auguste Comte's Positivism and Darwin's theory of natural selection. On the other hand, the novel may simply embody Machado's very skeptical view of a society rife with egotism, snobbery, and racism, and an all-consuming love of money, with, as his pawn, the innocent Rubião, whom he sends out into the big, bad world of Rio de Janeiro. Still worse, he has Rubião inherit a fortune, thus making him fair game for any predatory social climbers. As Machado puts it in Chapter XLIX: "his was eternally virgin soil in which anything could be planted." Before he has even arrived in the city, he meets Cristiano Palha and his wife Sofia on the train, a chance encounter that shapes his entire future: he misinterprets Sofia's meaningful glances as love, when she is merely following her husband's instructions to be nice to their rich friend, whom he intends to use for his own ends. When the arch political manipulator Dr. Camacho announces he is planning a career in politics for him, Rubião immediately accepts, just as he meekly accepts Camacho's subsequent dismissal of such plans. Set adrift in a society whose rules he doesn't understand, his life is a series of accidents. He very rarely makes a decision, and treats his one act of spontaneous heroism—when he saves a little boy from being run down by a carriage—as unimportant until, that is, he reads Camacho's overblown account of the incident, when it takes on a whole new significance to him. It's as if he only truly exists in the minds and opinions of others.

The other characters, with just three exceptions, all see him as a fool to be made use of, as a source of either money or food. As they clamber up the social ladder, they discard the less successful, the less beautiful, the less rich, and never once look back.

The only three good characters in this world are the genuinely selfless and kind Dona Fernanda, the devoted Quincas Borba the dog, and the appropriately named Angélica. When Dona Fernanda goes to fetch Quincas Borba the dog and reunite him with his master, Rubião, this is what happens:

> When Dona Fernanda stopped stroking him and stood up, he sat looking at her and she at him, so long and so deeply that they seemed to penetrate into each other's very soul. Universal sympathy, which was the essence of Dona Fernanda's soul, set aside all human considerations in the face of that obscure, prosaic misery, and she reached out to the dog with a part of herself, which wrapped about him, fascinating him and binding him to her. Thus, she felt the same pity for the dog as she had felt for his mad master, as if both were representatives of the same species.

It is that universal sympathy, so lacking in the other characters, and so opposed to the prevailing mores, that surfaces elsewhere in the novel. Chapter XXVIII provides the most extraordinary insight into a dog's mind, so steadfastly loyal and ready to forgive random acts of cruelty or neglect. Very like Rubião. And there is that seemingly unnecessary Chapter XLVI, in which an anonymous beggar and the night sky commune on terms of absolute equality:

> Beggar and sky stared at each other in a kind of game, daring the other to blink first, two serene, rival majesties, without a hint of arrogance or inferiority, as if the beggar were saying to the sky:
> "Well, you won't be falling in on me."
> And the sky to the beggar:
> "And you won't be clambering up to me."

The narrator also shows great sympathy for and understanding of Rubião's slide into madness, especially when he is still aware that he is going insane:

> When Rubião emerged from his delirium, that whole garrulous phantasmagoria became, briefly, a secret sadness. His conscious mind, which retained remnants of that previous state, struggled to detach itself from them. It was like a man's painful ascent from the abyss, clambering up the walls, grazing his shins, tearing his nails, struggling to reach the top and not fall in and be lost again.

Would Quincas Borba the philosopher have shown such empathy? Would Quincas Borba the dog? One possible answer to the question about the title might be that philosopher and dog represent two facets of society's philosophy: either a soulless dog-eat-dog mentality or the universal sympathy that is the essence of Dona Fernanda's soul. Is Rubião's madness then a response to the madness of contemporary society? So many questions that the reader soon finds his or her head spinning. Jealousy, madness, deception, and self-deception: Machado's references to *Hamlet*, *Tom Jones*, *Faust*, *Othello*, *Don Quixote*, and *The Tempest* signpost the way. Perhaps it is not just Rubião but the narrator himself who takes on the role of Prospero. A "sublime masque" indeed.

Margaret Jull Costa and Robin Patterson

Quincas Borba

Author's Preface to the Second Edition

Here is the second edition of *Quincas Borba*, issued with a few necessary and perhaps incomplete corrections. As pointed out in Chapter IV of the first edition, the title of this book is the name of a character who appeared in *Posthumous Memoirs of Brás Cubas*. If you choose to read both books, you will realize that this is the only connection between them, apart from their form, and even then, their form differs in the sense that the narrative here is more compact.

1896
MACHADO DE ASSIS

Author's Preface to the Third Edition

The second edition of this book sold out more quickly than the first. Here it is in its third edition, with no further changes beyond correcting a few typographical errors, so minor and so few that even had they been kept they would not have obscured the meaning.

An illustrious friend and colleague has urged me to give this book a sequel. "Together with *Posthumous Memoirs of Brás Cubas*, from which this one originates, you will then have a trilogy, with Sofia from *Quincas Borba* filling the third part." For some time, I thought the idea might work, but rereading these pages now I conclude that it would not. All of Sofia is here. To prolong her story would be to repeat her, and randomly repeating the same story would be quite wrong. I believe the same criticism has been leveled at me for this and some of the other books I have composed over the years in the silence of my life. There were some strong, generous voices that spoke out in my defense at the time; I have already thanked them individually; now I do so sincerely and publicly.

1899
M. de A.

Chapter I

RUBIÃO GAZED OUT across the water; it was eight o'clock in the morning. Anyone who saw him standing at the window of that large house in Botafogo with his thumbs tucked into the belt of his dressing gown would have thought he was admiring that small expanse of sea; but I can tell you that he was, in fact, thinking about something else entirely. He was comparing the past with the present. What was he a year ago? A schoolteacher. What was he now? A capitalist. He looked at himself, at his slippers (Tunisian slippers that his new friend, Cristiano Palha, had given him), at the house, the garden outside, the beach, the hills, and the sky. Everything, from slippers to sky, gave him the same sense of ownership.

"The Lord does indeed move in mysterious ways," he thought. "If my sister Piedade had married Quincas Borba, I would have had only a remote chance of inheriting anything. But she didn't marry him, both of them died, and now everything is mine; so what seemed to be a misfortune..."

Chapter II

WHAT A CHASM lies between head and heart! Troubled by that thought, the former schoolteacher's mind changed tack and alighted upon another subject, a skiff passing by; his heart, however, allowed itself a flutter of joy. What did he care about the skiff, or its skipper, as he gazed at them wide-eyed? His heart was telling him that since Piedade was destined to die anyway, it was a good thing she did not marry; there could have been a son or a daughter . . . What a fine skiff! So much the better! See how well it obeys the man's oars! One thing is certain: they are both now in heaven!

Chapter III

A SERVANT BROUGHT him his coffee. Rubião took the cup and, while adding the sugar, glanced furtively at the tray made of finely chased silver. Silver, gold—these were the metals he truly loved; he didn't care for bronze, although his friend Palha had told him that it was very valuable, which explained the pair of bronze figures here in the drawing room, a Mephistopheles and a Faust. If he had to choose, however, he would choose the salver—a masterpiece of fine silverware, impeccably executed. The servant was waiting, stiff and somber. He was Spanish, and it was only after some resistance that Rubião had accepted him from Cristiano, telling his new friend that he was accustomed to having his black slaves from Minas

Gerais around him, and that he didn't want any foreign languages spoken in his house. Palha had insisted, pointing out the necessity these days of having white servants.* Rubião reluctantly conceded. His good houseboy, whom he had wanted to install in the drawing room as a little reminder of the provinces, couldn't even be sent to the kitchen, where a Frenchman called Jean reigned; the boy was demoted and put to other uses.

"Quincas Borba is getting very impatient, you say?" Rubião asked, draining the last drops of his coffee and stealing one final glance at the salver.

"*Me parece que si.*"

"I'll go down and let him out."

He didn't go; he allowed himself to gaze for a while at the furniture. Seeing the small English prints hanging on the wall above the two bronzes, Rubião thought about Palha's wife, the beautiful Sofia, then took a few steps and sat down on the pouf in the middle of the room, staring into space . . .

"She was the one who recommended those two little prints, when the three of us went out shopping. How pretty she looked! But what I like best about her are her shoulders, which I saw at the colonel's ball. Such shoulders! As smooth and white as wax! Her arms too! Oh, her arms! Such shapely arms!"

Rubião sighed, crossed his legs, and drummed the tassels of his dressing gown on his knee. He sensed that he was not entirely happy, but he felt, too, that complete happiness was not far off. In his mind, he went over some of her mannerisms, her looks, her come-hither eyes, for which there could be no other explanation than that she loved him, and loved him a great deal. He was not

---

* Brazil was beginning its slow progress toward the abolition of slavery—see the introduction. Minas Gerais was a large inland province (now state), rich in mining and agriculture.

old; he would soon be forty-one, but seemed much younger. This thought was accompanied by a gesture: he stroked his chin, which he now had shaved every day; previously there had been no need for such unnecessary expense. A mere schoolteacher! He currently sported a pair of side-whiskers (which he would later develop into a full beard), so soft that he enjoyed running his fingers through them . . . And then he remembered their first meeting, at the Vassouras railroad station, where Sofia and her husband had boarded the train, the same carriage in which he was traveling down from Minas; it was there that he first met those luscious eyes that seemed to repeat the prophet's exhortation: "Come, all you who are thirsty, come to the waters." He had been unprepared for such an invitation; his head was filled with thoughts of the inheritance, the will, the inventory of his new possessions, all of which must first be explained, in order for you to understand both the present and the future. So let us leave Rubião in the drawing room in Botafogo, gently drumming the tassels of his dressing gown on his knee, and thinking of the beautiful Sofia. Come with me, reader, and let us take a look at him several months earlier, at the bedside of Quincas Borba.

Chapter IV

THIS QUINCAS BORBA IS, if you were perhaps kind enough to read *Posthumous Memoirs of Brás Cubas*, the very same castaway from reality who appears in my earlier book: a beggar, an unexpected heir, and the inventor of a philosophy. Now here you find him in the small town of Barbacena, Minas Gerais. As soon he arrived in

Barbacena, Quincas Borba fell in love with a widow, a lady of humble status and modest means, but so shy that the sighs of her new admirer went unanswered. Her name was Maria da Piedade. Her brother, the Rubião whom we have just met, did everything he could to encourage them to marry. Piedade resisted, then pleurisy carried her off.

It was this little fragment of a novel that connected the two men. Could Rubião have known that our Quincas Borba contained the seed of madness that a doctor had once diagnosed in him? Surely not; he merely considered him an eccentric. It is, however, certain that the tiny seed had not dislodged itself from Quincas Borba's brain, either before or after the illness that slowly consumed him. Quincas Borba once had relatives in Barbacena, but by then, in 1867, they were all dead; the last of them was an uncle who had made him heir to all his worldly goods. Rubião ended up being the philosopher's only friend. At the time, Rubião was running a school for boys, which he closed down in order to take care of the sick man. Before becoming a schoolteacher, he had tried his hand at running a number of businesses, all of which had foundered.

His job as Quincas Borba's nurse lasted nearly six months. Rubião, patient and good-humored, was genuinely devoted in his attentions. He dealt with everything, listening to the doctor's instructions, dispensing medicines at the designated times, taking the patient out for fresh air and exercise, forgetting nothing, either in the running of the house, or in reading out the newspapers the moment the mail coach arrived, either from the capital or from Ouro Preto.

"You're a good man, Rubião," Quincas Borba would say with a sigh.

"Well, it's hardly an onerous task! And, besides, you're a good man too!"

The doctor's ostensible prognosis was that Borba's illness would slowly pass. Then, one day, Rubião, while accompanying the doctor to the door, asked him how his friend was really doing. The doctor told him there was no hope, absolutely none, but that they should try to keep his spirits up. Why make death even more painful by telling him the stark facts—

"No, you're wrong there," said Rubião, interrupting. "For him, dying is an easy matter. Have you not read the book he wrote some years ago, some sort of philosophical tract . . . ?"

"I haven't, but philosophy is one thing and dying is another. Goodbye."

Chapter V

RUBIÃO HAD FOUND a rival in Quincas Borba's affections: a dog, a fine-looking dog of medium size, dark gray with black spots. Quincas Borba took him everywhere, and they slept in the same room. In the morning, it was the dog who woke his master, climbing onto the bed, where the two of them exchanged their first greetings of the day. One of the owner's eccentricities was to give the dog the same name as himself; he offered two reasons for this, one doctrinal, the other personal.

"Since, according to my doctrine, Humanitas is the source of all life and resides everywhere, it exists also in dogs, and thus dogs may be given human names, whether Christian or Muslim . . ."

"Very well, but why didn't you just call him Bernardo?" asked Rubião, thinking of a local political rival.

"All right, here is my real reason. If I die first, as I presume I shall, I will live on in the name of my trusty hound. You're laughing, aren't you?"

Rubião shook his head.

"Well, you should be, my dear fellow. Because immortality is my lot, or my legacy, or whatever you like to call it. I will live forever through my masterpiece of a book. Those, however, who cannot read, will call the dog Quincas Borba, and—"

Hearing his name, the dog ran over to the bed. Deeply touched, Quincas Borba looked at Quincas Borba.

"My poor friend! My good friend! My only friend!"

"Only!"

"Pardon me, you're my friend, too, I know, and I'm very grateful to you. People always forgive a sick man everything. Perhaps my delirium is beginning. Hand me the mirror."

Rubião did as he was asked. The patient stared for several seconds at his gaunt features and feverish gaze, in which he could see the suburbs of death toward which he was walking at a slow but steady pace. Then, with a wan, ironic smile, he said:

"Everything on the outside corresponds to what I feel here on the inside; I'm going to die, my dear Rubião . . . No, don't shake your head; I am going to die. And why should you be so afraid of dying, why so terrified?"

"I know you have your philosophies . . . But let's talk about supper. What shall it be this evening?"

Quincas Borba sat on the edge of the bed, letting his legs dangle, their bone-thinness visible even beneath his pajamas.

"What is it? What do you want?"

"Nothing," the patient replied, smiling. "'Your philosophies'! You say that with such disdain! Go on, say it again, I want to hear it again. 'Your philosophies'!"

"But it isn't disdain . . . And anyway, who am I to disdain philosophy? I'm only saying that you might well think death unimportant, because you have your reasons, your principles..."

Quincas Borba felt around with his feet for his slippers; Rubião pushed them toward him; Quincas Borba put them on and began to move around, stretching his legs. He patted the dog and lit a cigarette. Rubião wanted to wrap him up in something warm, and brought him a morning coat, a vest, a dressing gown, and a cloak for him to choose from. Quincas Borba dismissed them all with a wave of his hand. He now looked very different, his eyes turned inward as if following the workings of his brain. After much pacing, he stopped briefly before Rubião.

Chapter VI

"IN ORDER FOR YOU to really understand about life and death, I need only tell you how my grandmother died."

"How was that?"

"Sit down."

Rubião did as he was told, trying to look as interested as he could, while Quincas Borba continued pacing.

"It was in Rio de Janeiro," he said, "in front of the Imperial Chapel, which was then called the Royal Chapel, on the day of one of the major church festivals. My grandmother came out of the chapel and crossed the small enclosure, heading to where her sedan chair was waiting for her on Largo do Paço. The square was swarming with people, the crowds eager to catch a glimpse of the great ladies getting into their ornate carriages. Just at the moment my grandmother stepped into the street, one of the mules hitched to a waiting chaise was startled by something; the animal took off, the other one followed, there was commotion, uproar, my grandmother fell, and both the mules and the chaise ran straight over her. She was picked up and carried to a pharmacy on Rua Direita, a bloodletter arrived, but it was too late; her head was split open, her leg and shoulder broken, and she was covered in blood; she died within minutes."

"How awful," said Rubião.

"No, not at all."

"No?"

"Listen to the rest of the story. Here is how it happened. The owner of the chaise had also been waiting outside the church, and he was hungry, very hungry, because he had eaten only a light breakfast that morning and it was now getting late. From where he stood, he was able to wave to his coachman, who whipped the mules so as to go over and fetch their owner. The chaise encountered an obstacle in the middle of the road and ran straight over it; that obstacle was my grandmother. The first act in this series of acts was a mere impulse of self-preservation: Humanitas was hungry. Had the obstacle been a rat or dog, then it is true my dear grandmama would not have died, but the fact remains: Humanitas needs to eat. If instead of a rat or dog it had been a poet, let's say Byron or Gonçalves Dias, the incident would differ in the sense that it would have provided material for numerous obituaries, but would otherwise be the same. The universe has not yet ground to a halt for lack of a poem or two nipped in the bud while still in the mind of some brooding hero, whether illustrious or obscure; but Humanitas—and this is what matters—Humanitas needs to eat."

Rubião listened intently, genuinely wanting to understand; but he couldn't grasp what it was, that necessity to which his friend attributed the death of his grandmother. Surely even if the owner of the chaise had arrived home very late, he wouldn't have died of hunger, whereas the good lady had actually died, once and for all. He explained his doubts as best he could, and finished by asking:

"And what is this Humanitas?"

"Humanitas is the principle. But no, I won't go any further; you're not capable of understanding this, my dear Rubião. Let's talk about something else."

"Go on, tell me."

Quincas Borba, who was still pacing the room, stopped briefly.

"Would you like to be my disciple?"

"I would."

"Very well, you will gradually come to understand my philosophy; on the day when you have grasped it entirely, ah, on that day, the greatest pleasure in life will be yours, because there is no wine more intoxicating than truth. Believe me, Humanitism is the pinnacle of everything, and I, who formulated it, am the greatest man on earth. Look! See how my trusty Quincas Borba is looking at me? It isn't him, it's Humanitas..."

"But what is this Humanitas?"

"Humanitas is the principle. In all things there is a certain hidden and identical substance, a single common, universal, eternal, indivisible and indestructible principle—or, to use the language of our greatest poet, Camões:

> A truth that does within all things stir,
> And dwells in both seen and unseen.

"This substance or truth, this indestructible principle, is Humanitas. That's what I call it, because it encapsulates the universe, and the universe is man. Are you beginning to understand?"

"A little, but even so, how is it that your grandmother's death..."

"There is no death. The meeting of two expansions, or the expansion of two forms, can result in the suppression of one of them; but, strictly speaking, there is no death, only life, because the survival of one depends on the suppression of the other, and its destruction does not impinge upon the common universal principle. Hence the life-preserving and beneficial nature of war. Imagine for a moment a field of potatoes and two starving tribes. There are only enough potatoes to feed one tribe, which would thereby gain sufficient strength to cross the mountains and reach the other slope, where there is an abundance of potatoes. But if the two tribes divided the field of potatoes between them peacefully, there wouldn't be enough to nourish both tribes sufficiently, and they would all die of starvation. Peace, in this case, is destruction; war is preservation. One of the tribes exterminates the other and reaps the spoils. Hence the joy of victory, the hymns, acclamations, public recompense, and all the other effects of belligerent actions. If war was not thus, there would be no such response, for the practical reason that man only cherishes and commemorates what is pleasing or advantageous to him, and for the rational reason that no one extols an action that will potentially destroy them. To the vanquished, loathing or compassion; to the winner, the potatoes."

"But what about the views of the tribe that's been exterminated?"

"No one has been exterminated. The phenomenon disappears, the substance remains the same. Have you never watched water boiling? You'll have seen how the bubbles continuously form and unform, and yet it still remains the same water. Individuals are those transitory bubbles."

"Well then, the bubble's opinion . . ."

"A bubble has no opinion. Is there anything, at first appearance, more saddening than one of those terrible plagues that devastates some part of the globe? And yet this supposed evil is a godsend, not only because it eliminates those organisms that are weak and incapable of resistance, but also because it provides an opportunity for observation, and the discovery of a cure. Hygiene is the product of centuries of filth; it has come to us through millions of rotting and infected forebears. Nothing is lost, everything is gained. I repeat: The bubbles are still in the water. Do you see this book? It's *Don Quixote*. If I destroy my copy, I won't be destroying the work itself, for it lives on eternally in surviving copies and future editions. Eternally beautiful, beautifully eternal, just like this divine and super-divine world of ours."

Chapter VII

EXHAUSTED, QUINCAS BORBA stopped speaking and sat down, breathing hard. Rubião hurriedly fetched him some water and begged him to go to bed; but after a few minutes the patient replied that he was fine. He was simply unaccustomed now to making speeches, that's all. And, signaling to Rubião to stand back, so that he could see his face more clearly, he launched into a dazzling description of the world and its wonders. He interwove his own ideas with those of other people, images of every sort, idyllic and epic, to such an extent that Rubião began to ponder how a man mere days from death could expound so elegantly upon such matters.

"Go and rest a little."

Quincas Borba paused to think.

"No, I'm going for a walk."

"Not now you're very tired."

"Nonsense! I'm fine now."

He stood up and placed his hands on Rubião's shoulders in a paternal manner. "Are you my friend?"

"What a question!"

"Answer me."

"As much as or more than this animal here," replied Rubião, in a sudden outpouring of tenderness.

Quincas Borba squeezed his hands.

"Good."

Chapter VIII

THE FOLLOWING DAY, Quincas Borba awoke firmly resolved to go to Rio de Janeiro. He would return in a month; he had certain matters to deal with . . . Rubião was taken aback. What about his illness, and the doctor? The patient replied that the doctor was a charlatan, and that his illness needed a vacation, as did his health. Sickness and health were two sides of the same coin, two states of Humanitas.

"I need to attend to some personal matters," he concluded, "including a plan so sublime that not even you would understand it. You must excuse my frankness, but I would rather be frank with you than with any other person."

Rubião felt confident that the project would be quickly forgotten, like so many others, but he was mistaken. Moreover, the patient actually did seem to be getting better; he no longer stayed in bed, he went outside, and he wrote. A week later, he told Rubião to summon the notary.

"The notary?" his friend asked.

"Yes, I want to make my will. Or the two of us can go together . . ."

The three of them went, since the dog would not allow his master to go without him. Quincas Borba made his will, with all the usual formalities, and returned serenely home. Rubião could feel his heart pounding.

"Obviously I won't let you go to Rio on your own," he said to his friend.

"There's no need for that. In any case, Quincas Borba isn't going, and I won't entrust him to anyone but you. I'm leaving the house just as it is, and I'll be back in a month. I'll go tomorrow. I don't want him to know that I'm leaving. Take good care of him, Rubião."

"Yes, I will."

"Swear?"

"By this light that shines upon me! I'm not a child, you know."

"Give him milk at the proper times, all his meals as usual, and his baths; and when you take him out for a walk, make sure he doesn't run off. No, it would better if he didn't go out at all . . . don't take him out . . ."

"Don't worry, I won't."

Quincas Borba wept for Quincas Borba. He didn't even want to see him when he left. He wept real tears, whether of madness or of affection, let them fall upon the rich soil of Minas Gerais, like the last drops of sweat from a poor obscure soul about to fall into the abyss.

Chapter IX

SEVERAL HOURS LATER, Rubião had a horrible thought. People might think he had urged his friend to make the journey to hasten his death, assuming he really was included in the will. He felt terrible remorse. Why had he not tried harder to stop him? He saw

Quincas Borba's pale, stinking corpse fixing him with a vengeful stare; he decided that if things took a fatal turn during the trip, he would renounce the legacy.

For his part, the dog was constantly sniffing around, whining, and trying to escape; he couldn't sleep peacefully, and would get up many times during the night to roam around the house before returning to his usual corner. In the mornings, Rubião would call him into his bed, and the dog would come trotting gladly over to him, thinking that it was his real owner calling. When he saw that it wasn't, he accepted Rubião's caresses anyway, and returned them, too, as if Rubião would somehow pass these on to his friend, or bring him back from wherever he had gone. Besides, he had also taken a liking to Rubião, for he was the bridge that linked him to his previous existence. He didn't eat at all for the first few days. Since thirst was more difficult to endure, Rubião managed to get him to drink some milk; for a time, it was the dog's only nourishment. Later, he would lie for hours and hours locked in sad silence, curled up or stretched out with his head between his paws.

When the doctor called again, he was amazed at his patient's rash behavior. He should have been prevented from going; death was certain.

"Certain?"

"Sooner or later. Did he take that dog with him?"

"No, he's here with me. He asked me to look after him, and he wept, wept uncontrollably. Actually," continued Rubião, in his friend's defense, "that dog really does deserve his master's affections: he behaves like a real person."

The doctor removed his straw hat to adjust the hatband, and smiled. "A real person? In what way does he resemble a real person?"

Rubião insisted, then explained that he didn't mean that he was a person like other people, but he clearly had feelings, even intelligence. "Look, I was going to tell you a—"

"No, no, my dear fellow. Another time. I have to visit a patient suffering from erysipelas... If you receive any letters from Quincas Borba that aren't confidential, I would like to see them. And give my regards to the dog," he concluded as he left.

Some people began making fun of Rubião and his peculiar task of guarding the dog, when the dog should have been guarding him. First, there was giggling, then the nicknames rained down. How low had the schoolteacher stooped! A dog-guard! Rubião feared public opinion, and indeed felt ridiculous; he avoided the eyes of passersby, looked at the animal with distaste, cursed himself, and cursed his miserable life. If it wasn't for the hope of a legacy, however small... It was surely impossible he would not be left something.

Chapter X

SEVEN WEEKS LATER, the following letter arrived in Barbacena, postmarked from Rio de Janeiro and written in Quincas Borba's hand:

> My dear sir and friend,
> You must have found my silence rather odd. I did not write you for very particular reasons, etc. I will be returning shortly; but I wanted to inform you of a confidential, highly confidential, matter.
>> Who am I, Rubião? I am Saint Augustine. I know you will smile, because you are an ignoramus, Rubião; our friendship would allow me to use a cruder word, but I make you this concession, the very last one, ignoramus!

Now listen, ignoramus. I am Saint Augustine; I discovered this the day before yesterday. So listen and be quiet. Everything in our lives coincides. Both the saint and I have spent part of our time indulging in pleasure and in heresy, for I consider heresy to be everything that is not my doctrine of Humanitas. Both of us have stolen; he, as a boy, stole some pears in Carthage; I, as a young man, stole a watch from my friend Brás Cubas. Our mothers were chaste and religious. And he thought, as I do, that everything that exists is good, as he demonstrates in Book VII, Chapter XVI of his Confessions, *except that for him, evil is a deviation of the will, a delusion belonging to a backward age, a concession to error, since evil does not even exist, and only the first statement is true, that all things are good,* omnia bona, *and that's that.*

So farewell, ignoramus. Do not tell anyone what I have just confided to you, if you do not want to lose your ears. Say nothing, keep the secret, and thank your good fortune for having a great man like me as a friend, even though you don't understand me. You will understand me. As soon as I get back to Barbacena, I will explain to you, in clear, simple terms that even an ass would understand, what it means to be a great man. Farewell; give my best wishes to my poor Quincas Borba. Don't forget to give him his milk. Milk and baths. Farewell, farewell . . . Your devoted friend,

Quincas Borba

Rubião could scarcely hold the letter in his hands. A moment later, it occurred to him that his friend might be joking, and he reread the letter; but the second reading only confirmed his first impression. There was no doubt about it: the man was crazy. Poor Quincas Borba! All those eccentricities, the frequent changes in mood, the flights of fancy, the overblown expressions of affection, were nothing more than harbingers of his brain's total ruin. He was dying before he actually died. Such a good man! And so happy! He had his peculiarities, of course, but his illness explained all that. Rubião dabbed at his eyes, which had become moist with emotion. Then he remembered the possible legacy, and this distressed him even more, for it showed him what a good friend he was about to lose.

He read the letter again, slowly this time, analyzing the words, dissecting them in order to understand its meaning clearly and assess whether it was in fact a philosopher's prank. He was well used to his friend's way of playfully insulting him, but the rest of the letter confirmed his initial suspicions. Toward the end, he suddenly stopped reading. Was it possible, if the testator were proven to be mad, that the will would be declared null and void, and the legacy lost? Rubião felt almost faint. The letter was still in his hands when he saw the doctor; he had come for news of his patient, since the postmaster had told him a letter had arrived. Was that the one?

"It is, but . . ."

"Is there something confidential in it?"

"There is. It contains some confidential, highly confidential, information; personal matters. Would you mind?"

As he said this, Rubião put the letter in his pocket; when the doctor left, he took a deep breath. He had escaped the danger of making public so grave a document, one that could provide proof of Quincas Borba's mental state. But a few minutes later, he regretted not handing over the letter. Filled with remorse, he considered sending it to the doctor's house. He called for a slave, but by the time the slave arrived he had already changed his mind again; he decided that would be imprudent; the patient would return soon—in a few days—and was sure to ask about the letter; he would then accuse Rubião of being indiscreet, a tattletale . . . Easy remorse is easily overcome.

"Never mind," he said to the slave. And once again he thought of the legacy. He calculated the amount. It certainly wouldn't be less than ten *contos*.* He would buy a piece of land, a house, grow some crops, or mine for gold. At worst, it might be less, five *contos* . . . Five? It wasn't much, but perhaps that's all there would be. Even with five, well, yes, that would be less, but less was better than nothing. Five *contos* . . . It would be even worse if the will were declared void. All right, five *contos!*

Chapter XI

AT THE BEGINNING of the following week, when the newspapers (still subscribed to by Quincas Borba) arrived from the capital, Rubião read the following notice:

Senhor Joaquim Borba dos Santos passed away yesterday, following an illness that he endured with remarkable stoicism. He was a man of great wisdom, and battled tirelessly against the mean, sour pessimism that will one day reach us here in Brazil, for it is the sickness of our times. His last words were that pain was an illusion, and that Pangloss was not as foolish as Voltaire supposed . . . By then, he was already delirious. He leaves a large fortune. The will is in Barbacena.

---

* The main unit of currency at the time was the *mil-réis*. A *conto* was one thousand *mil-réis*.

Chapter XII

"HIS SUFFERING IS OVER," Rubião said with a sigh.

Then, on reading the article more closely, he saw that it spoke of a man of high esteem and merit, and alluded only to a philosophical struggle. No reference to madness. On the contrary, at the end it said only that he had been delirious in his final hours, as a result of his illness. Just as well! Rubião read Borba's letter again, and once again the hypothesis that it was all a joke seemed more likely. His friend had always had a keen sense of humor, and he had probably merely intended to poke fun at him; he had quoted Saint Augustine, just as he might have quoted Saint Ambrose or Saint Hilary, and had written him an enigmatic letter just to confuse him, no doubt for his own amusement when he returned. Poor friend! Perfectly sane—sane and dead. And now beyond suffering. Seeing the dog, Rubião sighed again.

"Poor Quincas Borba! If only you knew that your master was dead..."

Then, to himself:

"Now that my obligation is over, I'll give him to my friend Angélica."

⇒ *Chapter XII*

NEWS SPREAD RAPIDLY through the town the priest, the owner of the pharmacy, and the doctor all wanted to know if it was true. The postmaster, who had read about it in the newspapers, personally delivered a letter to Rubião that had come for him in the mailbag; it might be from the deceased, although the handwriting on the envelope was someone else's.

"So he's finally kicked the bucket?" he said as Rubião opened the letter, looking first for the signature, which read: *Brás Cubas*. It was a brief note:

> *My poor friend Quincas Borba died yesterday at my house, where he turned up some time ago looking ragged and filthy, the result of his illness. Before he died, he asked me to write and give you this news personally, along with his deepest gratitude, saying that the rest will follow in due course, in accordance with the usual legal formalities.*

At *deepest gratitude* the schoolteacher turned pale, but at *legal formalities* his blood returned. Rubião folded up the letter without a word; the postmaster said something or other and then left. Rubião ordered a slave to take the dog over to his friend Angélica, and to tell her that since she liked animals, here was another one; that she should treat the dog well since that was how he was used to being treated; and, finally, that the dog's name was the same as that of his recently deceased master, Quincas Borba.

Chapter XIV

WHEN THE WILL WAS READ, Rubião almost collapsed. You may guess why. He was named sole heir. Not five, or ten, or twenty *contos*, but everything, Quincas Borba's entire estate, including all his goods and chattels, his houses in Rio, one in Barbacena, his slaves, as well as government bonds, shares in the Bank of Brazil and other establishments, jewelry, cash, books—everything was left to Rubião, with no deductions, no bequests to other people, no charitable donations, no debts. There was only one condition in the will, which was that the heir must keep his poor dog Quincas Borba, a name he had bestowed on him as a token of his great affection. The will stipulated that the aforementioned Rubião must treat the dog as he would its former owner, doing everything he could to protect his well-being, guarding him from illnesses, from being stolen or from running away, and from death at the hands of miscreants. In short, he was to care for him not as a dog, but as a person. The will went on to state that when the dog died, he was to be given his own plot in the cemetery, which Rubião should cover with flowers and sweet-smelling plants; and that, at the appropriate juncture, the bones of said dog should then be disinterred and placed in a casket of fine wood, to be displayed in the most prominent position in the house.

=== Chapter XV

SUCH WAS THE CLAUSE. Rubião found it reasonable enough, since his one concern was to protect his inheritance. He had hoped for just a simple legacy, and here he was with all the man's worldly goods! He could scarcely believe his luck, and it took many firm, congratulatory handshakes to convince him it was not a mistake.

"Yes, sir, you've hit the jackpot!" said the pharmacist who had supplied Quincas Borba's medication.

To be an heir was quite something, but *sole* heir! For such a short word, it certainly plumped up the cheeks of any inheritance. Heir to everything, down to the last teaspoon. He wondered to himself how much it must all be worth. Houses, bonds, shares, slaves, clothing, china, a few paintings, which being a man of great taste and a connoisseur of art, he probably kept in Rio. And books? There must be a lot of books, since he was always quoting from them. But how much would it all amount to? A hundred *contos*? Maybe two hundred? It was possible; he wouldn't be surprised if it was three hundred. Three hundred *contos*! Three hundred! Rubião felt a sudden urge to go out and dance in the street. Then he calmed down. Even if it was two hundred, or one hundred, it was a dream that Our Lord God was bestowing upon him, one that would never end.

Eventually, the dog managed to gain a foothold in the swirling thoughts filling our man's head. Rubião thought the clause was reasonable but unnecessary, because he and the dog were firm pals and nothing was more certain than that they should stick together in remembrance of their third pal, the deceased, who was the author of their happiness. There were undoubtedly a few oddities in the clause, the business about the casket and some other things he couldn't quite remember, but everything would be followed to the letter, even if the sky fell in on him ... Or rather, "with God's help" he thought, piously correcting himself. A good dog! An excellent dog!

Rubião had not forgotten that he had tried many times to make a fortune through business ventures that had all come to nothing. At the time, he had put it down to his own ill luck, to being somehow jinxed, when the simple truth was that "God helps those who help themselves." It would no longer be impossible for him to become rich, because he *was* rich.

"Impossible? What's that?" he exclaimed aloud. "For God to sin, now, that would be impossible. God does not fail in his promises."

So off he went, up and down the streets of the town, not going home, but wandering aimlessly, his blood pounding in his veins. Suddenly a grave problem occurred to him: Should he go to live in Rio de Janeiro, or stay in Barbacena? He felt an itch to stay, to dazzle where once he had barely glimmered, to thumb his nose at those who had previously ignored him, and especially at those who had spoken scornfully of his friendship with Quincas Borba. But then came the image of Rio de Janeiro, a city he knew well, with all its charms, its hustle and bustle, with theaters on every corner, pretty girls dressed *à la mode française*. He decided this was the better option—after all, he could come back to his hometown as often as he liked.

Chapter XVI

"QUINCAS BORBA! Quincas Borba! Hey! Quincas Borba!" he shouted as he came into the house.

No sign of the dog. Only then did he remember that he had packed him off to his friend Angélica's. He rushed over to her house, which was quite a distance. Along the way all sorts of unpleasant thoughts tormented him, some of them extraordinary. One was that the dog could have escaped. Another, more extraordinary thought was that some enemy of his, on finding out about the clause in the will, and on then learning that he had given the dog away, might have immediately gone to see Angélica, stolen the dog, and then hidden or killed him. In which case, the inheritance . . . A cloud passed before his eyes; then he began to see more clearly.

"I don't know much about legal matters," he thought, "but it seems to me I have nothing to fear. The clause assumes that the dog is living with me, but if he runs away or dies, there is no need to invent another dog; therefore, the primary intention . . . But then, my enemies are capable of all sorts of chicanery. If the clause is not complied with . . ."

At this point, our friend's forehead and hands began to sweat. Another cloud passed before his eyes. And his heart beat faster and faster. The clause was beginning to seem excessive. Rubião threw himself upon the mercy of all the saints and promised to pay for a mass, ten masses . . . But there, straight ahead of him, was Angélica's house. Rubião quickened his pace; he saw someone; was it her? Yes, it was her, leaning against the door and laughing.

"What sort of a way is that to behave, my friend? Waving your arms around like a madman!"

Chapter XVII

"MY DEAR FRIEND, where is the dog?" asked Rubião with studied indifference, but looking very pale.

"Come in, and sit down," she replied. "What dog?"

"*What dog?*" asked Rubião, turning even paler. "The one I sent you. Don't you remember I sent a dog to stay here and rest for a few days, to see if . . . In short, a very dear pet. He isn't even mine. I've come to . . . But don't you remember?"

"Ah! Don't talk to me about that creature!" she blurted out.

She was small and trembled at the slightest thing, and, when she was excited, the veins in her neck stood out. Again she told him not to speak of the dog.

"But what did he do to you, dear friend?"

"What did he do? What doesn't he do, more like. He doesn't eat, he doesn't drink, he cries like a baby, and he's always looking for a way to escape."

Rubião gave a sigh of relief. She carried on listing the dog's irritating habits; Rubião said he would like to see him.

"He's out the back in the large pen. He's on his own so that the others don't bother him. Have you come to take him back? That's not what I was told. I thought they said the dog was for me, a gift."

"I'd give you five or six, if I could," replied Rubião. "This one I can't; I'm only taking care of him for someone else. But never mind, I promise you one of his puppies. I think the message must have got a bit muddled."

Rubião was already setting off, and, rather than showing him the way, Angélica ran along behind. There, inside the pen, was the dog, lying down some distance from a bowl of food. Outside the pen, other dogs and poultry jostled all around them; on one side was a henhouse, farther on were the pigs; beyond them a cow was lying down, asleep, with two hens alongside, pecking at her belly, pulling off ticks.

"Look at my peacock!" the woman said.

But Rubião's eyes were on Quincas Borba, who was impatiently sniffing the air, before lunging toward him as soon as a young scamp opened the gate of the pen. It was a scene of wild excitement; the dog returned Rubião's caresses by barking, jumping, and licking his hands.

"Good heavens! Such devotion!"

"You can't imagine, my friend. Goodbye, ma'am. I promise you a puppy."

Chapter XVIII

ON ENTERING THE HOUSE, both Rubião and the dog could smell and hear the lingering traces and the voice of their dearly departed friend. While the dog sniffed around, Rubião sat down on the same chair he had occupied when Quincas Borba had described his grandmother's death to him in scientific terms. His memory pieced together, albeit in muddled, fragmented form, his philosopher friend's arguments. For the first time, he paid close attention to the allegory of the starving tribes and understood the conclusion: "To the winner, the potatoes!" He distinctly heard the dead man's hoarse voice setting forth the situation the two tribes found themselves in, the conflict and the reason for the conflict, the extermination of one and the victory of the other, and he whispered softly:

"To the winner, the potatoes!"

So simple! So clear! He looked down at his threadbare trousers and his patched and darned frock coat, and realized that, until a short time ago, he had, so to speak, been one of the exterminated, a bubble. But not now; now he was a winner. There was no doubt; the potatoes were destined for whichever tribe eliminated the other one, so that they could then cross the mountains and reach the potatoes on the other side. Which was precisely his own case. He would leave Barbacena so as to pull up and eat the potatoes in the capital. He needed to be harsh and implacable, for he was powerful and strong. Jumping up from his chair, flushed with excitement, he raised his arms and exclaimed:

"To the winner, the potatoes!"

The formula appealed to him; he thought it clever, succinct, and eloquent, as well as being both profound and true. He imagined the potatoes in their various shapes, classifying them by taste, appearance, nutritional value, already eating his fill of the banquet of life. It was time to be done with those poor, shriveled roots that merely deceived the stomach, his paltry fare for many long years; now was the time for plentiful, solid sustenance in perpetuity, to eat until he died, and when he died it would be between silken sheets, which are infinitely better than rags. And he again determined to be harsh and implacable, and to embrace the formula from that allegory. In his head, he even designed himself a signet ring inscribed with the motto: TO THE WINNER, THE POTATOES!

He quickly forgot all about the signet ring, but the motto lingered in Rubião's thoughts for several days: To the winner, the potatoes! Before the will, he would not have understood it; on the contrary, as we have seen, he thought it obscure and meaningless. Proof, if proof were needed, that any landscape depends on how you look at it, and that the best way of truly appreciating the whip is to grip the handle yourself.

Chapter XIX

I MUSTN'T FORGET to mention that Rubião undertook to have a mass said for the soul of the departed, even though he knew or suspected that Quincas Borba was not a Catholic. He had never been rude about priests, or disparaged Catholic doctrines; but nor had he had a word to say about the church or its followers. On the other hand, his devotion to Humanitas strongly suggested to his heir that this was his true religion. Nevertheless, Rubião made arrangements for the mass to be said, taking the view that it was not so much a fulfillment of the dead man's wishes as a prayer for the living, and that it would be considered a scandal throughout the city if he, the man's heir, failed to give his benefactor the customary rites accorded to even the most miserly wretches of this world.

If there were some people who did not attend so as not to have to witness Rubião's triumph, many others—and by no means riffraff—did, and what they saw was the former schoolmaster's genuine sorrow.

Chapter XX

ONCE THE PRELIMINARY steps had been taken toward settling his inheritance, Rubião made arrangements to go to Rio de Janeiro, where he would stay until everything else was sorted out. There were things to be done both in Rio and in Barbacena, but matters promised to proceed swiftly.

Chapter XXI

SOFIA AND HER HUSBAND, Cristiano de Almeida e Palha, boarded the train at Vassouras. He was a hale young man of thirty-two, and she was around twenty-seven or twenty-eight. They chose the two seats facing Rubião, first stowing away their small baskets and parcels of souvenirs from Vassouras, where they had gone to spend a week, buttoning up their dustcoats, and exchanging a few whispered words.

Once the train set off again, Palha noticed Rubião. Among all those sullen and weary travelers, his was the only calm and contented face. Palha was the first to strike up a conversation, saying how tiring rail journeys were; Rubião agreed, adding that for those more accustomed to traveling by donkey, the railroad was particularly tiring and charmless, and yet one could not deny that it was progress . . .

"Indeed," agreed Palha. "Great progress."

"Are you a farmer?"

"No, sir."

"Do you live in the town?"

"Vassouras? No, we came to spend a week here. I live in Rio. I wouldn't be suited to farming, although I think it a fine and honorable occupation."

From farming they moved on to cattle, slavery, and politics. Cristiano Palha cursed the government, which had included a line about enslaved property in the Emperor's speech to parliament; but, to his great surprise, Rubião did not share his companion's indignation. Apart from one houseboy, he planned to sell all the slaves Quincas Borba had left him; if he got a bad price for them, the rest of the inheritance would make up the shortfall. In any case, the Emperor's speech, which he, too, had read, guaranteed current property rights. What did he care about future slaves if he was never going to buy any? The houseboy would be freed as soon as he, Rubião, came into possession of his inheritance. Palha changed the subject and turned to party politics, the Chamber, the Paraguayan War, and other general matters, to which Rubião listened with varying degrees of attention. Sofia was barely listening; she merely moved her eyes, which she knew to be pretty, gazing in turn at her husband and at the man he was speaking to.

"Will you stay in Rio or return to Barbacena?" asked Palha after twenty minutes of conversation.

"My wish is to stay, and that's what I will do," replied Rubião. "I'm tired of the provinces. I want to enjoy life. I might even go to Europe, but I'm not sure yet."

Palha's eyes suddenly lit up.

"Quite right. I would do the same, if I could. At the moment, I can't. No doubt you've already been there?"

"No, never. That's why I've been thinking about it. Sometimes we need to blow away those cobwebs! I don't yet know when I'll go, but I will . . ."

"You're right. They say there are lots of splendid things to see—no wonder, since they've been around longer than we have, but we'll catch up. And there are things here that are just as good, or even better. I'm not saying that Rio can compete with Paris or London, but it is beautiful, you'll see . . ."

"I have already."

"Already?"

"Many years ago."

"You'll find it even better now; there has been much progress. Later, when you go to Europe—"

"Have you been to Europe, senhora?" said Rubião, turning to Sofia.

"No, senhor."

"Oh, I forgot to introduce my wife to you," said Cristiano hurriedly. Rubião bowed his head respectfully and then, turning back to the husband, smiled.

"But won't you introduce yourself as well?" he said.

Palha smiled, too, realizing that neither of them knew the other's name, and quickly gave his own:

"Cristiano de Almeida e Palha."

"Pedro Rubião de Alvarenga, but everyone calls me Rubião."

Exchanging names put them even more at ease. Sofia, however, did not join in the conversation, instead giving her eyes full rein to wander wherever they wished. Rubião talked, smiled, and listened attentively to Palha's words, grateful for the friendliness shown to him by a young man he had never met before. He even suggested the idea of them going to Europe together.

"Oh! I won't be able to go, not for a couple of years," replied Palha.

"I'm not saying right now; I wouldn't go that soon myself. The desire that came upon me, as I was leaving Barbacena, was simply that, a desire with no deadline; I will go, of that there is no doubt, but at some point in the future, God willing."

Palha quickly replied:

"Ah, yes! When I said in a couple of years, I should also have added that the will of God might decide otherwise. Who knows, perhaps a few months from now? Divine Providence knows best."

The expression that accompanied these words was resolute and devout, but Sofia, who was looking down at her feet, did not notice, and Rubião did not even hear Palha's last few words.

He was bursting to tell him the reason that brought him to the capital. His mouth was brimming with confidences ready to be poured into his traveling companion's ear, and it was only a vestige of scruple, already weak, that was holding him back. And why should he hold back, since it wasn't a crime and would soon be public knowledge?

"I first have to draw up an inventory for a will," he finally murmured.

"Your father's?"

"No, a friend's. A great friend of mine, who has made me his sole heir."

"Ah!"

"Yes, sole heir. There are such friends in this world, but few like him. Pure gold. And what a mind! Such intelligence, such learning! He had been ill in recent years, which brought out some rather strange and erratic behavior. I'm sure you can imagine; wealthy and in poor health, with no family, he could certainly be rather demanding... But pure gold, fourteen-carat. When he took a liking to someone, there was no holding back. We were close friends, but he never said a word about his will. Then, when he died, the will was opened, and I discovered he'd left me everything. God's truth. Sole heir! Not a single bequest to anyone else. And no relatives. The only male relative he might have had would have been me, if he had married my sister as planned, but she died before him, poor thing! I went from being future brother-in-law to friend, and he certainly knew how to be a friend, don't you think?"

"He certainly did," agreed Palha.

His eyes were no longer shining, they were lost in deep reflection. Rubião, on the other hand, had plunged into dense woodland where all the birds were singing his good fortune; he was enjoying talking about his inheritance; he confessed he didn't yet know the total amount, but he could make a rough estimate—

"Best not to estimate anything," said Cristiano. "In any event, it's unlikely to be less than a hundred *contos*, I imagine."

"Oh, more than that!"

"Well, if it's more than that, best sit back and wait. And another thing—"

"I don't think it will be less than three hundred..."

"Another thing. Don't go telling strangers. I'm grateful for the trust you have placed in me, but don't take risks on a first meeting. Kind faces and discretion don't always go together."

Chapter XXII

WHEN THEY ARRIVED at the train station in Rio, they parted almost like old friends. Palha invited him to stay with them in Santa Teresa; the former schoolteacher, however, was heading to the União Hotel, so they promised to visit each other.

Chapter XXIII

THE FOLLOWING DAY, Rubião was keen to catch up once again with his new friend from the train, and decided to go to Santa Teresa that afternoon; however, it was Palha who found him first, that very morning. He had come to pay his respects, to see if he was comfortable in his hotel, or whether he might prefer to stay at his house, up on the hill. Rubião declined the offer, but accepted his suggestion of a lawyer, a distant relative of Palha's and one of the very best, despite his youth.

"You'd better take advantage of him now, before he starts charging for his reputation."

Rubião took his friend to lunch, then went with him to the lawyer's office, despite the protests of his dog, who wanted to go too. Everything was duly settled.

"Come and dine with me this evening in Santa Teresa," said Palha, as they parted. "No hesitating, now; I'll be expecting you."

Chapter XXIV

RUBIÃO FELT AWKWARD around Sofia, because he had no idea how to behave around ladies. Luckily, he remembered the promise he had made to himself to be strong and implacable, and he duly went to supper with them. Blessed decision! Where could he have spent a more delightful few hours? Sofia was far lovelier at home than she had been on the train. There, although her eyes were uncovered, she had been wearing a cape; here both eyes and body were visible, the latter elegantly sculpted in a cambric gown that revealed her very pretty hands and a little bit of forearm. Besides, here she was the lady of the house, she talked more and was a most attentive hostess. Rubião went back down the hill with his head in a daze.

Chapter XXV

HE DINED THERE many times, but remained shy and awkward. The frequency of his visits lessened that initial impression, but he always carried within him a hidden, if barely hidden, flame that he was unable to extinguish. While the process of drawing up the inventory dragged on, particularly when the will was challenged by someone alleging that Quincas Borba lacked testamentary capacity on account of his evident madness, our Rubião was somewhat distracted. The challenge, however, was rejected, and the inventory proceeded rapidly toward its conclusion. Palha celebrated the occasion with a supper, at which the three of them were joined by the lawyer, the procurator, and the probate registrar. That day, Sofia's eyes were the most beautiful in the world.

Chapter XXVI

"IT'S AS IF she had bought them in some mysterious factory," thought Rubião, as he made his way down the hill again. "I've never seen them as beautiful as they were today."

Soon afterward, he moved to the house in Botafogo, one of those he had inherited; it needed to be furnished, but once again his friend Palha was of great service to Rubião, guiding him in matters of taste and local knowledge, and accompanying him to furniture stores and auctions. At times, as we already know, all three of them went; because there are some things, as Sofia mischievously pointed out, that only a woman can choose. Rubião accepted gratefully, and dallied over his purchases, consulting her sometimes for no real reason, inventing things he needed, anything to keep the young lady by his side for as long as possible. She took it all in her stride—talking, explaining, demonstrating

Chapter XXVII

THESE ARE THE THOUGHTS that were passing through Rubião's head after his morning coffee, in the same place where we left him sitting earlier, gazing far, far away. He carried on drumming on his knee with the tassels of his dressing gown. Eventually he remembered to go let Quincas Borba out. This was his daily task. He stood up and went into the garden at the rear of the house.

Chapter XXVIII

"BUT WHAT IS THIS sin that torments me?" he thought as he walked. "She is married, on good terms with her husband, her husband is my friend, he trusts me absolutely... What temptations are these?"

Rubião stopped walking, and his temptations stopped too. He, a lay Saint Anthony, differed from the holy anchorite in that he liked the Devil's suggestions, given that the Devil was so insistent. Hence that alternating monologue:

"She's so pretty! And she really does seem rather keen on me! If that isn't love, then I don't know what is! She clasps my hand with such fervor, such warmth . . . I can't keep away; even if they would let me, I simply can't resist."

Quincas Borba heard his footsteps and began to bark. Rubião hurried to release him. A momentary release from his own travails too.

"Quincas Borba!" he cried, opening the gate.

The dog bounds out. Such joy! Such enthusiasm! Such leaps and bounds around his master! He starts licking Rubião's hand contentedly, but Rubião clips him on the nose, which hurts; he pulls back, downcast, his tail between his legs; then his master snaps his fingers, and suddenly he's back again, joyful as ever.

"Easy, boy, easy does it!"

Quincas Borba follows him through the garden, looping around the house, sometimes trotting, sometimes jumping. While he savors his freedom, he never lets his master out of his sight. Here he sniffs, there he stops to scratch an ear, farther on he picks out a flea from his belly fur, then, in one leap, he catches up, and is once again snapping at the heels of his master. He thinks Rubião's thoughts are only of him, and is walking back and forth solely to have him walk, too, and make up for all the time he was kept indoors. When Rubião stops, he looks up, waiting; naturally he must be thinking of him: It's some sort of plan for them to go out together, or something fun like that. He never considers the possibility of a sharp kick or a slap. He has a trusting nature and a very short memory when it comes to being hit. On the other hand, stroking makes a deep and lasting impression, no matter how distractedly it is done. He loves being loved. He's happy to believe that he is.

His life is neither entirely good nor entirely bad. There's a black boy who washes him every day in cold water, an evil custom that he never gets used to. Jean, the cook, likes him; the Spanish servant not at all. Rubião spends many hours away from home, but does not mistreat him. He allows him to come up into the house, even to be present during lunch and dinner, or to follow him into the drawing room or study. Sometimes he plays with him, and gets him to perform little jumps. If important visitors come, he has him taken inside or downstairs to the kitchens, and, since he always resists, the Spaniard leads him very gently at first, but soon gets his revenge, dragging him by an ear or a leg, hurling him far away, and blocking every means of return:

"*Perro del infierno!*"*

Bruised and separated from his friend, Quincas Borba goes to lie down in a corner and stays there, silent, for a long time; he shuffles around a little, until he finds a comfortable position, then closes his eyes. He doesn't sleep, but gathers his thoughts, pieces them together, remembers things. Distantly, very distantly, the blurred face of his dead friend sometimes appears to him, blurred fragments that then mingle with the face of his new friend, so that they both seem one person. Then there are other thoughts . . .

So many thoughts—too many, perhaps. In any event they are the thoughts of a dog, mere dust—even less than dust, you will no doubt say, dear reader. Yet the truth is that this eye, which from time to time opens and stares so expressively into space, seems to speak of something that shines deep within, hidden behind something else I cannot put a name to, something that, while it is intrinsically canine, is neither tail nor ears. Oh, the poverty of human language!

Eventually he dozes off. As he dreams, images of life play around his head, some recent, some blurred, shreds and patches from here

---

* "Wretched dog!"

and there. When he wakes, he has forgotten the bad parts; and yet he has an expression, which I will not call melancholic so as not to offend the reader. We can call a landscape melancholic, but we wouldn't say the same thing about a dog. The reason can only be that the landscape's melancholy lies within us, whereas attributing melancholy to a dog places the melancholy outside of ourselves. Whatever it might be, it is not the joy we saw only a short time earlier. Yet upon a whistle from the cook, or a gesture from his master, it all vanishes, his eyes shine, his snout sniffs the air with delight, and his legs fly like wings.

=== *Chapter XXIX*

RUBIÃO SPENT THE REST of the morning contentedly. It was Sunday; two friends had come for lunch, a young man of twenty-four, who was starting to nibble at the first trimmings of his mother's wealth, and a man of forty-four or forty-six who had nothing left to nibble.

The first man's name was Carlos Maria, and the second man was called Freitas. Rubião liked them both, but in different ways. It was not only age that drew him closer to Freitas, but also the man's nature. Freitas praised everything, saluting every dish and every wine with a few well-chosen and elegant words, and leaving with his pockets stuffed with cigars, thus proving that he preferred them to any others. Rubião had been introduced to him at a certain establishment on Rua Municipal, where they had once dined together. He had been told about the man's past, his reversals of fortune, but not in any detail. Rubião, though, rather turned up his nose at this, for Freitas was clearly a dissolute fellow, whose acquaintance would bring him neither personal pleasure nor public esteem. But Freitas quickly softened that first impression, for he was lively, interesting, full of anecdotes, and as cheerful as a man with an income of fifty *contos*. When Rubião mentioned the pretty roses in his garden, Freitas asked if he could come and see them: He was crazy about flowers. A couple of days later he appeared at Rubião's house and said he had come to see the beautiful roses, just for a few minutes, if that wouldn't inconvenience him, and if Rubião wasn't too busy. Rubião, on the contrary, was pleased to see that the man had not forgotten their conversation, and came down into the garden where Freitas was waiting, and showed him the roses. Freitas found them admirable, and examined them so minutely that he had to be dragged from one rosebush to the next. He knew the name of every one, and listed many other varieties that Rubião neither owned nor knew; as he listed them, he described each one in detail, its shape, its size (indicating this by making a circle with his thumb and forefinger), and then naming people who owned good specimens. But Rubião's were of the very best species; this one, for example, was extremely rare, and that one too. And so on. Rubião's gardener listened to him in awe. Once every rose had been examined, Rubião said:

"Come and have something to drink. What will it be?"

Freitas said he would be happy with anything. On entering the house, he commented on how well appointed it was. He examined the bronze figures, the paintings, the furniture, gazed out toward the sea.

"Yes indeed," he said, "you live as a true gentleman, sir!"

Rubião smiled; "gentleman" was certainly the kind of compliment he liked to hear. The Spanish servant entered the room bearing the silver salver, various liqueurs, and glasses, and Rubião glowed with pride. He offered his guest a choice of liqueurs, then recommended one he had been told was the best of its kind available on the market. Freitas gave a doubtful smile.

"That may be an exaggeration," he said.

He took a first sip, savoring it slowly, then a second, then a third. Finally, somewhat amazed, he admitted that it was indeed exceptional. Where had he bought it? Rubião replied that a friend of his, the owner of a large firm of wine importers, had given him a bottle as a present, and he had liked it so much that he had ordered three dozen more. Rubião and Freitas quickly became firm friends. And Freitas frequently returned for lunch or dinner—even more often than he himself really wanted to, or indeed should—because it's always hard to resist a man so amenable, and so friendly toward friendly faces.

Chapter XXX

RUBIÃO ONCE ASKED HIM:

"Tell me something, Senhor Freitas; if I took it upon myself to go to Europe, would you be able to accompany me?"

"No."

"Why not?"

"Because, as a friend, I prefer to be a free spirit, and we might well argue as soon as we set off."

"Well, that's a pity, because you're such a cheerful fellow."

"There you are mistaken, senhor; I keep up this cheerful appearance, but underneath I am sad. I am an architect of ruins. I'd go first to the ruins in Athens, then to the theater to see a sentimental drama called *The Pauper of the Ruins*, and then to the bankruptcy court, where ruined men go . . ."

And Rubião laughed; he liked his friend's frank, unreserved ways.

Chapter XXXI

WOULD YOU CARE TO see the reverse of this coin, curious reader? Then take a look at the other lunch guest, Carlos Maria. If Freitas is "frank and unreserved"—in the very best sense—then clearly Carlos Maria is the opposite. You will relish watching him enter the drawing room, slow, cold, and aloof, and being introduced to Freitas, his eyes averted. Freitas, who has already silently cursed him because of his lateness (it is almost midday), greets him warmly, with effusive courtesy.

You can also see for yourself that our Rubião, although he likes Freitas more, holds the other man in higher esteem; he had been waiting for him patiently, and would have waited until tomorrow. Carlos Maria, however, has no regard for either of them. Examine him closely; he is an elegant young man with large, placid eyes, very much his own master, and even more the master of others. He looks down his nose at them, and his smile is scornful rather than jovial. Now, as he sits down at the table, picks up his cutlery, and unfolds his napkin, everything is telling you that he's doing his host a great favor, perhaps even two: having lunch at his table, and not calling him an idiot.

And yet, despite this disparity in their natures, the lunch was a jolly affair. Freitas devoured his food, pausing briefly now and then, of course—and told himself that had the lunch been served at the designated time (eleven o'clock), it might not have been quite so tasty. Now he was busily engaged in polishing off the first few mouthfuls, those that best assuage the ravenous hunger of the shipwrecked man. After ten minutes or so, he was at last able to begin to speak, full of good cheer and laughter, growing ever more expansive in his gestures, working his way through a whole string of bon mots and picaresque anecdotes. To humiliate him, Carlos Maria listened to most of them with a straight face, so much so that Rubião, who found Freitas genuinely funny, no longer dared to laugh. Toward the end of the lunch, Carlos Maria relaxed a little, and alluded to a few amorous adventures involving other people; hoping to flatter him, Freitas asked him to recount one or two of his own. Carlos Maria burst out laughing.

"Which role would you like me to play?" he asked.

Freitas explained himself; he wasn't asking for some sort of apologia, just facts, a few interesting facts. There was nothing untoward in that, and no one could possibly imagine—

"Do you find it agreeable living here in Botafogo?" said Carlos Maria, interrupting him and addressing his host.

Freitas bit his lip at such impudence, and, for the second time, silently cursed the young man. He sat back in his chair, staring somberly at a painting on the wall. Rubião replied that he found Botafogo very agreeable indeed, and that the beach was beautiful.

"Yes, the view is pretty, but I was never able to stand the bad smell you get around here sometimes," said Carlos Maria. "What do you think?" he continued, turning to Freitas.

Freitas leaned forward and said everything he thought on the subject, adding that they might both be right; but he insisted that the shoreline, despite everything, was magnificent; he spoke without resentment or annoyance, even being so kind as to draw Carlos Maria's attention to a little bit of fruit clinging to the tip of his mustache.

They finished their lunch just after one o'clock. Rubião went over it all in his mind, dish by dish, gazing contentedly at the glasses with their residue of wine, the scattered crumbs, the appearance of the table after the meal, just before coffee. From time to time, he would glance at the footman's livery. He even caught a look of unalloyed pleasure on Carlos Maria's face as he took his first puff on one of the cigars that had been passed around. At that moment, the servant entered carrying a small basket covered with a fine cambric handkerchief, along with a letter, both of which had just been delivered.

Chapter XXXII

"WHO SENT THIS?" asked Rubião.

"Dona Sofia."

Rubião did not recognize the handwriting: it was the first time she had written to him. What could it be? His face and his fingers betrayed his excitement. While Rubião was opening the letter, Freitas casually uncovered the little basket: inside were strawberries. Trembling, Rubião read these lines:

> *I'm sending you these delicious fruits for lunch, assuming they arrive in time. And, on Cristiano's instructions you are invited to come dine with us this evening, without fail.*
>
> *Your true friend,*
> *Sofia*

"What type of fruit?" Rubião asked, folding the letter.

"Strawberries."

"They came too late. Strawberries, you say?" he repeated, his mind on other things.

"No need to blush, my friend," Freitas said, laughing, as soon as the servant left. "These things happen to those in love..."

"Those in love?" repeated Rubião, blushing deeply now. "But you can read the letter, see for yourself..."

He was about to show him the letter, but then held back and put it in his pocket. He was beside himself, half-baffled, half-euphoric; Carlos Maria took great delight in telling Rubião that he couldn't hide the fact that the gift was from a sweetheart. And there was nothing to be ashamed of in that; love was a law unto itself; if she was a married lady, then he praised his discretion—

"Good gracious, no!" his host interrupted.

"A widow, then? The same thing applies," Carlos Maria added. "In such cases discretion is a virtue. The greatest sin, apart from the sin itself, is publicizing it. If I were a lawmaker, I would propose that every man guilty of indiscretion in such matters should be burned at the stake, just like those accused during the Inquisition, except that rather than being dragged to the bonfire in sackcloth and ashes, they would wear a cloak made of parrot feathers..."

Freitas could not contain his laughter, and banged on the table to show his appreciation. Rubião, taken aback, replied that it was neither a married woman nor a widow...

"A single woman, then?" said Carlos Maria. "Do I hear wedding bells? Well, it's about time. Strawberries for the wedding party," he went on, picking up a couple with his fingers. "They smell of maidenly boudoirs and priestly Latin."

Rubião did not know quite what to say, then he decided it would be best to start over and explain. They were from the wife of a close friend of his. Carlos Maria winked; Freitas intervened to say that this did indeed explain everything, but that, at first, the air of mystery, the covered basket, the appearance of the strawberries themselves—adulterous strawberries, he said, laughing—all those things gave the matter an immoral and sinful appearance.

They sipped their coffee in silence, then went through to the drawing room. Rubião was even more attentive to his guests, but something was bothering him. After a few minutes, he decided that he was rather pleased with his two guests' initial assumption that it was an adulterous affair; he even wondered if he had defended himself too vigorously. Since he had mentioned no names, he could have confessed that it was indeed an intimate affair. But it was also possible that the very vehemence of his denial had left some doubt, some suspicion, in the two men's minds... He smiled at this consoling thought.

Carlos Maria consulted his watch; it was two o'clock, time for him to leave. Rubião thanked him profusely for coming, and asked him to come again; they could spend more Sundays like this in friendly conversation.

"I'll second that!" cried Freitas, joining them.

He had put half a dozen cigars in his pocket and, on leaving, whispered in Rubião's ear:

"My customary souvenir; six days of pleasure; one pleasure per day."

"Do take more."

"No, I'll get more next time."

Rubião accompanied the two men to the gate. As soon as Quincas Borba heard voices, he ran up from the far end of the garden to greet them, especially his master. He nuzzled up to Carlos Maria, trying to lick his hand; the young man drew back in disgust. Rubião gave the dog a kick, which made him yelp and run off. Finally, they all said goodbye.

"Which way are you going?" Carlos Maria asked Freitas.

Freitas assumed that Carlos Maria would be heading to visit someone over near São Clemente, and wanted to accompany him.

"I'm going to the end of the beach," he said.

"Well, I'm heading into town," replied the other.

Chapter XXXIII

RUBIÃO WATCHED THEM leave, then went back inside and sat down in the drawing room, where he reread Sofia's note. Each word of that unexpected letter was a mystery, the signature a capitulation. Just *Sofia*; no surname, either her own or her husband's. *Your true friend* was clearly a metaphor. As for the opening words—*I'm sending you these delicious fruits for lunch*—they exuded the innocence of a good and generous soul. Rubião saw, felt, and grasped all of this by pure instinct, and found himself kissing the piece of paper—or, rather, kissing the name, the name given to her at baptism, repeated by her mother, then surrendered to her husband as part of the wedding contract, and now stolen from all of those legitimate owners and sent to him, Rubião, at the bottom of a sheet of paper . . . Sofia! Sofia! Sofia!

Chapter XXXIV

"WHY SO LATE?" Sofia asked, when he arrived at the garden gate in Santa Teresa.

"Lunch didn't finish until two o'clock, and I had some papers to sort out. It isn't that late," Rubião continued, looking at his watch, "it's only half past four."

"For friends it's always late," Sofia replied with a reproachful look.

Rubião realized his mistake, but had no time to correct it. Facing him, in front of the house, four ladies were seated silently on wrought-iron benches, watching him curiously; they had come to visit Sofia and were awaiting the arrival of a wealthy man by the name of Rubião. Sofia introduced him. Three were married, the other was well on the way to spinsterhood. She was thirty-nine years old, with dark eyes that were weary of waiting. She was the daughter of a certain Major Siqueira, who appeared in the garden a few moments later.

"Our friend Palha has already told me all about you, sir," said the major after being introduced to Rubião. "A very worthy friend of yours, I'll wager. He told me you met by chance. Generally, those are the best friendships. Back in the thirties, during the last few years of the regency, I had a friend, the best friend I had back then, who I also met by chance, at Bernardes's Pharmacy, and who went by the nickname Fat Calves João . . . I think he used to wear padded stockings when he was young, between the years of 1801 and 1812. The nickname stuck. The pharmacy was on Rua de São José, where it meets Rua da Misericórdia . . . Fat Calves João . . . You see, the padding made his legs look thicker. Bernardes was his name, João Alves Bernardes. He owned the pharmacy on Rua de São José. People used to meet there, in the afternoons, or at night. Men would go in their cloaks, carrying canes; some even brought lanterns. Not me, I only took my cloak . . . Yes, we all brought our cloaks. Bernardes—João Alves Bernardes was his full name—was from Maricá, but grew up here in Rio de Janeiro . . . Fat Calves João was his nickname; they say he wore padded stockings as a young man, and it seems he was one of the dandies about town. I've never forgotten it: Fat Calves João . . . People wore cloaks then, you see . . ."

Rubião's mind was flailing about beneath this torrent of words; but he was up a blind alley with no way out. Walls all around him. No open doorway, no passageway to escape through, and down the torrent poured. Had he been able to glance over toward the ladies, he would have seen that at least he was an object of curiosity for all of them, in particular the major's daughter, Dona Tonica. But he could not escape, all he could do was listen to the major raining words down upon him. It was Palha who brought him an umbrella. Sofia had gone to tell her husband that Rubião had just arrived; moments later, Palha was in the garden, greeting his dear friend, and berating him for being so late. The major, who was yet again explaining the pharmacist's nickname, abandoned his prey and went over to the young ladies, then he left.

Chapter XXXV

THE MARRIED WOMEN were pretty; even the spinster had probably been pretty when she was twenty-five. Sofia, though, surpassed them all.

This is doubtless an understatement of what our friend was feeling. She was one of those women whom time, like a dawdling sculptor, does not finish straightaway, but spends long days polishing and perfecting. These slow sculptures are miraculous; Sofia was slowly approaching her twenty-eighth year; she was more beautiful than at twenty-seven, and the sculptor was presumably waiting for her to reach thirty before giving her the final touches, assuming, of course, that he didn't prolong his work for another two or three years.

Her eyes, for example, are no longer the same as on that first train journey, when they darted back and forth underscoring the conversation between our friend Rubião and Palha. Now they seem darker, and are no longer underscoring anything; they compose things all by themselves, in round, graceful letters, and not merely one or two lines, but entire chapters. Her mouth seems somehow younger. Her shoulders, hands, and arms have improved, too, and she makes the most of them with her well-chosen poses and gestures. And while her heavy eyebrows—a feature the lady herself hated, and one that Rubião himself at first found out of keeping with the rest of her face—have not grown thinner, they seem to give the whole ensemble a very striking appearance.

She dresses well, her waist and bust snugly contained by a simple bodice made of fine chestnut-colored wool, and she wears two real pearls as earrings—a gift our Rubião had given her at Easter.

This lovely lady is the daughter of an old civil servant. She married Cristiano de Almeida e Palha at twenty years old. A financial speculator, then age twenty-five, Palha earned good money, was sharp, quick-witted, and had a good nose for business and for people. In 1864, although still new to his trade, he somehow divined—there is no other word for it—that the banks were about to go bust.

"Something's bound to happen sooner or later; they're hanging by a thread. The slightest hint of alarm, and they'll all come crashing down."

The worst thing was that he was spending all his profits, and then some. He was partial to the finer things in life; social gatherings, expensive gowns and jewelry for his wife, household furnishings, especially if they were in the latest style, and new inventions—these consumed all of his earnings, both present and future. Apart from food, he spent little on himself. He went often to the theater, although he didn't enjoy it, and to balls, which he enjoyed somewhat; in truth, he went less for himself than to be seen alongside his wife's alluring eyes, and her fine bosom. This was his peculiar vanity, to display his wife's décolletage whenever he could, and even when he shouldn't, so as to show other men his own private good fortune. He was thus a sort of King Candaules,* in some respects more restrained, and in other respects more public.

At this point, we should do justice to our leading lady. At first she went along with her husband's desires somewhat unwillingly, but such was the flattery heaped upon her, and such is our ability to adapt to circumstances, that she ended up enjoying being seen, and very widely seen, for the entertainment and stimulus of others. We should not make her more of a saint than she was, but no less either. Her vanity was paid for only with her eyes, which were cheerful, restless, inviting, but only inviting: we could compare them to the lantern outside an inn where there are no rooms available for guests. The lantern, with its beautiful color and original design, makes everyone stop and look, before they go on their way. Why then fling wide the windows? In the end, though, she did fling them wide, but the door itself, if such can be called her heart, remained firmly locked and barred.

---

* According to Herodotus, King Candaules of Lydia was inordinately proud of his wife's beauty and compelled his bodyguard to sneak into her bedroom to see her naked. When the queen saw the bodyguard spying on her, she told him that he must kill the king and take his place.

Chapter XXXVI

"MY GOODNESS, she's pretty! If I'm not careful, I could cause a scandal!" thought Rubião that night, standing by a window, facing into the room and gazing at Sofia, who was gazing back at him.

One of the ladies was singing. The three husbands, who were also visiting, interrupted their card game in deference to the singer, and came into the drawing room for a few moments; the lady singing was the wife of one of them. Palha, who was accompanying her on the piano, did not see the gazes exchanged between his wife and his wealthy new friend. I do not know if the same was true for all the others. Or, rather, I do know that one of them—Dona Tonica, the major's daughter—did see them.

"My goodness, she's pretty! If I'm not careful, I could cause a scandal!" Rubião kept thinking, leaning against the window, facing into the room, his eyes lost in contemplation of the beautiful woman gazing back at him.

Chapter XXXVII

IT WAS ENTIRELY understandable that Dona Tonica should be watching that exchange of glances. Since Rubião arrived, she had thought of little else but how to attract his attention. Her weary thirty-nine-year-old eyes, eyes that had found no partners on this earth, and which were already slipping from weariness into despair, summoned up a few remaining sparks. Sweeping those eyes back and forth, languidly, invitingly, had long been her stock-in-trade. Now she had Rubião in her sights.

Her rather disenchanted heart began to beat faster again. Something told her that this rich new arrival from Minas Gerais was destined by heaven to resolve her matrimonial impasse. If truth be told, he was wealthier than she required; she wasn't seeking riches, she was seeking a husband. All of her previous campaigns had been waged without pecuniary considerations, and in recent times she had been lowering her expectations further and further; indeed, her last campaign had been waged against a penniless student. But who knows, perhaps heaven had destined her to marry a rich man. Dona Tonica had faith in her patron saint, Our Lady of the Immaculate Conception, and she set about assailing the fortress with great skill and valor.

"All the others are married," she said to herself.

It did not take long for her to notice that Rubião and Sofia's eyes tended to drift toward each other; she also noted, however, that Sofia's glances were less frequent and less lingering, a phenomenon that could, she thought, be explained by the caution for which the situation naturally called. Perhaps they were in love? This suspicion tormented her, but a combination of wishful thinking and hope told her that, after having one or more affairs, a man might turn to marriage. The trick was to lure him in; thoughts of marrying and having a family might well then kill off any other inclinations he might have.

And so she redoubled her efforts. She summoned up all her charms and, although somewhat faded, they answered the call. She tried everything: fluttering her fan, pouting her lips, shooting him sideways glances, and taking turns about the room to show off her slim waist and elegant profile. It was the old formula in action; it hadn't produced any results up until now, but it's the same with the lottery: one day you get a winning ticket that makes up for all your losses.

This evening, though, the singing accompanied by the piano got in the way of all that, and Dona Tonica could see that Rubião and Sofia were mesmerized by each other. There could be no doubt; these were not brief, casual glances as they had been before, but were a shared exchange that shut out the rest of the room. Dona Tonica could hear the old raven of despair croaking. *Quoth the Raven "Nevermore."*

Even so, her battle continued. She succeeded in getting Rubião to sit beside her for a few minutes, and tried to say a few nice things, phrases she remembered from novels, and others inspired by the melancholy of her own situation. Rubião listened and responded, but became restless whenever Sofia left the room, and even more so when she returned. At one point, his distraction was all too apparent. Dona Tonica was confiding in him her deep desire to visit Minas Gerais, in particular Barbacena: "How is the weather there?"

"The weather," he repeated mechanically.

He was looking at Sofia, who at that moment was standing with her back to him, talking to the other two ladies, who were sitting down. Rubião again admired her figure, her shapely torso, which filled out from a slender base and emerged from ample hips like a great bouquet of flowers from a vase. Her head could then be said to be like a single magnolia rising proudly from the center. It was this that Rubião was gazing at when Dona Tonica asked him about the weather in Barbacena and he repeated the word, without even giving it the form of a question.

Chapter XXXVIII

RUBIÃO'S MIND WAS made up. Never had Sofia's soul seemed so insistently to invite his own soul to fly away with hers to those clandestine lands, from which souls generally return feeling old and weary. Some never do return. Others stop halfway. A great number never go beyond their own rooftop.

Chapter XXXIX

THE MOON WAS magnificent. Up there on the hill, between the sky and the plain below, even the most timid of souls would be capable of taking on an enemy army and vanquishing it. Imagine what such a soul might do when faced with such a friendly foe. They were in the garden. Sofia had linked arms with him to go and look at the moon. She had invited Dona Tonica, but the unfortunate woman replied that her foot had gone to sleep and that she would join them shortly, but then did not.

The two of them stood in silence for some time. Through the open windows they could see the others chatting inside, even the men, who had finished their card game. It was a small garden, but the human voice has many modulations, and the two of them could easily have recited poems to each other without being overheard.

Rubião remembered an old simile, a very old one dredged up from goodness knows which ten-line stanza from the 1850s, or from any piece of prose from any age at all. He called Sofia's eyes the stars of the earth, and the stars the eyes of heaven. All this was said in a tremulous whisper.

Sofia was dumbstruck. Suddenly she straightened up, for until then she had been leaning on Rubião's arm. She had become so accustomed to his shyness and timidity ... Stars? Eyes? She was inclined to tell him not to tease her, but didn't know how to formulate her response without rejecting an opinion she, too, shared, or without encouraging him to go further. There was a long silence.

"With one difference," continued Rubião. "The stars are less beautiful than your eyes, and, besides, I don't even know what a star is; God put them up so high because they would lose much of their beauty if seen from close to ... But not your eyes, for they are right here beside me, large and shining brightly, far brighter than the starry sky ..."

Emboldened and loquacious, Rubião seemed a completely different person. He did not stop there; he said a great deal more, but always keeping within the same small circle of ideas. Of these he had few to begin with, and the situation, despite his rapid transformation, tended to stifle rather than inspire new ones. Sofia did not know what to do. She had clasped to her bosom a mild and gentle dove, only to find herself holding a hawk—a voracious, sharp-beaked hawk.

She needed to answer him, to make him stop, to tell him he was heading in a direction in which she did not wish to go, and all without making him angry or driving him away ... She tried to think of something but could not, because she kept bumping up against the same question, which for her was insoluble: Was it better to show that she understood, or to pretend that she didn't? At this point, she remembered her own gestures, her sweet words, her special attentions toward him, and came to the conclusion that, given the situation, she could not pretend to ignore the meaning of the man's compliments. Admitting that she understood, though, and not ordering him out of the house, well, therein lay the danger.

Chapter XL

UP ABOVE, the stars seemed to be laughing at this inextricable situation.

Let the moon see them, then! The moon does not know how to mock, and the poets, who think her sentimental, must have noticed that she, the moon, had once loved some wandering star, who abandoned her after many centuries. They may indeed still love each other. The moon's eclipses (if you will forgive my astronomy) are perhaps nothing more than amorous assignations. The myth of Diana descending to meet Endymion may well be true. Descending is the part that makes no sense. What harm is there in them meeting in midair, the way crickets do in the bushes here on earth? Night, that benevolent mother, takes it upon herself to watch over everyone.

But then, the moon is a solitary creature, and solitude makes a person serious. The stars, on the other hand, are like a gaggle of teenage girls: cheerful and chatty, laughing and talking about everything and everyone all at the same time.

I'm not saying they are not chaste; but that makes it even worse—they must have laughed at things they did not understand ... Chaste stars! That's how both Othello the terrible and Tristram Shandy the jovial describe them. These two extremes of heart and mind agree on one thing: the stars are chaste. And they (chaste stars!) heard everything, everything that Rubião's emboldened lips dared to pour into Sofia's startled soul. The man who had been quietly discreet for so many months was now (chaste stars!) neither more nor less than a libertine. You're probably saying that the Devil himself had set out to deceive the young lady with those two great archangel's wings that God had given him; then suddenly he popped them in his pocket and took off his hat, revealing the two evil horns sticking out of his forehead. And, laughing the ambiguous laugh of all evildoers, he offered to buy not only her soul, but both soul and body... Chaste stars!

=== *Chapter XLI*

"LET'S GO INSIDE," Sofia murmured.

She tried to pull away, but he held on to her arm. No. Why go inside? They were fine where they were... What could be better? Or was he boring her? Sofia hastened to say that he was not, indeed quite the contrary, but she needed to go in and attend to her guests... They'd been outside such a long time!

"Not even ten minutes," said Rubião. "And what's ten minutes?"

"But they might have noticed our absence..."

Rubião quivered at that possessive: *our* absence. He saw in it the beginnings of complicity. He agreed; they might have noticed *our* absence. She was right; they should part. He would ask her only one thing, or rather two things: the first was for her not to forget those ten sublime minutes, and the second was that every night, at ten o'clock, she would look up at the Southern Cross. He would look up, too, and their thoughts would find themselves joined in intimate communion, between God and mankind.

The invitation was poetic, but only the invitation. Rubião was devouring the young lady with fiery eyes, and gripping one of her hands to stop her from escaping. Neither his eyes nor his grip contained poetry of any sort. Sofia was on the verge of saying a few sharp words, but immediately swallowed them, remembering that Rubião was a good friend of her husband's. She wanted to laugh but couldn't; she went from annoyed, to resigned, to supplicatory, begging him in the name of his mother, who must be in heaven . . . Rubião knew nothing of heaven or his mother, or of anything. "Mother? Heaven? What are they?" his face seemed to say.

"Ouch! You're hurting my fingers!" whispered the young lady.

It was then that he began to come to his senses. He slackened his grip, but did not release it.

"Go," he said, "but first . . ."

He was leaning over to kiss her hand, when a voice, a few steps away, jolted him back to his senses.

Chapter XLII

"WELL, HELLO! Enjoying the moonlight? It really is delightful. It's a night for lovers, all right . . . Yes, delightful . . . Haven't seen a night like this for a long time . . . Just look at the streetlights down below . . . A delightful night for lovers! Lovers are always drawn to the moon. Back in my day, in Icaraí . . ."

It was Siqueira, the awful major. Rubião didn't know what to say; after a few moments, Sofia regained her composure; she replied that the night was indeed lovely, and added that Rubião was insisting that Rio nights could not be compared to those in Barbacena, and, on that very subject, he had been telling her an anecdote about a certain Father Mendes . . . It was Mendes, wasn't it?

"Yes, Mendes. Father Mendes," murmured Rubião.

The major had difficulty containing his surprise. He had seen their two clasped hands, Rubião's slightly bowed head, how quickly they had pulled apart when he strode into the garden; and now they were telling him it was all about some Father Mendes . . . He looked at Sofia and saw her smiling, calm and impenetrable. No fear, no embarrassment; she spoke so simply that the major wondered if his eyes had deceived him. Rubião spoiled everything, though. Irritated and sullen, he managed only to take out his watch and check the time, then put it to his ear as if he thought it had stopped working, and then slowly, very slowly, he wiped it with his handkerchief without looking at either Sofia or the major . . .

"Well then, I'll leave you two to talk," said Sofia. "I'm going in to sit with the ladies; they shouldn't be left on their own. Have the men finished their wretched game of cards?"

"Yes, they've finished," replied the major, eyeing Sofia inquisitively. "And they've been asking for this gentleman, which is why I came to see if I might find him in the garden. Have you been out here long?"

"Oh, no, no time at all," said Sofia.

Then, affectionately patting the major's shoulder, she went into the house; not via the door into the drawing room, but via the other door leading into the dining room, so that when she entered the drawing room, it would seem as if she had just given orders for tea to be served.

Coming to his senses, Rubião still didn't know what to say, and yet felt the need to say something. The Father Mendes anecdote had been a good idea; the problem was that neither priest nor anecdote existed, and he was incapable of inventing anything. The best he could come up with was:

"Ah, yes, Father Mendes! A very amusing fellow, Father Mendes!"

"I knew him," said the major, smiling. "Father Mendes, you say? Yes, I knew the fellow, he ended up a canon. Was he in Minas for some time?"

"I believe he was," murmured Rubião, terrified.

"He grew up down here, in Saquarema. He was one eye short, poor fellow—this one," the major continued, pointing to his left eye. "Knew him very well, if it's the same one, that is; might be a different one of course."

"Indeed."

"Ended up a canon. A man of good habits, but always had an eye for a pretty girl, only as one might admire a masterpiece, mind, and what greater artist is there than God?" said the major. "Dona Sofia, for example; every time he saw her on the street, he never failed to tell me: 'Today I saw that pretty wife of Palha's . . .' Ended up a canon, born in Saquarema . . . And he certainly had good taste. Our friend Palha's wife really is a beauty, a fine figure and a face to go with it; I'd still say, though, that I find her more well-proportioned than pretty . . . What do you think?"

"Yes, I'm sure you're right . . ."

"And a charming person, an excellent hostess," continued the major, lighting a cigar.

The light from his match gave the major's face a look of derision, or of something perhaps less scathing but no less dismissive. Rubião felt a chill run down his spine. Had the major heard something? Seen something? Or guessed? Was he a blabbermouth? A scandalmonger? The man's face gave nothing away; in any event, it was safer to think the worst. Here we have our hero, like someone who, after many years sailing close to shore, suddenly finds himself out on the heaving swell of the high seas; fortunately, fear is also the handmaiden of ideas, and it gave him one now: flattery. He wasted no time in finding the major interesting and witty, and in telling him that he owned a house on Botafogo Beach, number such-and-such, where he would always be welcome. It would be an honor to become better acquainted. He had so few friends here in Rio: there was Palha, who had been very kind to him, Dona Sofia, who was an unusually serious-minded lady, and three or four others. He lived alone; he might even be returning to Minas.

"So soon?"

"Perhaps not straightaway, but perhaps not before too long. For someone who's lived their whole life in one place, you know, it can be difficult to get used to somewhere else."

"That depends."

"Yes, it depends . . . But it's the general rule."

"It may be the general rule, but you will be an exception. Rio is a devil of a place; love spreads as easily as a cold; you only have to sit in a draft one day and you're done for. I'd wager that within six months you'll be married . . ."

"Ah, he didn't see anything," thought Rubião.

And then, cheerily:

"Perhaps, but people get married in Minas too; there's no lack of priests there either."

"Well, there's certainly no Father Mendes," replied the major with a chuckle.

Rubião smiled awkwardly, not knowing whether the major's remark was innocent or malicious. But the major then took up the reins of the conversation and steered it on to other subjects: the weather, the city, the government, the war, and Field Marshal López.* And see how the mood has changed: this new torrent of words, even greater than the previous one, fell now upon our

---

* The war against Paraguay had begun some three years earlier, in 1864—see this book's introduction. Francisco Solano López was dictator of Paraguay and widely seen as the instigator of the conflict.

friend Rubião like a ray of sunshine. His soul breathed a sigh of relief under the warmth of the major's endless discourse, interjecting a word or two here and there, wherever he could, and enthusiastically nodding in agreement throughout. And once again he thought to himself that, no, the major hadn't seen anything.

"Papa! Are you there, Papa?" asked a voice at the door that opened onto the garden.

It was Dona Tonica; she had come to ask the major to take her home. Yes, tea was on the table, but she couldn't stay longer; she had a headache, she told her father in a whisper. Then she held out her hand to Rubião, and he begged her not to leave just yet: "The esteemed major—"

"You're wasting your time," interrupted the major. "She rules me with a rod of iron."

Rubião again insisted that he come to visit; he even pressed him to name a day, that very week, but the major quickly replied that he couldn't give a specific date; he would come as soon as he could. He had a great deal of work to do, what with his duties at the arsenal, which were many, and then there was—

"Papa! Let's go!"

"Yes, dear. See? I can't talk for even a minute. Have you said your goodbyes? Where's my hat?"

Chapter XLIII

ALL THE WAY DOWN the hill, Dona Tonica listened to the rest of her father's lecture, which, while it frequently changed subject, continued in the same long-winded, rambling style. The words merely washed over her. She was entirely absorbed in her own thoughts, mulling over the evening's events, re-creating Sofia and Rubião's glances.

They arrived home in Rua do Senado; the father went straight to bed; the daughter didn't do so immediately, but sat in a little chair next to a chest of drawers on which she kept an image of the Virgin Mary, which did not bring her pure or peaceful thoughts. Though she knew nothing of love, she had heard about adultery, and she was horrified by Sofia's conduct. She saw her now as a monster, half person, half serpent; she felt that she hated her, and that she might get her revenge by setting an example and telling her husband everything.

"Yes, I'll tell Palha everything," she thought, "either in person or in a letter... No, not a letter. One day I'll tell him everything, in private."

And, imagining their conversation, she visualized his shock, followed by anger, then the curses, the harsh words he would say to his wife: vile, wretched, unworthy woman... All these names sounded sweet to the ears of her desire, and through them she channeled her own anger and desire for revenge; over and over she played out the woman's downfall, at the hands of her husband since she could not do it herself... Vile, wretched, unworthy woman...

This explosion of inner rage lasted for quite some time—nearly twenty minutes—until her spirits wearied and she regained her composure. With her imagination exhausted, reality came back into focus. She looked at her surroundings, her spinster's bedroom artfully arranged with an ingenuity that made chintz look like silk and turned an old offcut into a ribbon that embellishes, entwines, and enlivens as much as it can the barrenness of everyday objects, that adorns gloomy walls, and makes the best of a few humble sticks of furniture. Everything there seemed made to receive a beloved bridegroom.

Where have I read that on a certain night of the year, according to an ancient tradition, a virgin of Israel was made to wait for divine conception? Wherever it was, let us compare her to this other virgin, who differs only in not being limited to one specific night, but to every night of the year, every single one ... The wind whistling outside her window has never brought her the man she's been waiting for, nor has the pure maiden of dawn told her where upon the earth he lives. There was only waiting, waiting, waiting ...

Now, with her imagination soothed and her resentment assuaged, Tonica once again surveyed her lonely bedroom; she remembered her family and her closest friends from school, all now married. The last of them wed a naval officer when she was thirty, which had renewed Tonica's hopes; she didn't care too much about the rank, since a mere cadet's uniform had been the first thing to set her heart fluttering at the age of fifteen ... Where had the years gone? Another five years had passed; she was thirty-nine, and forty would soon follow. Forty years old and a spinster; Dona Tonica shuddered. She looked around again, remembering everything. Then she sprang to her feet, turned around twice, and flung herself onto the bed, weeping ...

Chapter XLIV

YOU MUST NOT BELIEVE, dear reader, that her pain was more real than her anger. In themselves they were equal; it was their effects that differed. Her anger led nowhere; her humiliation dissolved into justifiable tears. And yet she still felt an urge to throttle Sofia, trample her underfoot, rip out her heart piece by piece, saying to her face all the crude names she imagined her husband would say if he knew ... All, of course, mere imaginings. Believe me, there are tyrants who are only tyrants by intention. Who knows? Perhaps running through this lady's soul there is a tiny thread of a Caligula ...

Chapter XLV

AS ONE SOUL WEEPS, another laughs; such is the world, my good sir; it is a universal truth. Simply crying would be monotonous, simply laughing would be tiring; but a fair distribution of tears and polkas, sobs and sarabands, brings to the world's soul the variety it needs, and the balance of life is restored.

The one laughing is Rubião's soul. Listen, readers, to the bright, cheerful tune his soul sings as he walks down the hill, telling his most intimate secrets to the stars, a sort of rhapsody composed in a language no one has ever written down, since it would be impossible to find symbols that could represent its words. Back in the city, the empty streets seem to him thronged with people, the silence is deafening, and leaning from every window are the shapes of women with pretty faces and thick eyebrows, all of them Sofias merging into one single Sofia. Once or twice, it occurs to Rubião that he was reckless and indiscreet; he remembers the scene in the garden, the young woman's resistance, her annoyance, and he begins to repent; then he shudders, terrified at the thought that they might banish him from their house and cut him off entirely, and all because he had been too impetuous. Yes, he should have waited; it wasn't the right occasion—the guests, all those lights. What had he been thinking of, talking about love so recklessly, so shamelessly? She had been quite right to tell him to leave at once.

"I must have been out of my mind!" he said aloud.

He was not thinking about the supper, which had been sumptuous, or the wines, which had been copious, or the electric atmosphere of a drawing room graced by elegant ladies; no, he had been completely, utterly, out of his mind.

A few moments later, the same soul that had been so critical of itself was now finding excuses. Hadn't Sofia encouraged him, with her frequent glances that became stares, her manner and her languid gestures, her kindness in seating him next to her at supper, then giving him all her attention, melodiously murmuring all sorts of delightful things—what were these if not encouragement and invitation? And as for her reaction later on, in the garden, well, that could, he thought, be easily explained: it was the first time she had heard such words outside of a marital context, and within such close earshot of others—naturally she had trembled. Besides, he had been too open with her and tried to move things along too quickly. He should have taken things gradually, one step at a time, and certainly not gripped her hand so tightly that he hurt her. In short, he had been boorish. The fear returned that they might banish him from their house; but then he resorted to the consolation of hope, an analysis of the young lady's actions, her invention of that fictitious Father Mendes, her complicity in lying. He thought also about her husband's friendliness toward him . . . At this, he shuddered. Her husband's friendship gave him a pang of remorse. Not only did the man trust him, he had also borrowed money from him, and there were those three bills of exchange that Rubião had endorsed on Palha's behalf.

"I cannot and must not proceed any further," he said to himself, "it wouldn't be right. Strictly speaking, none of this is my doing; she's the one who, for quite some time now, has been leading me on. Well, she can try all she likes! Yes, I must resist her . . . I loaned him the money almost without being asked, because he was in great need of it, and I owed him favors; he did ask me to sign those bills of exchange, but he hasn't asked me for anything else. I know he's an honorable fellow, and hardworking too; it's that darned wife of his who spoiled things by coming between us, with her pretty eyes and her figure ... My goodness, what a remarkable figure she has! Tonight it was just divine. When her arm brushed against mine at the table, even through my sleeve ..."

Feeling bewildered and unsure what to do, he dwelled upon the loyalty he owed his friend, but his conscience was split in two, each part accusing the other, then one part explaining itself, until both were completely disoriented ...

Eventually, after wandering randomly around the city, he found himself in Praça da Constituição. He thought about going to the theater, but it was too late. So he headed toward Largo de São Francisco, from where he could catch a cab home to Botafogo. He found three cabs waiting, and they all hurried toward him, their drivers offering their services with particular praise for their respective horses: a fine horse, senhor—an excellent animal!

Chapter XLVI

THE SOUND OF VOICES and vehicles awoke a beggar who was sleeping on the steps of the church nearby. The poor fellow sat up, saw what was going on, then lay down again and stared up at the sky. The sky stared back at him just as impassively, but without the beggar's wrinkles, or his tattered shoes, or his rags; the sky was clear, starry, serenely Olympian, like the one that presided over Jacob's wedding and Lucretia's suicide. Beggar and sky stared at each other in a kind of game, daring the other to blink first, two serene, rival majesties, without a hint of arrogance or inferiority, as if the beggar were saying to the sky:

"Well, you won't be falling in on me."

And the sky to the beggar:

"And you won't be clambering up to me."

Chapter XLVII

RUBIÃO WAS NO PHILOSOPHER, and comparing his thoughts to those of the vagrant served only to make him jealous. "That scoundrel thinks about nothing," he said to himself. "Soon he'll be fast asleep, while I—"

"Get in, boss; she's a fine animal. We'll be there in fifteen minutes."

The other two cabdrivers were telling him the same thing, in almost the same words:

"Over here, boss—come and see . . ."

"Look here at my lovely little horse . . ."

"Please, senhor; it's a thirteen-minute ride. You'll be home in thirteen minutes."

After some hesitation, Rubião chose the cab closest to him, and with a crack of the whip they set off for Botafogo. He then remembered a long-forgotten incident, or perhaps it was the incident that unconsciously provided him with a solution. Either way, Rubião guided his thoughts in that direction, as a means of escaping the emotions of the evening.

It had happened many years ago. He was very young at the time, and poor. One day, at eight o'clock in the morning, he left the house, which was on Rua do Cano (now Rua Sete de Setembro), walked the short distance to Largo de São Francisco de Paula, and then turned onto Rua do Ouvidor. He had a few things on his mind, among them the fact that he was living in the house of a friend who was beginning to treat him like a three-day guest, when he had already been there for four weeks. It's said that guests begin to smell after three days; dead bodies begin to smell long before that, at least in hot climates like ours . . . What is certain is that our Rubião, a good and simple son of Minas Gerais, but as mistrustful as someone from São Paulo, was rather concerned and thinking about leaving as soon as possible. You can be sure that from the moment he left the house, entered Largo de São Francisco de Paula, and made his way down Rua do Ouvidor as far as Rua dos Ourives, he neither saw nor heard anything around him.

At the corner of Rua dos Ourives, he was stopped by a crowd of people and a strange procession. A man in judicial robes was reading out a document: a verdict. As well as the judge, there was a priest, soldiers, and various curious onlookers. But the principal figures were two black men. One of them, a scrawny, sallow-skinned fellow of medium height, had his hands tied, his head bowed, and a rope around his neck; the end of the rope was held by the other black man. This other man looked straight ahead and his skin had a firmer, darker sheen. He bravely endured the onlookers' curiosity. Once the verdict had been read out, the procession made its way along Rua dos Ourives; it had come from the jail and was heading toward Largo do Moura.

Naturally, all this made quite an impression on Rubião. For several seconds he found himself in the same quandary as when choosing his cab. Inner forces were, one might say, touting the services of their horses; some were urging him to turn back or carry on about his own business, while others urged him to go see the black man hanged. It was so rare to see a hanging! "Come on," said one, "it'll all be over in twenty minutes!" "No," said another, "we've got business to attend to!" And so our man closed his eyes and let himself be carried along by fate. And fate, rather than leading him on down Rua do Ouvidor toward Rua da Quitanda, turned his feet into Rua dos Ourives, following the procession. He wasn't going to watch the execution, he thought; no, he would just follow the condemned man's footsteps, see the hangman's face, the formalities... No, he didn't want to see the actual execution. From time to time, the procession stopped, people came to their doors and windows, and the court clerk again read out the sentence. Then the procession would start moving again with the same solemnity. The onlookers were regaling each other with details of the crime: a murder down near the slaughterhouse. The murderer was described as a cold and brutal man. News of these qualities made Rubião feel better; it gave him the strength to look the condemned man in the face, without being overcome with pity. The man's face, however, no longer reflected his crime; terror now concealed his savagery. Suddenly, without realizing, Rubião found himself at the place of execution. Quite a few people were already there. Along with those now arriving, they formed a dense throng.

"Let's go back," he said to himself.

The condemned man had not yet mounted the scaffold; he would not be put to death immediately, so there was still time to get away. And if he stayed, he could always close his eyes, as a certain Saint Alypius had once done at the Roman amphitheater.* It should be noted that Rubião knew nothing of that young man from

---

*   From Saint Augustine's *Confessions*, book V.

ancient times; he was entirely unaware not only that he had closed his eyes, but also that he had opened them shortly afterward, ever so slowly, out of curiosity . . .

And there before him was the condemned man, climbing the scaffold. An excited murmur passed through the crowd. The hangman set to work. It was at this point that Rubião's right foot swung outward in a graceful curve, obediently following a desire to turn around and leave; but the left foot, gripped by the opposite sentiment, stayed put; they tussled for several moments . . . "Look at my horse!" "See what a fine animal mine is!" "Don't be cruel!" "Don't be a coward!" Rubião remained frozen for several seconds, which was enough for the fatal moment to arrive. All eyes were fixed upon the same spot, his eyes included. Rubião could not figure out what beast it was that gnawed at his insides, nor what hands of iron clutched at his soul, preventing him from leaving. The fatal instant really was but an instant; the condemned man's legs thrashed about, then stiffened; the executioner leapt deftly and elegantly onto the man's shoulders; a deep murmur ran through the crowd; Rubião let out a scream, and saw nothing more.

Chapter XLVIII

"YOU MUST HAVE SEEN what a fine horse I have, senhor . . ."

Rubião opened his half-closed eyes, and saw the cabdriver lightly brush the animal with the tip of his whip in order to start it trotting. Inwardly, he was annoyed with the man, for hauling him out of his old memories. Not good memories, but old ones—old and salutary, because they provided him with an elixir that seemed to cure him completely of the present. And here was the cabdriver nudging him to wake him up. They were making their way up Rua da Lapa; the horse was racing along as if heading downhill.

"This horse," the driver went on, "has a fondness for me you wouldn't believe. I could tell you some extraordinary things. Some people say I'm lying, but no, senhor, I'm not. Everyone knows that horses and dogs are the animals that like us the most. Dogs seem to like us even more..."

The mention of dogs reminded Rubião of Quincas Borba, who must surely be anxiously awaiting him at home. Rubião had not forgotten the terms of the will; he had sworn to follow them to the letter. It must be said that mixed in with his fear of the dog running away was the fear of losing his inheritance. His lawyer's assurances counted for little; there was no clause in the will (the lawyer had told him) that would cause the inheritance to revert to some other party in the event of the dog running away; he could not be disinherited. What did he care if the dog ran away? It might even be better: one less thing to worry about! Rubião gave the impression of accepting the lawyer's explanation, but his doubts remained; there was the risk of long-drawn-out lawsuits, contradictory rulings on the same subject, actions by an envious or malevolent third party, and, encompassing everything, his terror of ending up with nothing. Hence the strictness with which the dog was kept captive, and also Rubião's remorse at having spent the whole afternoon and evening without thinking even once about Quincas Borba.

"I am an ungrateful fellow!" he thought.

He quickly corrected himself: it was even more ungrateful of him not to have thought once about the other Quincas Borba, who had left him everything. It suddenly occurred to him that perhaps the two Quincas Borbas were in fact one and the same, by virtue of the dead man's soul entering the body of the dog, not so much to purge the man's sins as to keep an eye on the dog's new owner. It was a black woman from São João del-Rei who had put this idea of transmigration into his head when he was a child. She used to say that sinful souls would end up in the bodies of animals; she even swore that she once knew a notary who'd ended up as a skunk—

"Don't forget, senhor, to tell me where the house is," the cabdriver said, interrupting Rubião's thoughts.

"Stop here."

Chapter XLIX

THE DOG BARKED from behind the gate, but as soon as Rubião entered, he greeted his master joyfully. Setting aside any feelings of annoyance, Rubião responded effusively. The possibility that his benefactor might be there inside the dog made him shiver. They climbed the stone steps together, then paused for several moments by the light of the lamp that Rubião had instructed be left on until his return. Rubião was more credulous than convinced; he had no particular reasons either to attack or to defend any theory on offer, for his was eternally virgin soil in which anything could be planted. Life in Rio had, however, given him one peculiarity: surrounded by incredulous people, he, too, was becoming incredulous.

He looked at the dog while he waited for the front door to be opened. The dog looked back at him in a way that suggested the late Quincas Borba himself was there inside him; the dog had the same ruminating gaze that the philosopher had when he peered into human affairs... Another shiver; but his fear, though great, was not so great as to tie his hands. Rubião cupped them around the animal's head, scratching his ears and neck.

"Poor old Quincas Borba! You like your master, don't you? Rubião's a good friend to Quincas Borba..."

And the dog slowly moved his head from side to side, thus ensuring an equal distribution of caresses to both of his floppy ears; he lifted his chin, so that Rubião could scratch beneath it, and his owner obeyed; but then the dog's eyes, half closed in enjoyment, took on something of the philosopher's eyes when he used to lie in bed telling Rubião things of which he understood little or nothing... Rubião closed his own eyes. The front door opened; he left the dog outside, but with such affection that it was tantamount to inviting him in. The Spanish servant took charge of carrying Quincas Borba back down the steps.

"Don't hit him," said Rubião.

The servant didn't hit the dog, but the descent was painful enough, and Rubião's dog-friend sat whimpering in the garden for quite some time. In the house, Rubião undressed and went to bed. Ah! His day had been filled with such various and contradictory sensations, from his morning recollections, the lunch with his two friends, right up to that last idea about metempsychosis. In between there had been the memory of the hanging, and a declaration of love that had not been accepted, but not exactly rejected either, and possibly guessed at by others... Everything was getting mixed up, and his mind bounced from one thing to another like a rubber ball thrown between children. Yet his overwhelming feeling was one of love. Rubião was amazed at his behavior, and felt pangs of remorse; but the remorse was a creature of his conscience, whereas his imagination would not relinquish Sofia's lovely figure at any price... One, two, three o'clock in the morning... Sofia so far away, the dog barking down below... Elusive sleep... Three o'clock already? Where had the time gone? Half-past three... Finally, after much imagining, sleep came to him, squeezed out the juice from its poppies, and that was that; by four o'clock, Rubião was fast asleep.

Chapter L

NO, MY DEAR LADY, this long day is not yet over: we still do not know what happened between Sofia and Palha after everyone had left. It may even be more to your taste than all that business about the hanged man.

Be patient, for we must return once again to Santa Teresa. The drawing room is still lit, but only by a single gas jet; the others have been extinguished, and this last one was just about to be, when Palha told the servant to wait a little longer Sofia was about to leave the room when her husband stopped her She trembled.

"It was a nice party," he said.

"Yes."

"That Siqueira fellow's such a bore, but never mind; he's a jolly sort. His daughter didn't look too bad, I thought. Did you see how Ramos gobbled up everything that was put on his plate? Just you watch, someday he'll swallow his own wife."

"His wife?" said Sofia, smiling.

"She's fat, I agree, but his first wife was even fatter, and I don't reckon she simply died either. He most likely ate her."

Reclining on the sofa, Sofia laughed at her husband's jokes. They commented on several other incidents from the afternoon and evening; then Sofia, stroking her husband's hair, said suddenly:

"And you still don't know the funniest thing that happened tonight."

"What was that?"

"Guess."

Palha said nothing for some time, looking at his wife, trying to guess what had been the funniest thing of the evening. He couldn't; he tried several possible answers, but each time Sofia shook her head.

"So what was it?"

"I don't know. Guess."

"I can't. Tell me!"

"On one condition," she replied. "I don't want any squabbles or arguments..."

Palha became more serious. "Squabbles? Arguments? What the devil could it be?" he wondered. He was no longer laughing; there was just a trace of a forced, resigned smile. He looked straight at her, and asked her what it was.

"Do you promise?" she said.

"All right. What was it?"

"Well then, you should know that tonight I heard a declaration of love, no less."

Palha turned pale. He hadn't promised not to turn pale. He was very fond of his wife, as we know, even to the extent of showing her off in public; he could not hear such news coolly. Sofia saw that change, and was pleased to see that he had reacted badly. To enjoy it even more, she leaned forward, loosened her hair, which was bothering her, gathered the hairpins in a handkerchief, then shook her head, took a deep breath, and clasped the hands of her husband, who had remained standing.

"It's true, my dear. Your wife was propositioned."

"Who was this scoundrel?" he asked impatiently.

"Well, if that's how you're going to react, I won't say a thing."

"Who was it? You want to know who it was? Then you must listen calmly. It was Rubião."

"Rubião?"

"It took me completely by surprise. He always seemed so shy and respectful, but appearances can certainly be deceptive. I've never heard a peep out of any of our other gentlemen visitors. I'm not exactly ugly, and so naturally they look at me . . . Why are you pacing back and forth like that? Stand still; I don't want to have to raise my voice . . . Good, that's better . . . Let's get to the point. Well, he didn't make an outright declaration—"

"Ah! He didn't?" her husband interrupted her.

"No, but it amounted to much the same thing."

And then she told him what had happened in the garden, from when the two of them stepped outside until the major appeared.

"That's all it was," she concluded. "But it's enough to show that the only reason he didn't mention love was because the word didn't reach his lips—but it did reach his hand, which squeezed my fingers . . . That's all, and it's more than enough. At least you aren't getting angry about it, but obviously we must stop inviting him here—either straightaway, or gradually. I would prefer immediately, but I can live with either. What do you think would be best?"

Palha stood biting his lip, staring at her like an idiot. Without a word, he sat down on the sofa. He turned the matter over in his mind. It was only natural that his wife's charms should captivate a man, and Rubião was as likely a candidate as any other. But he trusted Rubião so much that the note Sofia had sent him, along with the strawberries, had in fact been composed by Palha himself; his wife had merely written it out, signed it, and sent it. Never had it entered his mind that his friend might declare his love to anyone, much less Sofia, if it really was love. Maybe it was just a friendly jest? Rubião did look at her a lot, it's true; on some occasions Sofia seemed to reward him with looks of her own . . . The concessions of a pretty young woman! But then as long as her eyes remained his, a few glances here and there scarcely mattered. There was no point being jealous of an optic nerve, thought her husband.

Sofia stood up, went over to put the handkerchief with the hairpins on top of the piano, and looked in the mirror to see herself with her hair down. When she returned to the sofa, her husband took both her hands in his, and chuckled.

"I think you've been troubling yourself far more than the incident deserves. Comparing a young lady's eyes to the stars, and vice versa, is, after all, something that can be done in plain sight of everyone, within the family, or in prose or verse for publication. The blame lies with the person who has such pretty eyes. Besides, despite what you tell me, you know he's still just a country bumpkin..."

"Then the Devil's a country bumpkin, too, because that's what he seemed to me: the Devil. And what about him asking me to look up at the Southern Cross at a certain time, so that our souls might meet?"

"Well, yes, that certainly sounds like lovers' talk," Palha agreed. "But in some ways, it's rather sweet and innocent—the sort of thing a fifteen-year-old girl might say, or a fool at any time of life, and poets too; but then he is neither a young girl nor a poet."

"He certainly isn't. And what about grabbing my hands to keep me in the garden?"

Palha shuddered; the thought of their hands touching, and Sofia being held by force, was what mortified him most. Frankly, if he could, he would gladly throttle the man. Other thoughts, however, rushed in and drove out that initial urge; Sofia feared she had seriously irritated him, but then he merely shrugged, and replied that it was indeed a very rude thing to do.

"But, Sofia, whatever made you ask him to go and look at the moon in the first place?"

"I asked Dona Tonica to come with us."

"But when she refused, you should have found some excuse not to go into the garden. That's what you should have done. You gave him the opportunity . . ."

Sofia looked at him and scrunched up her thick eyebrows; she started to reply, but then stopped. Palha carried on in the same vein: that it was her fault, she shouldn't have given him the opportunity . . .

"But didn't you yourself tell me that we should treat him with extra consideration? I certainly wouldn't have gone into the garden with him if I'd known what was going to happen. But I never expected a man so mild-mannered, so . . . oh, I don't know what, would throw all caution to the winds and say such strange things to me . . ."

"Well, from now on, avoid moonlight and gardens," said her husband, trying to smile.

"But Cristiano, how do you want me to speak to him next time he comes over? I really don't think I'm up to it. Look, the best thing would be to break off the friendship completely."

Palha crossed his legs and began tapping his shoe. For several seconds, they remained silent. Palha was thinking over her proposal, not that he wanted to accept it, but he didn't know how else to reply to his wife, who was showing such anger and behaving with such dignity. He needed to say something that neither agreed nor disagreed with her proposal, and nothing came to mind. He stood up, put his hands in his trouser pockets and, after taking a few steps, stopped directly in front of Sofia.

"Perhaps we're getting all worked up about something that was simply the effect of too much wine. Clearly he's been a naughty boy; the wine went to his head, and then all it took was a slight jolt for everything inside him to be turned upside down . . . No, I won't deny that you probably made quite an impression on him, as would many other ladies. A few days ago, he went to a ball in Catete, and came back utterly charmed by the ladies he'd seen there, and by one in particular, the widow Mendes—"

Sofia interrupted him:

"So why didn't he ask that beauty to look up at the Southern Cross?"

"Because he hadn't been dining there, of course, and there was neither garden nor moonlight. What I'm trying to say is that *our friend* was not himself. Perhaps he's sorry now for what he did and feels thoroughly ashamed of himself, not knowing how to explain, or even whether he should try . . . It's entirely possible he'll stay away of his own accord . . ."

"It would be better if he did."

". . . unless we invite him."

"But why would we do that?"

"Sofia," said her husband, sitting down beside her. "I don't want to go into detail. I'll say only that I won't allow any man to show you disrespect . . ."

There was a slight pause; Sofia looked at him expectantly.

"I won't allow it, and heaven help any man who does so, and heaven help you if you let him. You know I'm adamant when it comes to things like that, and that it's only my certainty of your affections or—dare I say it—your love for me, that sets my mind at rest. Well, I have no concerns as regards Rubião. Believe me, Rubião is our friend, and I am indebted to him."

"A few gifts, a few bits of jewelry, boxes at the theater, are hardly reason enough for me to be gazing up at the Southern Cross with him."

"I wish to God it was only that!" said Palha with a sigh.

"What else is there?"

"Let's not go into detail . . . There are other things . . . We'll talk about it later . . . But rest assured that nothing would hold me back if I thought there was anything serious in what you've just told me. Anything at all. The man's an idiot."

"No, he isn't."

"Isn't he?"

Sofia stood up; she didn't want to go into detail either. Her husband grasped her hand; she stood there in silence. Leaning back on the sofa, Palha looked up at her and smiled not knowing what else to say. After a couple of minutes, he said that it was getting late, and that he was going to tell the servants to turn out the lights. After another brief silence, Palha added:

"Very well, tomorrow I'll write and tell him never to set foot here again."

He looked at his wife, waiting for some kind of objection. Sofia rubbed her eyebrows and said nothing. Palha repeated his solution, and perhaps this time he meant it.

"Listen, Cristiano," his wife replied wearily. "No one's asking you to write a letter. I wish now that I hadn't said anything. I told you about an act of discourtesy, and I said it would be better to break things off—either little by little or once and for all."

"And how do we go about breaking things off once and for all?"

"By not letting him in the house. But I'm not saying that. It would be enough, if you prefer, to do things gradually . . ."

It was a concession. Palha accepted it, but immediately grew somber; with a gesture of despair, he let go of his wife's hand. Then, putting his hands around her waist, he said in a voice that was louder than before:

"But, my dear, I owe him a great deal of money."

Sofia covered his mouth and glanced toward the hallway in alarm.

"All right," she said. "Let's drop the matter. I'll see how he behaves in the future, and I'll try to treat him more coolly... In that case, *you* mustn't change, so that it doesn't look as if you know about what happened. I'll see what I can do."

"You know how it is... business is tight, then there's a shortfall... a hole that needs plugging here, another there... darned creditors! That's why... But let's just treat it as a joke, darling; it isn't worth getting all hot and bothered. You know I trust you."

"Let's go to bed; it's late."

"Yes let's," replied Palha, kissing her on the cheek.

"I've got a terrible headache," she murmured. "I think it's the damp evening air, or this whole business... A terrible headache."

Chapter LI

BATHED, SHAVED, AND half-dressed, Palha was reading the newspapers before lunch, when he saw his wife coming into his study, looking somewhat pale.

"Are you feeling worse?"

Sofia responded with a movement of her lips that neither confirmed nor denied. Palha said he was sure her discomfort would pass as the day progressed; after all the fuss of the previous evening, the late supper... He then asked her to let him finish reading an article about some business at the stock exchange. It was a squabble between two merchants about letters of credit; one of them had given his version of events yesterday, and today the other was responding. "A very thorough response," said Palha, on finishing his reading, and he then explained at length to his wife the issue relating to the letters of credit, the intricacies of the transaction, the situation of the two adversaries, and the market rumors, all in the most technical of vocabulary. Sofia listened and sighed; but the despotism of the market gives no quarter to womanly sighs, nor to gentlemanly courtesy. Fortunately, lunch was served.

At around two o'clock, once she was alone, our friend, having taken only some light broth, went out to sit in the front garden. Naturally, her thoughts returned to the events of the previous evening. She was feeling neither entirely at ease nor outraged. She regretted having told her husband about the incident, and, at the same time, was annoyed with his attempts to explain it. In the midst of her reflections, she could distinctly hear the major's words: "Well, hello! Enjoying the moonlight?" as if the leaves in the garden had carefully absorbed those words and, stirred by the light morning breeze, were now repeating them back to her. Sofia shuddered. The major was indiscreet—indiscreet about sticking his nose into other people's business; would he go so far as to tell everyone else? Sofia considered that she was already the object of suspicion and gossip. She made up her mind. She wouldn't visit anyone at all; or she would go away, up into the mountains around Nova Friburgo or even farther afield. Her husband's insistence on continuing to receive Rubião just as they had before was too much, especially given his reasons. Not wanting either to obey or disobey, she considered leaving town, on some pretext or other.

"It was all my fault!" she thought.

Her fault lay in having paid special attention to the man, with her kind words, thoughtful gestures, and, yesterday evening, those lingering looks . . . If it hadn't been for that . . . Around and around in circles she went. Everything irritated her plants, furniture, a chirruping cricket, the sound of voices in the street, of clinking plates from within the house, the toing and froing of slave women, and even a poor old black man struggling up the hill in front of her house. Even his faltering footsteps got on her nerves.

Chapter LII

AT THIS POINT, a tall young man passed by, smiled, and greeted her with a casual wave. Sofia waved, too, somewhat taken aback by both the individual and his gesture.

"Who on earth is he?" she wondered.

She tried to place where she had met him, because there was indeed something familiar about his face, his manner, and his large, placid eyes. Where had she seen him? She mentally ran through the various houses she had visited in town, but without success; then she remembered a certain ball the month before, at the house of a lawyer celebrating his birthday. That was it; that's where she had seen him. They had danced a quadrille, a concession on his part, since he never danced; she remembered hearing him say many flattering things about feminine beauty, which, he said, lay mainly in the eyes and shoulders. Her shoulders, as we know, were magnificent. He spoke of little else besides eyes and shoulders, in relation to each of which he told several anecdotes about his personal experiences, some of which were of no interest at all, but he told them so well! And the subject was so relevant to her! Yes, indeed. She remembered now that as soon as their dance had finished, Palha came over and sat beside her, and told her the young man's name, because she hadn't quite heard it when they were first introduced. It was Carlos Maria—the same young man who had lunched with our very own Rubião.

"He's the most striking person in the room," said her husband, proud to see that the young man had spent so much time with her.

"Among the men, you mean," said Sofia.

"Among the ladies that would be you, of course," Palha quickly responded, gazing admiringly at his wife's bosom and then around the room, with an expression of ownership and possession that his wife knew well and appreciated.

By the time she had finished remembering everything, the young man was already far away; but at least this gave her a rest from the series of irritations assailing her. She had been suffering with a backache, which had retreated for a while. Now it returned, insistent and painful; Sofia tried to make herself comfortable in her chair and closed her eyes. She tried to doze off, but couldn't. Her thoughts were as insistent as the pain, and even more disagreeable. From time to time, a rapid beating of wings broke the silence: a neighbor's pigeons returning to their dovecote. The first couple of times this happened, Sofia opened her eyes, then she got accustomed to the sound. After a while, she heard footsteps in the street and looked up, assuming that it was Carlos Maria on his way back; it was a postman bringing her a letter from the country. He handed her the letter. On leaving the garden, the postman tripped over the foot of a bench and fell flat on his face, scattering all his letters. Sofia could not contain her laughter.

Chapter LIII

YOU MUST FORGIVE HER. I know very well that her discomfort, a bad night's sleep, and her fear of public opinion are all at odds with such ill-timed laughter. But, my dear lady reader, perhaps you have never seen a postman trip and fall over. On Olympus, once upon a time, Homer's gods—and they were gods, after all!—were having a serious, even furious, quarrel. Proud Juno, jealous of Thetis pleading with her husband Jupiter on behalf of Achilles, interrupted the son of Saturn. He, Jupiter, thundered and threatened; his wife trembled with anger. The others groaned and sighed. But when poor lame Vulcan brought the cup of sweet nectar and hobbled around to serve each of them, an enormous, inextinguishable roar of laughter broke out on Olympus. Why? My dear, clearly you have never seen a postman trip and fall.

Sometimes, he doesn't even need to fall; on other occasions, he doesn't even need to exist. It's enough to imagine or remember him. The merest shadow of some grotesque memory may intrude upon the most grievous of sorrows, and a smile will flicker across a face, faintly perhaps, even imperceptibly. So let's leave Sofia in peace, laughing and reading her letter from the country.

Chapter LIV

TWO WEEKS LATER, Rubião was at home when Sofia's husband turned up to see him. He wanted to know what had become of him, where he'd been hiding, whether he was ill, or simply avoiding the company of poor people. Rubião gave some mumbled response, unable to string together a single proper sentence. In the midst of this, Palha noticed that there was another man in the drawing room looking at the paintings, and so he lowered his voice.

"Oh, I'm sorry, I didn't see you had company," he said.

"No need to be sorry. He's a friend, just like you. Sir, allow me to introduce my friend Cristiano de Almeida e Palha. I believe I've already mentioned him to you. And this is my friend Senhor Camacho—João de Souza Camacho."

Camacho nodded, said a few words and got up to leave; but Rubião pressed him to stay. They were both good friends of his, and the moon would soon be shining over the beautiful waters of Botafogo.

The moon—the moon again—and that phrase: *I believe I've already mentioned him to you*—so disconcerted Palha that he was unable to speak for quite some time. I should add that his host was also at a loss for words. The three of them were seated, Rubião on the sofa, Palha and Camacho in armchairs facing one another. Camacho, who was still holding his cane, placed it vertically between his knees, tapping his nose and looking up at the ceiling. From outside came the sound of carriages, a clattering of horses, and some voices. It was half past seven in the evening, possibly later, nearly eight o'clock. The silence lasted longer than was appropriate for the situation, but neither Rubião nor Palha noticed. It was Camacho who, out of boredom, went over to the window and exclaimed to the other two:

"The moon's rising!"

Rubião started, and so did Palha, but both of them in such different ways! Rubião's instinct was to rush to the window; Palha's was to grab Rubião by the throat, impelled not so much by the possibility of Rubião and Sofia's moonlight encounter becoming public knowledge, as by the thought of how violently Rubião had gripped his wife's hands and pulled her toward him. Neither man moved, then Rubião, crossing left leg over right, turned to Palha and said:

"You know, of course, that I'm planning to leave you?"

Chapter LV

THIS WAS THE very last thing Palha was expecting. Hence the surprise into which all his anger dissolved; hence also a faint pang of sorrow, which is what you, reader, would least expect. Leave them? He, of course, meant that he would be leaving Rio, a punishment he was inflicting on himself for his actions that night in Santa Teresa. He had immediately felt ashamed and remorseful, and too embarrassed to face his friend's wife again. Such was Palha's initial conclusion, but other hypotheses also came to mind. For instance, Rubião's infatuation might still persist, and his departure was merely a means of distancing himself from the object of his affections. Or might there be some sort of marriage plan involved?

This latter hypothesis brought a new element to the look on Palha's face, which I struggle to give a name to. Disappointment? The elegant Garrett could find no better term for such emotions, and did not spurn it despite its English origins.* Let's go with "disappointment." Mix in with it the sorrow of separation, without forgetting that initial rumble of suppressed anger, and many of you will think that this man's soul is something of a patchwork quilt. Perhaps. Morally speaking, unpatched quilts are very rare indeed! The most important thing is that the colors do not clash, even when the patches do not obey the rules of symmetry and composition. This was the case with our man here. At first sight, he appeared to be a hodgepodge of emotions, however, if you looked more closely,

---

* João Batista de Almeida Garrett (1799–1854), Portugal's leading Romantic poet, often used an anglicism derived from "disappointment," in preference to the more common Portuguese word.

no matter how contradictory those emotions might seem, together they revealed the person as a single moral entity.

Chapter LVI

BUT WHY WAS Rubião leaving them? For what reason? To what end?

The morning after the events in Santa Teresa, Rubião woke in low spirits. He scarcely ate any breakfast. He couldn't focus on anything; he glumly put on his African slippers, and didn't even glance at the beautiful, or simply expensive, ornaments that filled his house. He could not endure the dog's nuzzling for more than two minutes; no sooner had Quincas Borba joined him in the drawing room than Rubião told the servants to take him away. The dog, however, promptly gave them the slip and returned to the drawing room, only to receive such a cuff on the ears from Rubião that he did not dare repeat his displays of affection; he simply lay down on the floor, gazing at his friend.

Rubião immediately felt sorry, annoyed, and ashamed. We have seen in Chapter X that remorse came easily to Rubião, but never lasted long; what we did not explain, however, was which kinds of actions might make his remorse last for a longer or shorter period of time. Back then, it was the letter written by the deceased Quincas Borba, so revealing of the author's state of mind, and which he had hidden from the doctor, despite its potential usefulness to science or the law. If he had shown the letter to the doctor, he would not have felt any remorse, nor perhaps would he have received any legacy—the small legacy he was then expecting from the dying man. In the present instance, his remorse had its roots in his attempt at adultery. Yes, he had pined after Sofia for quite some time, and felt certain urges, but it was only the young lady's unseemly vivacity, together with the excitement of the moment itself, that had prompted him to make his unwelcome declaration. Now, in the cold light of day, he felt not only embarrassment, but remorse. The sins are different; the moral is the same.

Let us skip over all the things he thought and felt during those first few days. By Sunday, he was expecting something, a note like the one she had sent before—with or without strawberries. By Monday, he was determined to return to Minas for a couple of months; he needed the fresh air of Barbacena to restore his spirits. He had failed to take into account Senhor Camacho.

"Leave us?" Palha asked.

"Yes, I think so; I'm going back to Minas."

Camacho, returning from the window, sat down in the armchair he had occupied previously.

"What do you mean, Minas?" he said, smiling. "Forget about Minas for now. You'll go there when you need to, and you won't stay long either."

Palha was no less surprised by Camacho's words than he had been by Rubião's. Where had this man come from, with his domineering attitude toward Rubião? Palha looked at him; he was of medium height, with a rather gaunt face, short beard, long chin, and large protruding ears. This was his first impression. He then noted that his clothes, while not luxurious, were of good quality, and that his feet were well shod. He did not examine his eyes, or his smile, or his manners; nor did he notice his incipient baldness or his bony, hairy hands.

Chapter LVII

CAMACHO WAS A POLITICIAN. He had qualified in law in 1844, at the faculty in Recife, and returned to his native province, where he began to practice. The law, however, was just a pretext. While still at college, he had already edited a political journal, not for any particular party, but which contained many ideas picked up here and there, and was set out in a style that managed to be both flimsy and bombastic. Someone who gathered those first fruits drew up an index of Camacho's principles and aspirations:—*Order through liberty, liberty through order;*—*Authority cannot abuse the law without slapping itself in the face;*—*Principles are a moral necessity for new nations as well as old;*—*Give me sound politics and I'll give you sound finances (Baron Louis);*—*Let us plunge into the Jordan of constitutionality;*—*Make way for the brave, ye men of power, for they will be your buttress,* etc., etc.

Once back in his native province, this set of ideas had to give way to others, and the same could be said of his style. He founded a newspaper there, but, since local politics were less abstract, Camacho clipped his stylistic wings and stooped to reporting public appointments, public works projects, contracts handed out, as well as picking fights with the opposing newspaper, and calling people names both proper and improper. The use of adjectives required great care. Pernicious, spendthrift, shameful, wicked—these were the terms required when attacking the government; but when, following a change of governor, he became a supporter, his adjectives also changed: energetic, enlightened, fair-minded, steadfast, an outstanding administration, etc., etc. This shooting match went on for three years, by the end of which a passion for politics held our young graduate firmly in its grip.

As a member of the provincial assembly, then the Chamber of Deputies, then governor of a second-rank province where, in a natural reversal of fortune, he read in the opposition's newspapers all the adjectives he had previously written himself—pernicious, spendthrift, shameful, wicked—Camacho had good days and bad, he paraded in and out of the chamber, gave speeches, wrote articles, and was constantly engaged in some battle or other. In due course he came to live in the imperial capital. As a deputy during the coalition, he saw the Marquis of Paraná come to power,* and was successful in pressing for several appointments; but whether or not the marquis ever sought his advice, or told him of his plans, no one could truly confirm, because when it came to matters of his own importance, Camacho had no difficulty in lying.

What can safely be believed is that he wanted to be a minister, and worked hard to that end. He joined various caucuses, wherever he felt his own best interests lay; in the chamber, he spoke at length on administrative issues, accumulated facts and figures, pieces of legislation, extracts of reports, quotations from French authors, albeit badly translated. But between ear of corn and hand stood that wall of which the poet spoke;† and for all that our fellow could stretch out the hand of his desires to pluck it, the ear of corn stayed stubbornly on the other side, where it was plucked by other hands, hands that were perhaps more, or less, voracious than his, or maybe even indifferent.

Politics also has its eternal bachelors. Camacho was slowly entering this melancholy category, in which all dreams of success

---

* The Marquis of Paraná's "conciliation" government lasted from 1853 until his death in 1856. It marked the beginning of a wider period of oligarchic consensus that continued until 1871.

† "*Tra la spiga e la man qual muro è messo*," from a sonnet by Petrarch quoted in Luís de Camões's *The Lusiads*.

slowly evaporate; but he did not have the good grace to abandon his ambitions. No one tasked with appointing a cabinet, even those who wanted him, dared to offer him a post. Camacho felt himself sinking; to give the appearance of influence, he would deal with the powerful figures of the day on familiar terms, and talk loudly of his visits to ministers and other public dignitaries.

He was not on the breadline. His family was small: a wife, a daughter approaching eighteen, and a nine-year-old godson, for all of whom his legal practice provided sufficient income. But politics was in his blood; he neither read nor thought about anything else. He had absolutely no interest in literature, natural science, history, philosophy, or the arts. Nor did he know a great deal about law; he retained something of what he had learned at college, plus his knowledge of subsequent legislation and his experience at the bar. Enough to get by in court and earn his crust.

Chapter LVIII

HE HAD SPOTTED RUBIÃO some days earlier, while spending the evening at the house of a counselor of state. The talk that evening was of the conservatives returning to power and the dissolution of parliament. Rubião had attended the meeting at which the Viscount of Itaboraí's new government presented its budget, and his voice still trembled when he recounted his impressions, describing the chamber, the rostrum, the galleries full to bursting, the speech by José Bonifácio, the motion, the vote . . . Of course his entire account was that of a simple soul, but his unruly gestures and heated words had all the eloquence of sincerity. Camacho listened attentively. He then found a way of drawing Rubião aside to a corner by the window, where he could impart his own considered opinion on the situation. Rubião responded with nods, or an approving word here and there. Finally, Camacho said:

"The conservatives won't be in power for long."

"Won't they?"

"No. They don't want war, so they'll be forced out. I've explained it all in my newspaper."

"Which newspaper?"

"Let's talk about that another time."

The following day, they lunched at the Hotel de la Bourse, at Camacho's invitation. Camacho told Rubião that a few months earlier he had started a newspaper with the sole aim of continuing the war at any cost . . . Disagreement among liberals was running high, and it seemed to him that the best way of serving his own party was to give it a neutral and nationalist terrain.

"And this now works to our advantage," he concluded, "because the government is leaning toward peace. There'll be a ferocious article of mine coming out tomorrow."

Rubião listened to every word, almost without taking his eyes off Camacho, and eating quickly during the brief intervals when Camacho bent his head over his own plate. He was enjoying imagining himself as a political confidant, and, to tell the truth, the idea of entering the fray in the hope of gaining something later on—a seat in the Chamber, for example—spread its golden wings in the mind of our dear friend. Camacho said nothing more to him; Rubião called on him the following day, but he wasn't in. And now, so soon after Camacho arriving, here was Palha turning up to interrupt them.

Chapter LIX

"YES, BUT I NEED to go to Minas," insisted Rubião.

"Whatever for?" asked Camacho.

Palha asked him the same question. Why on earth go to Minas, other than for a short visit to deal with business matters? Or was he already bored with Rio?

"No, I'm not bored, on the contrary..."

On the contrary, he liked it very much; but everyone misses their hometown, even if it's a rather ugly backwater, and all the more so when they leave it as a grown man. He wanted to see Barbacena. Barbacena was the best place in the world. For several minutes, Rubião divorced himself entirely from his two companions, wrapped entirely in his thoughts of home. Ambitions, petty vanities, ephemeral pleasures, all gave way to the man from Minas longing for his native province. If Rubião had at times been a crafty soul, and paid too much attention to his own interests, he was now simply a man weary of pleasure, and ill at ease with his own wealth.

Palha and Camacho looked at one another ... Oh, that look was like a calling card exchanged between two minds. Neither of them told its secret, but they saw the names on the cards, and greeted each other. Yes, Rubião must be prevented from leaving; Minas might well keep him for good. So they agreed with Rubião that he should indeed go, but later—in a few months' time. And perhaps Palha would go too. He'd never been to Minas; it would be an excellent opportunity.

"You?" asked Rubião.

"Yes, me. I've been wanting to go to Minas for quite some time, and to São Paulo. We've been on the verge of going for over a year now . . . Sofia's keen to go too. Remember when we met on that train? We were coming from Vassouras, but the Minas idea has always been there. The three of us will go."

Rubião seized upon the forthcoming elections, but Camacho intervened, assuring him that there was no need to be in Barbacena for them, and that the serpent ought to be crushed right here in the capital; there would be plenty of time afterward for him to assuage his homesickness and reap his reward. Rubião squirmed about on the sofa. The reward would no doubt be his seat in parliament. Such a magnificent vision! An ambition he had never, ever entertained, when he was a poor nobody . . . And yet here it was taking hold of him, whetting his appetite for greatness and glory. Still, however, he insisted on a short trip, although, to be precise, I should say that he did so rather hoping they would dissuade him.

By this stage, the moon was shining brightly; the bay, seen from the windows, had that seductive look which no native of Rio believes could ever exist anywhere else on earth. Sofia's shadow passed by in the distance, projected onto the side of the hill, before dissolving in the moonlight; the Chamber's final, tumultuous session still reverberated in Rubião's ears . . . Camacho went over to the window, then turned.

"But for how long?" he asked.

"I don't know, but not long."

"In any case, let's talk again tomorrow."

Camacho took his leave. Palha stayed a few moments longer, to tell Rubião that it would be very odd for him to return to Minas without them settling their accounts— Rubião interrupted him. Accounts? Was anyone asking him to settle accounts?

"You're clearly not a businessman," retorted Palha.

"I'm not, that's true. But accounts are paid whenever they can be. That's how it's been between us. Unless, perhaps . . . Now, please be frank: Do you need some money?"

"No, I don't, thank you. I have a business proposal for you, but that's for another time. I came here today so that I wouldn't have to put an ad in the newspapers: 'Friend missing, Rubião by name, owns a dog...'"

Rubião enjoyed the joke. Palha took his leave, with Rubião accompanying him as far as the corner of Rua Marquês de Abrantes. On saying good night, he promised to visit him in Santa Teresa, before going to Minas.

Chapter LX

POOR MINAS! Rubião headed home alone, walking slowly, thinking now of a way to avoid going there. And the words of both men darted around his brain, like goldfish in a glass bowl, shimmering: *"Here is where the serpent's head must be crushed"*; *"Sofia's keen to go too."* Poor Minas!

The following day, he received a newspaper he had never seen before, the *Sentinel*. The editorial excoriated the government; its conclusion, however, extended to all political parties and the entire nation: *Let us plunge into the Jordan of constitutionality*. Rubião thought it was excellent, and checked to see where the newspaper had been printed so that he could subscribe. The printer's address was in Rua da Ajuda; he went there straight from his house, and was informed that the editor was one Senhor Camacho. He then rushed over to Camacho's office.

On his way, though, on the same street, he heard a woman's frantic voice cry out from the door of a mattress-maker's shop:

"Deolindo! Deolindo!"

Rubião turned around and saw exactly what was happening. A carriage was hurtling down the street just as a three- or four-year-old child was crossing. Despite the coachman's attempts to rein the horses in, they were almost on top of the child. Rubião leapt into the path of the horses and pulled the boy to safety. When Rubião handed him to his mother, she was pale, trembling, and speechless. Several bystanders started remonstrating with the coachman, but the bald-headed man inside the carriage ordered him to keep moving. The coachman obeyed, and by the time the child's father came out of the mattress-maker's shop, the carriage was already turning into Rua de São José.

"He nearly died," said the mother. "If it hadn't been for this gentleman, I don't know what would have become of our poor boy."

News spread quickly. Neighbors came into the house to see what had happened to the boy; outside, children and street urchins stood gaping. The child had only a scratch on his left shoulder, from when he fell.

"It was nothing," said Rubião. "In any case, don't let the boy out into the street on his own; he's much too young."

"Thank you," replied the father, "but where is your hat?"

Rubião realized then that he had lost it. A ragged boy had picked it up and was standing at the door, waiting for the opportunity to return it. Rubião gave him a few coppers as a reward, something the boy had not been thinking of when he picked up the hat. He did so simply to play his part in the glorious rescue. Nevertheless, he gladly accepted the coins; it was perhaps the boy's first lesson in venality.

"But wait," said the mattress-maker, "are you injured?"

Indeed, our friend's hand was bleeding, a cut on the palm, just a scratch; he was only now beginning to feel it. The little boy's mother ran to fetch a basin and towel, despite Rubião saying that it was nothing serious, not worth bothering about. When the water arrived, he washed his hand while the mattress-maker hurried over to the nearby pharmacy and returned with some arnica. Rubião dressed the wound, and bound it up with his handkerchief; the mattress-maker's wife brushed his hat clean, and, when he left, both parents thanked him profusely for saving their son. The onlookers who had gathered at the door and on the sidewalk formed a guard of honor.

Chapter LXI

"WHAT'S THAT on your hand?" asked Camacho, as soon as Rubião entered his office.

Rubião told him about the incident in Rua da Ajuda. The lawyer asked him lots of questions about the child, the parents, the number of the house; but Rubião cut short his answers.

"Don't you at least know the little boy's name?"

"I heard them calling him Deolindo. But let's talk about important matters. I've come to subscribe to your newspaper. I received a copy, and I want to contribute toward—"

Camacho replied that he didn't need subscriptions. The newspaper was doing fine. What he needed were printing materials and more actual content for broadening the paper's scope, including more news, more special features, the translation of a novel for the supplement, reports on shipping, on the stock market, etc. And, as he had no doubt seen, there were advertisements too.

"Indeed."

"I have almost all the capital subscribed. Ten investors would be enough, and there are already eight of us, myself and seven others. Just two more shareholders and the company's capital will be complete."

"I wonder how much it would cost," thought Rubião.

Camacho was tapping the edge of his writing desk with a penknife, glancing silently at Rubião out of the corner of his eye. Rubião looked around the room; it was sparsely furnished, with some documents on a stool beside the lawyer, a bookshelf stacked with legal textbooks and a set of *Royal Ordinances*, and a portrait on the wall above the desk.

"Do you know him?" asked Camacho, pointing at the portrait.

"No, I don't."

"Look closely."

"I couldn't say. Nunes Machado, perhaps?"*

"No," replied the ex-deputy, putting on a pained expression. "I couldn't find a decent portrait of him. There are some lithographs for sale but I don't think they're very good. No, that's the marquis."

"Of Barbacena?"

"No, of Paraná; the great marquis, a personal friend of mine. He tried to bring the two parties together, which is how I got to know him. He died young, and his life's work died with him. Today, if he tried the same thing, he'd have me to contend with. No! Enough of conciliation and coalition; it's a fight to the death. We must destroy them. Read the *Sentinel*, my dear comrade-in-arms; it'll be delivered to your home . . ."

"No, sir."

"Whyever not?" Camacho asked.

Rubião lowered his eyes before Camacho's probing gaze.

"No, sir, I shan't hear of it. I would like to help my friends. Getting the newspaper for free . . ."

---

* A Liberal politician who played a leading role in the 1848 Pernambucan uprising.

"But I've already told you we have enough subscribers," retorted Camacho.

"Yes, but didn't you also mention that you still need two more shareholders?"

"That's right, two more. We have eight."

"How much is the capital of the company?"

"Fifty *contos*; five per person."

"Then count me in for five."

Camacho thanked Rubião in the name of the world of ideas. He had been intending to invite him to invest along with the rest of them; his new friend had earned the right through his conviction, his loyalty, and his passion for public affairs. He apologized for not asking him earlier, before Rubião himself had suggested it. He showed him the list of other shareholders; Camacho was the first; he had paid for his shares in kind, by contributing the newspaper itself, the articles, the subscribers, the whole Herculean labor ... He was about to correct himself, but thought better of it and repeated boldly: yes, a truly Herculean labor. Yes, he could call it that, without shame and without a false word; as a child, he, too, had grappled with serpents. Now it was an addiction; he relished the battle, and he would go down fighting, wrapped in the flag ...

== *Chapter LXII*

RUBIÃO SAID GOODBYE and left. A tall lady, dressed in black, passed him in the hallway with a rustling of silk and beads. From the top of the stairs he heard Camacho's voice, speaking more loudly than before: "Oh, it's you, Baroness!"

Rubião paused on the top step. The lady's silvery voice started to say a few words; it was about a lawsuit. A baroness! And our Rubião continued on down the stairs carefully, softly, so as not to appear to be eavesdropping. A fine, delicate aroma wafted into his nostrils, a dizzying sort of thing; the scent that trailed behind her. A baroness! He reached the door to the street; he saw a coupé waiting; the footman standing on the sidewalk, the coachman looking down from his seat, both men in livery... What novelty could there be in any of this? None whatsoever. A titled lady, perfumed and rich, perhaps bringing a lawsuit simply to relieve her boredom. But the thing about this particular incident was that Rubião, without knowing why, and despite his own wealth, suddenly felt he was once again that schoolteacher in Barbacena...

Chapter LXIII

OUT IN THE STREET, he ran into Sofia with another young lady and an older lady. He paid no attention to the appearance of the other two; he had eyes only for Sofia. They spoke awkwardly and for barely two minutes, then went their separate ways. Rubião stopped farther along the street and looked back, but the three ladies had carried on walking without turning around. After supper, he asked himself:

"Should I visit this evening?"

He pondered at length without reaching a decision. Yes, but then no. He thought she had behaved rather oddly, but remembered that she had at least smiled—briefly, but she had smiled. He decided to let fate decide. If the first carriage that passed his house came from the right, he would go; if it came from the left, he wouldn't. And he sat there on the pouf in the middle of the drawing room, staring out at the street. Soon a cab approached from the left. The fates had spoken: he would not go to Santa Teresa. But a voice inside him protested, insisting on the precise terms agreed: a carriage. A cab was not a carriage. It had to be something that was commonly called a carriage, whether a calèche, a coupé, or even a victoria. Within a few minutes, several calèches approached from the right, returning from a funeral. And so he went.

Chapter LXIV

SOFIA GREETED HIM KINDLY, holding out her hand without a hint of animosity. The two ladies she had been walking with earlier were in the drawing room with her, wearing their indoor clothes; she introduced them. The young lady was her cousin, the older one her aunt—the aunt from the countryside who had written the letter Sofia had received in her front garden from the postman's own hand just before he tripped and fell. The aunt's name was Dona Maria Augusta; she owned a small plantation, some slaves, and some debts, which her husband had left her along with some fond memories. Her daughter was called Maria Benedita—a name that embarrassed her as being, she said, an old woman's name; but her mother retorted that every old woman had once been a young woman and even a girl, and that whether a name "suited" someone was all down to the imaginings of poets and storytellers. Maria Benedita had been the name of her grandmother, the goddaughter of Luís de Vasconcelos, the viceroy. What more could she ask for?

This was all told to Rubião without any apparent annoyance on the part of Maria Benedita. Perhaps to alleviate the situation, or perhaps for some other reason, Sofia added that the ugliest of names could be beautiful, depending on the person. And Maria Benedita was exquisite.

"Don't you think so?" Sofia concluded, turning to Rubião.

"Stop teasing, cousin!" interrupted Maria Benedita, laughing.

We can safely assume that neither the old lady nor Rubião heard what she said—the old lady because she was beginning to doze off, and Rubião because he was busy stroking a little puppy that Sofia had recently been given; a small, spindly thing with dark eyes, a boisterous nature, and a little bell on its collar. But since his hostess insisted, he replied, "Yes," without knowing what he was agreeing to. Maria Benedita scowled. She was not, in truth, a beauty; she was not known for her captivating eyes, nor for one of those mouths that whisper secret thoughts even when silent; but she was natural, without any of the awkwardness of a country girl, and she had a charm all her own, which made up for any oddities in the way she dressed.

She had been born in the countryside and she liked it there. Her particular slice of countryside wasn't far: Iguaçu. She would very occasionally come to the city, to spend a few days; but after two days, she was already keen to go home. Her education had been perfunctory: reading, writing, religion, and some needlework. Recently (she was now nearly nineteen), Sofia had been pressing her to learn the piano. Her aunt consented, and so Maria Benedita came to stay with her cousin, this time for eighteen days. She couldn't stand it any longer than that; she missed her mother and went back to Iguaçu, much to the consternation of her music teacher, who had declared from the very beginning that she possessed a great musical talent.

"Oh, without doubt! A great talent!"

Maria Benedita laughed when her cousin told her this, and

could never again take the man seriously. At times, in the middle of a lesson, she would burst out laughing. Sofia would frown, as if scolding her, and the poor man would ask what was the matter, then, deciding that it must be some girlish thought, carry on with the lesson. Maria Benedita came to Rio knowing neither the piano nor French—another lacuna that Sofia found hard to excuse. Dona Maria Augusta couldn't understand her niece's consternation. Why French? Her niece informed her that it was indispensable for conversation, for shopping, for reading novels . . .

"I've always been perfectly happy without French," the old lady would reply. "And the same goes for colored folk speaking pidgin Portuguese: they're no worse off than the Europeans."

One day she added:

"There'll be no lack of suitors because of it. She can marry, I've already told her she can marry whenever she likes. After all, I myself married, and she can even leave me all alone in the countryside, to die like an old workhorse . . ."

"Mama!"

"Now, don't go feeling sorry for me; just you see what happens when a fiancé appears. When he does, you just go off with him and leave me be. You saw what Maria José did? She went off to live in Ceará."*

"But she had no choice; her husband's a judge," argued Sofia.

"Judge or crook, it's all the same to me! This old rag is staying here. Marry, Maria Benedita, and marry quickly; I will die with God. I won't have my children with me, but I will have Our Lady, who's the mother of us all. So go on, then, marry!"

All these grumblings were of course carefully calculated; the aim was to arouse fear and pity in her daughter, to dissuade her from

---

* A remote province in the far north-east of Brazil.

marriage. Or at least delay the inevitable. I doubt that she revealed this sin to her confessor, or even that she herself understood it; it was the product of the peevish selfishness of old age. Dona Maria Augusta had been loved all her life; her mother had doted on her, and her husband loved her with the same intensity until his very last day. Now that they were both dead, all of her filial and wifely affections had been placed on the heads of her two daughters.

One had escaped from her by marrying. Threatened by solitude, Dona Maria Augusta was doing everything she could to avoid such a disaster.

Chapter LXV

RUBIÃO'S VISIT WAS BRIEF. At nine o'clock, he discreetly stood up, expecting Sofia to say something, to ask him to stay a little longer, or that he should wait for her husband, who would be arriving soon, or some expression of surprise: "What, leaving already?" But no. Sofia held out her hand to him, but so briefly he barely brushed her fingers. She had, however, seemed so natural throughout his visit, so devoid of bitterness... Of course, her long, loquacious gazes were now a thing of the past; it seemed almost as if there had never been anything between them, neither good nor bad, neither strawberries nor moonlight. Rubião trembled and struggled for words; she found hers easily, and, when the need arose to look at him, she did so directly and calmly.

"My regards to Palha," he mumbled, hat and cane in hand.

"Thank you! He had to visit someone, but I think I hear footsteps. It must be him."

But it was Carlos Maria. Rubião was surprised to see him there, though perhaps he had come to visit Dona Maria Augusta and her daughter; they might even be related.

"I was just leaving," Rubião said to Carlos Maria, who had immediately sat down next to Dona Maria Augusta.

"Ah!" replied Carlos Maria, gazing at the portrait of Sofia.

Sofia accompanied Rubião to the front door, telling him that her husband would be sorry to have missed him, but that he had been called away on urgent business. He would apologize in person.

"Apologize? For what?" replied Rubião.

He seemed to want to say something more, but Sofia's brisk handshake and the neat curtsy that followed were the signal for him to leave. Rubião bowed. As he crossed the front garden, he could hear Carlos Maria's voice coming from the drawing room:

"I'm going to denounce your husband, senhora. He is a man of very poor taste."

Rubião stopped.

"Why?" asked Sofia.

"He has put this portrait of you in the drawing room," continued Carlos Maria. "Yet you are far more beautiful, infinitely more beautiful, than the painting. Judge for yourselves, ladies!"

Chapter LXVI

"SAYING THAT KIND of thing comes so naturally to him!" thought Rubião once he was at home, remembering Carlos Maria's words. "Criticizing the portrait simply to flatter the sitter! And yet the portrait is a very good likeness."

Chapter LXVII

THE NEXT MORNING, in bed, Rubião had quite a shock. The first newspaper he opened was the *Sentinel*. He read the editorial, one of the letters, and some news items. Suddenly he saw his own name.

"What's this?"

It was his very own name in glaring print, repeated several times over, an entire article about the incident in Rua da Ajuda. After his initial shock came annoyance. What impudence, to print a personal story like that, told in confidence! He had no desire to read any of it, now that he knew what it was about; he threw down the newspaper and picked up another one. Unfortunately, he had lost all concentration; he merely skimmed through an article, skipping some lines, not understanding others, and finding himself at the end of a column with no idea of how he had arrived there.

When he finally got up, he sat in an armchair beside the bed, and picked up the *Sentinel* again. He cast his eyes over the article; it was more than one column. "One and a bit columns for something so trifling!" he thought. And, just to see how Camacho had filled all the space, he read it all somewhat hastily, irritated by the adjectives and his dramatic description of the incident.

"Well, let that be a lesson to you!" he said out loud. "What was I thinking of, blabbering on like that?"

He took a bath, dressed, and combed his hair, all the while thinking of the newspaper's tittle-tattle. He felt embarrassed at the publication of something he considered trivial, and even more by the prominence the writer had given it, as if it were a matter worthy of political analysis. At breakfast, he picked up the newspaper again, to read some other items, on government appointments, a murder in Garanhuns, the weather forecast. But once again his eyes were drawn back to the article, and he read it again slowly. This time, Rubião admitted that he could well believe the author's sincerity. The enthusiastic language could be explained by the impression the incident had made upon Camacho, such that it prevented him from being more circumspect. Clearly this was the explanation. Rubião remembered going into Camacho's office, the way he had spoken; and from there he cast his mind back to the incident itself. Reclining in his study, he recalled the scene: the child, the carriage, the horses, the shout, how, in the grip of an irresistible impulse, he had leapt into the path of the horses. Even now he could not explain what had happened; it was as though a shadow had passed over his eyes . . . He threw himself at the child, and at the horses, impervious to sight or sound, or to the risk to himself . . . And there he might have stayed, under the horses, crushed by the wheels, dead or injured, preferably just injured . . . Could that have happened, or not? It was impossible to deny that it had been a serious situation . . . The proof was that the parents and the whole neighborhood—

Rubião interrupted his thinking to read the article one more time. That it was well written was beyond doubt. There were passages he reread with great satisfaction. It was as if the fellow had been right there at the scene. What a description! Such a vivid style! Some elements had been added—memory playing tricks, no doubt—but the additions did not detract. And did he sense a certain pride in the repetition of his name? "Our friend, our distinguished friend, our courageous friend . . ."

Over lunch, he chuckled: perhaps he had somewhat overreacted. After all, what was wrong with Camacho giving his readers a piece of news that was truthful, and interesting, and dramatic, and—most certainly—out of the ordinary? When he went out, he received several compliments; Freitas called him Saint Vincent de

Paul. And our friend smiled and thanked him, playing it down, saying that, really, it was nothing...

"Nothing?" someone replied. "Give me more of these 'nothings.' Risking your own life to save a child..."

Rubião listened and smiled and nodded; he described the scene to a number of interested listeners, who wanted to hear it straight from his own lips. Some replied with accounts of their own prowess: one who had once saved a man, another a little girl who had almost drowned going for a swim in the lagoon right beside the Passeio Público. There were also suicides that had been thwarted by the listener's intervention, snatching the pistol from the poor soul's hands and making him swear not to kill himself... Every little moment of glory pecked at its eggshell and stuck out its featherless, wide-eyed head, in homage to the supreme glory of Rubião. There were also some who were jealous, some who knew him only from hearing him being loudly praised. Rubião went to thank Camacho for writing the piece, not without first reproaching him for abusing his confidence, but only halfheartedly, for form's sake. Then he went to buy quite a few copies of the newspaper for his friends in Barbacena. None of the other papers had picked up the story, so Rubião, on Freitas's advice, had it reprinted in the Readers' Requests section of the *Jornal do Comércio*, in a large typeface.

Chapter LXVIII

MARIA BENEDITA FINALLY consented to learn French and the piano. For four days Sofia badgered her relentlessly, and with such effect that the girl's mother resolved to hasten their return to the plantation, for fear that her daughter might give in. Maria Benedita put up a brave fight; she told her cousin that such social accomplishments were superfluous, and of no use to a country girl like her. One night, however, when Carlos Maria was there, he asked her to play something. Maria Benedita turned bright red. Sofia came to her rescue with a lie:

"Don't ask her to do that; she hasn't played since she arrived. She says that these days she only plays for country folk."

"Well then, let's pretend that we're country folk!" the young man insisted.

But he quickly switched to another subject, the ball given by the Baroness of Piauí (the very same baroness that our friend Rubião had encountered at Camacho's office). Ah yes, a splendid ball! Really splendid! The baroness held him in very high esteem, he told them. The next day, Maria Benedita announced to her cousin that she was finally ready to learn the piano and French, plus the violin and even Russian, if that's what she wanted. The difficulty lay in convincing her mother, who, when she learned of her daughter's decision, threw up her hands in despair. French? And the piano? "Never!" she cried, saying that if she did, she'd be no daughter of hers; she could stay, and play, and sing, and speak Bantu or the Devil's tongue, for that matter—indeed, the Devil could carry off the whole lot of them! It was Palha who finally persuaded her; however superfluous such accomplishments might seem, they were the minimum requirements for a society education. "But I raised my daughter in the country and for the country," Sofia's aunt interrupted.

"For the country? Does anyone know what they raise their children for? My father had me destined for the priesthood; that's why I know a smattering of Latin. You won't live forever, and your financial affairs are somewhat precarious. Maria Benedita could one day end up destitute . . . Well, not exactly destitute; as long as Sofia and I are alive, we are all one family. But isn't it better to take a few precautions? In the worst case, if she had none of us to fall back on, she could live quite comfortably giving French and piano lessons. Simply by learning them she would be in a better position. She's a pretty girl, just as you were in your day; and she possesses rare moral qualities. She could find a rich husband. Did you know that I already have someone in mind, a serious candidate?"

"Is that right? So then she'll be learning French, piano, and flirting?"

"What do you mean, 'flirting'?" retorted Palha. "I am referring to a very confidential plan of my own, a plan I think could be most conducive to her happiness and yours . . . Because I've . . . Come, now, Aunt Augusta!"

Palha looked so concerned that the aunt abandoned her harsh tone for one that was merely sharp. She still resisted, but that night he gave her some sound advice. Her financial situation, and the possibility of a wealthy son-in-law, carried more weight than the other arguments. The best sons-in-law in the countryside usually married into other plantations, or other wealthy families with influence. Two days later, they reached a modus vivendi. Maria Benedita would stay with her cousin; the two of them would go to the country from time to time, and the aunt would also come to visit them in Rio. Palha even promised that as soon as market conditions permitted, he would arrange a means of liquidating her assets and bringing her to live here in the city. But to this the good lady shook her head.

Do not imagine that everything went as smoothly as it might appear. In practice, there were endless obstacles, tribulations, regrets, and revolts from Maria Benedita. Eighteen days after her mother returned to the plantation, she decided to go visit her, and Sofia went with her; they stayed there a week. Then two months later, her mother came to spend a couple of days in Rio. Sofia skillfully acquainted her cousin with the amusements of the city: theaters, social visits, strolls, and promenades, gatherings at home, fashionable dresses, pretty hats, and jewelry. Maria Benedita was a woman, albeit an unusual woman; she liked such things, but was convinced that whenever she wished, she could free herself of all ties and head back to the country. Sometimes the country came to her in a dream or reverie. When she returned home from her first two soirées, it was not the excitement of the evening's entertainment that filled her head, but a longing for Iguaçu. These longings increased at certain times of day, when the house and the street outside were completely still. Then she would wing her way back to the veranda of their old house, where she used to sit drinking coffee with her mother; she would think about the slaves, the old-fashioned furniture, the sturdy house slippers her godfather, a wealthy plantation owner from São João del-Rei, had sent her—and which remained back at home, because Sofia would not let her bring them to Rio.

Her French and piano teachers knew their trades. Sofia found a way to tell them privately that her cousin was embarrassed to be learning these skills so late, and asked them not to say a word to anyone about their new pupil. They promised they wouldn't; the piano teacher merely mentioned the request to a few colleagues, who found it amusing and in return told him other anecdotes about their clients. What is certain is that Maria Benedita learned with remarkable ease and studied diligently for hours at a time, to such an extent that even her cousin thought it wise to interrupt her.

"You must rest, poor thing!"

"I have to make up for lost time!" Maria Benedita replied, laughing.

Then Sofia would invent random excursions, to make her rest. One day she would take her on an errand to this neighborhood, the next day to another. On certain streets, Maria Benedita put her time to good use: she would read any shop signs that were in French, and ask Sofia about any nouns she didn't know. Sometimes her cousin didn't know, either, her vocabulary being strictly limited to dresses, coquetry, and drawing-room pleasantries.

But it was not only in these two disciplines that Maria Benedita made rapid progress. She had adjusted to her new environment more quickly than her natural inclinations might have suggested. She was already competing with her cousin, although the latter still possessed a certain elegance and a particular way of holding herself that, one might say, lent color to every line and movement of her figure. Despite this difference, Maria Benedita was certainly attracting looks and attention when they went out together, so much so that Sofia, who had once praised her at every opportunity, would now, while never actually denigrating her, listen to her cousin's admirers in silence. Maria Benedita spoke well; but when she went quiet, that silence would last for a long time—she always blamed it on "one of my moods." She danced the quadrille with a certain detachment, which is the perfect way of doing it, and she very much liked watching the polka and the waltz. Wondering if it was fear that prevented her from dancing the waltz or polka, Sofia suggested giving her a few lessons at home, just the two of them, with her husband at the piano. But her cousin always refused.

"Oh, that's just country prudishness," Sofia said to her on one occasion.

Maria Benedita smiled in such a peculiar way that her cousin did not insist. It wasn't a smile of embarrassment, or resentment, or disdain. And why would it be disdain? That smile could certainly, however, be seen as somewhat condescending. And it is equally certain that Sofia polkaed and waltzed enthusiastically, and no one clung better to her dancing partner's shoulder than she did; Carlos Maria, who rarely danced, would only waltz with Sofia—just two or three turns around the floor, he would say; one night Maria Benedita timed them—a whole fifteen minutes.

Chapter LXIX

THOSE FIFTEEN MINUTES were counted out on Rubião's pocket watch; he was standing beside Maria Benedita and she twice asked him what time it was, at the beginning of the waltz and at the end. She herself leaned over to see the minute-hand more clearly.

"Are you feeling tired?" asked Rubião.

Maria Benedita looked at him out of the corner of her eye and saw his placid face, entirely devoid of malice or mockery.

"No," she replied. "In fact, I'm rather worried that Cousin Sofia might want to go home early."

"She won't leave early. She no longer has the excuse that they'll have to go all the way up the hill to Santa Teresa. The new house is very close."

The Palhas had indeed moved. Sofia and her cousin now lived at Flamengo Beach, and the ball was being held on Rua dos Arcos.

I should tell you that eight months had passed since the beginning of the preceding chapter, and many things had changed. Rubião was now in partnership with Sofia's husband in a trading venture on Rua da Alfândega, which went by the name of Palha & Co. This was the business proposition Palha had come to propose to him on the night he had encountered Senhor Camacho at Rubião's house in Botafogo. Despite Rubião's usually trusting nature, he hesitated for some time before agreeing. He was being asked to invest a fair amount of money, and he had no experience of commerce nor any real inclination for it. Moreover, his personal outgoings were already very high; if color was to return to its cheeks and flesh to its bones, his capital needed a combination of sound investment and a little frugality. The business plan being proposed was not exactly clear; Rubião could not understand Palha's figures: profit forecasts, price lists, customs duties, and all the rest; but words spoken made up for the words written. Palha said the most extraordinary things, advising his friend to seize the opportunity to put his money to work and watch it multiply. If he was afraid, then that was a different matter; he, Palha, would set up the business with John Roberts, a former partner at Wilkinson & Co., founded in 1844, the head of which had returned to England and was now a member of parliament.

Rubião did not give in straightaway; he asked for five days to think about it. When he was alone, he felt freer to think, but this time freedom served only to bewilder him. He calculated the money he had already spent, and assessed the extent of the gaping holes in the fortune the philosopher had left him. Quincas Borba, who was with him in the study, lying on the floor, happened to lift his head and gaze at him. Rubião shuddered; the notion that the soul of the other Quincas Borba might be living within this canine Quincas Borba had never entirely left him. This time he could even see a look of reproach in the dog's eyes. He laughed: Nonsense, a dog could not be a man. Unconsciously, however, he reached down and stroked the animal's ears, in order to win him over.

Following immediately behind the reasons for saying no came the opposing arguments. What if the business made money? What if his investment really did increase? Furthermore, it was a respectable position to hold, and might be to his advantage in the elections, when it was time to stand for parliament, just like the former head of Wilkinson's. Another, even stronger reason was his fear of offending Palha, of appearing not to trust him with his money, when only a few days earlier Palha had reimbursed part of his old debt to him, promising to repay the other part within two months.

None of these motives were prompted by the others; they all came of their own accord. Sofia only appeared at the end, even though she had been there right from the start, a latent, subconscious thought, one of the most important factors in his decision, and the only one he concealed. Rubião shook his head to banish her from his mind, and stood up. Sofia (astute lady!) withdrew to his subconsciousness, respectful of his moral freedom, and left him to decide for himself that he would indeed go into business with her husband, subject to certain clauses that would safeguard his interests. So it was that the business was set up, and thus it was that Rubião legalized the frequency of his visits to the house.

"Senhor Rubião," said Maria Benedita after several moments' silence, "my cousin is very pretty, don't you think?"

"With no disrespect to you, madam, yes, I do."

"Pretty and with a fine figure?"

Rubião again agreed. The eyes of both Maria Benedita and Rubião followed the waltzing pair as they circled the ballroom. Sofia looked magnificent. She was wearing a dark blue dress, very décolleté—for the reasons stated in chapter XXXV. Her firm, bare arms had a golden hue, as did her shoulders and her bosom, all enhanced by the gaslight of the ballroom to which they were so accustomed. And she wore a tiara of cultured pearls so convincing that they were a perfect match for the two natural pearls adorning her ears, and which Rubião had given her some time ago.

Beside her, Carlos Maria cut an equally handsome figure. He was, as we know, an elegant young man, and had those same placid eyes we first saw when he lunched at Rubião's. He did not deploy the obsequious manners or deferential bows of other young men; he expressed himself with the graciousness of a benevolent king. Still, even if, at first sight, he appeared to be doing the lady a favor by dancing with her, he was also flattered to have in his arms the most elegant lady of the evening. There was nothing contradictory about these two sentiments; they both had their basis in this young man's adoration of himself. For him, having Sofia in his arms was like having a devoted follower prostrating herself before him. Nothing would surprise him. If, one day, he were to wake up as an emperor, the only thing that would surprise him would be his government's slowness in coming to pay their respects.

"I'm going to rest a little," said Sofia.

"Are you tired?" asked her dancing partner. "Or bored?"

"Oh, just tired!"

Regretting having mentioned the second hypothesis, Carlos Maria hurriedly ruled it out.

"Of course, why would you be bored? But I'm sure you could manage to dance for a little longer. Five minutes?"

"Five minutes."

"Not even a minute more? For my part, I could dance until eternity."

Sofia lowered her head.

"With you, of course," he added.

Sofia allowed herself to be carried along, keeping her eyes fixed firmly on the floor, not answering, not agreeing, and not even thanking him. It might have been no more than flattery, but flattery is usually rewarded with thanks. She had heard similar things from him in the past, praising her above all other women in the world, although she hadn't heard such comments for the last six months—the four months he had spent in Petrópolis,* plus a further two when he had simply not visited them at their house. Recently, he had resumed those visits and begun paying her such compliments, sometimes in private, sometimes in the presence of others. And so she allowed herself to be carried along, and on they went without a word, not a single word, until he broke that silence, telling her

---

* Petrópolis was the imperial summer capital and a fashionable retreat for Rio's elite, set in the hills about forty miles from the city.

how loudly the waves had been crashing on the shore opposite her house just last night.

"You were there?" asked Sofia.

"Yes, I was passing through on my way to Catete, it was rather late, and I decided to go down to the beach at Flamengo. It was a clear night, and I stayed for about an hour, between the sea and your house. I'll wager that I didn't even appear in your dreams, whereas I could almost hear your breathing."

Sofia tried to smile. He went on:

"The waves were pounding on the shore, it's true, but my heart was beating just as violently—the difference being that the sea beats mindlessly on without knowing why, while my heart knows that it beats for you."

"Oh," murmured Sofia.

With surprise? Indignation? Alarm? That's a lot of questions all at once. I suspect that the lady herself could not have answered precisely, such was her shock at the young man's declaration. And yet, she did not entirely disbelieve it. I cannot say more than that, except that her exclamation was so faint, so muffled, that he barely heard it. For his part, Carlos Maria skillfully concealed his feelings from the eyes of the rest of the ballroom; neither before, nor during, nor after his declaration did he show the slightest emotion; his lips even carried the hint of a sarcastic smile, the smile he always wore when making fun of someone; a casual observer might think he had just uttered some witticism. And yet, more than one woman's eyes were peering deep into Sofia's soul, studying the young lady's expression, her slight awkwardness, her stubbornly downcast eyes.

"You look a little troubled," he said. "Use your fan to distract attention."

Sofia mechanically began to fan herself and looked up. She saw that many eyes were trained on her, and she turned pale. The minutes ticked by with all the brevity of years; first five, and then another five; they were now into their thirteenth minute, and beyond it the fourteenth and fifteenth already beckoned. Sofia told her dancing partner that she would like to sit down.

"I'll take you to your seat and withdraw."

"No!" she said hastily.

Then, correcting herself:

"It's such a lovely ball."

"It is, but I want to take with me the best memory of the night. Any words I might hear tonight would be like hearing the croaking of frogs compared to the singing of some songbird, one of those songbirds you keep at home. Where would you like me to leave you?"

"Beside my cousin."

Chapter LXX

RUBIÃO GAVE UP his seat beside Maria Benedita and followed Carlos Maria, who crossed the ballroom and made his way to the vestibule, where the coats were kept and where a group of about ten men were chatting. Just before the younger man reached the vestibule, Rubião took him amicably by the arm in order to ask him something—anything would do—but, in reality, to detain him for a moment and sound him out on something. He was beginning to believe that an idea that had been tormenting him for many days might actually be true or at least possible. And now that long conversation, her manner . . .

Carlos Maria had no inkling of Rubião's long-standing passion, a painful secret he could not confess to anyone; a passion that made do with whatever comforts chance might bring, and contented itself with very little, the mere sight of her, a few sleepless nights, investing in certain business deals... Rubião was not in the least jealous of her husband. Their intimacies as a couple had never aroused in him any hatred toward her legitimate spouse. And months and months went by, with no change in his feelings, no end to his hopes. But the possibility of an outside rival really rattled him; and now, for the first time, jealousy took its first bite and drew blood.

"What is it?" asked Carlos Maria, turning around.

The ten men in the vestibule were discussing politics, because this ball—I almost forgot to mention—was being held at Camacho's house, in honor of his wife's birthday. When Carlos Maria and Rubião entered, the men were having a general conversation, and all talking at once—a swirl of slogans, assertions, and differing opinions... One of them, the most dogmatic, succeeded in subjugating the others, who momentarily fell silent, smoking their cigars.

"They can do whatever they like," said the dogmatist, "but there's no avoiding the moral consequences. The debts of the parties will be paid for with interest down to the very last penny and the very last generation. Principles do not die, and parties who forget this will perish in muck and ignominy.'

Another man, nearly bald, did not believe in moral retribution, and was explaining why; but a third man alluded to the dismissal of several revenue officials, at which point emotions, heady with doctrine, took hold once again. The officials were guilty of nothing but having an opinion; and their removal could certainly not be defended on the basis of the merits of their replacements, one of whom had an embezzlement hanging over him, while another was the brother-in-law of a fellow by the name of Marques who'd taken a pot shot at the local police chief in São José dos Campos... And as for those new lieutenant colonels... absolute crooks.

"Are you leaving already?" Rubião asked Carlos Maria, on seeing him pick up his overcoat.

"Yes, I'm feeling tired. Give me a hand with this sleeve, would you? I'm nearly nodding off."

"But it's still early; stay a bit longer. Our friend Camacho doesn't want the young men to leave; who's going to dance with the young ladies?"

Carlos Maria smiled and replied that he wasn't that keen on dancing. He had waltzed with Dona Sofia because she was so good at it; if she weren't, he wouldn't have bothered. No, he was tired and preferred his own bed to the orchestra. And he held out his hand benignly; Rubião, half-uncertain, shook it.

He didn't know what to think. The fact that Carlos Maria was going home, leaving her at the ball, rather than accompanying her to her carriage as on previous occasions... Perhaps he was mistaken... And he thought back to that night in Santa Teresa, when he had dared to declare his feelings to Sofia, squeezing her beautiful, delicate hand... The major had interrupted them, but why had he not persisted? She hadn't responded angrily, and her husband hadn't noticed anything... Here the thought of his potential rival returned; Carlos Maria had indeed gone home feeling weary, but what of her behavior? Rubião went over to the door leading into the ballroom, from where he could see Sofia, then he drifted off toward a quiet corner, or perhaps the card table, feeling restless and annoyed.

Chapter LXXI

AT HOME, AS SHE unpinned her hair, Sofia spoke of the ball as a tiresome ordeal. She was yawning, and her legs ached. Palha disagreed; she was just in a bad mood. If her legs ached, it was because she had danced too much. To which his wife retorted that if she hadn't danced, she would have died of boredom. She carried on taking out her hairpins, placing them in a glass dish; her hair gradually fell around her shoulders, which were loosely covered by her fine cambric nightgown. Palha, standing behind her, commented that Carlos Maria was certainly very good at the waltz. Sofia shuddered; she stared at him in the mirror, but his face was perfectly calm. She agreed that Carlos Maria really didn't waltz that badly.

"No, dear, he waltzes very well."

"You praise others because you know that no one waltzes better than you. Come, now, my conceited darling, I know you of old."

Palha reached out and pinched her chin, turning her face to look at him. Why conceited? Why was he conceited?

"Ouch!" squealed Sofia. "You're hurting me."

Palha kissed her shoulder; she smiled, with no trace of tiredness, no headache, unlike on that night in Santa Teresa when she had told her husband about Rubião's impertinent behavior. Was it just that beaches were healthier places than hills?

The next day, Sofia woke up early to the sound of chirruping birds in the house. They seemed to be sending her a message from someone. She stayed in bed and closed her eyes to see more clearly.

To see what more clearly? Certainly not those unhealthy hills. The beach was another matter. Standing at the window half an hour later, Sofia gazed out at the waves lapping on the shore in front of her, and at those farther off, rising and breaking over the bar at the entrance to the bay. That very imaginative lady wondered if the waves were waltzing, and she let herself be swept along by this current with neither sails nor oars to guide her. She caught herself looking at the street that ran by the shore, as if searching for signs of the man who had been there the night before last, in the dark . . . I can't swear to it, but I think she found those signs. What is certain, though, is that she compared what she found with the words of their conversation at the ball:

"It was a clear night, and I stayed for about an hour, between the sea and your house. I'll wager that I didn't even appear in your dreams, whereas I could almost hear your breathing. The waves were pounding on the shore, it's true, but my heart was beating just as violently—the difference being that the sea beats mindlessly on without knowing why, while my heart knows that it beats for you."

Sofia shuddered; she tried to forget his words, but they kept repeating over and over in her head: "It was a clear night . . ."

Chapter LXXII

BETWEEN TWO SENTENCES, she felt someone's hand on her shoulder; it was her husband, who had just finished his breakfast and was leaving for the city. They said goodbye affectionately; Cristiano mentioned Maria Benedita had woken up in a rather bad mood.

"She's up already?" exclaimed Sofia.

"When I went down, she was in the dining room. She was going on about returning to the country again. She'd had a dream or something . . . I don't know . . ."

"It must be one of her moods!" concluded Sofia.

And with her nimble fingers she fixed her husband's necktie, adjusted the collar of his morning coat, and once again they said goodbye. Palha went downstairs and into the street; Sofia remained standing at the window. Before disappearing around the corner, he turned his head and, in their usual way, husband and wife waved.

Chapter LXXII

"IT WAS A clear night, and I stayed for about an hour, between the sea and your house. I'll wager that..."

By the time Sofia managed to pull herself away from the window, the clock downstairs was striking nine o'clock. Angry and contrite, she swore to herself, on her mother's soul, to think no more of the episode. She decided it didn't mean anything; the mistake had been letting the young man get so far with his impertinences. At least in the way she had dealt with it, she had avoided a major scandal, since he would have been perfectly capable of accompanying her back to her seat and continuing to confess all in front of other people. And that "confession" repeated itself once more in her mind, like a musical refrain that wouldn't go away, the same words, and the same voice: "It was a clear night, and I stayed for about an hour..."

Chapter LXXIV

WHILE SOFIA WAS repeating the previous night's declaration, Carlos Maria opened his eyes, stretched his limbs, and, before taking a bath, getting dressed, and going out for a ride on his horse, he reconstructed the previous night's events. It was a habit of his; he always found something said or done that made him feel good. This was where his mind would linger; these were his staging posts, where he would dismount from his horse and drink a leisurely draft of cool, fresh water. If there were no such incidents, or only disagreeable ones, then no matter; the merest hint of a word that he himself had said, a gesture he had made, the contemplation of his own existence, or the joy of feeling alive, would be enough to ensure that the previous evening had not been wasted.

The previous evening included Sofia. She was, indeed, the principal feature of that reconstruction, the main façade of the entire edifice, stately and magnificent. Carlos Maria savored from memory the evening's conversation, but when he came to his declaration of love, he felt both good and bad. It was a commitment, a hindrance, an obligation; and even though the benefits compensated for any tedious consequences, the young man felt caught between the two feelings, unsure of what to do next. On remembering that he'd told her he had gone to Flamengo Beach the night before, he burst out laughing, because it was simply not true. The idea had come to him during their conversation, but he had neither gone there nor even considered doing so. Eventually he managed to contain his laughter, and even felt guilty about laughing; the fact of having lied made him feel rather base, and that took the wind out of his sails. He wondered about amending what he had said when he next saw

Sofia, but realized that the emendation would be worse than the sonnet, and there are plenty of very pretty but mendacious sonnets.

His spirits quickly rose. In his mind's eye he saw the ballroom, the men, the women, the impatiently fluttering fans, the bristling mustaches, and he wallowed in a warm bath of envy and admiration. Other people's envy, of course: he himself was a stranger to that unpleasant sentiment. It was the envy and admiration of others that now gave him such inner pleasure. The queen of the ball was falling for him. That alone established Sofia's superiority, although he recognized she had one major shortcoming: her upbringing. He judged that the young lady's polished manners had been acquired by imitating others as an adult, only after, or shortly before, her marriage, and even then, they weren't much better than the milieu in which she lived.

Chapter LXXV

OTHER WOMEN ALSO came to mind those who preferred him to other men for his company and physical allure. Were they all women he was wooing or had wooed? Who can say? Some of them, no doubt. What is certain is that he relished all of them. Among them were women of proven virtue who liked having him at their side, to enjoy the company of a good-looking man without either the presence or the risk of sin—rather like a theatergoer who revels in Othello's passion, yet leaves the theater with his hands unsullied by Desdemona's death.

All these women came and stood around Carlos Maria's bed, weaving him the same garland. Not all were in the first flower of youth, but elegance made up for youth. Carlos Maria received them as an ancient god fixed in marble should receive his beautiful devotees and their offerings. In the general murmuring he could pick out their voices; not all at once, but three or four at a time.

The last of these was Sofia's, the most recent; he listened to it feeling still enamored, but without the same initial excitement, because the memory of his other admirers, all ladies of quality, diminished her importance. Nevertheless, he could not deny that she was very attractive and that she waltzed perfectly. Would he ever love passionately? At this, he remembered again his lie about Flamengo Beach. He got out of bed feeling annoyed.

"What the devil made me say such a thing?"

Once again he felt a desire to set the record straight, this time more seriously than before. Lying, he thought, was for scoundrels and their ilk.

Half an hour later, he mounted his horse and set off from his house, which was on Rua dos Inválidos. As he passed through Catete, he remembered that Sofia's house was nearby on Flamengo Beach; there would be nothing more natural, surely, than for him to pull on the reins, turn left into one of the streets heading down toward the sea, and pass by the front door of his waltzing partner. He might perhaps find her standing at her window; he would see her blush and wave to him. All this passed through the young man's head in a matter of seconds; he even gave a tug on the reins, but his soul—not the horse, but his soul—bridled; it was too soon to be chasing after her. He gave another tug on the reins and continued his ride.

≡ *Chapter LXXVI*

HE RODE WELL. No one passing by or standing in a doorway could fail to admire the young man's posture, his elegance, his regal tranquility. Carlos Maria—and this was the point on which he yielded to the crowd—gathered in all these expressions of admiration, no matter how lowly. For the purposes of venerating Carlos Maria, all men were part of humanity.

≡ *Chapter LXXVII*

"UP ALREADY?" repeated Sofia, on seeing her cousin reading the newspapers.

Maria Benedita jumped, but quickly regained her composure; she had slept badly, and woken early. She was not one for these late-night revelries, she said; but Sofia quickly replied that she would need to get used to it, because life in Rio de Janeiro was not the same as the country, where the rule was "to bed with the hens and up with the rooster." She then asked for her impressions of the ball; Maria Benedita gave an indifferent shrug, but said she had enjoyed it. Her words were brief and unenthusiastic Sofia, meanwhile, commented that she, Maria Benedita, had danced a lot, but not the polkas or waltzes. Why not polkas or waltzes? Her cousin shot her an angry look.

"I don't like them."

"What do you mean, you don't like them? It's just fear."
"Fear?"
"Lack of practice," explained Sofia.
"I don't like it when a man holds my body close to his, and parades me around the floor like that, in front of everyone. I think it's embarrassing."

Sofia grew serious, but then changed the subject, talking about the countryside, asking if what Cristiano had told her was true, that she wanted to return home. Her cousin, who was randomly leafing through the newspapers, replied emphatically that it was indeed true; she was missing her mother terribly.

"But why? Haven't you been happy staying with us?"

Maria Benedita said nothing; she scanned one of the newspapers, as if looking for something, biting her lip, trembling, anxious. Sofia persisted in trying to find out the reason for this sudden change; she clasped her cousin's hands and thought they felt cold.

"You need to marry," she said finally. "I already have a fiancé in mind."

The fiancé in question was Rubião. Palha was keen on the idea of marrying his business partner to his cousin; as he said to his wife, it would keep everything in the family. Sofia undertook to guide things in the right direction. Now she remembered her promise; she had a fiancé ready and waiting.

"Who?" asked Maria Benedita.
"Someone."

Would you believe it, future generations? Sofia could not bring herself to say Rubião's name. She had told her husband once already that she had proposed it to Maria Benedita, and she had lied. And now, just as she really was about to propose it, the name would not pass her lips. Jealousy? It would be very odd for this woman, who had no love for that man, to be unwilling to give him as fiancé to her cousin. But human nature is capable of anything, my friend. It invented the jealousies of Othello and of the Chevalier des Grieux,* and it could certainly invent the jealousy of someone who doesn't want to relinquish what they don't even want to possess.

"But who?" repeated Maria Benedita.

"I'll tell you later. Leave it to me to arrange matters," replied Sofia, before changing the subject.

Maria Benedita's expression underwent an immediate transformation. Her face lit up with a smile, one of happiness and hope. Her eyes glowed with gratitude and spoke words no one could hear or understand: "Keen on waltzing—that's the clue."

Who was keen on waltzing? Her cousin, for one. She had waltzed so much the night before, with the very same Carlos Maria, that she might well have been using the dance as a pretext. Maria Benedita now concluded that this was the only possible motive. They had spoken at length between dances, and clearly they had been talking about her, since her cousin was bent on finding her a husband—hadn't she just told her to leave her to arrange matters? Maybe he thought she was ugly, or clumsy. If her cousin wanted to arrange things, though . . . This is what those glowing eyes were saying.

Chapter LXXVIII

RUBIÃO'S SUSPICIONS WERE not so easily allayed. He decided he would speak to Carlos Maria and ask him outright, and even went

---

* The lover of the inconstant Manon Lescaut in Abbé Prévost's 1731 novel, and subsequent operatic adaptations.

to Rua dos Inválidos three times the following day to do so. Not finding his rival, he changed his mind and cloistered himself at home for several days. Major Siqueira drew him out of his solitude, arriving to inform him that he had moved to Rua Dois de Dezembro, in Catete. He admired our friend's house, its furnishings, its magnificence, all its little gewgaws, gildings, and drapes. He held forth on the subject at length, fondly recalling the furniture of an earlier age. Then he broke off suddenly to say that Rubião seemed bored; it was only natural, for in all this comfort there was still something lacking.

"You're obviously happy here, but there's something else you need; you need a wife. You should marry. Get yourself a wife, and then tell me I'm wrong."

Rubião remembered Santa Teresa—the famous evening of his conversation with Sofia—and felt a chill run down his spine; but there was no sarcasm in the major's voice. Nor was he motivated by self-interest. His daughter was still the same as we left her in Chapter XLIII, except that she had now turned forty. Forty and a spinster. When she woke up on her birthday, she groaned; she put neither ribbon nor rose in her hair that morning. There was no party, just a speech by her father over lunch, reminding her of her childhood, followed by a few anecdotes about her mother and grandmother, a hooded cloak she had worn at a masked ball, a baptism in 1848, a certain Colonel Clodomiro's tapeworm, and a whole ragbag of things to fill the time. Dona Tonica barely heard, too absorbed in her own thoughts, chewing on the dry crusts of her spiritual solitude, while at the same time regretting her more recent efforts at procuring a husband. Forty years old; it was time to stop.

None of this crossed the major's mind as he spoke to Rubião. He meant what he said; he felt that Rubião's house lacked soul. And, on leaving, he repeated:

"Get yourself a wife, and then tell me I'm wrong."

Chapter LXXIX

"AND WHY NOT?" a voice asked after the major departed.

Terrified, Rubião looked around him, but saw only the dog, who was looking at him. It was too absurd to think that the voice had come from Quincas Borba—or rather from the other Quincas Borba, whose spirit might be inside the dog. Our friend smiled at him scornfully, but nevertheless repeated the same trick he had performed in Chapter XLIX: he reached out and fondly scratched the dog's ears and neck—an act intended, just in case, to placate the dead man's spirit.

It was thus that our dear friend hedged his bets, with no audience and with only himself as witness.

Chapter LXXX

BUT THE VOICE REPEATED: "And why not?"

"Yes, why shouldn't I get married?" Rubião thought. It would put an end to the passion that was slowly consuming him, with neither hope nor consolation. Besides, it was the gateway to a mystery. Yes, marry. Marry soon, and marry well.

He was standing at the gate when this idea began to blossom; he turned and went inside, going up the stone steps, opening the front door, totally oblivious to everything. As he closed the door, Quincas Borba, who had followed him, jumped up and brought him to his senses. Where had the major gone? Rubião made as if to go back down to see him, but remembered in time that he had just accompanied him out into the street. His legs had done all the work; they had carried him all by themselves, lucid, straight, and without stumbling, so that all his head would have to do was think. Good legs! Friendly legs! The mind's natural crutches!

Saintly legs! They carried him onward to the couch, where they slowly stretched out with him, while his mind worked on the idea of marriage. It was a way of escaping Sofia; it might even be something more.

Yes, it might also be a way of restoring the unity his life had lost with his change of surroundings and fortune; but this latter consideration was not strictly the offspring of either mind or legs, but of something else, which, like the spider, he could distinguish neither clearly nor unclearly. What does a spider know about Mozart? Nothing, and yet it enjoys listening to one of his sonatas. The cat, who has never read Kant, may well be a metaphysical animal. Marriage could indeed be the bond that would restore his lost unity. Rubião felt strangely discombobulated; his traveling companions, to whom he was so attached and who showered him with attentions, gave his life the feeling of a journey in which the language changed with each city, today Spanish, tomorrow Turkish. Sofia contributed to this state of mind; she herself was so unpredictable, one thing one day, another thing the next, that the days slipped by with no firm agreement and no definitive disillusion.

Rubião had nothing to do. To fill his long, empty days, he would attend proceedings at the courthouse or the Chamber of Deputies, watch military parades, go for long walks, pay unnecessary social calls in the evenings, or go to the theater, which he did not enjoy. His house still provided a refuge for his soul, with its glittering luxury and the dreams that floated in the air.

Recently, he had been doing a lot of reading; he had read novels, but only historical ones by Alexandre Dumas *père*, or contemporary ones by Octave Feuillet, the latter with some difficulty, since his French wasn't very good. As for Dumas, there were plenty of translations. He tried a few other authors provided they had the same sort of royal or aristocratic settings as Dumas and Feuillet. Those scenes from the French court, invented by the wonderful Dumas, along with his swashbuckling noblemen and adventurers, and Feuillet's countesses and dukes in their luxuriant palm houses, all speaking in polished, convoluted sentences, sometimes haughty, sometimes witty, made the time speed past. He would almost always end up staring into space and thinking, with the book lying by his side. Perhaps some long-dead marquis was telling him stories from another era.

Chapter LXXXI

RUBIÃO GAVE MORE THOUGHT to the wedding than to the bride. That day and during the days that followed, he planned the sumptuous celebrations, the carriages—he wondered if they still had the luxurious ones he had seen in engravings in books about times past. Such large and magnificent carriages! How he enjoyed, on great state occasions, going to wait for the Emperor at the palace gates, to see the arrival of the imperial procession, especially His Majesty's coach with its generous proportions, powerful springs, finely painted panels, and four or five pairs of horses driven by a grave and dignified coachman! Other coaches would follow, smaller in size, but still large enough to impress.

One of these other carriages, or even something a little smaller, might have fit the bill for his wedding, if only the whole of society hadn't been brought down to the same level by the vulgar coupé. Oh, well, a coupé would have to do; he imagined it sumptuously upholstered, but in what? For the moment he couldn't quite decide, but it would have to be an unusual fabric that he could not himself name, but which would give the vehicle the distinction it currently lacked. A fine pair of horses. A coachman in gold livery. But a gold that had never been seen before! Guests of the very highest rank: generals, diplomats, senators, one or two ministers, many prominent businessmen. And what about the ladies, the great ladies? Rubião named them from memory, watched them arrive, him standing at the top of a palatial staircase, gazing down at the rich tapestry spread out beneath him: the ladies crossing the entrance lobby, treading lightly up the stairs in their dainty satin slippers; at first only a few, and then more, and yet more. Carriage after carriage . . . Here were the count and countess of so-and-so, a dashing gentleman and a striking lady . . . "Here we are, my dear friend," the count would say, loud enough for all to hear; and, later on, the countess: "What a splendid party, Senhor Rubião . . ."

Then, all of a sudden, the internuncio would arrive. Yes, indeed; he had forgotten that the internuncio himself would marry them; there he was—with his large Neapolitan eyes and wearing the purple socks of a monsignor—deep in conversation with the Russian ambassador. The gold and crystal chandeliers shining down upon the most beautiful bosoms in the city; frock coats standing erect, others bending over, listening to the ladies' fans as they opened and closed; tiaras and epaulets; the orchestra striking up a waltz. And then the black-sleeved arms, sharply bent, went in search of the bare arms, gloved to the elbow, and the couples began to whirl around the dance floor: five, seven, ten, twelve, twenty couples. A splendid supper. Bohemian crystal, Hungarian porcelain, Sèvres glassware, nimble footmen in livery, with Rubião's initials on their collars.

Chapter LXXXII

THESE DREAMS CAME and went. How mysterious... Was it thus that Prospero transformed an ordinary island into a sublime masque? "Go, Ariel, bring the rabble here, for I must bestow upon the eyes of this young couple some vanity of mine art." The words were much the same as the play's, but the island was different, both the island and the masque. The former was our friend's own head, and the latter was composed not of goddesses nor of verse, but of human beings and drawing-room prose. But it was all very lavish. Let us not forget that Shakespeare's Prospero was Duke of Milan; perhaps this is why he washed up on our friend's island.

For indeed, the brides who appeared at Rubião's side during those nuptial dreams were always titled ladies. Their names were the most resonant and best-known of our august peerage. Here is the explanation: a few weeks earlier, Rubião had picked up a copy of *Laemmert's Almanac* and, leafing through it, had come across the chapter on titled nobility. Although he had heard of some, he certainly didn't know all of them. He bought his own copy and read it over and over, running his eyes down the page from marquises to barons and back again, repeating the beautiful names and learning many of them by heart. Sometimes he took pen and paper, picked one of the titles ancient or modern, and wrote it out again and again, as if it belonged to him and he were signing something:

                    Marquis of Barbacena
Marquis of Barbacena
                         Marquis of Barbacena
                                      Marquis of Barbacena
Marquis of Barbacena
                                   Marquis of Barbacena

He carried on down to the bottom of the page, changing his handwriting each time, sometimes large, sometimes tiny, upright or slanting, in every conceivable style. When he finished the page, he picked it up and compared the signatures, then put it down and stared into space. Hence his hierarchy of brides. The worst of it was that they all had Sofia's face; at first they might resemble a neighbor of his, or the girl he'd tipped his hat to that afternoon in the street; they might start off very thin or very plump; but they didn't take long to change shape, fill out or slim down, and take on the resplendent face of the beautiful Sofia, with her eyes, rebellious or at rest. Was there no way of escaping her, even by marrying? One evening as he left their house, after hearing her say all sorts of vague and charming things, Rubião even went so far as to imagine Palha dying. He felt an overwhelming sense of happiness, even as he instantly rejected the idea as an evil omen. A few days later, when her behavior toward him changed, he reverted to his previous plans. More than once, it was Palha himself who awakened him from these conjugal dreams:

"Are you going anywhere this evening?"

"No."

"Then take one of these tickets for the opera. We're in box number eight, first tier, left-hand side."

Rubião would get there early and wait for them, offering Sofia his arm. If she was in a good mood, it would be one of the best evenings ever. If not, it was torture, as he himself said to the dog one day.

"Last night was sheer torture, my poor friend."

"Get yourself a wife, and then tell me I'm wrong," barked Quincas Borba in reply.

"Yes, you're right, my poor friend," replied Rubião, picking up the dog's front paws and placing them on his knees. "You need an indulgent mistress who will give you the kind of attention you won't get from me. Do you still remember, Quincas Borba, our very own Quincas Borba? He was a good friend of mine, a great friend, and I was a friend to him. Two great friends. If he were alive, he would be best man at my wedding. He would propose the toasts—at least the most important one, to the newlyweds—and it would be from a golden goblet encrusted with diamonds, which I would ask him to have specially made for the occasion . . . Great Quincas Borba!"

And Rubião's mind hovered over the abyss.

Chapter LXXXIII

ONE DAY, HAVING LEFT the house earlier than usual and unable to decide where to spend his time, he walked over to the warehouse. He hadn't been to Flamengo for a week, because Sofia was going through one of her silent phases. When he reached the warehouse, he found Palha dressed in mourning; his wife's aunt, Dona Maria Augusta, had died at her plantation; the news had reached them two days earlier, in the afternoon.

"That young girl's mother?"

"The very one."

Palha spoke of the dead woman with great affection, and then of Maria Benedita's grief, which was painful to see. He suggested to Rubião that he come over to Flamengo that same evening, to help them take her mind off it. Rubião promised he would.

"Good, you would be doing us a great favor; besides, the poor thing deserves all the help she can get. Such a delightful creature. A good, strict upbringing and, as regards social accomplishments, while she may not have acquired them as a child, she has certainly made up for lost time. Thanks to Sofia. And as for running a household? I doubt, my friend, if you'd find anyone her age better prepared. From now on, she'll be living with us. She has a sister, Maria José, who is married to a judge in Ceará; she also has a godfather in São João del-Rei. Her mother was always singing his praises. I don't think he will send for her, though, but even if he does, I won't give her up. She's ours now. We won't let go of her just because her godfather might decide to leave her something in his will. She's staying put," he concluded, picking a speck of dust off Rubião's collar.

Rubião thanked him. Then, since they were in the office, at the rear of the premises, he looked out through the railings and saw a couple of bales being delivered to the warehouse. He asked what was in them.

"Some English calico."

"English calico," repeated Rubião impassively.

"Talking of which, did you know that Morais & Cunha is paying all its creditors, in full?"

Rubião didn't even know such a firm existed, nor whether he and Palha were among its creditors; he said he was very glad, and stood up to leave. But his partner detained him a few moments longer. He was cheerful now; you would never have thought there had been a death in the family. He spoke again about Maria Benedita. He intended to marry her well; she wasn't the type to fall for a dandy, nor was she the kind to be carried away by foolish fantasies; she was a sensible girl and deserved a good husband, a man of substance.

"Yes, indeed," said Rubião.

"Look here," his partner suddenly said in a low voice, "don't be surprised at what I'm about to say. I think you should be the one to marry her."

"Me?" replied Rubião, astonished. "No, sir." And then, to soften the impact of his refusal: "I'm not denying she is a worthy and wonderful girl, but . . . for the time being . . . I have no thoughts of marriage . . ."

"No one is suggesting you do it tomorrow or the day after; marriage isn't something to be rushed into. What I'm saying is that I have a little hunch. Never underestimate a hunch. Has Sofia not told you about my little hunch?"

"No, never."

"That's odd; she told me she'd mentioned it to you once or even twice, I think."

"Oh, possibly; I'm rather absent-minded You mean about the two of you wanting me to marry the girl?"

"No, about my little hunch. But let's drop the matter for now. All in good time."

"Goodbye."

"Goodbye, and be sure to come early tonight."

Chapter LXXXIV

"SO, SOFIA WANTS to marry me off?" Rubião thought; this was clearly the most efficient way of getting rid of him. Marry him off and make him her cousin. Rubião trudged along many streets before coming to a very different hypothesis: perhaps Sofia hadn't, in fact, forgotten to talk to him about Maria Benedita, and was deliberately lying to her husband in order to frustrate his plans. In that case her feelings were entirely different. This explanation seemed perfectly logical, and his mind regained its earlier serenity.

Chapter LXXXV

BUT NO AMOUNT of serenity can trim so much as a minute off the passing hours, when a person has no way of making time run faster. On the contrary, Rubião's impatience to go to Flamengo that evening made the hours drag even more slowly. It was still too early for anything, too early to go to the cafés in Rua do Ouvidor, too early to return to Botafogo. Senhor Camacho was in Vassouras, defending a client in court. There were no public amusements that day, no religious festivals or sermons. Nothing. Profoundly bored, Rubião wandered aimlessly, reading shop signs or being waylaid by something as banal as the sight of two carts colliding. He had never been so bored in Minas; why was that? He could find no solution to this enigma, since Rio had far more in the way of amusements, and ones that really did amuse him, but there were also hours and hours of deadly boredom.

Fortunately, there is a god for the bored. Rubião suddenly remembered that Freitas—that cheery fellow Freitas whom we met earlier—was gravely ill. Rubião hailed a cab and went to visit him at Formosa Beach.* He spent nearly two hours there, talking to the patient. When the man dozed off, Rubião said goodbye to the mother—a shriveled old lady—and, at the door before leaving, added:

"You've probably had to tighten your belt," said Rubião. Seeing her bite her lip and lower her eyes, he added: "Don't be embarrassed; poverty is painful, but nothing to be ashamed of. I would like you to accept a little something from me to help with expenses; you can pay me back someday, if you're able to . . ."

He opened his wallet and took out six twenty-*mil-réis* notes, folded them up, and pressed them into her hand. Then he opened the door and left. The old woman was too taken aback to thank him; it was only when the cab set off that she rushed to the window, but by then her benefactor was already out of sight.

Chapter LXXXVI

ALL OF THIS happened so spontaneously that Rubião only had time to reflect on it in the cab. It seems he did manage to draw back the

---

* Formosa Beach was located on the less salubrious side of Rio, away from Flamengo and Botafogo. By the time the novel was being written, the beach had disappeared under a vast land reclamation project.

little curtain over the peephole behind him; he could just see part of the old woman's arm as she turned to go inside. Rubião felt all the advantages of not being an invalid. He leaned back, gave a deep sigh, and gazed over at the beach; then he leaned forward again for a better view; on the way there he had hardly been able to see it.

"Enjoying the view, senhor?" asked the cabdriver, pleased to have such a good customer.

"Yes, it's very pretty."

"Haven't you been here before?"

"I think I have, but many years ago, when I was in Rio de Janeiro for the first time. I'm from Minas . . . Stop here, will you, boy?"

The driver stopped the horse; Rubião got out and told him to follow on slowly.

It was indeed an unusual sight. Those great clumps of vegetation, bursting forth from the mud, right there in front of Rubião's face, made him want to go up and touch them. So close to the street too! Rubião didn't even feel the sun. He had forgotten all about the sick man and his mother. "Ah, yes," he said to himself, "if only the sea was like this everywhere, dotted with islands and greenery, then it would be worth exploring." Farther on was Lázaro Beach, and São Cristóvão Beach. Just a short stroll away.

"*Praia Formosa*—the beautiful beach," he murmured. "A well-chosen name."

Meanwhile, the shoreline was changing. He was turning the corner toward Alferes, and there were now houses between the road and the sea. Here and there were overturned canoes, hauled up onto the mud or dry land. Around one of these canoes he could see some young boys playing, in shirtsleeves and barefoot, around a man who was lying facedown. They were all laughing; one boy was laughing more than the others because he couldn't manage to get the man's foot to touch the ground. He was only a toddler, three years old; he kept grabbing the man's leg and pulling it down toward the ground, but each time the man lifted both foot and boy up into the air.

Rubião paused for several minutes. The boy, seeing he had an audience, redoubled his efforts, no longer innocently unselfconscious. The other boys, who were older, stopped to watch in surprise. But Rubião didn't notice anything; everything he saw was a blur. He carried on walking for quite some time toward the city, past Alferes and on past Gamboa; he stopped at the English cemetery, with its old gravestones clambering up the hillside, and finally he reached Saúde. He saw its cramped, steep streets and alleyways, a jumble of houses running up and over the rocky slopes, many of the houses very old, some dating back to the time of the king, with their shabby, cracked, and crumbling walls, blackened limewash exteriors, and teeming with life inside. And all this gave him a feeling of nostalgia . . . A nostalgia for rags and tatters, for a meager life, humble but peaceful. This did not last long, though; the sorcerer within him waved his wand and transformed everything. How good it was not to be poor!

Chapter LXXXVI

RUBIÃO REACHED THE END of Rua da Saúde but he continued to wander aimlessly, not paying attention to where he was going. A woman passed by him; she wasn't pretty, but nor was she plain or completely lacking in distinction; poor rather than well-off, but with a freshness in her features; she was around twenty-five years old, and she was holding a little boy by the hand. The boy somehow got himself tangled up in Rubião's legs.

"Mind where you're going, little one," said the young woman, tugging her son by the arm.

Rubião bent down to help the child.

"Sorry, sir. Much obliged," she said, smiling; and she bobbed a short curtsy.

Rubião lifted his hat and smiled back. Once again, images of family life assailed him: "Get yourself a wife, and then tell me I'm wrong!" He paused, looked back, watched the woman walking away, *tick-tack*, and the little boy scampering along beside her trying to keep up. Then he carried on walking, slowly, thinking about various women he might well choose to perform a conjugal piano duet with him, steady, serious, classical music. He even considered the major's daughter, who knew only a few old mazurkas. Suddenly he could hear the guitar of sin, plucked by Sofia's fingers, which both delighted and dazzled him, and out went that chaste piano duet. He tried once more to switch compositions; he thought about the young woman in Saúde, with such nice manners, holding her little boy by the hand . . .

Chapter LXXXVIII

THE SIGHT OF the cab reminded him of his sick friend at Formosa Beach.

"Poor Freitas!" he thought.

Immediately after that, he thought about the money he had given the sick man's mother, and decided he had done the right thing. Perhaps the idea that he might have given her one or two notes too many fluttered briefly through the mind of our friend; he quickly shooed it away, annoyed at himself for entertaining it, and in order to banish it completely, he exclaimed aloud:

"Dear lady! Poor old lady!"

Chapter LXXXIX

WHEN THE IDEA kept coming back, Rubião hurried over to the cab, climbed in, and sat down, speaking to the driver as a way of escaping his own thoughts.

"I've had a good long walk; yes, indeed, it's rather pretty here, unusual; those beaches, those streets, it's different from other neighborhoods. I like it here. I must come more often."

The cabdriver smiled to himself in such an odd way that it made Rubião suspicious. He couldn't figure out the reason for that smile; perhaps he had let slip a word that in Rio de Janeiro had negative connotations, but he repeated them in his head and could find nothing untoward—they were all perfectly normal, anodyne words. And yet the driver was still smiling, wearing the same expression as before, half-subservient, half-roguish. Rubião was on the point of questioning him, but stopped himself in time. It was the driver who picked up the conversation.

"So you're very taken with this neighborhood, senhor? If you'll allow me to say so, senhor, and let's not get into an argument about it, for I wouldn't want to offend—I'd never be one to cause offense to a serious customer like your good self—but I don't believe it's the neighborhood you're taken with, senhor."

"Why do you say that?" ventured Rubião

The driver shook his head and said again that he didn't believe him—not because the neighborhood wasn't worthy of appreciation, but because he must, of course, already know it very well. Rubião repeated that he had been there many years before, on a previous visit to Rio de Janeiro, but had no recollection of the place. The cabdriver laughed; and the more Rubião insisted, the more familiar he became, making all sorts of negative gestures with his hands, lips, and nose.

"I know all about these things," he concluded. "And I'm not blind. Do you perhaps think, senhor, that I didn't see the way you looked at that young woman who passed by just now? That alone is enough to show you've a fine eye and a liking for . . ."

Flattered, Rubião allowed himself a faint smile, but quickly corrected himself:

"What young woman?"

"What did I tell you?" the man retorted. "You're the discreet type, sir, and quite right too; but I know how to keep a secret, and this carriage has been used for many such comings and goings. Only a few days ago, I brought a fine young man, very well dressed, smart fellow—clearly chasing a bit of skirt."

"But I . . ." Rubião began.

He could scarcely contain himself; the supposition appealed to him; the driver thought he was hiding some guilty secret.

"Look, I've seen it all before," the driver continued. "Just like that fine young man from Rua dos Inválidos. You can rest assured, senhor, I won't say a thing; it's all part of the job. But do you expect me to believe that someone, with a cab at his disposal, walks all the way from Formosa Beach to here just for the sake of it? If you ask me, you came to the appointed meeting place, but the person in question didn't turn up."

"What person? I came to see a sick man, a friend of mine who's dying."

"Just like the young man from Rua dos Inválidos," repeated the driver. "He came to see a seamstress on behalf of his wife—as if he were married..."

"From Rua dos Inválidos?" asked Rubião, only now paying attention to the name of the street.

"I won't say a word more," replied the driver. "He was from Rua dos Inválidos, handsome fellow with a mustache and large eyes, very large. Oh, yes, I might fall in love with him myself, if I were a woman... As for her, I've no idea where she was from, and if I did, I wouldn't say; I only know that she was a fine figure of a woman."

And, seeing that his customer was listening to him wide-eyed:

"Oh! You've no idea, senhor! She was tall, good figure, her face half-covered by a veil, very fancy. I might be poor, but I still know a good thing when I see it."

"But... what happened?" murmured Rubião.

"What happened? He arrived just like your good self, in my cab. He got out and went into a house with latticed shutters; he said he was going to see his wife's seamstress. Since I hadn't asked him, and he'd been silent throughout the journey, very full of himself, I got the message straightaway. Now, of course, it could well be the truth, for there is indeed a seamstress who lives in that house on Rua da Harmonia..."

"Rua da Harmonia?" repeated Rubião.

"Now, now, you're trying to get me to tell you my secret. Let's change the subject; I won't say another word."

Rubião stared in astonishment at the cabdriver, who did indeed stop talking for two or three minutes, but then began again:

"In any event, there isn't much more to say. The young man went inside, and I waited for him; half an hour later, I saw a woman's figure in the distance, and I suspected right away she was heading for the same place. And I was spot-on; she approached very slowly, looking all around her; when she reached the house—now, keep all this to yourself—she didn't even need to knock; as if by magic the door opened all by itself and in she went. Oh, I've seen it all before. How else do you think folk like me earn a few extra pennies? The price of the fare hardly gives us enough to eat; we have to make do with these little extras."

Chapter XC

"NO, IT COULDN'T BE HER," Rubião reflected when he was back at his house, putting on his evening clothes.

Since arriving home, he could think of nothing else but the incident the cabdriver had described. He tried to forget about it by putting his papers in order, or reading, or clicking his fingers to make Quincas Borba jump up; but the image kept pursuing him. Reason told him that there were many ladies with fine figures, and there was no proof that she was the one seen in Rua da Harmonia; but the beneficial effects of this thought were short-lived. A few moments later, there in the distance, walking along slowly, head bowed, he saw a woman, who was none other than Sofia herself, and who suddenly entered a house through a door that closed quickly behind her ... The vision was so clear that, at one point, our friend stood staring at the wall, as if the latticed shutters of Rua da Harmonia were there before him. He imagined himself knocking, then entering, grabbing the seamstress by the throat, and demanding the truth or her life. Threatened with death, the poor woman confessed everything, and took him to see the lady, who was someone else, not Sofia. When Rubião returned to his senses, he felt ashamed.

"No, it couldn't be her."

He put on his vest and went to button it up in front of one of the windows at the back of the house. At that same moment, a column of ants was making its way across the windowsill. How many such processions had he seen before! But this time, for reasons that escaped him, he picked up a towel and flicked it twice at the poor ants, killing a good many of them. Perhaps one of them looked like that "fine figure of a woman." He immediately regretted his actions; for what did the ants have to do with his suspicions? Fortunately, a cicada began chirruping, with such relevance and meaning that our friend stopped at the fourth button on his vest. *Soooo . . . fia, fia, fia, fia, fia . . . Soooo . . . fia, fia, fia, fia . . .*

Ah! The sublime, merciful foresight of nature, compensating for twenty dead ants with a joyously living cicada! That, dear reader, is of course your idea. It could not be Rubião's. He was incapable of putting two things together and drawing a conclusion, nor would he be doing so now as he reached the last button on his vest, all ears, all cicada . . . Poor dead ants! Go now to your Gallic Homer, and may fame reward you; the cicada is the one laughing now, amending the text as follows:

Vous marchiez? J'en suis fort aise.
Eh bien! Mourez maintenant.*

---

* "Were you walking? I'm so pleased. Well, now you die." Turning on its head Jean de La Fontaine's fable "The Ant and the Grasshopper."

Chapter XCI

THE BELL RANG for supper; Rubião composed himself, so that his usual guests (there were always four or five) would not notice anything amiss. He found them in the drawing room, chatting while they waited. They all stood and came forward eagerly to shake his hand. Rubião felt an inexplicable urge to hold out his hand for them to kiss. He refrained just in time, shocked at himself.

Chapter XCII

AFTER SUPPER, HE HURRIED over to Flamengo Beach. He wasn't able to speak to Maria Benedita, who was upstairs in her room with two friends of hers, young ladies from the neighborhood. Sofia came to greet him at the front door, and took him into a side room where two seamstresses were busy making the mourning dresses. Her husband had just got home, and had not yet come downstairs.

"Sit here," she said.

She was attentive toward him; she was divine. Her words were both affectionate and serious, her smiles friendly and honest. She talked to him about her aunt, her cousin, the weather, the servants, the theater, the water shortages, and a whole host of other things, banal or otherwise, but which took on an entirely different character when they came from her lips. Rubião listened enraptured. Not wanting to be idle, she carried on with her sewing as she spoke, and when the conversation paused, Rubião could barely stop himself from devouring the sight of her nimble hands that seemed to merely play with the needle.

"Did you know that I'm setting up a ladies' committee?"

"No, I didn't. What for?"

"Didn't you read the news of that epidemic in a town in Alagoas?"

She told him she had been so distressed by the news that she had immediately decided to set up a committee of ladies to raise donations. Her aunt's death had interrupted her initial efforts, but she would carry on with it once the seventh-day mass was over. She asked him what he thought about it.

"I think it's a very good idea. Aren't there any gentlemen on the committee?"

"Only ladies. The men can donate money, but that's all," she concluded with a smile.

In his head, Rubião immediately made a large donation, in order to oblige those who followed to do likewise. Everything she said was true. It was also true that the committee would raise Sofia's profile, and give her a big push upward in society. The ladies selected were above her own social circle, and only one of them would greet her in the street; but through the good offices of a certain widow, who had dazzled in the 1840s and still retained the refinement of and a nostalgia for those times, she had succeeded in getting them all to join her committee. For several days, she had thought of little else. Sometimes, in the evenings, before tea, she might seem to be dozing in her rocking chair, but she wasn't asleep; she was merely closing her eyes to picture herself among her new companions, people of quality. Understandably, this was the main subject of conversation, but Sofia did return from time to time to Rubião. Why such long absences? Eight, ten, fifteen days or more? Rubião replied that there was no particular reason, but he said this with such feeling that one of the seamstresses tapped the other one's foot. From then on, even when there was a prolonged silence, interrupted only by the sound of scissors, the tearing of fabric, and needles passing through merino wool, neither of the seamstresses took their eyes off our friend, whose own eyes were fixed firmly on the lady of the house.

A man, the director of a bank, arrived to offer his condolences. Someone went to fetch Palha, who came downstairs to receive the visitor. Sofia asked Rubião to excuse her for a few moments; she was going up to see Maria Benedita.

Chapter XCIII

LEFT ALONE WITH the two women, Rubião began pacing back and forth, walking as quietly as possible so as not to bother anyone. From the drawing room he could hear a few words here and there from Palha: "In any case, you can rest assured . . ."—"Running a bank isn't child's play . . ."—"Of course not . . ." The director said very little, speaking in a low, terse voice. One of the seamstresses folded up her sewing and hurriedly tidied away any scraps of material, as well as scissors, spools of thread, and sewing silk. It was getting late and she was leaving.

"Wait a minute, Dondon, and I'll come with you."

"No, I can't wait. Could you tell me what time it is, senhor?"

"It's half past eight," replied Rubião.

"Goodness, it is late."

Just to say something, Rubião asked her why she couldn't wait as the other woman had asked.

"I'll just wait for Dona Sofia to come down," replied Dondon respectfully. "But do you know where my friend lives? She lives close by in Rua do Passeio. But I'm off to rest my bones in Rua da Harmonia, and from here to Rua da Harmonia is a fair old walk."

Chapter XCIV

SOFIA CAME DOWN soon after; she found Rubião looking terribly upset, unable to meet her eye. She asked him what was wrong and he said it was nothing, just a headache. Dondon left, and the bank director said good night; Palha thanked him for his kindness and wished him good health. Now, where was his hat? Palha found it, and also handed him his overcoat; and, sensing he was looking for something else, asked him if it was his cane.

"No, my umbrella. I think it's this one; yes, this is the one. Good night."

"Once again, thank you, thank you very much indeed," said Palha. "Do put your hat on; it's damp outside, no need to stand on ceremony. And thank you, thank you very much," he concluded, grasping the man's hand in both of his, and bowing sharply from the waist.

Returning to the study, he found his business partner, who was also keen to leave. Palha urged him to stay and have a cup of tea, insisting that his headache would soon pass. Rubião refused.

"Your hand's very cold," Sofia remarked as she shook it. "Why don't you wait awhile? A little lemon balm works wonders. I'll fetch some."

Rubião stopped her; there was no need; he knew all about these minor ailments; a good night's sleep was the best cure. Palha wanted to send for a cab, but Rubião replied that the night air would do him good, and that he would find one on his way through Catete.

≋ *Chapter XCV*

"I'LL CATCH HER before she reaches Catete," Rubião said to himself as he walked up Rua do Príncipe.

That was the route he thought the seamstress would have taken. He could make out several figures in the distance, on either side of the street; one of them looked like a woman. It must be her, he thought, and quickened his pace. It goes without saying that his head was in a spin: Rua da Harmonia, a seamstress, a lady, and all the latticed doors and windows wide open. Don't be surprised to learn that, feeling almost at his wits' end and walking very briskly, he collided with a man who was proceeding very slowly, head down. Rubião didn't even apologize; seeing that the woman was also walking briskly, he merely increased his speed.

≋ *Chapter XCVI*

AS FOR THE MAN he bumped into, he scarcely felt the impact. He, too, was lost in his own thoughts, strolling happily along and in an expansive mood, free from any cares or concerns. It was the bank director, the one who had just visited Palha. He wasn't in the least annoyed by the impact; he simply adjusted his overcoat and gathered his thoughts, and walked serenely on.

To explain the man's indifference, I should perhaps tell you that he had, within the space of an hour, experienced a whole slew of completely contradictory emotions. First, he had gone to the house of a government minister to make a request on behalf of his brother. The minister, who had just finished having dinner, was peacefully, silently smoking a cigar as the director launched into a somewhat confused explanation of the request, circling back and forth, tying himself in knots. As he sat respectfully on the edge of his seat, his mouth was fixed in a deferential smile; and he bowed frequently, apologizing for the intrusion. The minister asked a few questions; the director replied enthusiastically and at length, great length, and ended by handing the minister a written memorandum. Then he stood up, thanked the minister, shook his hand, and the minister accompanied him out to the veranda. There the director bowed twice—the first time deeply, before descending the steps, and the second time from the front garden at the bottom of the steps; the latter bow, however, was witnessed only by the frosted glass door and the gas lamp hanging from the roof. He put on his hat and left, humiliated and annoyed with himself. It wasn't making the request that bothered him, but his overly effusive greetings, his many apologies, and his craven demeanor—a whole rosary of futile actions. It was in this mood that he had arrived at Palha's house.

Within ten minutes, his mind was refreshed and restored to its former self, such was the warmth of Palha's welcome, his nods of approval and his fixed and gleaming smile, not to mention the offers of tea and cigars. The director immediately became stern, superior, cold, terse; he even disdainfully curled his left nostril in response to a suggestion of Palha's, who immediately retracted it and agreed that it was absurd. The director replicated the minister's languid gestures. As he left, the bowing came not from him, but from Palha.

He was a different man by the time he reached the street; hence his untroubled and contented pace, his expansive mood restored, and the indifference with which he met Rubião's colliding shoulder. Memories of his own bowing and scraping were fading away, and now it was he who savored the bowing and scraping of Cristiano Palha.

== Chapter XCVII

WHEN RUBIÃO REACHED the corner of Rua do Catete, the seamstress was talking with a man who had been waiting for her, and who immediately offered her his arm; Rubião watched them head off, like husband and wife, toward Glória. Were they married? Friends? They disappeared around the first bend in the road, while Rubião stood motionless, remembering the cabdriver's words, the latticed shutters, the mustachioed young man, the fine figure of a woman, Rua da Harmonia . . . Yes, Rua da Harmonia; she had said Rua da Harmonia.

He went to bed late, having spent some of the time standing at the window, brooding and smoking a cigar, trying in vain to come up with an explanation. Dondon was clearly the go-between in the affair; her shifty eyes told him so.

"I'll go there tomorrow. I'll leave the house early and wait for her at the corner. I'll give her a hundred *mil-réis*, two hundred, even five hundred, and she'll confess the whole thing."

When he grew tired, he looked up at the sky; there was the Southern Cross . . . Oh! If only she had agreed to gaze up at the Southern Cross! Their lives would have been so different. The constellation, shining unusually brightly, seemed to confirm his feelings, and Rubião stood there gazing and imagining countless charming scenes of love—the life that could have been. When his heart had had its fill of these unfulfilled moments, it occurred to our friend that the Southern Cross was not only a constellation, but also an order of merit. This led him to an entirely different series of thoughts. He thought what a very clever idea it had been to make the Southern Cross into a national honor of the highest distinction. He had seen its insignia adorning the chests of several public servants. It was beautiful, but above all, rare.

"All the better!" he said out loud.

It was nearly two o'clock when he left the window; he closed it and got into bed, falling asleep almost instantly. He awoke to the sound of his Spanish servant telling him that a letter had come for him.

Chapter XCVIII

RUBIÃO SAT UP in bed, still half asleep, opened the letter without noticing the handwriting on the envelope, and read:

> We were rather concerned yesterday after you left. Cristiano isn't heading over to see you this morning because he woke up very late, and he has a meeting with the customs inspector. Send us word if you are feeling better. Fond regards from Maria Benedita and from
>
> Your grateful friend,
> Sofia

"Tell the messenger to wait."

Twenty minutes later, the reply reached the hands of the black boy who had brought the letter; Rubião himself gave it to him and asked after the ladies of the house. Informed that they were both well, he gave the lad a few coins, and advised him to come back and see him whenever he needed some money. Eyes wide with surprise, the boy promised that he would.

"Goodbye, then!" said Rubião benevolently.

And he waited as the boy went down the short flight of steps. When he was halfway across the front garden, the boy heard a shout:

"Wait!"

He turned around; Rubião was already coming down the steps; they walked toward each other, and stopped in silence. Two minutes passed before Rubião said anything. Finally, he asked a question: Were the ladies of the house well? It was the same question he had just asked; the servant confirmed his answer. Then Rubião let his eyes wander over the garden. The roses and daisies were so beautiful and fresh, some carnations were starting to open, and the other flowers and the greenery, the begonias and climbers, indeed that whole little world seemed to turn their invisible eyes toward Rubião, and cry out:

"O feeble heart, put an end to this and follow your desires; pick us, send us . . ."

"Well," said Rubião finally, "do give my regards to the ladies. And don't forget what I told you. Anytime you need me, you know where I am. Do you have my letter?"

"Here it is, sir."

"You'd better put it in your pocket. But be careful not to crumple it."

"No, sir, I won't crumple it," replied the boy, putting the letter away.

Chapter XCIX

THE BOY LEFT. Rubião paced around the garden, hands thrust in the pockets of his dressing gown, gazing at the flowers. Why shouldn't he send her some? It would be a perfectly normal thing to do, even an obligatory one, repaying one courtesy with another. He had made the wrong decision; he ran to the gate, but the boy was already far away; then Rubião remembered that mourning ruled out any such cheerful gifts, and he felt relieved.

Just as he turned back toward the garden, however, he saw a letter lying next to one of the flower beds. He leaned down, picked it up, and read the envelope ... The handwriting was hers, undoubtedly hers; he compared it to the letter he had just received; it was the same. The name on the envelope was that scoundrel Carlos Maria's.

"Yes, that's what must have happened," thought Rubião after a few minutes. "The boy was carrying this letter as well, and dropped it."

And, staring at the envelope, front and back, he wondered what the letter might contain. Ah, the contents! What could be written on that murderous piece of paper? Wickedness, depravity, all the language of lust and insanity, condensed into two or three lines. He held it up to the light, to see if he could read a few words; the paper was too thick and he couldn't make out a thing. Then, realizing that the boy, when he missed the letter, would come back looking for it, Rubião stuffed it in his pocket, and hurried into the house.

Once inside, he took the letter out and looked at it again; his hands hesitated, mirroring his state of mind. If he opened the letter, he would know everything. Once he had read it and burned it, no one else would know its contents, and he would have put an end to this terrible fascination that tormented him as he stood staring into the abyss of opprobrium . . . These are not, dear reader, my words; they are his; he is the one using these terrifying words, and others besides; it is he who stops dead in the middle of the room, staring down at the carpet, with its pattern that features an indolent Turk, smoking his pipe and gazing out at the Bosporus . . . Yes, it must be the Bosporus.

"Infernal letter!" he snarled under his breath, repeating a phrase he had heard at the theater a few weeks earlier and then forgotten, and which now came to him as an expression of the moral equivalence between spectacle and spectator.

He felt an urge to open it; it was only one small gesture, one small act. No one would see it; the portraits on the wall hung there still and indifferent, the Turk on the carpet carried on smoking and looking out at the Bosporus. And yet he had his scruples; although he had found it in his garden, the letter did not belong to him. It belonged to Carlos Maria. If it had been a wad of money, would he not return it to its owner? Irritated, he put it back in his pocket. Caught between sending the letter to its addressee or returning it to Sofia, he chose the second option, which had the advantage of allowing him to read the truth in the face of the author herself.

"I'll tell her I found a letter and so on," thought Rubião, "and before giving it to her, I'll see clearly from her face whether she is terrified or not. Maybe she'll turn pale; in which case I'll really scare her by mentioning Rua da Harmonia; I'll swear to her that I'm willing to spend three hundred, eight hundred, one thousand, two thousand *contos*, thirty thousand *contos*, whatever it takes, to strangle that scoundrel . . ."

Chapter C

NONE OF HIS usual guests appeared for lunch. Rubião waited another ten minutes, even sending a servant to the front door to see if anyone was coming. No one; he had to lunch alone.

Generally speaking, he found such solitary meals unbearable; he was so accustomed to his friends' conversation, their observations and witty remarks, not to mention their respect and gratitude, that to eat alone was tantamount to not eating at all. Now, though, he was like Saul in need of a David to drive out the malignant spirit that had slipped inside him. He felt positively angry with the bearer of the letter for having dropped it; it would be so much better not to know. Then, however, his conscience wavered, shifting back and forth between returning the letter and not returning it, and keeping it indefinitely. Rubião was afraid of knowing; one minute, he wanted to be able to read something on Sofia's face; the next, he would have preferred to read nothing. His desire to know everything was, in short, the hope of finding that there was, in fact, nothing at all.

A David finally appeared, in between the cheese course and the coffee, in the person of Senhor Camacho, who had traveled back from Vassouras the previous night. As in the Bible, he brought a donkey laden with bread, a bottle of wine, and a kid goat. He had been visiting a deputy from Minas Gerais who was currently lying gravely ill in Vassouras, and he had already begun preparing Rubião's candidature by writing to all the most influential people in Minas, or so he said in between sips of coffee.

"Me? A candidate?"

"Of course, who else?"

Camacho explained why there could be no better candidate. Had Rubião not done useful work while he was in Minas?

"Well, a little, yes."

"And here you have achieved some other very important things. Helping me to keep alive that highly principled organ, my newspaper, and, out of solidarity, taking many blows intended for me, not to mention the inevitable financial sacrifices we have all had to make. So, please, not a word. I am here to tell you that I will do whatever I can. Besides, you are the surest way of staving off a possible split."

"A split?"

"They say that should a vacancy occur, Senhor Hermenegildo from Catas Altas and Colonel Romualdo both intend to stand, which would mean splitting the vote . . ."

"It would indeed, but what if they insist on standing?"

"I doubt if they will when I send them confirmation of your candidature by the party leaders, because that was one of the things they threw in my face, that I had no say when it came to choosing the candidate; and I admitted that, in such unforeseen circumstances, they were right, but that I did enjoy the confidence of the leaders, who would be sure to give me the go-ahead. It's all settled. What do you think? Why else would I invest all this time and effort and money, plus a smidgen of talent, if not to help a friend who has shown himself so loyal to our principles? Why else? No, don't you worry, they'll listen to me and will be sure to adopt my proposed candidate."

Rubião was touched and asked a few more questions about the forthcoming election battle and victory: Was any immediate expenditure needed, any letter of recommendation or a formal application to stand as candidate, and how would they go about receiving regular news of the dying man's condition, etc.? Camacho answered all these questions, but urged caution. In politics, he said, the slightest thing can send a campaign off course and hand victory to your opponent. However, even if he didn't win, it would be to Rubião's advantage to have had his name approved as a candidate—a useful precedent.

"Resolve and patience," he concluded, adding:

"Am I myself not a fine example of patience and resolve? My province is currently in the hands of a horde of bandits; there's no other word for the Pinheiro faction; besides (and I say this with great sadness and strictly between you and me), I have friends who are plotting against me, certain unscrupulous self-seekers who want to see me ousted from the party purely so that they can take my place ... the villains! Ah, my dear Rubião, politics can rightly be compared to the passion of Our Lord Jesus Christ, for it's all there: The disciple who denies him and the one who betrays him. The crown of thorns, the beatings, and, finally, dying nailed to the cross of one's ideas by the nails of envy, calumny, and ingratitude ..."

This last phrase, which came to him in the heat of conversation, seemed to him worthy of an article; he made a mental note of it, and, before going to sleep, wrote the phrase down on a strip of paper. At the time, though, while the doctor was fixing those words in his memory, Rubião was telling him not to worry, that he was sure Camacho was just the man for a big campaign, and that he shouldn't be frightened off by such impostors.

"Certainly not. I wouldn't even be frightened by a real-life ogre, if such things existed. Let them do their worst, I say! They'd better watch out when we rise to power, though. Then they'll be sorry. One piece of advice: In politics, no one ever forgives or forgets. You pay back any trickery in kind, and, believe me, revenge is sweet," he went on with a smile. "Positively delicious ... Nevertheless, when you weigh up the good and the bad things about politics, the good still outweighs the bad. There are always going to be ungrateful so-and-sos, but they either resign or are thrown in prison. Or they're driven out..."

Rubião listened meekly. Camacho, his eyes shining, was very commanding. Curses and anathemata poured from his lips as if from the mouth of Isaiah; triumphal palms seemed to grow lush and green in his hands. His every gesture was like a moral principle. When he flung wide his arms, scything the air, it was as if he were unfurling a whole manifesto, growing drunk on hopes, on the wine of joy. Then he stood before Rubião:

"Come, now, Mr. Deputy, how about a speech calling for the debate to be closed: 'Mr. Speaker...' Come on, say after me: 'Mr. Speaker, I humbly ask Your Excellency...'"

Rubião sprang to his feet, feeling almost dizzy. He could see himself entering the Chamber to take his oath, with all the other deputies watching, and a shudder ran through him. This was a very difficult step, and yet there he was crossing the room, going up to the Speaker's rostrum, and taking the usual oath... His voice perhaps quavering a little...

Chapter CI

IT WAS WHILE he was still thinking about all this that the news of Freitas's death came to find him. Privately, he wept a tear or two; he took it upon himself to pay for the cost of the funeral and the following afternoon he accompanied the deceased to the cemetery. When Freitas's old mother saw Rubião enter the room where the body was still lying, she made as if to kneel before him, but Rubião immediately embraced her and thus prevented her from doing so. This action made a great impression on the other guests. One man came over and shook his hand, and later, in a corner, confided quietly to Rubião that he had been unfairly dismissed only days before, a dismissal intended to wound or provoke and one that was clearly the result of intrigues . . .

"You may not know this, but that place is a den of thieves (if you'll forgive the expression) . . ."

Then it was time for the body to be conveyed to the cemetery; the mother's farewell to her son was painful to behold; a whole heartrending mixture of kisses, sobs, and cries. None of the women could detach her from her son's coffin, and, in the end, two men and the servant had to physically drag her away; even then, she kept crying out and struggling to return to the corpse, crying: "My son, my poor son!"

"An utter scandal!" the dismissed employee went on. "They say the minister himself disapproved, but you know how it is, no one wanted the director to lose face . . ."

Then came the dull thud of hammer on coffin lid—bang, bang, bang . . .

Rubião agreed to help carry the coffin, and abandoned the dismissed employee. A few onlookers were waiting outside; the neighbors were all at their windows, crammed in elbow to elbow, their eyes full of the curiosity that death always inspires in the living. And then there was Rubião's coupé, which stood out among the other older carriages. The dead man's friend had already been the object of much talk, and his presence at the house only confirmed the rumors. The deceased was now spoken of with new respect.

At the cemetery, not content with scattering a little earth on the coffin—which, at everyone's request, he was the first to do—Rubião waited, his eyes moist with tears, until the gravediggers, with their large spades, had finished their task. Then he left, flanked by the other mourners, and, at the gate, raising his hat just once to right and left, he bade farewell to their bare, bowed heads. As he got into his coupé, he heard someone mutter:

"He must be a senator or a high court judge or something..."

Chapter CII

NIGHT HAD FALLEN. Rubião was returning home, still thinking about the poor wretch he had just buried, when, on Rua de São Cristóvão, he passed another coupé escorted by two orderlies on horseback. The man inside was clearly a minister on his way to some government meeting. Rubião craned his neck to see, then promptly drew back, and despite the clatter made by the other horses in the street, all he could hear was the sound of those particular horses' hooves, so regular, so distinctive. Such was our friend's heightened state of mind that he could still hear them even when distance rendered this quite impossible. Clip-clop... clip-clop... clip-clop...

Chapter CIII

ON THE SEVENTH DAY following the death of Dona Maria Augusta, the usual mass was held in São Francisco de Paula; Rubião duly attended and there he saw Carlos Maria, and this was enough to precipitate the return of the letter. Three days later, he put it in his pocket and rushed over to Flamengo. It was two o'clock in the afternoon. Maria Benedita had gone to visit some neighborhood friends who had accompanied her during the early days of her grief; Sofia was alone and was dressed to go out.

"It doesn't matter, though," she said, inviting him to sit down. "I'll stay, I can always go out afterward."

Rubião replied brusquely that he wouldn't be long; he had merely come in order to give her a piece of paper.

"Well, sit down anyway. You can just as easily give me a piece of paper while seated."

She looked so lovely that he could not, at first, bring himself to utter the harsh words he had prepared. Mourning really did become her, and her dress fit her like a glove. When sitting, she revealed half her foot, her shoe, her silk stocking, all of which cried out for his mercy and forgiveness. As for the sword in that sheath—as one poet described the soul—it appeared to lack any sharp blade and never to have known war; it was an innocent ivory letter opener. Rubião very nearly weakened; then one word brought the others in its train.

"What's this piece of paper, then?" asked Sofia.

"One that I believe to be of grave importance," he replied, trying to keep calm. "Do you not remember losing a letter? Or were you even aware in the first place that you had?"

"No."

"Do you write many letters?"

"I've written a few, but whether they were of grave importance, I can't recall. Let me see it."

By now Rubião was almost wild-eyed. For a moment, he neither said nor did anything. He stood up intending to leave, then did not leave. After a few moments of awkward silence, he said very calmly:

"It will come as no surprise if I tell you that I love you. You know this, but you neither send me away nor acknowledge me;

indeed, you encourage me with your charming manners. I have still not forgotten that night in Santa Teresa, or when I first met you and your husband on the train. Do you remember? That journey was my downfall; ever since then you have held me captive. You are a wicked woman with the soul of a serpent; what did I ever do to you? You may well not love me, but why not make that clear from the start?"

"People are coming," Sofia broke in, standing up now and looking over at the door. "Be quiet."

No one came, but it was true that anyone could have heard him because Rubião's voice was growing in volume and in feeling. It grew still louder. He was no longer simply pleading his cause, he was opening up his soul and pouring out its contents.

"I don't care if they hear me," he bawled. "Let them! I will say everything I have to say, and then you can throw me out and that will be the end of it. You can't allow a poor man to suffer like this . . ."

"For the love of God, be quiet!"

"God? What God? Hear me out, for I am determined to leave nothing unsaid—"

Beside herself now, and genuinely afraid that a servant might hear, Sofia raised her hand and covered his mouth. This sudden contact with that beloved epidermis completely silenced Rubião. Sofia withdrew her hand and made as if to leave the room; however, on reaching the door, she stopped. Rubião had gone over to the window to recover from that explosion of emotion.

Chapter CIV

AFTER STANDING AT the door listening for a few seconds, Sofia came back into the room and, with a great rustle of skirts, sat down on the blue satin ottoman, which had only been purchased a few days before. Rubião turned and saw her shaking her head reprovingly. Before he could speak again, Sofia silenced him by placing one finger on her lips, then beckoned him over. Rubião obeyed.

"Sit on that chair," she ordered; then, once he was seated, she went on. "I would be perfectly within my rights to tell you off, but I won't because I know you to be a good man and, I believe, sincere. Say you're sorry for what you just said, and all will be forgiven."

Sofia brushed the right side of her dress with her fan in order to smooth out any creases, then she raised her arms slightly, setting her black glass bracelets tinkling. Finally, she brought them to rest on her knees, and sat there, repeatedly opening and closing her fan, while she awaited his response. Contrary to expectations, Rubião shook his head.

"I'm not sorry," he said, "and I would prefer you not to forgive me. You will stay in my heart whether you like it or not. I could lie, but where would that get me? You're the one who has been less than sincere, because you have deceived me . . ."

Sofia stiffened.

"Please don't be angry, I have no wish to offend you, but allow me to say that you are the one who has deceived me, cruelly and without a hint of compassion. That you should love your husband I accept and forgive, but that you—"

"But that I what?" she asked in alarm.

Rubião pulled the letter from his pocket and handed it to her.

When Sofia saw Carlos Maria's name, every drop of blood drained from her face, a change Rubião could not help but notice. However, she immediately regained her composure and asked him what the letter was and why he was bringing it to show her.

"It's your handwriting."

"It is, but whatever do you imagine I said in the letter?" she continued serenely. "Who gave it to you?"

Rubião was about to explain how he had found it, but realized that he had gone far enough, and so bowed and made as if to leave.

"Forgive me," she said. "Why don't *you* open the letter?"

"No, I have nothing further to do here."

"Stay and open the letter. Here, read it all," she said, grabbing his sleeve, but Rubião drew away violently, then went to fetch his hat and left. Fearing the servants, Sofia remained in the room.

Chapter CV

DURING THE MOMENTS that followed, she felt so agitated that she nearly forgot about the letter. Afterward, though, she turned it this way and that, unable to think what it could contain; gradually, once she had calmed down, she realized that it must be the circular from the newly founded Alagoas committee. She tore open the letter: Yes, it was the circular. How could such a letter have found its way into Rubião's hands? And where had his suspicions come from? Were they his or someone else's? Was there some rumor going around? She went to find the servant who had taken the circular to Carlos Maria and asked if he had delivered it, knowing full well that he had not. When the servant had arrived at the house in Rua dos

Inválidos, he realized he no longer had the envelope in his pocket and was then too afraid to tell his mistress.

Sofia returned to the drawing room, determined now to stay in. She picked up the letter and the envelope, intending to show them to Rubião, so that he could see it was nothing at all, but he would doubtless assume she had replaced the letter with the circular. "Wretched man," she murmured. And she began aimlessly pacing.

Memories swarmed into Sofia's mind. The image of Carlos Maria entered and stood before her, with those large eyes of his, the eyes of a specter both loved and loathed. Sofia tried to drive him away, but failed; he paced along beside her, never for one moment losing his elegant, masculine charm or his sublimely ironic air. Sometimes she would see him lean toward her, uttering the same words he had said one night at a ball, words that had cost her many sleepless hours and many days of hopeful waiting, until they dissolved into unreality. Sofia had never understood where that affair went wrong. He appeared to be genuinely in love, and why else would he declare his love so boldly, or walk past her windows late at night, as he had told her he did? She recalled other meetings, snatched conversations, warm, lingering looks, and she could not understand why such passion should come to nothing. There had probably been no passion, and it was a mere flirtation or, at most, a way of honing his powers of seduction . . . The actions of a cynical, shallow dandy.

Why even bother pondering such a mystery? He was a superficial fellow. Her feelings of disgust and disdain grew. She even laughed at him; she could face him again now with no feelings of remorse. And she continued her pacing, thinking vengeful thoughts about that fool—that's what she called him, a "fool"—fixing the empty air with her virginal eyes. She really was worrying about nothing; she began to curse Rubião for summoning up such a man, a man she had quite forgotten, and all because of that silly circular... Then she returned to those early memories, to Carlos Maria's words. Since everyone thought her beautiful, why should he be any different, and why should he not tell her so? Perhaps she would have had him at her beck and call if she hadn't shown herself to be so pathetically grateful, so easily flattered...

Suddenly the maid, who was in the next room, heard the sound of something breaking, and rushed in to find her mistress standing there alone.

"It's all right," said Sofia.

"I thought I heard—"

"It was that figurine. It fell off the shelf. Pick up the pieces, will you?"

"Oh, the Chinese one!" cried the maid.

It was indeed a porcelain mandarin, who, poor thing, had been quietly sitting on a shelf, minding his own business. Sofia had found herself holding him, without knowing why; remembering her own voluntary humiliation, she was gripped by a sudden impulse—possibly anger at herself—and she had hurled him to the floor. Poor mandarin! The fact that he was made of porcelain didn't save him from her wrath, nor did the fact that he had been a present from Palha.

"But, madam, how did it...?"

"Go away!"

Sofia remembered how she had behaved with Carlos Maria, how easily she had acquiesced, forgiven him in advance, recalled her yearning glances, their lingering handshakes... Yes, she had thrown herself at him. Then the feeling changed. After all, it was only natural that he should admire her, and their deep shared understanding seemed to exclude the possibility of one abandoning the other. Perhaps the fault lay elsewhere. She delved deep for other possible reasons, some harsh or cold gesture on her part, perhaps she had proved inattentive; she did recall that, once, afraid to receive him alone, she had sent word that she was not at home. Yes, maybe that was it. Carlos Maria was a proud man, the slightest snub could wound him. He knew it was a lie . . . Yes, that was the reason.

Chapter CVI

. . . OR, RATHER, a chapter in which the disoriented reader, finding it hard to marry Sofia's anxieties with the cabdriver's story, will ask in some bewilderment: "So that meeting in Rua da Harmonia between Sofia and Carlos Maria, that clash of sweet and dissonant rhymes, is mere gossip?" A calumny created by the reader and by Rubião, not by the poor cabdriver, who mentioned no names and wasn't even telling a true story. You would have realized this had you read more carefully. Yes, poor reader, just think how unlikely it was that a man engaged in such an affair would have his cab stop right outside the chosen rendezvous. That would be like arranging to have a witness to a crime. There are far more streets in heaven and earth than are dreamt of in your philosophy—side streets for a start, where the cab could wait.

"All right, so the cabdriver didn't know what he was talking about, but why would he invent a tale like that?"

He had driven Rubião to a house, where our friend had stayed for nearly two hours, having told the driver to wait; he had then watched him come out of the house, get back in the cab, only to get out again and continue on foot, ordering him to follow. The driver concluded that this was a most valuable customer, but it still did not occur to him to invent anything. However, when a lady walked past with a child—the lady in Rua da Saúde—Rubião stood looking after her with sad, loving eyes. Here is where the cabdriver assumed his passenger was not only generous, but also a libertine, and decided to offer him his services. If he mentioned Rua da Harmonia, this was only because it reminded him of the district from which they had just come; and if he said he had brought a young man from Rua dos Inválidos, it was because he had, naturally enough, picked up someone—possibly even Carlos Maria—from there the day before, or because he himself lived there or kept his horses there, or for some other reason that proved useful in improvising a story, just as things seen during the day serve as material for our dreams. Not all cabdrivers are imaginative. It's hard enough just to be able to stitch together the everyday scraps of reality.

All that remains is the coincidence that one of the seamstresses making the mourning garments lived in Rua da Harmonia. Now, that certainly does seem to have been laid on by Fate. But the fault lies with the seamstress; she could easily find a house nearer the center of town if she wanted to leave both needle and husband. Alas, she loves them both more than anything in the world. Not that this is any reason for me to delete the episode, or interrupt the book.

Chapter CVII

THERE IS, THOUGH, no need to explain Sofia's thoughts. They all had a toe in the truth. It was true, very true, that Carlos Maria had not matched up to her first hopes—nor to her second or third— because she had planted hopes in various flower beds, albeit somewhat less green and flourishing. As for the cause, we have seen that

Sofia, for want of one cause, immediately came up with three more. It never once occurred to her that Carlos Maria might have found a new love, thus rendering all others dull and insipid. That would be a fourth cause, and possibly the real one.

Chapter CVIII

FOR A FEW MONTHS, Rubião stopped going to Flamengo. This was not an easy resolution to keep. He frequently hesitated and frequently repented; more than once he even set off fully intending to visit Sofia and ask her forgiveness. But forgiveness for what? He didn't know, he just wanted to be forgiven. Whenever he experienced such temptations, the thought of Carlos Maria always stopped him in his tracks. Then, after a certain point, it was the number of days or weeks that had elapsed since his last visit that held him back; it would be distinctly odd just to turn up there one day, like a sad prodigal son, in the hope of being granted a fond look from the beautiful eyes of the mistress of the house. He did, however, continue to visit Palha at the warehouse; after five weeks, though, Palha reproached him for his long absence from their home, and, after two months, asked Rubião if he was deliberately avoiding them.

"I've had an awful lot to do," said Rubião, "these political matters take up all my time. I'll come on Sunday."

Sofia got dressed up specially to receive him. She was determined to find an opportunity to explain the true nature of the letter, meanwhile swearing by all that was holy that she was telling the truth, then he would see that truth was indeed on her side. All in vain; Rubião did not appear. Another Sunday came and went, and more Sundays followed. Nevertheless, one day Sofia sent him a donation form for the Alagoas committee, and he signed up to give five *contos*.

"That's a lot," said Palha when Rubião came to the warehouse to hand him the form.

"I wouldn't want to give any less."

"You can still be generous without going over the top, you know. Besides, this isn't a small affair, with only half a dozen donors. There are plenty of ladies involved and some gentlemen, too, and the form is in all the shops in the Praça do Comércio, and so on. Why not make a slightly smaller donation?"

"But I've already filled out the form."

"You could easily make that five into a three. Three *contos* is still a very decent amount. There have been larger donations, but they're from people whose wealth or position obliges them to give more; Bonfim, for example, signed up for ten *contos*."

Rubião gave an ironic smile, then shook his head and refused to alter the amount. The only change he would be prepared to make would be to put a one in front of the five, making it fifteen *contos*, thus outdoing Bonfim.

"You can give five, ten, or fifteen, or whatever you like," said Palha, "but you need to look after your capital, you're starting to eat into it . . . and you're already earning less interest."

Palha was now the custodian of Rubião's investments (shares, bonds, title deeds), which were kept locked up in the warehouse safe. He collected the interest for him, as well as the dividends and the rent on three houses he had persuaded Rubião to buy at rock-bottom prices and which had proved a highly lucrative investment. He also kept a small cache of gold coins for him, because Rubião loved collecting them, purely for the pleasure of looking at them now and then. Palha knew the sum total of Rubião's wealth better than he did, and was aware that holes were beginning to appear in the ship's hull even though there was no storm raging and the sea was smooth as silk. Three *contos* was quite enough, he said again; and if proof of his sincerity were needed, was he not the husband of the person who had set up the committee? Rubião, though, refused to budge and took the opportunity to ask for another ten *contos*. Palha scratched his head.

"Forgive my asking," he said after a few moments, "but what do you need the ten *contos* for? You'll only end up losing them, or run the risk of doing so."

Rubião laughed at this objection.

"If I really thought I would lose them, I wouldn't come here asking for them. There might be some risk involved, but you know what they say: nothing ventured, nothing gained. I need them for a business enterprise, or, rather, for three different enterprises. Two are secured loans and only amount to one and a half *contos*. The remaining eight and a half *contos* are for a business investment. Why are you shaking your head when you don't even know what it is?"

"For that very reason. If you were to consult me first and tell me what this enterprise was and who were the people involved, I would be able to tell you at once if it was worth the risk, which I very much doubt; instead, it'll just be more money down the drain. Do you remember those shares you bought in that so-called Union of Honest Investors? I told you straightaway that such a brazenly worthy name was a sure sign that it was a ruse to con people out of their money while providing employment for ne'er-do-wells. You wouldn't believe me, of course, and fell for it hook, line, and sinker. The share price has since plummeted, and in the last six months there have been no dividends whatsoever."

"Well, sell those shares at once, then, and I'll take the cash. Or else give me the ten *contos* from our business here . . . I'll drop by later if you like, or you can send it over to me in Botafogo. Or borrow some money against my government bonds, whatever you think best . . ."

"I'll do nothing of the sort, and I won't give you the ten *contos* either," Palha responded angrily. "I'm no longer going to give in to your every whim, it is my duty to resist. Secured loans? They're not loans. Don't you see that these people just take your money and have no intention of ever paying you back? They're the sort who dine with their creditor each night, like that fellow Carneiro, who I've often seen at your house. I don't know if your other guests are also in your debt, but that seems highly likely. It's just too much. I'm speaking to you as a friend, so that you don't come to me later and say I didn't warn you. What will you live on if you squander everything you have? Our whole business could collapse."

"It won't collapse," said Rubião.

"It could, anything can collapse. I watched Souto the banker go under in 1864."

Rubião pondered his friend's advice, not because he thought it was good advice or because he thought his predictions were likely to come true, but because he saw in his friend's blunt way of putting things a genuine desire to help. He wholeheartedly thanked Palha for his advice, but still rejected it. He would try to be more prudent in the future, and promised to be less gullible. Besides, he had more than enough money, money to spare . . .

"But not to give away," Palha added.

Then, after a moment, he said:

"It's late now, but I'll bring you the ten *contos* tomorrow. Or why don't you come and collect the money from our house in Flamengo? Have we offended you in some way? Or have the women upset you? Because it seems that you're angry with them rather than with me, given that you're happy enough to meet me here. What did they do to you, that you feel such a need to punish them?" he asked with a chuckle.

Rubião looked away, for Palha's words seemed to him tinged with irony, as if he knew everything and were mocking him. When he looked again into Palha's eyes, he saw that same interrogative expression and said:

"They didn't do anything. I'll drop by tomorrow evening."

"Yes, come to supper."

"No, I can't, I have friends visiting. I'll pop around later on." And, trying to make light of the whole matter, he added: "I'm not 'punishing' them. Why would I?"

"Someone's been getting at him," Palha thought as soon as Rubião left, "someone who's jealous of our friendship . . . Or perhaps Sofia did something to drive him away . . ."

Rubião appeared at the door again, having not even gotten as far as the street corner. He came to say that, since he needed the money quickly, he would come back to the warehouse to collect it, then visit them at home in the evening. He had to have the money by two o'clock that afternoon.

Chapter CIX

THAT NIGHT, RUBIÃO DREAMED about Sofia and Maria Benedita. He saw them standing in a large square, wearing only skirts, their backs completely bare; Sofia's husband, armed with a metal-tipped cat-o'-nine-tails, was furiously whipping them. They writhed about, their backs running with blood and with lumps of flesh gouged out of them, and all the time they were screaming and begging for mercy. Now, quite why Sofia was the Empress Eugénie, and Maria Benedita her maid, I really don't know. "Dreams, dreams, Penseroso!" cried a character in a play by our own Álvares de Azevedo. But I prefer old Polonius's response to some nonsensical comment by Hamlet: "Though this be madness, yet there is method in't." There's method, too, in that blending of Sofia with the Empress Eugénie, and there's even method in what happened afterward, and which seems still madder.

Incensed, Rubião ordered the punishment to cease at once, for Palha to be hanged and the victims to be rescued. One of them, Sofia, accepted a seat in the open carriage that was waiting for Rubião, and off they set at a gallop, she elegant and unscathed, he glorious and masterful. The horses, of which there were two when they started, soon became eight: four fine pairs. Streets and windows were crammed with people, flowers rained down on them, there were cries of acclamation . . . Rubião felt that he was Emperor Louis Napoleon; the dog was with them in the carriage, curled up at Sofia's feet . . .

The dream merely fizzled out. Rubião opened his eyes; perhaps he had been bitten by a flea or something: "Dreams, dreams, Penseroso!" No, I still prefer Polonius's words: "Though this be madness, yet there is method in't."

Chapter CX

RUBIÃO PAID OUT the two loans and made that promised investment in a company called the Company for the Improvement of Embarkation and Disembarkation in the Port of Rio de Janeiro. One of the loans was to pay off a long-overdue bill for paper supplies that had been run up by the *Sentinel*. Had it been left unpaid, the newspaper would have been under threat of closure.

"Wonderful," said Camacho when Rubião brought him the money. "Many thanks. You see how, for a footling amount of money, our newspaper could so easily be silenced. The inevitable thorns in the path. People are just not well educated enough; they neither recognize nor support those who work for their benefit, those who enter the arena every day in defense of their constitutional liberties. Just imagine, if we hadn't had this money, all would be lost, we would each have to go about our own business and leave our principles bereft of their loyal proponents."

"Never!" cried Rubião.

"You're right. We will redouble our efforts. The *Sentinel* will be like that mythological figure, Antaeus. Each time it falls, it will rise again with renewed vigor."

Camacho then contemplated the bundle of notes. "One *conto* two hundred *mil-reis*, right?" he asked, stuffing the money into his jacket pocket. He said again that they were quite safe now, the newspaper could continue its journey under full sail and with a following wind. He had a few substantial changes in mind, namely:

"We need to develop our program, to give our fellow supporters a nudge, or even attack them if need be . . ."

"How?"

"What do you mean 'how'? Why, by attacking, of course. Well, 'attack' is a manner of speaking, 'correct' would be a better word. It's clear that the party newspaper is growing lax. I say 'the party newspaper,' because *our* publication is the party's organ for ideas, if you see what I mean?"

"Oh, I do."

"Yes, it's definitely growing lax," Camacho went on, an unlit cigar poised between his fingers. "We need to re-state our principles, but in a frank, noble, honest fashion. Our leaders need to hear this from their friends and supporters. I have never rejected the idea of coalition between the parties, indeed, I have fought for precisely that; but coalition is no easy matter. To give you an example, in my own province, the Pinheiro crowd enjoys the support of the government purely and simply as a way of keeping me out; and my fellow party members in Rio, instead of fighting back, given that they have the strength of the government behind them, what do you think they do? They support the Pinheiros too."

"The Pinheiros do have some influence, then?"

"No, none at all," said Camacho, snapping shut the matchbox he was opening. "Among their numbers they count a criminal and another fellow who was apprenticed to a barber. Admittedly, he did go to Recife Law School, in 1855 I think, after his godfather died and left him some money, but his political career has been an absolute scandal: no sooner did he graduate than he entered the provincial assembly. He's an arrogant fool, and about as much of a university graduate as I am the Pope!"

Camacho and Rubião reached an agreement on the political changes to be made to their publication. Camacho reminded Rubião that his candidature had failed precisely because it had been opposed by the party leaders. Well, by some of them, he was quick to add. Rubião nodded; his friend had told him as much at the time, and the memory revived the resentment he had felt at such an abject failure. He could and should have been in the Chamber. Those people had rejected him, but just wait, thought Rubião, they would come to regret their mistake. They would watch goggle-eyed with amazement as he rose from deputy to senator to minister . . . All it took was one spark from Camacho to set our friend's mind ablaze, not with hatred, not with envy, but with naive ambition and heartfelt certainty, with the dazzling vision of greatnesses to come. Camacho was pleased to find him in agreement.

"Our people are of the same mind," he said. "I don't think issuing a little threat to our friends will do any harm."

That same night, he read Rubião the article in which he, Camacho, warned the party of the importance of not succumbing to the perfidious allure of power and supporting certain corrupt, worthless individuals in certain provinces. Here is his conclusion:

"The parties must remain united and disciplined. Some believe (*mirabile dictu!*) that such discipline and union is all very well, but not if it means rejecting any favors they receive at the expense of their opponents. *Risum teneatis!* Who can utter such blasphemy without a shudder? However, let us suppose that it is so, that the opposition can, now and again, close its eyes to the government's misguided ways, to their cavalier attitude to the law, to their abuses of power, to their all-too-evident evil and sophistry. *Quid inde?* Such cases—albeit rare—can only be allowed when they favor the good and not the bad. Every party has its dissidents and its sycophants. It is in the interests of our opponents to see us grow lax, in exchange for the boost this gives to the corrupt element in the party. This is the truth: to deny it would be to plunge us into an internecine war, that is, to tear apart the nation's soul . . . But no, ideas do not die; they are the flag of justice. The vendors shall be driven from the temple; only the believers and the pure of heart shall remain, those who place the enduring victory of our principles above mean, local, ephemeral interests. We will oppose anything less. *Alea jacta est.*"

Chapter CXI

RUBIÃO PRAISED THE ARTICLE; he thought it excellent. Although did it perhaps lack a certain energy? "Vendors," for example was spot-on, but wouldn't "vile vendors" be even better?

"Vile vendors? There's just one thing wrong," said Camacho. "And that's the repetition of the *v*. Vile vendors; doesn't that sound rather ugly to you?"

"Earlier on, though, you have the same repetition . . ."

"Ah, you mean *vae victis*. But that's a Latin saying. We could find an alternative: 'vile merchants.'"

"Oh, yes, 'vile merchants' is good."

"Then again, 'merchants' doesn't have the same force as 'vendors.'"

"Why not leave 'vendors,' then? 'Vile vendors' is very strong, no one will notice the alliteration. I never do. What I like is energy. Vile vendors."

"Vile vendors, vile vendors," Camacho repeated to himself. "I'm beginning to like it now. Vile vendors. Yes, I accept your suggestion," he said at last, and having made the correction, he reread the final passage: "The vile vendors shall be driven from the temple; only the believers and the pure of heart shall remain, those who place the enduring victory of our principles above mean, local, ephemeral interests. We will oppose anything less. *Alea jacta est.*"

"Excellent!" said Rubião, feeling that he was, in some small part, the author of the article.

"Do you like it?" asked Camacho, beaming. "Some people think my style still has the freshness of my student days. I don't know, I can't say, but the tone and the intention are the same. I will chastise them; *we* will chastise them."

Chapter CXII

IT IS AT THIS POINT that I wish I had used the method favored by so many other writers—all of them old—in which the substance of the chapter was placed at the beginning as a heading: "In which this happens and then that." You find it in the work of Bernardim Ribeiro and in that of other glorious authors. In the literature of other languages, without going as far back as Cervantes or Rabelais, one need think only of Fielding and Smollett, many of whose chapters are only read for their headings. Pick up *Tom Jones*, Book IV, Chapter I, and read this: "Containing five pages of paper." It's clear, it's simple, it deceives no one: there are five pages of paper, and that's that, if you don't want to read them, don't; and if you do, then do, and for those who do, the author concludes kindly: "And now, without any further preface, we proceed to our next chapter."

Chapter CXIII

WERE I TO USE that method, here's a heading that would explain everything: "In which Rubião, feeling pleased with his emendation to Camacho's article, then went on to compose and ponder so many other sentences that he ended up writing all the books he had ever read."

There will inevitably be at least one reader who would find this unsatisfactory. He, or she, would, naturally, want a detailed analysis of our character's mental process, not realizing that to do so would require more than Fielding's five pages. There is a great chasm between Rubião being coauthor of that one sentence and him being the author of all the books he had ever read; the fact is that what he found most difficult was going from writing that one sentence to rewriting the first book—thereafter the operation grew faster. No matter; any analysis would still prove long and tedious. Best just to say this: for a few minutes, Rubião *felt* he was the author of many another author's work.

Chapter CXIV

ON THE OTHER HAND, I'm not sure if the following chapter could be summarized in a heading.

Chapter CXV

RUBIÃO REMAINED TRUE to his resolve not to see Sofia again, in that he stopped going to her house. However, he did one day spot her riding past in a carriage, accompanied by one of the ladies from the Alagoas committee; she nodded and smiled and waved to him. He reciprocated by doffing his hat, with just a hint of embarrassment, but he did not stand rooted to the spot as he would have done before; he merely glanced at the carriage as it moved on. Then he, too, moved on—and, thinking about that business of the letter, he couldn't understand that wave, which contained not a trace of hatred or annoyance, as if nothing had ever happened between them. It could be that the work of the committee and the presence of her companion were enough to explain Sofia's elegantly benevolent attitude, but Rubião did not consider that hypothesis.

"Has she really so little pride?" he wondered. "Has she forgotten the letter I found, sent by her to that young whippersnapper from Rua dos Inválidos? The cheek of it! There was almost something defiant about her, as if she were saying that she didn't care, that she would write as many letters as she wanted. Let her, then, but she might at least go to the expense of buying a stamp and sending them by post; it wasn't that expensive . . ."

He thought this rather witty and laughed to himself. This rescued him from those bitter memories, as did a man who bowed deeply as he walked by, and then Rubião forgot all about the matter and concentrated on another, which took him to the offices of the Bank of Brazil.

As he entered the bank, he bumped into Palha, who was about to leave.

"I believe I just saw Dona Sofia," Rubião said.

"Where?"

"In Rua dos Ourives. She was in a carriage with a lady I didn't know. How have you been?"

"So you saw her, but that didn't jog your memory?" said Palha, without responding to the question. "You've completely forgotten that it's her birthday the day after tomorrow, this Wednesday. I won't invite you to supper, I wouldn't dare; I'd hate to bore you, but a cup of tea is quickly drunk. Would you do me that favor?"

Rubião did not reply at once, then he said:

"I could come to supper if you like. Wednesday, you say? I'll be there. I admit I had forgotten, but I have so many things to think about at the moment . . . Meet me in half an hour at the warehouse."

In fact, he arrived there earlier in order to ask Palha to give him two *contos*. Palha no longer protested at the progressive erosion of Rubião's capital, and apart from the occasional mild reprimand, he now simply handed over the money. Before going home, Rubião bought a magnificent diamond, which he sent to Sofia on that Wednesday along with a visiting card wishing her a happy birthday.

Sofia was alone in her dressing room, putting on her shoes, when the maid handed her the package. It was the third present of the day; the maid waited for her to open it so that she, too, could see what it was. Sofia was overwhelmed when she opened the box and saw the beautiful jewel exquisitely set in a necklace. She had been expecting something pretty, but after all that had happened, she could hardly believe such generosity. Her heart beat faster.

"Is the person who brought it still there?"

"No, he's gone. But isn't it lovely, madam?"

Sofia closed the box and put on her shoes. She paused for a moment and sat there alone remembering things past, then stood up, thinking:

"That man adores me."

She was about to finish getting dressed, but on passing the mirror, she paused for a few moments. She took pleasure in contemplating herself, her opulent curves, her bare arms, her own contemplative eyes. She was twenty-nine, and it seemed to her that she hadn't changed since she was twenty-five, and she was quite right. Once she had laced up her corset, still standing before the mirror, she lovingly arranged her breasts to show off her magnificent décolletage. She then decided to see how the new necklace looked on her. Perfect. She turned first to the right, then to the left, moved closer, adopted various poses, even adjusted the flame of the gas lamp in the dressing room. Perfect. She took off the necklace and put it away. And again she thought:

"That man adores me."

On his way to supper in Flamengo, Rubião was thinking: *"He'll probably be there this evening, but I very much doubt he'll have given her a finer present."*

Carlos Maria was indeed there, chatting with Maria Benedita and one of the committee members. It was a small gathering; it had been a conscious decision to invite only a few select guests. Major Siqueira wasn't there, nor was his daughter, nor the ladies and gentlemen whom Rubião had met at that other supper, in Santa Teresa. There were some ladies from the Alagoas committee, as well as the director of the bank—the one who had visited the minister—with his wife and daughters, another man from the world of banking, an English merchant, a deputy, a judge, a counselor, a few other wealthy men, and that was about it.

Although Sofia was clearly the glorious center of attention, she forgot all the other guests when she saw Rubião enter the room and walk straight toward her. Whether he had actually changed or whether she had simply grown unaccustomed to seeing him, it seemed to her that he was different, that he walked more confidently, with his head held high; he was, in short, the very opposite of his former shy, shrinking self. Sofia clasped his hand firmly and whispered a thank-you. At supper, she had him sit next to her, with the chairlady of the committee on her other side. Rubião cast a superior eye over everything. He was unimpressed by the quality of the guests, the ceremonious atmosphere, and the lavish table setting; it all left him cold. However agreeable Sofia's attentions, they did not dizzy him as once they did. And for her part, she was more solicitous, her gaze exceptionally fond and obliging. Rubião looked around for Carlos Maria; there he was, sitting between the same two young women—Maria Benedita and the committee member.

He saw that Carlos Maria was entirely taken up with them and did not so much as glance at Sofia, who, in turn, didn't look at him.

"Unless they're pretending," he thought.

It seemed to him, as they left the table, that the two did eventually exchange a look, but in the general flurry he might have been wrong, and he thought no more about it. Sofia was quick to take Rubião's arm. As they walked, she said:

"I've been wanting to speak to you ever since your last visit, but you never came back. And I was perfectly within my rights to demand that you did, so that I could explain properly. We'll talk later."

Shortly afterward, Rubião went into the smoking room. He listened in silence to the other men talking and looked around ambivalently. When they left, he lingered, slumped on a leather sofa, his mind a blank. His imagination continued to work, though, albeit somewhat slowly—perhaps he had eaten too much. Outside, the after-supper guests were just arriving; the house was filling up, the buzz of conversation growing, while our friend remained absorbed in his delightful reverie. Not even the sound of the piano, which silenced all the other noises, brought him back to earth. But then a rustle of silks coming into the room made him sit bolt upright, suddenly alert.

"Ah, there you are," said Sofia, "hiding away to escape boredom. Don't you even want to hear some good music? I thought perhaps you'd left. I've come to speak to you."

And without further ado, because there was not a minute to be lost, she explained to him what we already know about the letter found in the Botafogo garden; she reminded him that, before she opened it, she had asked him to do the same and to read it. What clearer proof of innocence! She spoke quickly, seriously, with great dignity and emotion. At one point, her eyes even grew moist and red, and she dabbed at them with her handkerchief. Rubião clasped her hand and saw a tear—a tiny tear—run down her cheek to the corner of her mouth. Then he swore he believed every word she had said. There was no need to cry. Sofia dried her eyes and gratefully shook his proffered hand.

"I must go," she said.

Rubião pointed out that the piano was still playing. As long as the others were listening to the music, no one would bother them.

"But I can't leave my guests for long," said Sofia. "Besides, I have orders to give. I must go."

"No, please, listen," Rubião insisted.

Sofia waited.

"Listen, allow me to say, possibly for the last time—"

"For the last time?"

"Who knows? It could be the last time. I really don't care if that man is alive or dead, but I might occasionally run into him here, and I don't want any unpleasant scenes."

"Well, he'll be here every day. Didn't Cristiano tell you? Carlos Maria is going to marry Maria Benedita."

Rubião drew back.

"Yes, they're going to marry," she went on. "It took us by surprise, I must say, either they kept very quiet about it or it all happened very fast. Anyway, they're getting married. Maria Benedita gave me her version of events, which was confirmed by someone else; in the end, though, it's the same old story. They fell in love, and that's that. They intend to marry quite soon. When he asked Cristiano for his blessing, Cristiano told him that it was up to me . . . as if I were her mother! I said yes straightaway, and I hope they'll be very happy. He seems a decent fellow, and she's an excellent young woman; and they're sure to be happy. It's a good match too. He's inherited all his parents' wealth, and although Maria Benedita has no money of her own, she does have the education I gave her. You must remember that when she first came to stay here, she was terribly shy, a real country bumpkin, and knew almost nothing; I was the one who educated her. My aunt deserved nothing less, nor did she. Anyway, yes, they're to marry very soon. Didn't you notice how inseparable they are? It's not official yet, so we're only telling close family friends."

For someone in such a hurry, this was far too long a speech, as Sofia realized a little too late, then she again told Rubião that she really must go back to the main room. The piano had stopped and there was a discreet murmur of applause and conversation.

Chapter CXVI

THEY WERE GOING to marry? But how, then, was it that . . . ? Maria Benedita—Maria Benedita was going to marry Carlos Maria, so then Carlos Maria . . . Ah, now he understood; it had all been a mistake; what appeared to involve one person actually involved another, which is precisely the kind of misunderstanding that can lead to all kinds of calumnies and even crimes.

This is what Rubião was thinking as he went back into the dining room, where the servants were already clearing the supper table. And as he walked the length of the room, he went on: "And to think that Palha wanted to marry me off to his cousin, unaware that fate had quite another bridegroom in mind. He's not bad-looking, and certainly much better-looking than her. Beside Sofia, Maria Benedita is almost nothing, but that's love for you . . . They're getting married, and soon too . . . Will it be a big affair? Probably. Palha is doing much better now financially." And Rubião looked around at the furniture, the china, the glasses, the door hangings. "Yes, it's sure to be a big wedding, and the bridegroom is rich . . ." Rubião imagined the carriage and the horses; he had seen a magnificent pair in Engenho Velho just days before, one that would suit the couple perfectly. He would order another one just like it, and to hell with the cost; he would, after all, have to give the bride a present. And just as he was thinking this, in she came.

"Do you know where Cousin Sofia is?" she asked.

"No, I don't, she was here a moment ago."

And, seeing that she was about to leave the room, he asked if they could have a word and hoped she wouldn't be embarrassed by what he was going to say. Maria Benedita waited, and he, without hesitation, offered her his congratulations. He knew she was about to be married . . . Maria Benedita blushed scarlet and begged him not to tell anyone. The servants had all left by then, and Rubião took her hand and clasped it between his.

"I'm an old friend of the family," he said, "and you deserve to be very happy, and I hope you will be."

A little frightened, Maria Benedita pulled her hand away, smiling so as not to offend him. There was no need; he was utterly delighted. We know that she wasn't exactly pretty, but happiness had made her beautiful. Nature seemed to have endowed her with all its graces. Still smiling, Rubião went on:

"Your cousin told me, and said I must keep it a secret, and I will say nothing until the time is right. But why shouldn't I speak to you about it? You're a good girl and deserve the very best in life. There's no need to look so embarrassed; getting married is nothing to be ashamed of. Come on, chin up and smile."

Maria Benedita fixed him with radiant eyes

"That's it!" said Rubião approvingly. "Where's the harm in telling a friend? Shall I tell you what I think: I think you will be happy, but that he will be even happier. Don't you agree? You'll see if I'm right or not; he himself will tell you his feelings and if he's sincere, then you'll see how accurate my predictions were. I know there are no scales on which one can weigh feelings, but all I'm saying is that you're a good and lovely creature . . . Right, off you go; if you don't, I'll keep burbling on, and you're blushing quite enough already . . ."

Maria Benedita was indeed blushing with pleasure on hearing Rubião's effusive words. In the house, the marriage had been greeted with only lukewarm acquiescence, nothing more. Carlos Maria himself wasn't exactly effusive and loved her only circumspectly. He spoke to her of conjugal bliss as if it were a debt owed to her by destiny—a debt that would be paid in full. Nor did she need him to treat her any differently; she would still adore him more than anything else in the world. Rubião again urged her to go, and stood gazing after her as if she were his daughter. He watched her cross the room, looking so bright and happy—so different from the way she used to look—and disappear through one of the doors. He couldn't help but say:

"What a dear, lovely girl!"

Chapter CXVII

THE STORY OF how Maria Benedita came to be married is a brief one, and although Sofia may have found it rather banal, it's worth telling all the same. It has to be said that were it not for the epidemic in Alagoas, there might never have been a marriage, which leads one to conclude that disasters are useful and even necessary. There are more than enough examples of this, but let's make do with a little tale I heard when I was a child, and which I give here in abbreviated form. Once upon a time, there was a roadside shack being consumed by flames; a few feet away, squatting on the ground, the owner—a poor ragged wretch of a woman—was bewailing her fate. Then a drunken man wandered by, saw the fire, saw the woman, and asked if it was her house that was burning down.

"It is, sir, and it's all I have in the world."

"Would you allow me to light my cigar on the flames?"

The priest who told me the story doubtless amended the original text, for you don't have to be drunk to light a cigar on another person's misery. "Good, kind Father Chagas," for that was his name, "you were more than just kind to me; for many years, you instilled in me the consoling idea that no one in his right mind should profit from the misfortunes of others; not to mention the respect shown by the drunk for the principle of ownership, going so far as to ask permission from the mistress of the ruins before lighting his cigar on the flames. All very consoling ideas. Good old Father Chagas!"

Chapter CXVIII

FAREWELL, FATHER CHAGAS! I will now tell the story of the marriage. Ever since the ball in Rua dos Arcos when Carlos Maria and Sofia had danced so many waltzes together, it had been clear as day that Maria Benedita was in love with him. We saw Maria Benedita the following morning, ready to go back home to the countryside, and how her cousin had won her over with the promise that she was in the process of finding her a suitor. Maria Benedita assumed it was the waltzer from the previous night, and so she waited. She said nothing to her cousin—initially out of embarrassment and later so as not to spoil the element of surprise when Sofia revealed his name to her. If she were to confess straightaway, her cousin might slacken her pace, and then all might be lost. But let's ignore all that as being simply a young woman's intricate calculations.

Then came the epidemic in Alagoas. Sofia organized a charitable committee, and this brought the Palha family new social contacts. Maria Benedita worked closely with all the ladies on one of the subcommittees, but gained the affection of one in particular, Dona Fernanda, the wife of a deputy. Dona Fernanda was in her early thirties, she was a cheerful, friendly woman, fresh-faced and sturdy; she had been born in Porto Alegre, had married a university graduate from Alagoas, who was now a deputy for another province, and was, or so people said, poised to become a government minister. The fact that her husband had been born in Alagoas was the reason she was selected to be on the committee, and she proved to be an excellent choice because she was extremely commanding, with no qualms about asking for favors and unwilling to take no for an answer. Carlos Maria, who was her cousin, went to visit her as soon as she arrived in Rio de Janeiro. He thought her even more beautiful than she had been in 1865, which was the last time he had seen her, and perhaps she really was; he concluded that the air in southern Brazil must have an invigorating effect on people, enhancing their charms, and he promised her that he would go there to end his days.

"Let's go right now and I'll arrange a wife for you," she said. "I know a girl from Pelotas who is a real gem, and she'll only marry a young man from Rio."

"Meaning me, of course."

"A young man from Rio with large eyes. Really, I'm not joking. She's a child of the *pampa*, none better. Look, I have a picture of her here," and Dona Fernanda opened an album and showed him a photograph.

"Hm, not bad-looking," he agreed.

"Is that all you have to say?"

"No, you're right, she's pretty."

"Since when have you been so picky, cousin?"

Carlos Maria smiled, but did not reply; he disliked that word "picky." He tried to change the subject, but Dona Fernanda returned to his possible marriage to that friend of hers in Pelotas. She was looking at the photograph, bringing it to life with words, telling him what the young woman's eyes were like, her hair, her skin; and then she provided him with a brief biography of Sonora. Such a pretty name. The priest who baptized her wasn't sure whether to allow it, despite her father being a highly respected and influential man, a wealthy cattle farmer; in the end, though, he agreed, thinking that the virtues of the person bearing that name could well add it to the list of saints.

"Do you think she will become a saint?" asked Carlos Maria.

"Yes, if she marries you."

"That's not saying much. She would still become a saint if she married the Devil, because that would be tantamount to a martyrdom. Saint Sonora's not a bad name, though, and suitably sonorous . . . Anyway, cousin—"

"You're such a skeptic," she broke in. "So you reject my girl from the *pampa*, do you?" she went on, putting the album back in its place.

"I don't reject her, but allow me to continue my life of celibacy, which is my personal road to heaven."

Dona Fernanda burst out laughing.

"Lord have mercy! Do you really think you're going to heaven?"

"I've been there for the last twenty minutes. What else is this quiet, cool room, so far from the world outside? Here the two of us are free to talk, without having to listen to any blasphemous comments or the babblings of some other crippled, consumptive, scrofular, unbearable souls, in other words, in hell. This is heaven—or a piece of heaven; and as long as we're in it, that's eternity enough for me. Let's talk about Saint Sonora, Saint Carlos Maria, and Saint Fernanda, who, unlike Saint Gonçalo of Amarante, specializes in marrying off not ageing spinsters, but young women. Where would you find another heaven like this?"

"In Pelotas."

"Pelotas is too far away!" he said with a sigh, stretching out his legs and gazing up at the chandelier.

"All right, but this is only my first attempt; I'll keep trying until you finally give in."

Carlos Maria smiled and looked at the tassels on the silk belt she wore tied with a loose bow about her waist. Did he do so because he liked the tassels, or in order to admire her slender figure? He noted again that his cousin was a beautiful creature. Her figure drew his gaze, while respect made him look away; but it wasn't only friendship that made him linger in that room, and which brought him back to that house time and again. Carlos Maria enjoyed the conversation of women as much, generally speaking, as he loathed that of men. He found men loud and coarse, wearisome, boring, frivolous, vulgar, and trivial. Women, on the other hand, were neither coarse nor declamatory nor boring. A little vanity rather suited them, and even the occasional flaw was not entirely unbecoming; besides, they had the natural grace and gentleness of their sex. There was, he thought, always something to be gleaned from even the least significant of women. Whenever he found them dull or stupid, he would think that they were merely trying to be men.

Meanwhile, the friendship between Dona Fernanda and Maria Benedita was becoming closer. The latter, as well as being shy, was rather sad at the time, and it was precisely this disparity in character and situation that drew them together. Dona Fernanda possessed both sympathy and compassion in very large measure; she loved the weak and the sad because she felt a need to make them happy and bold. She was known to have performed many acts of mercy and devotion.

"What's wrong?" she asked her young friend one day. "You almost never laugh and you always have a rather pensive, frightened look in your eyes..."

Maria Benedita replied saying that there was nothing wrong, it was just the way she was, and she smiled when she said this, purely out of politeness. She mentioned the loss of her mother as one of the causes of her melancholy. Dona Fernanda began taking her out and about, inviting her to supper or reserving a place for her in their private box at the theater, and thanks to this and to her own lively personality, she managed to shoo away the hateful crows roosting in the young woman's soul. Habit and affection soon made them firm friends, and yet Maria Benedita continued to keep her private mystery to herself.

"Whatever that mystery is," thought Dona Fernanda one day, "I think it would be best to marry her to Carlos Maria; Sonora can wait."

"You know, Maria Benedita, you really ought to marry," she said to her a couple of days later, in the garden of her large house in Rua de Matacavalos. Maria Benedita had gone to the theater with her the previous evening and had stayed the night. "Now, don't make a fuss, you need to marry and you will marry. I've been meaning to say as much since the day before yesterday, but such matters have no real weight if talked about in a drawing room or in the street. Here in a private garden, it's different. And if you have the energy, I'm sure you'll feel much better if you come for a little walk with me up that hill. Shall we?"

"It's very hot..."

"That makes it all the more poetic, my dear. You bloodless *cariocas* have only water in your veins! All right, let's sit on this bench. Yes, you sit there, and I'll sit here beside you, armed and ready for anything. Either you marry or you die. Don't say a word." Then, in a different tone, she went on: "You're not happy, regardless of what I try to do to cheer you up, you're just not enjoying life. Tell me frankly, are you in love with someone? Tell me, and I'll send for him immediately."

"No, there's no one."

"Really? Well, good, that's exactly what we want. No need to put any *For Rent* signs on your heart, because I already have a good tenant in mind."

Maria Benedita turned to face her, mouth agape and eyes wide. She seemed to both dread the proposal and yearn for it. Dona Fernanda, still unsure of her friend's real state of mind, took her by the hand and asked her to tell her everything. She clearly did love someone, she could see it in her eyes, she urged and pleaded with her to tell her—she would invoke the law if necessary. Maria Benedita's hand grew cold, her eyes bored into the ground, and, for a few moments, neither of them said anything.

"Come on, speak," said Dona Fernanda again.

"I have nothing to say."

Dona Fernanda looked utterly incredulous, then drew Maria Benedita closer, put her arm around her waist, and embraced her, whispering that she felt as if she were her mother. And she kissed her cheek, her ear, the back of her neck, made her rest her head on her shoulder, meanwhile stroking her with her free hand. Everything, everything, she wanted to know everything. If her beloved was on the moon, she would send for him there, or wherever he was, unless, of course, he was in the cemetery, although if he was, she would find her a still better beloved who would make her forget her first love in a matter of days. Maria Benedita heard all this and trembled, her heart racing, not knowing how she could escape, wanting to confess, but then saying nothing, as if she were defending her modesty. She neither denied nor confessed, but since she also did not smile and was trembling with emotion, it was easy to guess at least half the truth.

"Am I not your friend, then? Don't you trust me? Pretend I'm your mother."

Maria Benedita gave in; she no longer had the energy to resist and felt the need to at least reveal something. Dona Fernanda listened to her, deeply touched. The sun was now licking around the bench where they were sitting, soon it had climbed up onto their shoes, the hems of their dresses, their knees; but neither of them noticed. Love absorbed them both; what one said cast a rare spell over the other. It was a passion never known or shared or even guessed at; a passion that was gradually changing its nature and becoming pure adoration. At first, whenever she saw her beloved, she would experience two very different sorts of emotion—the first she couldn't really define, but it took the form of excitement, dizziness, palpitations, almost swooning; the second was a kind of contemplative state. Now, it was this second state that tended to prevail. She had wept profusely in secret, had spent endless nights yearning for him, and had paid a high price for such ambitious hopes. However, she would never lose her certainty that he was superior to all other men, a divine being, who, even if he paid no attention to her, would still deserve to be adored.

"Right," said Dona Fernanda when her friend finally fell silent. "Let's get straight to the point, which is to stop all this aimless pining. No, my dear, adoring a man who doesn't even notice you is the stuff of poetry. Enough of poetry. You're the only loser, because he'll end up marrying someone else, the years will pass, and love will climb up onto their backs and gallop away; and one day, when you're least expecting it, you'll wake up with no love and no husband. Anyway, who is this barbarian?"

"That I won't tell you," said Maria Benedita, getting up from the bench.

"Well, don't, then," said Dona Fernanda, grasping her wrists and drawing her down onto her lap. "The main thing is to marry, if not him, then another."

"No, I won't marry."

"You mean you would only marry him?"

"I don't even know if I would marry him," said Maria Benedita after a brief pause. "I love him as I love God who is in Heaven."

"Holy Mother of God! What blasphemy! No, two blasphemies! The first is that you should never love anyone as much as you love God, and the second is that a husband, even a bad one, is always better than the very best of dreams."

Chapter CXIX

"A HUSBAND, EVEN A bad one, is always better than the very best of dreams."

Not exactly an idealistic maxim, and Maria Benedita duly rebelled against it. Wasn't it better to dream than to weep? A dream will come to an end, or else change, whereas bad husbands can live a very long time.

"You say that," said Maria Benedita, "because God gave you an angel for a husband . . . look, here he comes."

"Don't worry. You, too, will find your angel. I have a magnificent one just waiting for you. All the angels come to seek me out."

Teófilo, Dona Fernanda's husband, who had seen them from afar, came to join them; he was carrying a crumpled newspaper in one hand. He did not even greet their guest, but spoke directly to his wife.

"Do you know what they've done to me, Nanã?" he said through gritted teeth. "The speech I gave on the fifth of this month has just been published. Look at this. What I said was: *When in doubt, do nowt, as the wise saying goes* . . . And what have they put? *When in debt, do nowt* . . . It's unspeakable! And I happened to be talking about a loan taken out by the Admiralty, arguing in the debate that a lot of unnecessary money had been spent. It could look like a comment made in the very worst possible taste, as if I were encouraging such profligacy. Anyway, it's absurd!"

"Didn't you read the proofs?"

"I did, but the author is always the least well qualified person to read proofs. *When in debt, do nowt,*" he read again, his eyes fixed on the printed page, before adding with an angry snort: "Honestly, it's just unbelievable . . ."

He was genuinely upset. He was a man of talent, serious and hardworking, but, at that moment, every major undertaking, the most daunting of problems, the most decisive of battles, the profoundest of revolutions, the sun and the moon and the stars, and all the dumb creatures of the earth and all of humanity were of less importance than that typographical error. Maria Benedita looked at him, uncomprehending. She thought hers was the greater sadness, but there was another as great as her own, and far more painful. So, the tormenting melancholy of a young woman was on a par with a typographical error. Teófilo, who only then noticed her presence, held out his hand to her; it was cold. No one can pretend to have cold hands; he really must be suffering. Moments later, he flung the newspaper violently down on the ground and left.

"But Teófilo, it can easily be corrected tomorrow," said Dona Fernanda, getting up.

Teófilo turned his back on them and stalked off in despair. His wife ran after him, and Maria Benedita followed in some alarm. The bench was left alone to bask in the rays of the sun, and the sun neither loves nor makes speeches. Dona Fernanda led her husband into his office, and there, by dint of many kisses, consoled him. By lunchtime, he was already smiling again, albeit rather wanly; to divert him from his worries, Dona Fernanda told him about her plan to find a husband for Maria Benedita, and how he would have to be a deputy—if there were any bachelors in the Chamber—regardless of political persuasion. He could be pro-government, a member of the opposition, or both those things or neither—just as long as he was a husband. She made a few lively, witty comments on the subject, which were intended to fill the time and stop her husband from thinking about that typographical error, merciful creature that she was! Teófilo listened to his wife and gradually grew more cheerful, agreeing with her that a husband should be found for Maria Benedita.

"The trouble is," said Dona Fernanda, glancing at her friend, "she loves someone already and refuses to reveal his name."

"She doesn't need to," said her husband, wiping his lips, "anyone can see that she's in love with your cousin."

== Chapter CXX

THE FOLLOWING SUNDAY, Dona Fernanda went to the Church of Santo Antônio dos Pobres. After mass, she spotted emerging from among the other faithful—who were all either busily greeting each other or genuflecting before the altar—none other than her cousin, looking very cheerful and proper in his Sunday best and holding out his hand to her.

"You? At mass?" she asked, astonished.

"Yes, me."

"Do you come regularly?"

"No, but fairly often."

"Frankly, I never suspected you were that devout. Men, in general, are an impious lot. Teófilo will only set foot in the church to have his children baptized. So, are you religious?"

"I couldn't answer with any certainty, but I have a horror of vulgarity, and it's vulgar to speak ill of religion. Anyway, I came to attend mass, not to confess; I will now accompany you home and, if you invite me, I will have lunch with you and your husband. Unless you want to come and have lunch at my house, which, as you know, is here on this street."

"I'll come on my own, if you don't mind, because I have some news to tell you, which could take a while."

"Let us walk slowly, then," said Carlos Maria, standing at the door of the church and offering her his arm. A few steps farther on, he asked: "Is it important news?"

"Important and delightful."

"Could it be that God in his mercy is going to take to his bosom our own dear Teófilo, your husband, and thus abandon to her lonely fate the loveliest of all widows . . . Now, don't look like that, cousin, and don't pull away. Come on, tell me your news. Has the girl from Pelotas arrived in Rio, is that it?"

"I'll only tell you if you promise to be serious."

"I am being serious."

Dona Fernanda confessed that she had her doubts about marrying him to that native of Pelotas, but there was no need to be disappointed, because she had found someone in Rio who felt an immense love for him. Carlos Maria smiled and was about to make a joke, but this news pricked his curiosity. Immense love?

Yes, immense love, a violent passion, said his cousin, adding that this definition might no longer be an accurate description of the person's current feelings. What she felt now was a steadfast, unspoken adoration. She had wept over him for nights on end and had done so for as long as she had some hope . . . And Dona Fernanda told him everything that Maria Benedita had told her, but without revealing her name. Carlos Maria asked who this person was, but she refused to say. She was not at liberty to tell him. Why should she give him the pleasure of knowing who it was who adored him if he did not share those feelings? It was best to leave it a mystery. The young woman had stopped crying now; modest and unambitious, she had lost all hope of being loved by him, and with time she had become a mere devotee, but one quite without equal, who did not even expect to be heard or one day favored with a benevolent glance from her beloved god.

"Cousin, you . . ."

"What?"

Carlos Maria concluded by saying that she was certainly an eloquent spokeswoman for her cause. If this young woman really did adore him, it was only right and natural that his cousin should put her case with such passion. But why not tell him her name?

"I can't tell you now, but one day . . . You can understand why I would find it difficult to marry you off to my fellow southerner when I know that another person loves you so very much. And yet it could be that the young lady here would not be that upset if she did see you marry someone else. Yes, I know it seems absurd, but you don't know her as I do; I will say only that as long as you were happy, she might well bless her beautiful rival."

"This no longer smacks of romanticism but of mysticism," said Carlos Maria after taking a few more steps, his eyes fixed on the ground. "It's hardly in tune with our times. And do you have evidence of such a soul as this?"

"I do... This is your house, isn't it?" asked Dona Fernanda, stopping outside.

"It is."

"A lovely building and solidly built."

"Very solidly."

"One, two, three, four... seven windows. Does the salon run the whole width of the house? An excellent place for a ball."

Then, walking on, she added:

"If I had a bigger house, I would give a really grand ball before I go back to Rio Grande. I love parties, and my two children are not much trouble. By the way, I want to find a school for Lopo, do you know a good one?"

Carlos Maria was thinking about that unknown devotee, his thoughts many miles from education and its establishments. How good it was to feel like a god, and to be worshipped as the gospel recommends, with the devotee alone in a room, with the door locked, in secret, not in the synagogues in full sight of everyone. "And your Father, who sees in secret, will reward you." And he would definitely reward her if he knew who she was. Might she be married? No, impossible, she wouldn't tell anyone about her feelings; she must be either a widow or single, preferably single. He sensed she was the latter. In what room would she shut herself up in order to pray and think of him and weep for him and bless him? He no longer insisted on knowing her name, but if he could at least know about that room.

"Where would I find a good school?" Dona Fernanda asked again.

"School? I've no idea. I'm still thinking about that mystery woman. Surely someone who adores me in silence and with no hope of being requited deserves my full attention. Is she tall or short?"

"It's Maria Benedita."

Carlos stopped in his tracks.

"Her? No, it can't be. I've talked to her often and never noticed anything particular about her behavior toward me. In fact, she always seemed rather reserved. There must be some mistake. Has she mentioned me to you by name?"

"No, she wouldn't tell me, however hard I begged her. She confessed to the miracle, but without naming the saint, and that's a miracle in itself! No one has ever been so adored before. You should feel proud. Whose house is that?"

"You do exaggerate, cousin. 'No one has ever been so adored before'? Really! And how did you find out it was me?"

"Teófilo was the first to pick up on it, and when he said your name, she turned bright red. She again roundly denied it to me, and she hasn't been back to the house since."

Thus their love began. Carlos Maria was flattered to be loved like that in silence, and all his prejudices turned to affection. He began to seek her out, enjoying her embarrassment, her shyness, her joy, her modesty, her almost imploring looks, a combination of actions and feelings that proved the apotheosis of the object of her love. Thus it began and thus it continued. This is how we saw them at the party held to celebrate Dona Sofia, to whom he had once whispered such sweet nothings. But then this is what men are like, no different from the rushing waters and the roaring winds.

Chapter CXXI

"GOOD, SO HE's going to marry, all the better!" thought Rubião.

Between that night and the wedding day, Rubião did catch in the air a few suspiciously alluring glances from Sofia, but if Carlos Maria reciprocated, it was more out of politeness than anything else. Rubião, however, concluded that this was all purely fortuitous; he could still remember the tear Sofia had shed on the night of her birthday party, when she had explained to him about the letter.

Ah, happy, unexpected tear! You, who were enough to persuade one man, may prove inexplicable to others, but then that's the way of the world. What does it matter if those eyes were unaccustomed to crying, or if the occasion was more likely to provoke very different feelings, and certainly not melancholy? Rubião saw the tear fall, and he could still see it in his mind's eye. But Rubião's confidence was based not only on that tear, it came also from the current Sofia, for she had never been so solicitous or so attentive. She appeared to have repented of the pain she had caused, eager to salve it either through a belated show of affection or through the failure of that earlier affair. Some virtual crimes can lie dormant, just as there are operas waiting inside a maestro's head for the first few notes of inspiration to sound.

Chapter CXXII

"YES, JUST AS WELL he's getting married!" Rubião thought again.

The wedding took place soon afterward, only three weeks later. On the morning of the appointed day, Carlos Maria woke up feeling slightly alarmed. Was he really going to get married? Yes, there was no doubt about it; he looked at himself in the mirror, yes, it was him. He thought over the last few days, how quickly events had moved, the genuine affection he felt for his bride-to-be, and, ultimately, the pure happiness he would give her. This last idea filled him with a rare feeling of great satisfaction. And he continued to ponder these ideas as he set off on his usual morning ride, this time choosing a route through Engenho Velho.

Although he was accustomed to receiving admiring glances, it seemed to him from the expression on people's faces that they had all heard the news of his imminent marriage. The casuarina trees in a large garden he passed, and which had been quite still before, said very particular things to him, things that more frivolous minds would attribute to the passing breeze, but which wiser folk would know to be neither more nor less than the casuarinas' nuptial language. Birds hopped about here and there, piping a madrigal. A pair of butterflies—which the Japanese hold to be a symbol of fidelity, having observed that as they fly from flower to flower, they almost always go in twos—a pair of them accompanied him for a long time, following the hedge of a garden bordering the road, fluttering here and there, so light, so yellow. Wrapped around all this was the cool air, the blue sky, the happy faces of men riding past on their donkeys, people leaning out of carriage windows to see him in his bridegroomly elegance. It really was hard to believe that all those looks and gestures on the part of people, creatures, and trees could express anything other than Nature's homage to marriage.

The butterflies vanished into one of the denser shrubs in the hedge. Another country estate came in view, bare of trees, with its gates wide open to reveal, set farther back, an old house, whose five deep-set windows—as if they had grown weary of waiting for someone to move in—resembled five frowning eyes. They, too, had seen weddings and parties, in the early part of the century, when they had been young and green and full of hope.

Don't imagine that this sight saddened the heart of our rider, though. On the contrary, he possessed the singular gift of restoring ruins to youthful vigor, and drawing life from the former lives of things. He even rather enjoyed seeing the faded old house, which contrasted with the liveliness of the butterflies earlier. He reined in his horse; he summoned up the ladies who would once have lived there, the different clothes and faces and manners. Perhaps the ghosts of those happy but now-dead people actually came out to greet him, saying with their invisible lips all the sublime things they thought about him. He even heard them and smiled. But a strident voice interrupted the concert—a parrot in a cage hanging from a wall of the house: "Parrot-Portugal, para-ta-ta-royale; who's a pretty boy, then? Parrrupu-pa-pa. Grrr .. Grrr . . ." The ghosts fled, the horse moved on. Carlos hated parrots, as he hated monkeys, both fraudulent imitations of humans, he used to say.

"Will the happiness I give her also be interrupted?" he wondered as he rode.

Wrens flittered back and forth across his path, singing in their own language, restoring his spirits. Their wordless tongue was perfectly intelligible, saying many clear and beautiful things. Carlos Maria could even see a symbol of himself in their language. When his wife, deafened by the parrots of this world, felt she could bear it no longer, he would raise her up with the chirruping of those divine birds, who carried within them golden ideas spoken in a golden voice. Oh, how happy *he* would make *her*! He could already see her kneeling before him, her arms resting on his knees, her head in her hands, and her eyes fixed on him, grateful, devoted, loving, pure supplication, pure nothing at all.

Chapter CXXIII

NOW, THAT EXACT same image, at the very moment it appeared in the bridegroom's imagination, was there in the bride's mind too.

Maria Benedita, sitting at the window, gazing out at the waves breaking in the distance and on the beach down below, could see herself kneeling at her husband's feet, meek and contrite, as if she were kneeling at the Communion table to receive the host of happiness. And she was saying to herself: "Oh, how happy *he* will make *me*!" The words and the thought were different, but the attitude and the hour were the same.

Chapter CXXIV

THEY MARRIED, and three months later, they left for Europe. As she said goodbye to them, Dona Fernanda was as happy as if she were already welcoming them back; she didn't cry at all. The pleasure of seeing them so happy was greater than the pain of separation.

"Are you happy?" she asked Maria Benedita one last time as she stood by the ship's rail.

"Oh, very happy!"

Dona Fernanda's fresh, ingenuous soul leaned out of those windows of her soul, her eyes, and sang a few lines from an Italian aria—because our proud southerner preferred Italian music—perhaps this one from *Lucia di Lammermoor*: *Ó bell'alma innamorata*. Or this from *The Barber of Seville*:

> *Ecco, ridente in cielo*
> *Spunta la bella aurora.*

Chapter CXXV

SOFIA DID NOT GO ONBOARD; she felt ill and sent her husband instead. Don't go thinking this was out of grief or sorrow; on the day of the wedding, she had behaved most discreetly, taking care of the bride's trousseau and bidding farewell to her with many kisses and tears. Boarding the ship, however, seemed to her embarrassing, almost a humiliation, which was why she fell ill; and to lend truth to her excuse, she stayed in her room. She picked up a recently published novel, which had been given to her by Rubião. Other objects reminded her of him, too, all kinds of knickknacks, not to mention pieces of jewelry safely locked away. Finally, something he had said on the night of her cousin's wedding came to be added to her inventory of memories of him.

"Now you are the queen of all women," he said softly, "but wait a little and I will make you an empress."

Sofia could not understand the meaning of those enigmatic words. She imagined this might be a way of luring her into becoming his mistress by a promise of greater things, but she dismissed this as pure vanity. While Rubião was no longer the timid, shrinking fellow he once had been, she did not believe him to be so presumptuous. But what, then, did his words mean? Perhaps it was a figurative way of saying that he would love her still more. Sofia thought anything was possible. She did not lack for suitors; she had even heard that declaration from Carlos Maria and had probably heard others, which merely flattered her vanity. And none had lasted, only Rubião. There had been the occasional hiatus, provoked by his suspicions, but these went as easily as they came.

"*He deserves to be loved,*" Sofia read when she returned to her novel; she closed the book, closed her eyes, and became lost in her thoughts. The slave-woman appeared shortly afterward, bringing her a bowl of soup, but, assuming that her mistress was asleep, she tiptoed back out again.

Chapter CXXVI

MEANWHILE, RUBIÃO AND PALHA were getting off the steamship into the boat that would bring them back to the quayside. They were both pensive and silent. Palha was the first to speak:

"For some time now, Rubião, there's been something important I've wanted to tell you."

Chapter CXXVII

RUBIÃO CAME TO. This had been his first experience of being on a steamship. He was returning to shore with his soul full of the sounds of life onboard: the hustle and bustle of people coming and going, Brazilians, foreigners of every stripe, French, English, German, Argentinian, Italian, a babel of languages, a gallimaufry of hats, trunks, ropes, sofas, binoculars, men going up and down stairwells inside the ship, women, some crying, some curious, others roaring with laughter, and many bearing flowers and fruit they had brought with them—everything to him was new. In the distance, the bar at the entrance to the bay from where the steamship would begin its voyage. Beyond that, the vast sea, the brooding sky, and solitude. Rubião reinvented old dreams of the ancient world, creating an Atlantis, even though he knew nothing of the traditional story. Having no notion of geography, he had only a vague idea about other countries, and his imagination surrounded them with a mysterious nimbus. Since it cost him nothing to travel like that, he sailed on for some time in his mind on that tall, long steamship, with no seasickness, no waves, no winds, no clouds.

Chapter CXXVIII

"TO TELL ME?" Rubião asked after a few seconds.

"Yes, you," said Palha. "I should have told you before, but I was so caught up with all this wedding business, the Alagoas committee, and so on, that I haven't had a chance. Now, though, before lunch . . . You are having lunch with me, aren't you?"

"Of course, but what have you got to tell me?"

"Something important."

As he said this, he took out a cigarette, unrolled it, thinned out the tobacco between his fingers, rolled it up again, and struck a match, but the wind blew out the flame. Then he asked Rubião to please hold his hat so that he could light another. Rubião obeyed somewhat impatiently. It might be that his colleague was keeping him waiting on purpose so that he would think it was some terrible disaster and then the reality would seem like nothing. Palha took two puffs of his cigarette before saying

"I'm planning to close the business. I've been invited to take up the directorship of a bank and I think I'll accept."

Rubião breathed again:

"I see, but you mean to close it straightaway?"

"No, but definitely by the end of next year."

"Do you need to?"

"As far as I'm concerned, yes. If the offer from the bank wasn't definite, I wouldn't risk it; you know, a bird in the hand and all that, but the offer is guaranteed."

"So at the end of next year we cut the ties that bind us . . ."

Palha cleared his throat.

"No, actually, before that, by the end of this year."

Rubião could not understand, but Palha explained that it was best to dissolve their partnership now, so that he could proceed with the sale of the business on his own. He wasn't sure when he would start working at the bank, and he didn't want to subject his friend to such uncertainty. Besides, Senhor Camacho had assured him that Rubião would soon be entering the Chamber, and that the government was sure to collapse.

"Anyway," he concluded, "the sensible thing would be to dissolve our partnership ahead of time. You don't depend on the business to live; you simply put in the capital that was needed at the time, just as you could have given it to another business or even kept it for yourself."

"Yes, I'm sure you're right," said Rubião.

Then, after a brief pause:

"But tell me something, is there some hidden reason behind this proposal? Is this personal, the end of a friendship? Please, be frank . . ."

"Don't talk such nonsense!" said Palha. "What do you mean, 'the end of a friendship'? Are you mad? The swaying of the ship must have affected your mind. Would I, who have worked so hard for you, introduced you to all my friends, treated you like family, like a brother, would I seek to quarrel with you for no reason? If you hadn't refused, you would have been the one to marry Maria Benedita, not Carlos Maria. It's possible to break one tie without breaking them all. To do otherwise would be absurd. Should all our friends and family be partners in the business? And what of those who aren't?"

Rubião thought this reasoning excellent and went to embrace Palha, who shook him by the hand, feeling very pleased with himself. He would be free of a partner whose growing extravagance could prove dangerous. The business was very solid, and it would be easy enough to give Rubião his share, minus the personal loans that the two of them had previously entered into. There were still some of those old debts that Palha had confessed to his wife that night in Santa Teresa (see Chapter L). Few had been repaid, and it was usually Rubião who wouldn't hear of settling the matter. One day, Palha, trying to force him to take some money as a repayment, repeated the old proverb: "Pay what you owe and then see what's left." But Rubião had responded with a joke:

"Well, if you don't pay, you'll find you're left with much more."

"That's a good one!" Palha responded, laughing and putting the money back in his pocket.

Chapter CXXIX

THERE WAS NO BANK and no directorship, either, nor was he intending to sell the business, but how could Palha possibly justify that proposed separation by telling Rubião the truth? Hence the lie, which, given Palha's love of banks and his longing to become the director of one, had been easy enough to come up with. His career was definitely on the up and he was beginning to be noticed. Business was booming, and one of the reasons for the separation was simply so as not to have to split any future profits with someone else. Palha also owned shares in all kinds of companies, gilt-edged stock from the Paraguayan War loan, and, in association with an influential partner, he had won two contracts to supply the army which had brought in a lot of money. He had already arranged with an architect to build a mansion, and even had his eye on a peerage.

Chapter CXXX

"WHO'D HAVE THOUGHT Palha's people would treat us in such a way? We're clearly of no use to them anymore. No, no, don't try to defend them . . ."

"I'm not defending them, I'm explaining. There must have been some mistake."

"A birthday party, a cousin's marriage, and not one invitation for the major, the great major, the dear dear major, our old friend the major. That's what they used to call me, yes, I was a dear old friend, a great man, et cetera. But now, nothing, not a single invitation, not even by word of mouth from a messenger boy: 'It's Madam's birthday or her cousin is getting married, and you're both invited, formal dress.' We wouldn't go, of course, because we don't have the right clothes, but that would at least be something, a message, a messenger, for the dear, dear major—"

"Papa!"

Dona Tonica's interruption encouraged Rubião to persist in defending the Palha family. He was at the major's home, which was no longer on Rua Dois de Dezembro, but a modest dwelling above a shop on Rua dos Barbonos. Rubião had happened to be passing, and the major, standing at the window, had beckoned him in. Dona Tonica didn't even have time to leave the living room and check her appearance in the mirror; she could only smooth her hair, straighten the bow around her neck, and give her dress a downward tug to cover her rather shabby shoes.

"As I say, there must have been a mistake," insisted Rubião. "They're so busy over there with the Alagoas committee."

"I would remind you," said Major Siqueira, interrupting, "that they did not ask my daughter to be on that committee. And why? I noticed this change a while back. Before, they never had a party without inviting us. We were the heart and soul of everything. Then things began to change, they began to treat us rather coolly, and the husband started going out of his way to avoid me. That all happened some time ago, but before that, they never used to do anything without us. What do you mean, 'a mistake'? The day before her birthday party, I suspected they wouldn't be inviting us and so I went to see him at the warehouse. He hardly said a word and was clearly hiding something. Finally, I said: 'Yesterday at home, Tonica and I were talking about when Dona Sofia's birthday was; she said it had already passed, and I said no, it was either today or tomorrow.' He didn't answer, pretended to be concentrating on some accounting problem or other, he even called in the bookkeeper and asked him to explain. I could see what the rotten fellow was up to, though, and so I repeated what I'd said, and he reacted in exactly the same way. I left. That jumped-up nobody Palha! He's obviously ashamed to know me now. In the old days, it was: Make a toast, Major. And I made many toasts, I had a certain gift for it. We used to play cards together. Now he's too grand for the likes of us;

he moves in more refined circles. Ah, vanity of vanities! I even saw his wife the other day with some other woman, riding in a coupé. Sofia in a coupé! She pretended she hadn't seen me, but I could tell she was looking at me out of the corner of her eye just to see if I was watching her, admiring her. Ah, vanity of vanities! If you ask me, it's all going to her head."

"Forgive me, but the work of the committee does require a certain degree of pomp."

"Oh, of course," said Siqueira, "that's why my daughter wasn't invited to be on the committee, so as not to ruin the look of the carriages . . ."

"Besides, the coupé might have belonged to the lady who was with her."

The major took a few steps, hands clasped behind his back, then came to a halt in front of Rubião:

"Yes . . . or to Father Mendes. How is the good Father? Living the high life, no doubt."

"But, Papa, she may have nothing against us at all," said Dona Tonica. "She's always very kind to me, and when I was ill last month, she sent a messenger boy to ask after me—twice, in fact . . ."

"A boy!" roared her father. "A boy! How gracious of her! 'Boy, go to the house of that old major and ask if his daughter is feeling better. I can't go myself because I'm polishing my nails.' Some favor! *You* don't polish your nails. You work. You are a worthy daughter of mine! Poor, but honest!"

At this point, the major began to weep, but just as suddenly stopped. His daughter, touched by his distress, was equally upset. The house certainly spoke of their poverty, a handful of chairs, an old round table, a threadbare settee; on the walls two lithographs in pinewood frames painted black: one showed the major in 1857, the other depicted *Veronese in Venice* and had been bought on Rua do Senhor dos Passos. However, Dona Tonica's hard work was apparent in everything; the furniture positively gleamed, the table was covered with a lace tablecloth that she herself had made, and there was a cushion on the settee. And it wasn't true that Dona Tonica didn't polish her nails; she might not have the requisite powder and buffer, but every morning she rubbed away at them with a bit of cloth.

Chapter CXXXI

TO PREVENT ANY further distress, Rubião stopped defending the Palhas and treated the major and his daughter with great kindness. He took his leave shortly afterward, promising, even though he had not been invited, to come and dine with them "one of these days."

"It'll be a poor man's supper," said the major, "so give us due warning."

"I'm not expecting a banquet. I'll just drop by when I can."

He said goodbye. Dona Tonica went as far as the landing, but no farther because of her shabby shoes, then rushed over to the window to watch him leave.

Chapter CXXXII

AS SOON AS Rubião had turned the corner into Rua das Mangueiras, Dona Tonica returned to the room and rejoined her father, who had lain down on the settee to reread an old copy of *St. Clair* of the Isles; or, The Outlaws of Barra. This was the first novel he had ever read, and that copy was more than twenty years old. Indeed, it was their entire library. Siqueira opened the first volume and his eyes fell on the opening words of Chapter III, which he knew by heart. Given his recent upsets, they seemed to him particularly appropriate:

> Fill your goblets, nay fill to the brim, my pledge is—May the generous soul prosper, and the oppressor sink into deserved infamy!

"Do you know what we should do, Papa? Tomorrow you can buy some canned fish and peas and so on. Then if he ever does come to supper, we just have to heat them up on the stove and we can give him a decentish meal."

"But I only have enough money for your dress."

"My dress? Oh, we can buy that next month or the one after. I can wait."

"I thought you'd ordered it already."

"I can always un-order it. I can wait."

"What if there isn't another one at the same price?"

"I'm sure there will be. I can wait, Papa."

Chapter CXXXIII

I HAVEN'T YET mentioned this—because the chapters are positively jostling to leave my pen—but here is one to say that, by this time, Rubião's social circle had widened considerably. Camacho had put him in touch with various politicians; the Alagoas committee with many ladies, banks, and other companies within the world of commerce and finance; the theaters with regular theatergoers; and Rua do Ouvidor with everyone else. He was now a familiar figure, whose name was often on people's lips. Whenever a beard and a long mustache, well-cut frock coat, broad chest, a cane bearing the head of a unicorn, and a firm, gentlemanly step appeared, people would immediately know it was Rubião, a very wealthy man from Minas.

A legend had grown up around him. He was said to be the disciple of a great philosopher, who had bequeathed to him his vast wealth—one thousand, three thousand, five thousand *contos*. Some were puzzled as to why he never talked about philosophy, but the legend explained this silence as being his master's philosophical method, which consisted in teaching only men of goodwill. And where were those disciples? They went to his house every day, sometimes twice, morning and evening; and thus received the name of disciples. Not that they were disciples, they were simply men of goodwill. With hunger gnawing at them, they would wait and listen silently and cheerfully to their host's speeches. There was a certain rivalry between the old guests and the new, with the former eager to show their greater familiarity by giving orders to the servants, asking for cigars, sauntering into the other rooms, whistling, and so on. But habit taught them solidarity and they all ended up gladly singing the praises of their host's many qualities. After some time, even the newer guests owed him money, either in cash or in the form of a guarantee to a tailor or an endorsement on a bill of exchange, which he would secretly pay, so as not to humiliate his debtors.

They all showered Quincas Borba with affection. They would click their fingers to make him do tricks; some would even plant kisses on his forehead; one of the cleverer ones found a way of having him sit on his lap all through lunch or supper so that he could feed him bread crumbs. The first time, Rubião protested:

"No, really, that's too much!"

"Why?" retorted the guest. "We're all friends here."

Rubião thought for a moment, then said:

"And it is true that inside him dwells a very great man."

"Ah, yes, the philosopher, the other Quincas Borba," said the guest, giving the novices a knowing look, just to show them how close he and Rubião were; but this did not work to his advantage alone, for the other friends of the same vintage would all chorus:

"Yes, the philosopher."

And Rubião would explain this allusion to the novices, as well as the reason for the dog's name. Quincas Borba (the deceased one) was described and talked about as one of the greatest men of his time, far superior to his fellow countrymen from Minas. A great philosopher, a great soul, and a great friend. And finally, after a brief silence, during which he drummed his fingers on the edge of the table, Rubião would exclaim:

"If he were alive today, I'd make him a government minister!"

And one of the guests, with little conviction and purely out of duty, would cry:

"Indeed!"

None of those men, however, knew the sacrifices Rubião made for them. He turned down invitations to supper parties, to jaunts in the countryside; he interrupted pleasurable conversations simply to rush home and have supper with them. One day, he found a way of reconciling these calls on his time. If he was not home by six o'clock on the dot, the servants were to serve his friends their supper. There were protests; no, they would wait for him until seven or eight o'clock. A supper without him was no fun at all.

"But I can't be there," Rubião would say.

And so it was. The guests all set their watches by the clocks in Rubião's house in Botafogo, and at six o'clock, they would be seated at the table. During the first couple of days there was some hesitation, but the servants had been given strict orders. Sometimes Rubião would arrive shortly afterward, and there would be laughter, witty comments, amusing anecdotes. One guest pretended that he had wanted to wait, but that the others... the others would then deny this, saying that *he* was the one who had dragged them to the table because he was so hungry, so much so that only the empty plates were left. And Rubião would laugh along with them.

Chapter CXXXIV

IT WILL SEEM FRIVOLOUS even to the frivolous to write a chapter simply to say that, at first, when Rubião wasn't there, the guests would smoke their own cigars after supper; however, more thoughtful readers will say that there is something of interest in this apparently trivial circumstance.

In fact, one night it occurred to one of the older guests to go into Rubião's study; he had been there before on a few occasions and knew that this was where Rubião kept his boxes of cigars, many of them open, not just four or five boxes, but twenty or thirty of all different makes and sizes. A servant (the Spaniard) lit the gas lamp. The other guests followed and chose cigars, and those who were unfamiliar with the study admired the furnishings, all beautifully made and arranged. They particularly admired the desk, a very tasteful, solid piece made of exquisitely carved ebony. A novelty awaited them there, for on the desk stood marble busts of the two Napoleons, the first and the third.

"When did they arrive?"

"Today at midday," said the servant.

Two magnificent busts. Next to the uncle's eagle eyes, the nephew's more pensive eyes gazed off into space. The servant recounted how his master, as soon as he had received the busts and put them in their current position, had spent a long time lost in admiration, so oblivious to everything else that he, the servant, had been able to stand looking at them, too, although in his case without a hint of admiration. *No me dicen nada estos dos pícaros,** he said, making a sweepingly dismissive gesture.

≡ Chapter CXXXV

RUBIÃO WAS A generous supporter of the arts. Any book dedicated to him went to the press with a guaranteed print-run of two or three hundred copies. He had received diploma after diploma from different societies, literary, theatrical, charitable, and he was a member of both a Catholic congregation and a Protestant guild, having forgotten about one by the time he joined the other; what he did, though, was make a monthly contribution to both. He subscribed to newspapers that he never read. One day, as he was about to pay a subscription, he learned from the man collecting the money that the paper supported the government party. He told the poor man to go to the Devil.

* I've no time for those two rogues.

Chapter CXXXVI

THE MAN DID NOT go to the Devil; he took the subscription money and, with the naturally acute mind of all payment collectors, he left, muttering:

"Here's a man who hates the newspaper, but pays for it anyway; think of all the people who love it and never pay a penny!"

Chapter CXXXVII

HOWEVER—THANKS TO a stroke of good fortune, thanks to Nature's equanimity—while our friend's profligacy had no remedy, it did have its compensations. Time no longer passed as it would for some feckless idler without an idea in his head. Rubião, though he may have lacked ideas, now had imagination. Before, he had lived more from other people than from himself, he felt he had no inner equilibrium, and idleness made the hours stretch out endlessly. Now everything was changing; his imagination tended to fixate on one thing. He could spend a whole morning sitting in Bernardo's shop, without once feeling wearied by time or hemmed in by the narrowness of Rua do Ouvidor. Delightful visions filled his mind, like that of his imagined wedding (see Chapter LXXXI), which remained charming despite the pomp and grandeur. He had often been seen leaping to his feet to watch someone passing by his door. Did he know them? Or was it someone who happened to resemble the imaginary creature he had been gazing upon? Too many questions for one chapter; suffice it to say that, on one such occasion, there was no passerby, and he himself, realizing it was an illusion, went back into the shop and, before leaving, bought a piece of jewelry for Camacho's daughter, whose birthday it was and who was soon to be married.

Chapter CXXXVIII

"AND SOFIA?" asks the reader impatiently, just as Orgon repeatedly asks: "And Tartuffe?" Ah, dear friend, the answer is, of course, the same—she, too, ate heartily and slept snugly in her warm bed—neither of which things prevent a person from loving another person, when she wants to love them. If this last thought is the secret reason behind your question, let me just say that you are extremely indiscreet, and I much prefer the company of dissemblers.

I repeat, she ate heartily and slept snugly in her warm bed. She had brought the work of the Alagoas committee to a close and been highly praised in the press; the *Sentinel* called her "the angel of consolation." Don't go thinking, though, that she liked this title; on the contrary, making Sofia the center of all that charitable work might annoy her new friends and ruin the work of many long months in a single day. This would explain the article that appeared in the next edition of that same newspaper, in which the other committee members were all named and celebrated as "stars of the highest order."

Not all these friendships survived, but most did, and our lady had the necessary talent to make them last. Her husband, on the other hand, tended to be overly effusive and obsequious, making it clear that the favors and the kindnesses being heaped on him were entirely unexpected and possibly undeserved. In an attempt to mend his ways, Sofia pestered him with criticism and advice:

"You were just unbearable today; you behaved like a servant," she told him, laughing.

"Cristiano, do show a little more self-control. When we have visitors, don't roll your eyes and dance around like a child being given a piece of candy..."

He would deny this, and try to explain and justify himself, but he always ended up agreeing that she was right, that he shouldn't behave as if he did not merit their kindness, but appear merely polite, affable, and nothing more...

"Yes, but don't go to the opposite extreme, either," said Sofia, "and go all grumpy..."

Palha became both those things: grumpy and, initially at least, cold, almost scornful; then either a conscious decision or a purely unconscious impulse would restore him to his usual animated self, and this, depending on the circumstance, often tipped over into excess and bluster. Sofia was the one who smoothed everything over. She watched and imitated. Necessity and a natural vocation helped her gradually to acquire what neither birth nor fortune had given her. She was, moreover, at that middle age when women inspire the trust of both twenty-year-old girls and forty-year-old matrons. Some adored her and many sang her praises.

This was how, little by little, our friend Sofia transformed their life at home. She broke off relations with old friends and family members, some so close that it was very hard to sever the connection; but the art of greeting people coolly, listening to them without the slightest interest, and saying goodbye without a moment's regret wasn't the least of her many gifts; and one by one, off they went, those poor modest creatures, who lacked both manners and fashionable clothes; friends of little account, with homely habits, simple and undistinguished. With the men she did exactly as the major had described when he saw her pass in a carriage—which, by the way, *was* hers. The difference was that now she no longer bothered to see if they were watching. The honeymoon period of her rise in society was over; now she would look determinedly the other way, thus avoiding the risk of any hesitation, and obliging old friends *not* to doff their hats to her.

Chapter CXXXIX

RUBIÃO DID TRY to intercede again on the major's behalf, but the irritated way in which Sofia interrupted him was enough to make him ask instead if they were still going up to Tijuca the following morning, rain permitting.

"I've spoken to Cristiano, and he says he has some business to deal with, so it'll have to wait until Sunday."

After a pause, Rubião said:

"Why don't we go, just the two of us? We could leave early, have lunch there, and we'd be back by three or four o'clock."

Sofia gave him a look that was so clearly saying yes that Rubião did not even wait for her to answer.

"It's agreed, then, we'll go," he said.

"No."

"Why not?"

And when she refused to explain, he repeated the question, even though the reason was more than obvious. Finally, when forced to answer, she said that her husband would be jealous and might postpone his business meeting in order to go with them. She didn't want to get in the way of his business, and they could easily wait a week. Sofia's eyes accompanied this explanation rather like a bugle accompanying an Our Father. Oh, how she wanted to go! How she wanted to go the very next morning with Rubião, riding down the road, sitting firmly in the saddle, not engaging in vain, poetic daydreams, but bold, her face ablaze, entirely *in* the world, galloping, trotting, stopping. And when they reached the top, she would dismount for a moment, quite alone, with the city in the distance and the sky above. Leaning against her horse, combing its mane with her fingers, she would hear Rubião praising her courage and her elegance . . . She even felt a kiss on the back of her neck . . .

Chapter CXL

SPEAKING OF HORSES, it seems appropriate to say that Sofia's imagination was now a fiery, spirited steed capable of climbing hills and forging a path through the densest undergrowth. In other circumstances, we would make a different comparison, but "fiery steed" is the most suitable one here. It carries within it the idea of energy and blood and riding at full tilt, as well as the serenity with which said steed returns to the straight homeward path, and, finally, the stable.

Chapter CXLI

"RIGHT, THEN, we'll go tomorrow," Rubião said again, aware of Sofia's flushed cheeks.

The fiery steed had returned weary from its ride and meekly entered the stable intent on sleep. Sofia was a different person now; the dizzy excitement, the imagined passion, the pleasure of riding along the road with him to Tijuca, were all gone. When Rubião said he would ask her husband if he would allow her to go on that ride, she replied wanly:

"Don't be silly! It'll have to wait until next Sunday!"

And she fixed her gaze on the trivial bit of sewing she was engaged in—"tatting," it's called—while Rubião turned his gaze on a little patch of garden next to the small sewing room where they were sitting. In a corner seat by the window, Sofia was working nimbly away with her fingers. Rubião meanwhile was looking at two very ordinary roses and seeing a sumptuous imperial party, and had completely forgotten about the room, the woman, and himself. It's impossible to say exactly how long the two of them remained there, silent, absorbed, and remote from one another. It took a maid bringing in coffee to rouse them both from their reveries. Once he had drunk his coffee, Rubião smoothed his beard, took out his watch, and said goodbye to Sofia, who had been waiting for him to leave, and felt pleased when he did, although she covered her pleasure with mock surprise.

"Are you going already?"

"I have to meet someone at four o'clock," said Rubião. "Anyway, we're agreed—tomorrow's excursion is off. I'll cancel the horses. But we'll definitely go next Sunday?"

"I can't say for certain, but assuming Cristiano makes up his mind in time, yes. It's my husband who creates the obstacles."

Sofia accompanied him to the door, held out one indifferent hand, responded with a smile to some trivial remark, then returned to the room she had just left—the same corner seat, the same window. She didn't immediately resume her work, but crossed her legs, and out of sheer habit carefully rearranged the hem of her dress; then she looked out at the garden, at the two roses that had given our friend that imperial vision. Sofia saw only two silent roses. However, she did study them for a few moments before picking up her lacework, continuing for a while, then stopping for another while, her hands resting on her lap; then she again went back to her work and again put it down. Suddenly she stood up and threw the shuttle and the thread into the small wicker workbasket. The basket was another present from Rubião.

"Tedious fellow!"

She leaned out of the window that gave onto the little patch of garden, where those two ordinary roses were slowly fading. Roses, when they're new, care little or nothing about other people's vexations, but as they fade, they look for every opportunity to wound the human heart. I'd like to believe this has to do with the brevity of life. Someone once wrote: "For roses, the gardener is eternal." And what better way of annoying that eternal being than by mocking his little tantrums? I will die and you will remain; all I did was flower and give off perfume, I served as a love letter to ladies and young women, I adorned the buttonholes of men, and even if I await death here on this bush, every hand, every eye treated me and looked on me with admiration and affection. Not like you, O eternal one: you get angry, you suffer, you weep, you torment yourself! Your eternity is not worth a single one of my minutes.

Thus, when Sofia looked out of the window that gave onto the garden, both the roses laughed their petals off. One said that it served her right, served her right, served her right!

"I can understand why you're angry, lovely creature," it added, "but it's really yourself you should be angry with, not him. What is he, after all? A sad man with few charms, he might be a good friend and even generous, but he's pretty repellent, don't you think? And you, so sought-after by other men, why on earth should you even bother with him, one of life's failures? Admit it, proud creature, you are the cause of your own ills. You swear to forget him, but you don't. Do you even need to forget him? Isn't it enough just to look at him and listen to him in order to despise him? What has that man got to say to you, O strange one, and you—"

"Now, that's not quite fair," broke in the other rose in a weary, ironic voice. "He does have something to say, and he's been saying it ad nauseam for a long time now; he's steadfast, he sets aside sadness and believes in hope. His entire love life is like that trip to Tijuca the two of you were talking about just now: 'It'll have to wait until next Sunday!' At least have a little pity, yes, be merciful, O kind Sofia! If you have to love someone outside of marriage, then love him, for he truly does love you and he's discreet. Go on, take back what you said earlier. What has he ever done to you, and is it his fault that you're pretty? And if anyone is to blame, it's not that workbasket, just because he bought it, still less the threads and the shuttle you yourself ordered the maid to buy. You're wicked, Sofia, unfair..."

Chapter CXLII

FOR SOME TIME, Sofia carried on listening, listening... She questioned other plants, and they said the same thing. Such fine examples of consensus are not unknown. Anyone who knows the soil and subsoil of life knows very well that a stretch of wall, a bench, a carpet, an umbrella, are all rich in ideas or feelings, when, that is, we are, too, and this exchange of ideas between men and things is one of the most interesting phenomena on earth. The expression "to consult with one's pillow" may seem to be a mere metaphor, but it has a very real and direct meaning. Our pillow works synchronously with us; it forms a kind of parliament, comfortable and cheap, and one that always votes in favor of any motion we propose.

Chapter CXLIII

THE TRIP TO TIJUCA duly took place, and the only incident was a fall from a horse on the way back. It wasn't Rubião who fell, or Palha, but the latter's wife, who, thinking about who knows what, had furiously whipped her horse, which took fright and threw her to the ground. Sofia fell very gracefully. In her riding outfit, with its tight bodice, she looked extremely slender and alluring. If Othello had seen her, he would have cried: "O, my fair warrior!" At the beginning of their ride, Rubião said only: "You're an angel!"

≡ *Chapter CXLIV*

"I'VE HURT MY KNEE," she said as she limped into the house.

"Let me see."

In their dressing room, Sofia put her foot up on a stool and showed her husband her bruised knee; it had swollen a little, very little, but when he touched it, she groaned. Not wanting to hurt her, Palha merely brushed her knee with his lips.

"Did my skirts ride up at all when I fell?"

"No, I mean, with a skirt that long . . . you can hardly see the tip of your shoes. Really, it was fine."

"Do you swear?"

"Have you so little confidence in me, Sofia? I swear by all that's most sacred, by the sun that lights me and by Our Lord God. Now are you satisfied?"

Sofia was covering up her knee.

"Let me have another look. I don't think it's anything serious, but you should put some cream on it. Ask the pharmacist."

"All right, but now let me get undressed," she said, struggling out of her clothes.

Palha, though, had shifted his gaze from her knee to the rest of her leg, where it disappeared into her boot. Nature really had outdone herself. Her silk stocking showed off the shape of her leg to perfection. Palha jokingly asked if she had bruised herself here or here or here, indicating the different places as he slid his hand down her leg. If a tiny piece of this masterpiece were to be revealed, the sky and the trees would be astonished, he said while his wife let her dress fall and removed her foot from the stool.

"Possibly, but the sky and the trees weren't the only ones there; there were Rubião's eyes too," she said.

"Ah, of course, Rubião! But he's never repeated any of the nonsense he spouted that night in Santa Teresa, has he?"

"Never, but I still wouldn't like it if... Do you really swear, Cristiano?"

"You just want me to rise ever upward from sacred to sacred to the most sacred thing of all. I swore by God, but that wasn't enough. All right, I swear by you. Now are you satisfied?"

A lover's sentimental twaddle. He finally left Sofia's room and went to his own. Sofia's display of fearful, incredulous modesty pleased him. It showed that she was his, all his, and precisely because she was, he felt it appropriate in a great lord not to be overly concerned if someone else caught a chance, momentary glimpse of a hidden part of his realm. And he was sorry that the chance glimpse had ended at the tip of her boot. That was merely the frontier, the territory's first villages, the outskirts of the city bruised by the fall, and would give others an idea of a sublime and perfect civilization. And as he soaped his hands, washing face and neck and head in the vast silver basin, before brushing his hair, drying and perfuming himself, Palha was imagining the amazement and envy of the accident's sole witness, had more been revealed.

Chapter CXLV

IT WAS AROUND this time that Rubião astonished all his friends. On the Tuesday after the Sunday outing (it was now January 1870), he asked a barber-cum-hairdresser in Rua do Ouvidor to send a man to his house the following morning at nine o'clock. The man in question was a Frenchman named Lucien, who went straight into Rubião's study as instructed by the servant.

"Uhm!" growled Quincas Borba from his position on Rubião's lap.

Lucien bowed to the master of the house, who, however, did not see the bow, just as he had not heard Quincas Borba's warning growl. He was reclining on a chaise longue—the perfect refuge for his imagination, which had risen up through the ceiling and drifted off into the air. How many leagues had he traveled? Neither condor nor eagle could say. On his way to the moon, he saw below only endless good fortune, which had rained down upon him ever since he was in his cradle, gently rocked by fairies, who had then carried him all the way to Botafogo Beach on a path strewn with roses and jasmine. No setbacks, no failures, no poverty—a placid life rich in pleasures and with an ample income. On his way to the moon.

The barber glanced around the room, which was dominated by the desk on which sat the two busts: Napoleon and Louis Napoleon. In homage to the latter, there was an engraving or lithograph depicting the Battle of Solferino, and a portrait of the Empress Eugénie.

Rubião was wearing a pair of damask slippers embroidered in gold; on his head a cap with a black silk tassel. On his lips a pale blue smile.

Chapter CXLVI

"SIR . . ."

"Uhm!" said Quincas Borba again, standing up now on his master's lap.

Rubião came to and noticed the barber. Having seen him recently in his shop, he recognized him and sat up. Quincas Borba was barking now, as if defending his master against an intruder.

"Be quiet! Shut up!" said Rubião, and the dog, ears flattened against his head, scurried off to hide behind the wastepaper basket. Meanwhile, Lucien was preparing his instruments.

"You're going to lose a very handsome beard," he said in French. "I know men who have done the same in order to please a lady. I have been the confidant of many respectable men and—"

"Precisely!" said Rubião, interrupting him.

He had understood nothing; he may have known a little French, but—as we know—he could barely understand written French, and not a word of it when spoken. The curious thing is, though, he had not responded like that as a way of pretending he had understood; he heard the words as if they were a compliment or an acclamation; even more curious is that while he responded in Portuguese, he thought he was speaking French.

"Precisely!" he said again. "I wish to restore my face to its former appearance, as it is over there."

And since he was pointing at the bust of Napoleon III, the barber responded in Portuguese:

"Ah, the emperor! A fine bust indeed. An excellent piece of work. Did you buy it here or have it sent from Paris? They're both magnificent. And there's the first Napoleon, the great man; now, he was a genius. Had he not been betrayed, ah... But traitors, sir, traitors are worse than any Orsini bombs."*

"Huh, Orsini! Miserable wretch!"

"He paid dearly."

"He paid what he owed, but no bombs and no Orsinis can get in the way of a great man," Rubião continued. "When the fate of a nation places the imperial crown upon the head of a great man, no evil can touch him... Orsini, bah! A fool!"

The barber quickly began demolishing Rubião's luxuriant beard, leaving him with only Napoleon III's goatee and mustache; he rather exaggerated the difficulty of the task, saying it was very hard to copy something so exactly. And as he was snipping away at Rubião's beard, he praised it, saying: "Such fine whiskers! This is a real sacrifice you're making..."

"You're a presumptuous fellow, *Mister* Barber," Rubião said. "I've told you what I want, to restore my face to its previous appearance. You have the bust there to guide you."

"Of course, sir, I'll do exactly that, and soon you'll see how alike you are."

And he snip-snipped away at the last remnants of Rubião's beard, then began carefully shaving his cheeks and chin. It was a lengthy operation, with the barber serenely shaving, comparing, glancing back and forth between bust and man. Sometimes, the better to compare the two, he would take two steps back and look first at one, then at the other, sometimes bending over and asking the man to turn to one side or the other, then studying the corresponding side of the bust.

---

* Felice Orsini was an Italian nationalist who tried to assassinate Napoleon III by throwing bombs at the carriage of Napoleon and Empress Eugénie on their way to the opera in Paris. He was arrested and executed.

"How does it look?" asked Rubião.

Lucien silenced him with a gesture, and carried on. He shaped the goatee, left the mustache much as it was, then shaved the rest of his face painstakingly, slowly, lovingly, tediously, feeling with his fingers for some imperceptible piece of stubble. Sometimes Rubião, weary of staring up at the ceiling while the other man perfected his cheeks, would ask to rest, and while he rested, he patted his face and felt by touch the change in himself.

"The mustache is not quite long enough," he remarked.

"I still have to do the ends: I have some tongs to make sure the mustache curves over the lip, and then we will deal with the ends. Creating ten original works is so much easier than making one copy."

Another ten minutes passed before mustache and goatee were finished to perfection. When it was done, Rubião leapt to his feet and ran to look in the mirror in his bedroom, which was just next door; he was the other, he was both, he was, in short, himself.

"Precisely!" he cried, returning to his study, where the barber, having tidied away all his implements, was now fussing over Quincas Borba.

Going to his desk, Rubião opened a drawer, took out a twenty-*mil-réis* note, and gave it to the barber.

"I don't have any change," he said.

"No need," said Rubião with a regal gesture. "Pay whatever you owe to your boss and keep the change."

Chapter CXLVII

ONCE HE WAS alone again, Rubião flung himself down in an armchair and watched as several splendid scenes passed before his eyes. He was in Biarritz or Compiègne, although it wasn't clear which. He ruled over a vast empire, he listened to the advice of ministers and ambassadors, he danced, he dined—and other such things spoken of in newspaper articles he had read and which stuck in his memory. Not even Quincas Borba's whining could rouse him. He was far away and very high up. Compiègne was en route to the moon. Yes, to the moon!

Chapter CXLVIII

WHEN HE CAME DOWN from the moon, he heard the dog whimpering and felt a certain chill on his face. He ran to the mirror and saw what a huge difference there was between a bearded face and a shaven face, but the latter rather suited him. His guests reached the same conclusion.

"It looks really good! You should have done it ages ago. Not that the long beard detracted from your noble features, but you look just as good now, and with a modern touch..."

"A modern touch," repeated the host.

In the outside world, he met with the same astonished reaction. And everyone genuinely thought this new look suited him better than the old one. Only one person, Senhor Camacho, dissented. While he agreed that the mustache and goatee really did suit his friend, he wondered if it was wise to alter the appearance of one's face, which, as the true mirror of the soul, should reflect the soul's steadfast, constant nature.

"I don't wish to take myself as an example," he said, "but my face will always remain the same. It is like a moral necessity. My life, entirely given over to principles—because I have never tried to make terms with principles, only with men—my life, I say, is a faithful image of my face, and vice versa.'

Rubião listened gravely and nodded his agreement. He felt then that he was the French emperor traveling incognito; once out in the street again, though, he returned to his former self. Dante, who saw so many extraordinary things, says that in hell he witnessed the punishment of a Florentine soul, who was so tightly embraced by a six-footed serpent that their bodies became fused, and, in the end, it was impossible to tell if they were one being or two. Rubião was still two. His own self and the French emperor did not intermingle in him; they took turns and even forgot about each other entirely. When he was only Rubião, he was his usual self. When the emperor took precedence, he was pure emperor. They balanced each other out, neither one imposing on the other, both essential parts of his being.

Chapter CXLIX

"WHY SUCH A radical change?" asked Sofia when he visited her over the weekend.

"I came to ask about your knee. Is it better?"
"Yes, thank you."

It was two o'clock in the afternoon. Sofia was just getting dressed to go out when the maid came to tell her that Rubião was there, his face so altered that he looked like a different man. Filled with curiosity, Sofia went downstairs to see him; she found him standing in the drawing room reading the various visiting cards.

"Why such a radical change?" she asked again.

Rubião responded very unimperially that he thought he would look better with just a mustache and a goatee.

"Or am I uglier?"

"No, you look better, much better."

And Sofia wondered if perhaps she was the reason for that change. She sat down on the sofa and started to pull on her gloves.

"Are you going out?"

"Yes, I am, but the carriage hasn't yet arrived."

She dropped one of her gloves. Rubião bent down to pick it up, she did the same, and in doing so, their faces met and her nose collided with his; their mouths remained intact enough to laugh, however, and they did.

"Did I hurt you?"

"No, I was about to ask you the same thing . . ."

And they laughed again. Sofia pulled on her glove. Rubião noticed one of her feet surreptitiously tapping until the servant came in to announce that the carriage was at the door. They both stood up, and again they laughed.

Chapter CL

STANDING VERY ERECT and bareheaded, the footman opened the door to the coupé as soon as Sofia appeared. Rubião offered her his hand to help her in and she gratefully accepted.

"See you on—"

She didn't manage to finish the sentence, because Rubião climbed into the carriage as well and sat down beside her; the footman closed the door, got into his seat, and the carriage set off.

Chapter CLI

THIS ALL HAPPENED so quickly that Sofia lost both voice and the ability to react, but after a few seconds she said:

"What are you doing? Senhor Rubião order the carriage to stop."

"To stop? But didn't you say you were going out and were waiting for your carriage?"

"I wasn't planning to go out with you, sir . . . Don't you see that . . . Tell the driver to stop . . ."

Almost beside herself, she made as if to give the order, but fearing that this might cause a scene, she held back. The coupé entered Rua Bela da Princesa. Sofia once more begged Rubião to see how wrong it was for them to be traveling together like that, in the sight of God and everyone else. Rubião agreed and suggested they close the curtains.

"I don't think it matters if people see us," he said, "but if we close the curtains, no one will. Shall I?"

Without waiting for an answer, he closed the curtains on both sides, and there they were alone; although from the inside they could see the occasional passerby, from the outside no one could see them. Alone, completely alone, just as they had been that other day in her house, and at that very same hour of two o'clock, when Rubião had spoken so frankly of his despair. Then, she had at least been free to leave, but here, inside this closed carriage, who knows what might happen?

Rubião meanwhile made himself more comfortable and said nothing.

Chapter CLII

SOFIA SHRANK BACK into a corner. It may have been the strangeness of the situation, it may have been fear, but mainly it was a feeling of repugnance. She had never before felt such aversion, such revulsion for that man, or, if you prefer something less harsh—how can I put this without offending your ears?—an incompatibility, an epidermal incompatibility. What had become of her dreams of recent days? In response to a simple invitation to go for a ride to Tijuca, she had galloped with him into the hills, dismounted, heard his adoring words, and felt a kiss on the back of her neck. What had become of those imaginings? What had become of the long looks, the friendly handclasps, the restless feet, the tender words, and the compassionate ears that heard them? All forgotten, all vanished, now that they were actually alone, imprisoned by the carriage and by scandal.

And the horses continued drawing the carriage slowly onward, their hooves clip-clopping over the cobbles of Rua Bela da Princesa. What would she do when they reached Catete? Would she proceed into town with him? She thought of getting out at a friend's house and ordering the driver to drive on, leaving Rubião alone in the carriage. She would tell her husband everything. In the midst of this agony of doubt, a few banal memories, which had nothing to do with the current situation, flitted through her mind: the news of a jewelry theft she had read about in the morning paper, yesterday evening's strong winds, a hat. Finally, she fixated on one problem only. What was Rubião going to say to her? She saw that he was still looking straight ahead, silent, resting his chin on the handle of his cane. This pose, calm, serious, almost indifferent, was even rather becoming, but then why had he gotten into the carriage? Sofia tried to break the silence; twice she nervously wrung her hands; she found the man's impassivity almost irritating, given that his actions could only be explained by a violent, long-standing passion. Then it occurred to her that he himself might have regretted what he had done, and she said as much.

"I don't see why I should have any reason to regret anything," he said, turning to face her. "You said it was wrong of us to be traveling together like this in the public eye, and so I closed the curtains. I didn't agree with you, but I obeyed."

"We've reached Catete," she said. "Shall I drop you off at your house? We can't continue together like this into town."

"We could just ride along aimlessly."

"What?"

"The horses can trot aimlessly along and we can talk, without anyone hearing us or suspecting . . ."

"Dear God, don't talk like that. Leave, get out, or else I'll get out here, and you can do what you like. What can you possibly have to say to me that would take more than a few minutes? Look, we're heading into town; tell the driver to go to Botafogo. I'll leave you at your door..."

"But I've only just left home, and since I'm heading into town, why shouldn't you take me there? If it's because you don't want anyone to see us, you can let me out anywhere, at Praia de Santa Luzia, for example... by the sea..."

"It would be best if you got out right here."

"But why can't we continue on into town?"

"No, that's impossible. I'm begging you by all you hold most sacred, please, don't make a scene. What must I do for you to grant me such a simple wish? Shall I kneel before you?"

Despite the cramped space, she did actually make as if to kneel, but Rubião immediately urged her to sit.

"There's no need to kneel," he said gently.

"Thank you. In that case, I ask you in the name of God, in the name of your dear mother, may she rest in peace..."

"Yes, she must be in heaven now," said Rubião. "She was a real saint. All mothers are good, but anyone who knew my mother would say the same: She was a saint. And such a wonderful hostess! If we had guests, she didn't mind if there were five or fifty, it was all the same, she dealt with whatever needed to be done promptly and without fuss, she was known for it. The slaves called her Sinhá Mãe, because she really was a mother to everyone. Yes, she must be in heaven now!"

"Fine, fine," said Sofia, "well then, do me this favor out of love for your mother. Will you?"

"Do what?"

"Get out—here."

"What, and walk into town? I can't. You're worrying about

nothing, no one can see us. And these horses of yours are just so magnificent. Have you noticed how steadily they trot along, clip ... clop ... clip ... clop ... ?"

Weary with asking, Sofia fell silent, folded her arms, and, were it possible, shrank even farther into her corner of the carriage.

"I know," she thought. "I'll tell the driver to stop outside Cristiano's warehouse, and tell Cristiano how this man got into the carriage with me, how I begged him to leave, and how he refused. That would be better than having him making a suspicious exit in some street or other."

Rubião, meanwhile, was sitting very still. Now and then he would play with the ring on his finger, a splendid solitaire diamond. He wasn't looking at her, he wasn't saying or asking her anything. They were riding along like a very bored married couple. Sofia was beginning to wonder what had led him to get into the carriage in the first place. It couldn't be because he needed a ride. Nor could it be vanity; he had closed the curtains as soon as she complained that they might be seen together. Not a single amorous word, not even some timid remark, adoring and supplicant. There was just no understanding him; he was a monster.

=== Chapter CLIII

"SOFIA," RUBIÃO SAID suddenly, then without a pause went on. "Sofia, time passes, but no man ever forgets the woman who truly loved him; if he does, he doesn't deserve to be called a man. Our love will never be forgotten, certainly not by me, nor, I'm sure, by you. You gave me everything, Sofia, even at the risk of your own life. True, my lovely, I would have taken my revenge, and if revenge can bring pleasure to the dead, then the greatest possible pleasure would be yours. Luckily, my destiny protected us, and we could love each other without hindrance and with no blood spilled."

Sofia was staring at him in horror.

"Fear not," he said, "we will not part, no, I am not speaking of us parting. Don't tell me you would die; I know you would weep many tears. I would not, for I did not come into the world to weep, but my sorrow would be no less than yours; on the contrary, secret sorrows hurt more than any other. Tears are a good thing because they allow a person to vent their feelings. Dear friend, I am speaking to you like this because we must be careful; our insatiable passion might forget that need for caution. We have acted rashly, Sofia; since we were born for one another, it seems to us that we are married, and so, yes, we have acted rashly. Listen, my love, listen, soul of my soul . . . Life is beautiful! Life is magnificent! Life is sublime! With you, though, what name can I give to life? Do you remember our first rendezvous?"

When Rubião uttered that last word, he tried to take her hand. Sofia withdrew in time; she felt utterly bewildered, uncomprehending, and afraid. His voice was growing louder, the driver might hear . . . She was shaken by a suspicion; perhaps Rubião's intention was precisely to make himself heard, to terrorize her into succumbing . . . or was he simply bent on ruining her reputation? She was tempted to throw herself at him, cry out for help, and save herself through scandal.

After the briefest of pauses, he said almost in a whisper:

"I remember it as if it were yesterday. You arrived in a carriage, not like this one, a hired carriage, a calèche. You were so afraid and you had a veil over your face; you were trembling like a leaf . . . But my arms were there to support you . . . That day, the sun must have stopped, just as when Joshua commanded it to . . . And yet, my flower, for some reason those hours were devilishly long; strictly speaking, they should have been short. This was perhaps because our passion was endless, unending, and it never will end... In compensation, we did not see the sun again that day; it was sinking down behind the mountains when my Sofia, still fearful, stepped out into the street and took another calèche. Was it another or the same one? I think it was the same one. You can't imagine my feelings; I was almost dizzy, I kissed everything you had touched; I even kissed the doorstep. I think I've told you that before. Imagine that, the doorstep. And I almost, almost went down on my knees to kiss each stair... I didn't, though, I went back inside and shut myself in so as not to lose the smell of you, violets, I seem to recall..."

No, Rubião clearly wasn't intending that the driver would hear and believe such a slanderous lie. He was speaking so quietly that Sofia could barely hear him, but if it was hard to hear his words, it was quite impossible to understand them. Why was he telling her this story that had never happened? Anyone hearing it would think it was all true, such was the sincerity with which he told it, the tender expressions and the realism of every detail. And he continued to sigh over those beautiful memories...

"Is this some kind of joke?" Sofia finally asked.

Our friend did not answer; he was focused on the image before his eyes, and didn't even hear the questions, but carried on talking. He mentioned a concert by Gottschalk. The divine pianist was playing beautifully; they were listening, but that devilish music made them turn to look into each other's eyes, and they both forgot everything else. When the music stopped, the audience burst into applause, and they awoke. Poor wretches! They awoke to Palha's gaze, the gaze of a fierce jaguar. That night, he was convinced Palha would kill her.

"Senhor Rubião..."

"No, don't call me Napoleon, call me Louis. I am your Louis, aren't I, precious creature? Yours, yours ... say that I am yours, your Louis, your beloved Louis. Ah, if you knew how I love to hear you say those two words: 'My Louis!' You are my Sofia, my heart's sweet, loving Sofia. Let us not waste these moments; let us call each other tender names, but softly, very softly, so that neither the driver nor the footman will hear. Why do there have to be such people in the world? Without them, the carriage would drive itself, we could talk easily then and go to the ends of the earth."

They were driving along by the Passeio Público now, but Sofia didn't even notice. She was staring hard at Rubião; no, behind his words there was no evil intent, no mockery either ... Madness, yes, that was what it was. He said these things with such sincerity, like someone who could actually see the things he was describing.

"I have to get him out of this carriage," she thought, and, plucking up her courage, she said:

"Where are we? It's time for us to go our separate ways. Look out the window. Where are we? It looks like the convent. Yes, we're in Largo da Ajuda. Tell the driver to stop or, if you like, you can get out in Largo da Carioca. My husband—"

"I intend to appoint him ambassador," said Rubião. "Or senator, if you prefer. Yes, senator would be better, then you will both stay here in Rio. Were he ambassador, I could not allow you to go away with him, and you can imagine the gossip ... You know what criticism I face, the calumnies ... Vile people! The convent, you say? What's that to you? Do you want to become a nun?"

"No, I'm just saying that we have already passed the convent. I'm going to leave you in Largo da Carioca. Or shall we carry on to my husband's warehouse?"

Sofia returned to that second option; that way the driver would suspect nothing, it would be further proof to Palha of her innocence, and she could then tell him everything, from Rubião's unexpectedly climbing into her carriage to his madness. But what had caused that madness? Sofia thought that she herself might be the cause, and this possibility made her smile sympathetically.

"Why do that?" said Rubião. "I'm going to get out right here, it's safer. Why should we run the risk of him suspecting us and then mistreating you? I could punish him, but I would never be free of my feelings of remorse for the harm he would do you. No, my lovely flower, my friend; even if the wind dared to touch your person, believe me, I would send it away as being unworthy. You don't yet know the extent of my power, Sofia; come, now, admit that you don't."

When Sofia would admit to nothing, Rubião praised her beauty and offered her his diamond ring; much as she loved jewels, and had a particular penchant for diamonds, she fearfully refused the offer.

"I can perfectly understand your scruples," he said, "but you will not be the loser, because I will give you an even more beautiful jewel, and it will be a gift from your husband. I will make you a duchess. Do you hear? I will give him the title, but you are the reason. Duke . . . but duke of what? I'll look for some pretty title, or you can choose one yourself, because the title is for you, not for him, but for you, my precious one. There's no need to choose now, go home and think about it. There's no hurry, just let me know which title appeals to you most, and I will have the decree drawn up at once. Or you could do something else: choose and give me your answer when we meet again in the usual place. I want to be the first to call you duchess. Dear duchess . . . The decree will come later. My heart's duchess!"

"Yes, yes," she said wildly, "but first tell the driver to take us to Cristiano's place of business."

"No, no, I'll get out here . . . Stop, stop!"

Rubião drew back the curtains, and the footman came to open the door. Sofia, so as to avoid all suspicion, again asked Rubião to go with her to see her husband, saying that he needed to speak to him urgently. Rubião looked with some alarm at her, at the footman, at the street, and then said no, he would go later.

Chapter CLIV

THE MOMENT THEY PARTED, each reacted quite differently.

Once in the street, Rubião turned around, and reality began to take hold of him again as his madness vanished. He strolled along, stopped outside a shop, crossed the road, greeted an acquaintance and engaged him in conversation; an unconscious effort to shake off that borrowed personality.

On the other hand, once Sofia had recovered from her terror, her mind plunged into a state of reverie; Rubião's invented stories and allusions filled her with a kind of nostalgia, but nostalgia for what? Perhaps a "nostalgia for heaven," as Father Bernardes called every good Christian's natural yearning. Sundry names flickered like lightning across the blue sky of that possibility. Such an interesting detail! Sofia reconstructed the old calèche, into which she quickly climbed only to leave again, trembling, in order to slip back into the hallway, go up the stairs, and find a man—a man who said the sweetest of sweet nothings to her and was repeating them now, sitting right next to her in the carriage, but who wasn't and couldn't be Rubião. Who was it, then? Sundry names flickered like lightning across the blue sky of that possibility.

Chapter CLV

NEWS OF RUBIÃO'S madness spread. Some people, who had not encountered him during one of his bouts of delirium, would try to see if the rumors were true; they would turn the conversation to matters French and Napoleonic. Rubião would slide rapidly down into the abyss, and his visitors would leave convinced that he was indeed insane.

Chapter CLVI

A FEW MONTHS PASSED, the Franco-Prussian War began, and Rubião's crises became more acute and more frequent. When the mail from Europe arrived early, Rubião would leave Botafogo before breakfast and rush down to the port to await the newspapers; he would buy the *Correspondência de Portugal* and go read it at Carceler's Patisserie. Whatever the news, he would interpret it as a victory. He would count the dead and wounded and always find the balance in his favor. The fall of Napoleon III became for him the capture of King Wilhelm I, the revolution of September 4 a banquet for the Bonapartists.

At home, his supper friends made no attempt to dissuade him. Nor in each other's presence did they agree with him, for that would have been too shameful. They merely smiled and changed the subject. All of them, meanwhile, had their military ranks—Marshal

Torres, Marshal Pio, Marshal Ribeiro—and they would answer to their respective titles. Rubião imagined them all in uniform; he would order a reconnaissance mission, an attack, but there was no need for them to leave the house in order to obey; their host's brain did that for them. When Rubião left the field of battle to return to the table, what a change had taken place. There was no silverware, barely any china or glasses, and yet in Rubião's eyes, the table was lavishly set. To him, poor scrawny chickens were pheasants; meager cottage pies and miserable roasts were the earth's finest delicacies. The guests did complain to each other—or to the cook—but Lucullus always dined with Lucullus,* It was the same in the rest of the house, which had grown shabby with neglect, the carpets faded, the furniture battered and rickety, the curtains grubby and stained, but to him it looked quite different, glossy and magnificent. His language had changed, too, and become more peremptory and verbose, as had his ideas, some of them as extraordinary as those of his late friend Quincas Borba—theories he had never understood when he heard them in Barbacena, but which he now repeated with utter, heartfelt lucidity—sometimes using the philosopher's very words. How to explain this repetition of the obscure, this knowledge of the inexplicable, when both thoughts and words appeared to have been carried away by the winds of former days? And why did all these reminiscences vanish when reason returned?

---

* Lucullus (118–57/56 BC) was a Roman general and statesman famous for his banqueting. Once, it is said, his steward, hearing that he would have no guests for dinner, served only one not especially impressive course. Lucullus reprimanded him, saying, "What, did not you know, then, that today Lucullus dines with Lucullus?"

Chapter CLVII

SOFIA'S COMPASSION—once she had explained Rubião's madness to herself as being a result of his love for her—was a halfway house of a feeling, neither pure sympathy nor stubborn egotism, but a little of both. As long as she avoided a repeat of that encounter in the coupé, everything was fine. When Rubião was lucid, she would listen and speak to him with interest—because his illness, which made him bold when in the grip of one of his crises, only redoubled his timidity when he was behaving normally. She did not, like Palha, smirk when Rubião ascended to his throne or commanded an army. Believing herself to be the cause of the illness, she forgave him, and the idea of being loved to the point of madness filled her with a new respect for the man.

Chapter CLVIII

"CAN'T HE GET treatment for it?" asked Dona Fernanda one evening, for she had met Rubião the year before. "There might be a cure."

"It doesn't seem that serious," said Palha. "He does have these attacks, but they're quite harmless, as you've seen, delusions of grandeur, which soon pass; and apart from that, he can still hold a reasonable conversation. You never know, though . . . What do you think, sir?"

Teófilo, Dona Fernanda's husband, responded saying that there might be a cure, and asked:

"What did he do, or what does he do now?"

"Nothing, either now or before. He was rich, but a spendthrift. We met when he first came here from Minas, and we were, in a way, his guides in Rio, where he hadn't been for many years. He's a good man, but he has always lived too high on the hog, you see. No amount of wealth is inexhaustible, not once you start eating into your capital, which is what he has done. I don't believe he has much left now . . ."

"You might be able to save the little that's left by making yourself his trustee while he gets the treatment he needs. I'm no doctor, but your friend might then recover."

"You may be right. And it really is a shame. . . . He gets on well with everyone and is always ready to help. He very nearly became one of the family, you know. He wanted to marry Maria Benedita."

"On the subject of Maria Benedita," said Dona Fernanda, "I almost forgot that I've brought a letter from her to show Sofia. I received it yesterday. As you probably know, they'll be home soon. Here it is."

She handed the letter to Sofia, who opened it unenthusiastically and read it with a weary expression on her face. It was more than just an ordinary letter from across the ocean, it was a whole repository of sentiments, the full and intimate confession of a happy, grateful person. She described their most recent adventures in a somewhat confused fashion, because the travelers themselves were superimposed on everything, and man or nature's most exquisite works were nothing compared to the eyes that gazed upon them. Sometimes she expended more words on an incident at a hotel or in the street, and always for the simple reason that they highlighted her husband's many qualities. Maria Benedita loved him as much as, or even more than, she had in the beginning. At the end, in a timid little postscript, asking Dona Fernanda to tell no one, she confessed to her that she was expecting.

Sofia folded the letter, no longer weary but resentful, and for two contradictory reasons, but then contradiction is part of life. When she compared this letter with the ones *she* had received from Maria Benedita, she felt as if she were a mere acquaintance, with no ties of blood or affection; on the other hand, she had no wish to hear such happiness whispered to her from across the ocean, full of details and adjectives and exclamations, full of Carlos Maria's name, Carlos Maria's eyes, Carlos Maria's witty comments, and, finally, Carlos Maria's child. It felt so deliberate, so provocative, that she almost wondered if Dona Fernanda was an accomplice in all this.

She was clever enough, though, to control her feelings and disguise her resentment, and to smile as she handed back her cousin's letter. She wanted to say that, judging by what she'd read, Maria Benedita's happiness was as perfect as when she had left Rio, but the words got stuck in her throat. Dona Fernanda provided the conclusion:

"Yes, she seems very happy, doesn't she?"

"Yes, she does."

Chapter CLIX

HAD THE NEXT MORNING not been rainy, Sofia might have been in a different mood. The sun is not always the bringer of cheerful thoughts, but at least it allows you to go out and about, and a change of scenery can change one's feelings. When Sofia woke up, the rain was falling hard and steadily, and the clouds were so low and the mist so dense that sea and sky were one.

Tedium inside and out. No distant views upon which to rest her gaze and allow her soul some repose. Sofia put her soul in a cedarwood coffin, which she then placed inside the lead coffin of the dreary day, and allowed herself to feel well and truly dead. She didn't know that the dead think, that a swarm of new ideas rush in to replace the old ones, and that they sally forth full of critical comments about the world, rather like an audience leaving the theater bristling with criticisms of the play and the actors. She, the dead woman, discovered that certain ideas and feelings remained alive. They were a mixed bunch, but all had the same starting point—the letter she had read the previous evening and the memories it had brought back of Carlos Maria.

She thought she had long since driven away that hated figure, but there he was again, smiling and gazing at her and whispering in her ear the same words that the egotistical, infatuated idler had spoken when he invited her to waltz the waltz of adultery with him, before abandoning her in the middle of the dance floor. Other people came in his wake: Maria Benedita, for example, that charmless nonentity, whom she had brought from the countryside to give her a little urban luster, and who then forgot all about the benefits she had given her in order to concentrate solely on her own ambitions. And there was Dona Fernanda, too, the fairy godmother of Maria Benedita's love story, who had deliberately brought that letter yesterday, complete with confidential postscript. She didn't for one moment think that her friend's pleasure in Maria Benedita's happiness was enough to explain her forgetting to conceal the postscript; she was even less inclined to consider whether it was in Dona Fernanda's nature to behave this way. Other thoughts and images followed, then the earlier ones returned, all of them connecting and disconnecting. Among them was another memory from the previous evening. Dona Fernanda's husband had given Sofia a particularly long, admiring look. True, she had been at her very best, her dress emphasizing to perfection her bust, her slender waist, and the gentle curve of her hips—the dress was made of pale foulard silk.

"They call this shade *cor de palha*," said Sofia with a laugh, when Dona Fernanda complimented her on the color soon after she arrived; *cor de palha*—straw-colored, like a gentle reminder of her husband.

It's always hard to disguise one's pleasure at a flattering remark, and Palha beamed proudly, trying to read in the eyes of the other guests the effect of that clear proof of her love. Teófilo also praised the dress, but it was difficult to look at the dress without also looking at its owner's body; this explained his long, admiring look, devoid of lust, it must be said, and that look happened only once, or almost only once. That memory—an uninvited look, an unwanted admiration—intervened again now, while Sofia was mulling over Dona Fernanda's malign behavior.

Carlos Maria, Teófilo... and other names flickered like lightning across the sky of that possibility, as I put it in Chapter CLIV. And now all those names appeared again because the rain continued to fall, and the sky and the sea were still melded into one by the mist. Yes, all those names appeared, along with their respective faces, and even certain nameless faces—the adventitious and the unknown—belonging to men who had once walked past her, sung a hymn of admiration, and received the obolus of a grateful look. Why had she not stopped one of those many men to hear his song and reward him richly? Not that anyone grows rich on oboli, but there are coins of greater worth. Why had she not held on to one of those many elegant and even illustrious names? This unspoken question ran through her veins, her nerves, her brain, and the only response was a feeling of agitation and curiosity.

Chapter CLX

AT THIS POINT the rain eased a little, and a ray of sun managed to break through the mist—one of those moist rays that seems to have fallen from tearful eyes. Sofia thought that there was still time for her to go out for a stroll; she was eager to see things, to walk around, to shake off that torpor, and she waited for the sun to sweep away the rain and regain full control of the sky and the earth; but that great star, realizing that she intended to use him as Diogenes' lamp,* said to that moist ray: "Come back, come back to me, chaste and virtuous ray; I won't allow you to lead her where her desires wish to lead her. Let her love if she so chooses; let her answer love letters—if she receives them and doesn't burn them—but I will not have you serve as her torch, light of my bosom, child of my womb, brother of all my many rays . . ."

And the ray obeyed, withdrawing into the main source, slightly alarmed by the fears expressed by the sun, which had seen so many ordinary and extraordinary things. Then the veil of clouds grew thick again, and darker, and the rain once more began to beat down.

---

* The Greek philosopher Diogenes was said to have carried a lamp during the day in his search for an honest man.

Chapter CLXI

SOFIA RESIGNED HERSELF to staying indoors. Her soul was now as confused and diffuse as the scene outside. All those images and names fused into the one desire: to love. It should be said that when she returned from these vague, obscure states of mind, she did try to drive them away and steer her thoughts on to other matters; but, as with those who fight against sleep and struggle to stay awake, their eyes close each time they open, and open only to close again. Finally, she left the rain and the mist; she was tired, so, to relax a little, she took up the most recent issue of *Revue des Deux Mondes*. One day, while engaged on work for the Alagoas committee, one of Rio's most elegant ladies, the wife of a senator, had asked her:

"Are you reading Feuillet's latest novel in the *Revue des Deux Mondes*?"

"I am," said Sofia. "It's very interesting."

She wasn't in fact reading the novel nor had she even heard of the magazine, but the following day she asked her husband to buy a subscription. She read the first installment, and all the subsequent ones, then talked freely about the other novels she had read or was reading. Having leafed through that current issue and read a short story, Sofia withdrew to her room and lay down on the bed. She had slept badly the night before and so found it easy to fall into a long, deep, dreamless sleep; well, dreamless up until the very end, when she had a nightmare She was lost in that same mist, but this time she was out at sea, lying facedown in a boat and writing a name in the water—Carlos Maria. And there the letters remained, as if engraved on the surface clearly outlined in foam. So far there was nothing very troubling about this, apart from the mystery of it all, but as everyone knows, in dreams mysteries seem perfectly natural. Then the wall of mist was torn asunder, and the owner of the name appeared before Sofia's eyes; he walked toward her, took her in his arms, and spoke tender words, similar to those she had heard Rubião say some months earlier. His words did not distress her, however; on the contrary, she listened with pleasure, half-reclining, as if in a swoon. She was no longer on a boat, but in a carriage, in which she was traveling with her new cousin, their hands clasped, and he was wooing her in words of gold and sandalwood. There was still no reason to feel terrified. The terror came when the carriage stopped, and they found themselves surrounded by a number of masked men, who killed the driver, ripped off the doors, stabbed Carlos Maria, and left him for dead. Then one of the men, who appeared to be the leader, took the dead man's place, removed his mask, and told Sofia not to be afraid, that he loved her a thousand times more than that other man. He grasped her wrists and kissed her, but his kiss was moist with blood and smelled of it. Sofia let out a cry of horror and woke up. Her husband was standing by the bed.

"What's wrong?" he asked.

"Oh!" said Sofia, taking a breath. "Did I scream?"

Palha said nothing; he was staring into space, absorbed in his business affairs. Then Sofia was assailed by a fear: What if she had spoken, murmured some word or someone's name—the name she had written on water? Stretching out her arms, she placed them on her husband's shoulders, closed her fingers around the back of his neck, and, half-happy, half-sad, murmured:

"I dreamed someone was killing you."

Palha was touched. Knowing that she had been afraid for his life, even in a dream, filled him with pity, a pleasurable pity, a very particular emotion, intimate, deep, that made him wish she would have more such nightmares, in which someone would again murder him while she looked on, so that she would again utter that anguished, impassioned cry, in a voice filled with sorrow and fear.

Chapter CLXII

THE FOLLOWING DAY, the sun rose bright and warm, the sky clear and the air fresh. Sofia summoned the carriage and set off to visit friends as a way of compensating for the previous day's enforced seclusion. Just the sight of this beautiful day did her good. She sang as she dressed. The warm welcome she received from the ladies she visited and those she met on Rua do Ouvidor, the hustle and bustle in the streets, the society gossip, the kindness of so many fine, friendly people, were enough to banish from her soul all of yesterday's anxieties.

Chapter CLXIII

AND SO WHAT HAD seemed to be an unstoppable impulse shrank to being a mere whim and, after a few hours, all evil thoughts withdrew to their bedchambers. Were you to ask me if Sofia showed any sign of remorse, I really wouldn't know what to say. There are degrees of resentment and reproach. It is not only with actions that the conscience shifts gradually from novelty to habit, and from fear to indifference. Sins of thought are subject to the same change, and just becoming used to thinking certain things so accustoms us to them that our mind no longer finds them strange or repellent. And in such cases there is always a moral refuge to be found in an appearance of impartiality, which, put more plainly, is the body without blemish.

Chapter CLXIV

A SINGLE INCIDENT troubled Sofia on that pure, bright day, and this was a close encounter with Rubião. She had gone into a bookshop on Rua do Ouvidor to buy a novel; he came in while she was waiting for her change. She quickly turned away and perused the books on the shelf before her—books on anatomy and statistics. She took her change, put it away, and, head down, shot out of the door as fast as an arrow and set off up the street. Her pulse only slowed when she was safely past the corner of Rua dos Ourives.

Days later, as she was entering Dona Fernanda's house, she ran into Rubião in the hallway. She assumed he had just arrived and so prepared to go upstairs with him, albeit with some misgivings; Rubião, however, was just leaving, and they shook hands in friendly fashion and said goodbye.

"Does he come here often?" Sofia asked Dona Fernanda, when she mentioned that she had seen him in the hallway.

"This is the fourth time, the fourth or fifth, but he was only in one of his mad phases on his second visit. Otherwise, he is as you saw him now, very calm and even chatty. There's always something about him, though, that tells you he's not quite right. Did you notice the slightly vague look in his eyes? That's what I mean, and yet he happily joins in the conversation. Believe me, Dona Sofia, that man could be cured. Why don't you ask your husband to do something?"

"Cristiano has mentioned sending him to be examined and treated, but I'll hurry him along."

"Yes, do, because he appears to be great friends with you and your husband."

"Could he have made some inappropriate remark about me in his madness?" Sofia thought. "Should I tell her the truth?"

She decided against this; Rubião's madness would surely be enough to explain any such remarks. She promised that she would ask her husband to make haste, and indeed, she spoke to Palha about it that same evening. His tart response was that it would be "a frightful bore." And he wondered why Dona Fernanda had brought the subject up again. Why didn't *she* deal with it? It would be a real drag having to take care of Rubião, go with him to the doctor and no doubt pick him up, too, not to mention managing what little money the fellow still had, thus becoming in effect his trustee, as Senhor Teófilo had suggested. It would be the very devil of a nuisance.

"I have a heavy enough burden to carry as it is, Sofia. And what would we end up doing? Bringing him here to live with us? I don't think so. Or arranging for him to live somewhere else? In a sanatorium, perhaps . . . Yes, but would they take him? I couldn't possibly send him to the mental hospital at Praia Vermelha . . . Who would pay? Did you promise her you'd talk to me about it?"

"I did, and I promised that you would take care of it," said Sofia with a smile. "It might not turn out to be as difficult as you think."

Sofia was very insistent. She had been deeply impressed by Dona Fernanda's compassion; there was something so distinguished and noble about her, and she felt that if Dona Fernanda—who had met Rubião only recently and was not even a close friend of his—took such an interest in him, then it was only right and proper that they should be equally generous.

Chapter CLXV

IT WAS ALL DONE very easily and discreetly. Palha rented a small house in nearby Rua do Príncipe, close to the sea, where he installed Rubião, along with a few bits of furniture and his canine friend. Rubião accepted the arrangement quite happily, indeed even enthusiastically when his madness returned and he believed himself to be living in the Château de Saint-Cloud.

Rubião's regular visitors did not feel the same; the news of this move seemed to them more like a decree of exile. They felt completely at home with everything in his former house, the garden, the railings, the flower beds, the stone steps, the view of the bay. They had the whole routine down pat. They would enter, leave their hats, then go and wait in the drawing room. They had entirely forgotten that this was someone else's house or that they were favored guests. Then there were the neighbors. Every one of Rubião's friends was so accustomed to seeing the locals, the familiar morning faces and the evening faces, some of whom would even greet them as if they really were their neighbors. There was nothing to be done. They would go now into Babylon like the exiles of Zion. Wherever the Euphrates was, they would find willow trees on which to hang their harps, or, rather, hatstands on which to hang their hats. The difference between them and the prophets was that, after only a week, they would once again pick up their harps and play them with the same elegance and energy as before; they would sing the old hymns, as new as on the very first day, and Babel would become their new Zion, lost and regained.

"Our friend needs to rest for a while," Palha told them in Botafogo, on the eve of the move. "You must have noticed that he's not been well; he sometimes forgets himself, becomes disturbed, confused, and he will receive treatment, but for now he needs to rest. I've rented him a small house, but it may be that he'll have to move to a sanatorium of some sort."

The friends listened, astonished. One of them, Pio, recovering from the shock more quickly than the others, agreed that this was something that should have been done some time ago, but to do so required someone with a decisive influence over Rubião's mind.

"I often said to him, politely of course, that he really should consult a doctor because it seemed to me that he had something wrong with his stomach . . . That was a roundabout way of telling him he needed help, you understand. But he always said that he was fine, that he had no problems with his digestion . . . 'But you're eating less,' I would say, 'on some days you hardly eat anything; you've grown thinner and your color's not good . . .' I couldn't tell him the truth. I even consulted a doctor myself, but our dear friend Rubião refused to see him."

The other four nodded to confirm the truth of this outright lie; this was all anyone could expect of them and all they could manage after the blow they had just received. They concluded by asking for the number of the new house so that they could go and visit Rubião. Poor man! When they were leaving and saying goodbye to each other, an unexpected phenomenon occurred: they could hardly bear to part. Not that they were bound by friendship or mutual esteem; their respective self-interest made them more like rivals. However, the habit of seeing each other every day at lunch and supper and always at the same table had somehow welded them together; they had, out of necessity, learned to put up with each other and time had made them mutually indispensable. In short, each man's eyes would feel the absence of their companions' faces, gestures, side-whiskers, mustaches, bald pates, personal tics, and ways of eating, speaking, and being, to which they had all become accustomed. It was more than a separation, it was an amputation.

Chapter CLXVI

WHEN RUBIÃO NOTICED that his visitors did not accompany him to the new house, he sent for them, but none came, and during the first few weeks their absence filled our friend with sadness. His "family" had abandoned him. Rubião wondered if he had perhaps wounded them in some way, by word or deed, but he could think of nothing.

Chapter CLXVII

"I'VE TALKED TO the man and he did have some crazy ideas. However, while I may not be an alienist myself, I believe he could be cured . . . Shall I tell you an interesting discovery I have made?"

"You think he could be cured, then?" asked Dona Fernanda, ignoring Dr. Falcão's question.

Dr. Falcão was both a deputy and a doctor, a friend of the family, an erudite man, skeptical and cold. Dona Fernanda had asked him to examine Rubião shortly after our friend moved to the house in Rua do Príncipe.

"Yes, I think so, as long as he receives regular treatment. It may be that there's no family history of the illness. Send him to a specialist. But don't you want to know about my interesting discovery?"

"What's that?"

"A person of your acquaintance may have played some part in his illness," he replied, smiling.

"Who?"

"Dona Sofia."

"But how?"

"He spoke of her with great enthusiasm, and told me she was the most splendid woman in the world, and that he had made her a duchess because he couldn't make her Empress; were he pressed, though, he was capable of doing as his uncle had done, and divorce his wife so as to marry Dona Sofia. I concluded that he had been in love with the young woman, and if you'd heard the familiar way he spoke of her, Sofia this and Sofia that . . . Forgive me, but I think they were lovers . . ."

"No!"

"Dona Fernanda, I really do believe they were lovers. Why are you so surprised? I hardly know her, and it seems you haven't known her for long, either, nor are you close. They may have been in love and so very passionately that . . . Let's assume that she, one day, banished him from her house . . . True he does suffer from a *folie de grandeur*, but that might explain it . . ."

Dona Fernanda averted her gaze, annoyed even to hear such a theory, and, given the delicacy of the matter, she avoided talking about it further. She thought his suspicions were quite without foundation, absurd, improbable; she would never believe in that hypothetical love affair even if Rubião himself told her about it. He was, after all, mad. And even if he wasn't, she probably wouldn't believe it either. No, she wouldn't. She couldn't believe that Sofia had been in love with that man, not because of him, but because she herself was so proper and so pure. It was impossible. She was tempted to defend Sofia, and yet, however well she knew Dr. Falcão, she again drew back and instead repeated the question she had asked earlier:

"You think he can be cured, then?"

"Yes, but you need someone else to examine him. As you know, in these matters it's always best to consult a specialist."

When Dr. Falcão left shortly afterward, he smiled to himself at Dona Fernanda's refusal to accept his hypothesis. "There was definitely something," he thought, "he's good-looking, and although he's no dandy, he's attractive and has a fiery look in his eyes. Yes, there's definitely something . . ." And in his head he repeated a few of the things Rubião had said, and as he recalled the expression on his face and the tender tone in which he spoke, his suspicions only grew in weight. "Yes, there was definitely something . . ." He was quite certain that they had been in love, and Dona Fernanda's opposition seemed to him ingenuous—unless that had been her way of changing the subject and not talking about it. Yes, that's what it was . . .

At this point, the deputy stopped in his tracks, assailed by a new suspicion. After a few brief moments, though, he shook his head as if to deny it, as if he found it too absurd, and continued walking. The suspicion, however, proved stubborn, and any suspicion that takes up residence in a man's mind pays no heed to his head or to his gestures. "Who knows, perhaps Dona Fernanda sighed for him too? Could her interest in him be just a prolongation of that love?" Still more questions arose and found an affirmative response inside Dr. Falcão's mind. He resisted nonetheless, well, he was a friend of the family, had great respect for Dona Fernanda and knew her to be honest, but—he carried on thinking—it could have been a secret love, unspoken, possibly provoked by Dona Sofia's passion. Such temptations do occur. Leprosy poisons even the purest blood, and one pitiful bacillus can destroy the most robust of organisms.

His hesitant resistance gave way gradually to the idea of possibility, probability, and then certainty. He knew of other acts of charity performed by Dona Fernanda, but this was different. The special interest she was taking in a man who was not a regular visitor to the house or an old friend, not a relative, a dependent, a colleague of her husband's, or anything related to their domestic life through acquaintances, blood, or habit, could only be explained by some secret motive. Probably love; the curiosity of an honest woman, which can degenerate into vice and remorse. She would certainly have stepped back before anything happened, but would have been left with a kind of morbid sympathy ... And beyond that, who knows?

Chapter CLXVIII

AND BEYOND THAT, who knows? Dr. Falcão repeated these words to himself the following morning. A night's sleep had not dissipated his suspicions. And beyond that, who knows? No, it wouldn't be just some rather soppy sentiment. Without knowing Shakespeare, he amended Hamlet: "There are more things in heaven and earth, Horatio, than are dreamt of in your *philanthropy*." The hand of love was definitely there. And he neither mocked nor condemned it. As I said, he was a skeptic, but since he was also discreet, he told no one else of his conclusions.

Chapter CLXIX

THE RETURN OF Carlos Maria and his wife interrupted Dona Fernanda's preoccupation with Rubião. She went aboard the ship to welcome them, then drove them to Tijuca, where an old family friend of Carlos Maria's had rented and furnished a house on his orders. Sofia did not go onboard; she sent the coupé to wait for them on the quayside, but Dona Fernanda had already arranged a calèche to transport the happy couple, along with herself and Palha, to their new home. Sofia went to visit the new arrivals later that afternoon.

Dona Fernanda was brimming over with contentment. According to Maria Benedita's letters, the couple were very happy, but Dona Fernanda did not immediately see this confirmed in the eyes and manners of the couple. Maria Benedita could not hold back her tears when she embraced her friend, nor could Dona Fernanda, and they held each other close like two sisters. The following day, Dona Fernanda asked Maria Benedita if she and her husband were happy, and when Maria Benedita said that they were, she clasped her hands and gazed at her, speechless. All she could do was repeat her question:

"Are you happy?"

"We are," said Maria Benedita.

"You don't know how pleased I am to know that. Not just because I would feel guilty if you didn't enjoy the happiness I had hoped to give you, but because it's always so lovely to see other people happy. Does he love you as much as he did on the first day?"

"I think he may love me even more, because I adore him."

Dona Fernanda did not understand these words. *I think he may love me even more, because I adore him.* It did not seem quite logical, and called for another slightly amended version of Hamlet: "There are more things in heaven and earth, Horatio, than are dreamt of in your *dialectic*." Maria Benedita began telling her about their travels, unpicking all her impressions and memories; and when her husband came over to join them shortly afterward, she resorted to his memory in order to fill any lacunae.

"What happened then, Carlos Maria?"

Carlos Maria would remember, explain, or rectify, but rather reluctantly, almost impatiently. He sensed that Maria Benedita had just been telling her friend how happy she was, and he could barely disguise the unpleasant effect this had on him. Why bother saying she was happy with him when she couldn't possibly be anything else? And why broadcast his affectionate words and gestures, which were, after all, the merciful actions of a great, kindly god?

He had only agreed to return to Rio de Janeiro to please Maria Benedita. She wanted to have their child there, and he had given in to her, with difficulty, but he had given in. Why with difficulty? That's hard to explain, still less understand. On the subject of pregnancy, Carlos Maria had some very personal and rather unusual ideas, ideas he kept strictly to himself. He thought it immodest, almost disreputable, of nature, to make human gestation such a public phenomenon, there for everyone to see, growing larger and larger to the point of deformity. This explained his desire for solitude, mystery, and absence. He would happily live out the final days of her pregnancy inside some solitary house high up on a hill, cut off from the world, and from whence his wife would one day descend with her babe in her arms and divinity in her eyes.

He said nothing of this to his wife. It would mean an argument, and he disliked arguments; he preferred to give in. Maria Benedita's feelings were, of course, completely different: she considered herself to be a chaste, divine temple, in which there lived a god, the child of another god. Her pregnancy had been at times tedious, painful, uncomfortable, but she had done her best to conceal this from her husband, and besides, it only made her future child seem still more precious. She put up with any discomforts with resignation, even joy, since it was what she had to go through in order to bear fruit. She happily accepted the duty of the species and silently repeated the words of Mary of Nazareth: "Behold, I am the handmaid of the Lord; let it be unto me according to thy word."

Chapter CLXX

"WHAT'S WRONG?" Maria Benedita asked her husband as soon as they were alone.
"Nothing. Why?"
"You seemed to be annoyed."
"No, I wasn't."
"Yes, you were," she insisted.

Carlos Maria smiled, but said nothing. Maria Benedita already knew that strangely inexpressive smile, pale and superficial, neither tender nor tetchy. She didn't ask again, but bit her lip and withdrew.

She sat for some time in her bedroom, pondering what that wan, silent smile could mean; it was clearly a sign that something had annoyed him, and she must be the cause. She went over the whole conversation, every one of her words and gestures, and she could find nothing to explain Carlos Maria's coolness or whatever it was. Perhaps she had talked too much, which she always did when she was happy, taking her heart in her hands and sharing it out among friends and strangers. Carlos Maria disapproved of such generosity, because it made his emotional and domestic state seem like some big lottery prize he had won, and because it seemed to him banal and vulgar. Maria Benedita remembered that during the time they spent among the Brazilian "colony" in Paris, she had more than once experienced the aftereffect of her overly chatty nature. But surely Dona Fernanda did not belong in the same category? Was she not the author of their happiness? She rejected this hypothesis and searched for another. Failing to find one, she returned to the first, and, as always happened, she decided that her husband was right. However close a friend Dona Fernanda was, and however grateful she was to her, she shouldn't tell her the details of their domestic life, that was mere frivolousness on her part . . .

Nausea interrupted her thoughts at this point. Nature was reminding her of a *raison d'état*—or *raison d'espèce*—far more urgent and more important than her husband's irritation. She gave in to necessity, but only moments later she was standing next to Carlos Maria and wrapping her right arm around his neck. He was sitting down, reading an English magazine; he took her hand, which was resting on his chest, and finished the page he was on.

"Do you forgive me?" she asked, when he put down the magazine. "I promise I'll be less of a chatterbox in the future."

Smiling and nodding, Carlos Maria clasped her hand in both of his, and it was as if he had shone a great wave of light on her; happiness penetrated her very soul. You might almost think that the fetus itself reflected back that feeling and showered blessings on its father.

Chapter CLXXI

"PERFECT! THAT'S WHAT I like to see!" boomed a voice from the veranda.

Maria Benedita immediately drew away from her husband. Three doors separated the veranda from the drawing room, and one of those doors stood open. This was where the voice had come from, and there was Rubião's beaming face peering in. This was the first time they had seen him since their return. Carlos Maria remained seated and simply looked at him gravely, waiting. And the beaming face—complete with a finely waxed mustache—laughed, looking from one to the other, then said again:

"Perfect! That's what I like to see!"

Rubião entered the room, holding out his hand, which they received rather coolly; then he heaped flattering, adulatory words on Maria Benedita, she was so graceful, he so elegant; he noted, too, that they both bore the name Maria, which must be a kind of predestination, and finally, he announced the collapse of the government.

"The government?" Carlos Maria could not help but ask.

"They're talking of nothing else in town. Now, since you haven't offered me a chair, I'm going to sit down without asking if I may," he went on, taking hold of the cane he had been carrying under his arm and resting his hands on the handle. "Yes, the cabinet have all resigned. I'm going to arrange another one. Palha, our Palha—your cousin Palha—and you, of course, if you want, will be ministers. I need a good cabinet, full of strong, supportive people, willing to lay down their lives for me. I will summon Morny, Pio, Camacho, Rouher, and Major Siqueira. You remember the major, don't you, senhora? I think he'll be Minister of War. I don't know a better man for dealing with military matters."

Feeling bored and impatient, Maria Benedita was pacing up and down the room, waiting for her husband to tell her what to do; with a glance he said that she should leave, and she gladly made her excuses and left. When she had gone, Rubião praised her again—a flower, he said—then corrected himself with a chuckle: "No, two flowers, for I believe there are now two flowers, not just one, God bless them!" Carlos Maria held out his hand as a signal to Rubião that he should say his goodbyes.

"My dear sir . . ."

"May I include you in the cabinet?" asked Rubião.

Receiving no response, he took this as a yes and promised him an interesting position. The major would be Minister of War and Camacho would be Minister of Justice. Did he not know them? "Two great men, Camacho even greater than the major." And in following Carlos Maria, who was heading toward the door, Rubião was leaving without realizing that he was; but he did not leave at once. On the veranda, before going down the steps, he recounted various facts about the war. For example, he had restored Germany to the Germans; that was the kind and politic thing to do. He had already given Venice to the Italians. He didn't need more territory, apart from the Rhine provinces, of course, but there was plenty of time to get those.

"My dear sir," Carlos Maria said again, holding out his hand.

He said goodbye and closed the door; Rubião uttered a few more words, then went down the steps. Maria Benedita, who was waiting in the background, came over to her husband, clasped his hand, and stood watching as Rubião crossed the garden. He did not proceed in a straight line, nor was he in a hurry, nor was he silent; he stopped now and then to gesticulate or pick up a twig, or gaze up at a thousand things in the air, all of them more graceful than the lady of the house, and more elegant than the master of the house. They watched our friend through the glass, and when he made a particularly grotesque gesture, Maria Benedita could not help but burst out laughing; Carlos Maria, meanwhile, watched serenely.

Chapter CLXXII

"IF THE GOVERNMENT really has fallen," she said, "guess who's going to be a minister?"

"Who?" Carlos Maria asked with his eyes.

"Your cousin Teófilo. Nanã told me he's had hopes in that direction for a while, and that's why he stayed in Rio this year. He had a feeling, or perhaps there was already talk of a collapse, no, perhaps he just had a feeling. I can't quite remember what she told me now, but apparently he's joining the cabinet."

"It's possible."

"Look, there's Rubião. He's stopped stock-still and is gazing up at something. Maybe he's waiting for a cab or a carriage. He used to have a carriage. No, he's walking . . . off he goes."

Chapter CLXXIII

"SO TEÓFILO'S GOING TO be a minister!" cried Carlos Maria.

Then, a moment later:

"I think he'll do a good job. Would you like it if I were a minister too?"

"If that's what you wanted, what could I do?"

"Meaning that if it was up to you, you'd rather I wasn't?" asked Carlos Maria.

"What do you want me to say?"

Laughing, he said:

"Admit that you would still adore me even if I were a mere orderly to a minister."

"Of course!" she cried, throwing her arms around his neck.

Carlos Maria stroked her hair and murmured gravely:

"Bernadotte was king and Bonaparte was emperor. Would you like to be the queen mother of Sweden?"*

Maria Benedita didn't understand the question, and he didn't explain. To do so, he would have had to say that she possibly carried in her womb another Bernadotte; however, such a supposition implied a desire, and that desire implied an admission of inferiority. Carlos Maria again stroked his wife's hair, a gesture that seemed to mean: "Maria, you made the right choice . . ." And she seemed to understand.

"Yes, yes, I would!"

Her husband smiled and went back to reading his English magazine. Leaning on the back of his armchair, she ran her fingers through his hair, very gently so as not to disturb him. He carried on reading, reading, reading. Maria Benedita's caresses gradually slowed and ceased entirely when she slowly withdrew her fingers and finally left the room, where Carlos Maria continued to read an essay by Sir Charles Little, MP, on the famous statue of Narcissus in the Museum of Naples.

---

* Jean Bernadotte (1763–1844), one of Napoleon Bonaparte's loyal lieutenants, was made King of Sweden in 1818. Unlike Bonaparte's, his dynasty proved long-lived.

Chapter CLXXIV

WHEN RUBIÃO WENT to Dona Fernanda's house later that afternoon, the servant told him that he couldn't come in. His mistress was feeling unwell; his master was with her, and they were apparently waiting for the doctor. Our friend did not insist and left.

In fact, the opposite was true: it was the master who was ill and the mistress who was sitting with him; however, the servant could not alter the message he had been given. Another servant, it's true, thought that the master was ill and not her, because he had seen him arrive home looking very dejected. Up above, in their bedroom, there was the occasional sound of voices, now loud, now soft, interspersed with silences. A young maid, who had tiptoed up to the room, came down saying that she had heard her master complaining; the mistress must be terribly upset. Down below, muttered conversations, cocked ears, conjecturings; it was noted that no one upstairs called for water or medicine or even soup. The table was laid, the servant in his livery, the cook proud and impatient... It was one of his best suppers too!

What was wrong? Teófilo looked as dejected as when he had arrived; he was sitting on a sofa in his shirtsleeves and staring into space. Sitting next to him, holding his hand, was Dona Fernanda begging him to calm down, insisting it really wasn't that important. And she leaned in closer to peer into his face, asking him to look at her and to rest his head on her shoulder.

"No, stop it," murmured her husband.

"It's just not that important, Teófilo! Do you really want to be a minister? Is it worth taking on a job that won't last long and, while it does, will be full of unpleasantnesses, insults, hard work, and to what end? Isn't it preferable to lead a quiet life? Yes, it is unfair when you've worked so hard, but is it such a loss? Come on, my love, cheer up. Let's go and have supper."

Teófilo was biting his lip and tugging at one of his side-whiskers. He had heard none of what his wife had said, neither her exhortations nor her consolations. He heard instead the conversations that had taken place the previous night and that morning, too, with the political lists being drawn up, various names mentioned, some rejected and others accepted. Not one of those lists included his name, even though he had spoken to many people about the true nature of the situation. He was listened to intently by some, impatiently by others. Once, the glasses worn by the organizer of the meeting seemed to gaze at him interrogatively, but that look proved brief and illusory. Teófilo was reliving the intensity of all those hours and places—he remembered those who shot him sideways glances, those who smiled at him, those who wore the same expression on their faces as he did. By the end, he had stopped speaking, his last hopes burning out in his eyes like an oil lamp in the dawn light. He heard the names of the ministers and was obliged to agree that they were excellent choices, but what a struggle it had been to stay silent! He feared they would notice his dejection or indignation, but his efforts to disguise his feelings only made them more obvious. He grew pale, his hands trembled.

Chapter CLXXV

"COME ON, LET'S GO down to supper," Dona Fernanda said again.
Teófilo slapped his knee with his hand and stood up, spitting

out a few angry words, pacing up and down, stamping his foot, and uttering threats. Dona Fernanda could do nothing to quell the violence of this new rage, she just hoped it would prove short-lived, which it did; Teófilo went over to an armchair, shaking his head, and slumped down in it. Dona Fernanda took a chair and sat down next to him.

"You're quite right, Teófilo, but you have to be a man about this. You're young and strong, you still have a future ahead of you, possibly a great future. Who knows, by joining the cabinet now, you might lose out later on. You'll join another one. Sometimes what appears to be a misfortune turns out to be a blessing."

Teófilo squeezed her hand gratefully.

"It's all treachery and intrigue," he murmured, gazing at her. "I know this rabble. If I were to tell you everything that went on . . . but what would be the point? I prefer to forget all about it. I'm not angry because I haven't been given some miserable ministerial post," he went on after a few moments. "They're worthless anyway. Anyone with enough talent, who's prepared to work hard, can do without them and show he's better than that. Most of those people, Nanã, aren't fit to tie my shoelaces. I know that and so do they. A bunch of intriguers, the lot of them. Where would they find more honesty, more loyalty, and more passion for the fight? Who wrote more articles for the press while we were out of power? Their excuse is that cabinets are chosen by the Emperor himself . . . Oh, how I'd like to have a word with the Emperor!"

"Teófilo!"

"I would say to him: 'Your Majesty, you have no idea what it's like, this brand of politics, carried on in corridors and side rooms. You want the best men working on your committees, but it's the mediocrities who get the jobs . . . Merit counts for nothing.' That's what I'll say to him one day, possibly tomorrow."

He fell silent. Then, after a long pause, he stood up and went into his study, which was next to their bedroom; his wife followed. It was dark by then and so he lit the gas lamp and wandered around the room, his eyes veiled in melancholy. There were four large bookcases full of books, reports, budgets, and treasury accounts. The desk was very tidy. Three tall, open cabinets were home to his manuscripts, notes, memoranda, estimates, jottings, all arranged in methodical, carefully labeled piles: *extraordinary loans, additional loans, war loans, navy loans, loans from 1868, railways, internal debt, fiscal year '61–'62, '62–'63, '63–'64*, etc. This was where he worked day and night, adding and subtracting, gathering facts for his speeches and reports, because he was a member of three parliamentary committees, and generally did his own work plus that of his six colleagues; they simply listened to what he had to say and added their signature. When the reports were very long, one of them would sign without even bothering to listen.

"You're the expert, and that's enough for me," he would say, "just hand me the pen."

The whole room exuded attention, care, and assiduous, meticulous, useful work. On the wall, hanging from hooks, were the week's newspapers, which were then taken down, stored away, and finally bound together every six months as a source of reference. His speeches, printed in pamphlet form, stood in a row on a shelf. Not a single painting or bust or ornament, nothing to engage the eye or to admire—everything unadorned, exact, administrative.

"What's the point of all this?" Teófilo asked his wife after sadly surveying the scene. "Long, weary hours of work, sometimes through the night . . . No one could say this was the study of an idle man; work gets done here. You know how hard I work. But to what end?"

"Work consoles you," she murmured.

He retorted bitterly:

"Some consolation! No, I'm done with all this, I'm having nothing more to do with it. In the Chamber, they all consult me, even the ministers, because they know I really apply myself to administrative matters. And what is my reward? To turn up here in May and applaud our new lords and masters?"

"You don't need to applaud anyone," said his wife gently. "Would you like to do something to please me? Let's go to Europe, in March or April, and not come back for a year. You can write to the Speaker from wherever we happen to be—Warsaw, for example, I'd love to go to Warsaw—and tell him you're taking a sabbatical," she went on, smiling and tenderly cupping his face in her hands. "Say yes, and I'll write to Rio Grande today, because the mail boat leaves tomorrow. Are we agreed? Shall we go to Warsaw?"

"Don't joke, Nanã. This is no joking matter."

"I'm perfectly serious. I've been wanting to suggest such a trip for a long time now; you need a rest from all this infernal paperwork. It's too much, Teófilo! You scarcely have time to visit friends, let alone go on holiday. You barely speak. Our children hardly see their father, because no one is allowed in here when you're working. You need a rest; please, take a year off. I'm serious. Let's go to Europe in March."

"No, that's not possible," he managed to say.

"Why not?"

It really was impossible. It was like asking him to leave behind his own skin. Politics was everything. Yes, politics went on elsewhere, too, but what was that to him? Teófilo knew nothing about what went on outside Brazil, apart from the names of half a dozen economists and the country's debt to the banks in London. Nevertheless, he thanked his wife for her kind suggestion:

"You're very good to me."

And a vaguely hopeful note restored to his voice the gentleness it had lost during that great moral crisis. The papers in the room breathed life into him. He gazed upon that mass of documents much as a farmer gazes upon a field that has been fertilized and sown with seeds. Eventually they would germinate, and all his hard work would be rewarded; one day, sooner or later, the seeds would sprout and the tree would bear fruit. This was precisely what his wife had said more directly and more eloquently, but only now did he see the possibility of a harvest. He felt vexed by his own angry, indignant, despairing outbursts, his complaints of only a short time earlier. He tried to laugh, but couldn't. Over supper and coffee, he talked to his children, who went to bed later than usual that night. Nuno, who was already in school, where he had heard about the change of government, told his father that he wanted to be a minister. Teófilo grew serious.

"My son," he said, "choose to be anything but a minister."

"They say it's really smashing, Papa, they say you get to ride around in a carriage with a soldier on the back."

"I'll give you your own carriage."

"Were you ever a minister, Papa?"

Teófilo again attempted a smile and glanced at his wife, who seized the opportunity to send the children off to bed.

"Yes, I have been a minister," said Teófilo, planting a kiss on Nuno's head. "But I don't want to be anymore, it's a horrible job and hard work too. You will be a chaplain."

"What's a chaplain?"

"Chaplain means bed," responded Dona Fernanda. "Time to go to sleep, Nuno."

Chapter CLXXVI

AT LUNCH THE next day, Teófilo received a letter from an orderly.

"An orderly?"

"Yes, senhor, he says he was sent by the president of the Council of Ministers."

Teófilo opened the letter with trembling hands. What could it be? He had seen the list of new ministers in the newspaper, the cabinet was full, and the names were as previously announced. What could it be? Sitting opposite her husband, Dona Fernanda tried to read on his face the contents of the letter. She saw a light dawn; she saw on his lips a repressed smile of satisfaction, or at least hope.

"Tell him to wait," Teófilo told the servant.

He went into his study and returned a few minutes later with the reply. He sat down at the table again, but said nothing, allowing time for the servant to give his response to the orderly. This time, as expected, he heard the sound of horse's hooves, then heard it galloping down the street, and he felt better.

"Read it," he said.

Dona Fernanda read the letter, in which the president of the Council of Ministers invited Teófilo to go and see him at two o'clock that afternoon.

"But the cabinet—"

"Is full," he said, interrupting her, "the ministers have all been appointed."

He didn't entirely believe what he was saying. He imagined there was some last-minute vacancy and an urgent need to fill it.

"It must be some policy meeting, or perhaps he wants to discuss the budget with me—or to ask me to write some report or other."

He said this in order to distract his wife, but immediately plunged into gloom again when he saw that these invented hypotheses were all too probable; a couple of minutes later, though, the butterflies of hope were fluttering about him again, a whole cloud of them, filling the air.

Chapter CLXXVII

DONA FERNANDA WAITED as anxiously as if she herself were going to be appointed minister, and as if the news would bring her something other than bitter and vexatious problems. As long as her husband was happy, that was all that mattered. Teófilo returned at half past five. She could tell from his expression that he was pleased. She ran to meet him and clasp his hands.

"What happened?"

"Poor Nanã! We're going to have to pack our bags again. The marquis asked me straight-out to accept the governorship of one of our most important provinces. He hadn't been able to give me a cabinet position, although he had, in fact, reserved a place for me, but he wanted, indeed begged, me to share in the government's political and administrative responsibilities by taking on a governorship. He couldn't possibly do without a man of my prestige (his words), and he hopes that I'll also assume the post of majority leader in the Chamber. What do you say?"

"We'd better pack our bags," said Dona Fernanda.

"Could I have said no?"

"No."

"No, I couldn't. You can't refuse to work with a government

who are on the same side as you; if you did, you might as well leave politics. And he couldn't have been nicer; I already knew he was an excellent fellow, but he was so friendly and affable, you can't imagine. He wants me to go to a meeting with the ministers and a few friends, not many, half a dozen at most. He's already given me his program for government, in strict confidence, of course . . ."

"When do we leave?"

"I don't know. I'm meeting him again tomorrow night at eight . . . I did the right thing in accepting, didn't I?"

"Of course."

"Yes, because had I refused, I would have been in for a lot of criticism, and quite right too. In politics, the first thing you lose is your liberty. If you prefer, you can stay here; the next session of parliament will start in five—or even four—months from now, so I'll barely have time to arrive and have a look around before I'm back."

Chapter CLXXVIII

DONA FERNANDA ACCEPTED this proposal, as it would avoid any interruption to their son's education, and they would, after all, only be apart for four months. Teófilo set off a few days later. Very early on the morning of his departure, he went to bid farewell to his study. He took one last look at his books, reports, budgets, manuscripts, the part of his family who spoke only to him and were of interest only to him. He had tied all his papers and pamphlets into bundles so that nothing would go astray, and he gave detailed instructions to his wife. Standing in the middle of the room, he surveyed the shelves and left a little of his heart on all of them. He said goodbye to his household gods and friends with genuine regret. For Dona Fernanda, who was standing next to him, that farewell lasted only ten minutes, for Teófilo it lasted many years.

"Don't worry, I'll look after them. I'll dust them myself every day."

Teófilo gave her a kiss . . . Another woman would have received that kiss rather glumly, seeing how much he loved his books, possibly more than he loved her. Dona Fernanda, however, felt very fortunate.

Chapter CLXXIX

RUBIÃO DID NOT RETURN to Dona Fernanda's house after that government crisis; he knew nothing about Teófilo's promotion to governor, nor that he had already set off to his new post. He lived alone with his dog and his servant, with no major crises nor any long intervals between crises. The servant did a decent job, and received generous tips and, quite often, the title of marquis. Otherwise, he amused himself. When he came upon his master talking to the walls, he would eavesdrop on the dialogue, because Rubião took on both roles, responding as if the walls had asked him a question. At night, the servant would go and chat with his friends in the neighborhood.

"How's the crazy fool doing?"

"Very well. Today he asked the dog to sing and the dog barked and barked, and he just loved it, and made such a big deal out of it. When he's having one of his turns, he behaves like someone who rules the world. Just yesterday, over lunch, he said to me: 'Marquis Raimundo, I'd like you to . . .' and then rambled on about something or other, but I couldn't understand a word. In the end, though, he gave me ten *tostões*."

"Which you quickly pocketed . . ."

"You bet!"

When Rubião emerged from his delirium, that whole garrulous phantasmagoria became, briefly, a secret sadness. His conscious mind, which retained remnants of that previous state, struggled to detach itself from them. It was like a man's painful ascent from the abyss, clambering up the walls, grazing his shins, tearing his nails, struggling to reach the top and not fall in and be lost again. Then he would go and visit friends, some new, some old, like the major and Senhor Camacho, for example.

For some time, Camacho had been less talkative. Even politics did not provide enough matter for his former tirades. When he saw Rubião appear at his office door, he would make a face, which he immediately suppressed, but Rubião noticed the change and wondered long and hard if he had unwittingly offended him or if Camacho was beginning to find him boring. And to dispel the tedium or those hypothetical feelings of resentment, he would smile and speak very softly, and leave long respectful pauses, in the hope that Camacho would say something. In vain he appealed to the Marquis of Paraná, whose portrait was still there on the wall; he repeated the things Camacho used to say about him: The great marquis! The consummate statesman! Camacho would nod his head while continuing to write, consulting his law reports and textbooks on legal procedure, quoting, scoring out, apologizing. He had a brief to prepare for that day. He broke off to go over to the bookshelves.

"Excuse me . . ."

Rubião drew in his legs to allow him to pass; Camacho took down a volume of *Royal Ordinances* and leafed through it, then leafed through it again, randomly jumping ahead and turning back, not actually looking for anything, purely as a way of getting rid of his importunate visitor; alas, the importunate visitor stayed for that very reason, and they exchanged covert glances. Camacho picked up his brief again. In order to read while sitting down, he leaned over to the left to catch the light, thus turning his back on Rubião.

"It's dark in here," Rubião remarked.

But he received no reply, so intent was the lawyer on his reading, or so it seemed. Perhaps his presence really was importunate, thought our friend. He studied Camacho's hard, serious face, and the way he gripped his pen in order to continue writing that interminable brief. Twenty minutes more of absolute silence. Then Rubião saw him put down the pen, straighten his back, stretch his arms, and rub his eyes. He said earnestly:

"You must be tired."

Camacho nodded and prepared to carry on writing. Then our friend stood up and took advantage of that pause to say his goodbyes.

"I'll come back when you're not so busy."

He held out his hand, which Camacho shook rather halfheartedly before returning to his papers. Rubião went down the stairs, bemused and hurt by his illustrious friend's coldness. What had he done to deserve that?

Chapter CLXXX

ON THAT OCCASION, he had the good fortune to run into Major Siqueira.

"I was just about to come to your house," Rubião said. "Are you going there now?"

"I am, but we're not in the same house anymore. We've moved to Rua da Princesa, over in Cajueiros . . ."

"Well, wherever it is, let's go."

Rubião was in great need of a piece of string to tether him to reality, because his mind was beginning to succumb to the vertigo of madness. However, he spoke in such a sane, sensible way that the major, assuming Rubião was in full possession of his faculties, said:

"I have a very important piece of news to tell you."

"What is it?"

"It will have to wait until we get home."

They arrived home, which was a two-story house; Dona Tonica came to open the gate for them. She was wearing a new dress and earrings.

"Now take a good look at her," said the major, playfully pinching her chin.

Dona Tonica drew back in embarrassment.

"I'm looking," said Rubião.

"Well, isn't it obvious that she's about to be married?"

"Really? Well, congratulations!"

"Yes, it's true, she's going to be married. It took a bit of work, but she made it. She's found a fiancé who simply adores her, as all fiancés do; when I was young, oh, how I adored my dear late wife, you've never seen the like of it . . . Yes, she's going to be married. It took a bit of doing, but she made it. He's a serious fellow, middle-aged; he comes and spends the evenings with us. In the morning, when he walks by on his way to the office, I think he knocks on her window, or else she waits for him; I pretend not to notice . . ."

Dona Tonica shook her head, but smiled in a way that seemed to say yes, it was true. She was so lively! She had quite forgotten that she had once set her sights on Rubião, that he was one of her last hopes, indeed, the very last. They had gone into the living room;

Dona Tonica went over to the window, then wandered aimlessly back, her head held high, quite contented with life.

"He's a good man," said the major, "a kind man... Tonica, go and fetch his picture, go on, go and fetch your fiancé..."

Dona Tonica did as asked. The picture was a photograph of a middle-aged man with short, sparse hair, staring out in some alarm, his face gaunt, his neck thin, and his jacket tightly buttoned up.

"What do you think?"

"Excellent."

Dona Tonica took the photo from him and gazed at it for a few moments, then looked away and sat down, while her imagination set off to wait for Rodrigues. That was his name. He was shorter than her—which the photo did not show—and worked for the Ministry of War. He was a widower, with two children, one of whom was an army cadet, while the other, who was only twelve, had tuberculosis and was doomed to die. Never mind. He was her fiancé, and every night, before going to bed, Dona Tonica would kneel before the image of Our Lady, her patron saint, to thank her and pray for happiness. She was already dreaming of having a son, who would be called Álvaro.

Chapter CLXXXI

RUBIÃO LISTENED in silence to the major's ramblings. The marriage was to take place in a month and a half; her fiancé had to put the finishing touches to his house, he was not wealthy, but lived on his salary and sometimes resorted to taking out loans. The house was the one he currently lived in, and there would be no need to buy new or expensive furniture, but there are always a few odds and ends ... In short, in a month and a half or even less, they would be united by the bonds of holy matrimony.

"And I'll be free of an encumbrance," said the major.

"Oh, really!" cried Rubião.

Dona Tonica laughed; she was used to her father's jokes and, besides, she was so happy that nothing could vex her; she didn't even mind when her father referred to her being over forty, when most brides are fifteen.

"He'll come looking for you later when he starts to miss you," Rubião said to Dona Tonica.

"What do you mean?" said the major. "Why, I might get married too!"

Rubião suddenly sprang to his feet and took a few steps around the room; the major could not see the expression on his face, and didn't realize that Rubião's mind was possibly about to go off the rails, and that Rubião himself could sense this. He told Rubião to sit down and talked to him about his marriage and his campaigns. By the time the major had reached the Battle of Caseros—full of the marches and countermarches he always indulged in when telling a story—the person before him had become Napoleon III. At first Rubião remained silent, but then he uttered a few words of praise, cited the Battles of Solferino and Magenta, and promised Major Siqueira a medal. Father and daughter exchanged glances, and the major commented that heavy rain was forecast. The sky had indeed darkened a little. It would be best if Rubião left before the rain started; he hadn't brought an umbrella with him, and the only one he had in the house was very old ...

"My carriage will come for me," said Rubião serenely.

"No, it's waiting for you in Campo da Aclamação. Can't you see it from the window, Tonica?"

Dona Tonica made a vague, reluctant gesture. She didn't want to lie, but then again, she felt afraid and wanted Rubião to leave. It was impossible to see the square from their house. Then the major took Rubião's arm and led him to the door.

"Come back tomorrow or the day after, whenever you want."

"But why can't I wait here for my carriage?" asked Rubião. "The Empress mustn't get wet . . ."

"The Empress has already left."

"Well, she shouldn't have. That was very naughty of her. General . . . because why should you be forever a major? General, I saw the portrait of your son-in-law, and I would like to give you a portrait of myself. Ask the Tuileries Palace to send you one. Where is my carriage?"

"It's in the square, waiting."

"Well, send someone for it."

Dona Tonica, who was standing at the window, said to her father:

"Rodrigues is coming."

And she again looked back down the street, leaning out and smiling, while, in the living room, her father continued, gently but firmly, to steer Rubião toward the door. Rubião stopped and said reprovingly:

"General, I am your Emperor!"

"Of course, but, please, come this way, Your Majesty . . ."

They had reached the door, and the major was opening the gate just as Rodrigues was about to come up the steps. Dona Tonica came out to greet her fiancé, but the way was blocked by her father and Rubião. Rodrigues doffed his hat, revealing his coarse, grizzled hair; he had a few freckles on his sunken cheeks, but his smile was kind and humble—rather more humble than kind—and despite the banality of his face and person, he was very pleasant. He no longer had the look of alarm he wore in the photo, which had come about because of his excessive concern that every part of his person should be absolutely perfect so that he would be seen at his very best.

"This gentleman is my future son-in-law," said the major. "Did you just see a carriage and a squadron of cavalry in the square?" he asked Rodrigues with a wink.

"Yes, I believe I did, sir."

"You see?" said Siqueira, turning to Rubião. "Off you go, turn left down Rua de São Lourenço and Campo da Aclamação is straight ahead of you. Goodbye now, see you tomorrow."

Rubião went down three of the five steps and stopped in front of the new arrival, fixing him with his gaze for a few moments before declaring that he was delighted to meet him and urging him to be a good husband and a good son-in-law. What, he asked, was his name?

"João José Rodrigues."

"Rodrigues. I will have a nice little ribbon sent for you to put in your buttonhole. A wedding present. Remind me to do that, Siqueira."

Siqueira again took his arm and propelled him down the last two steps and into the street.

"Campo da Aclamação, you say?"

"Precisely."

"Goodbye."

From the street, Rubião kept looking up at the windows, doffing his hat to Dona Tonica, but Dona Tonica was in the living room, which Rodrigues had just entered, as fresh and lovely as the first rose of summer.

Chapter CLXXXII

RUBIÃO FORGOT ALL about the carriage and the cavalry. He ended up some distance away, having wandered down various streets only to find himself now climbing Rua de São José. Since passing the imperial palace, he had been gesticulating and talking to a person with whom he imagined himself to be strolling along, arm in arm: the Empress. Was she Eugénie or Sofia? Two women in one—or, rather, the second bearing the name of the first. Passersby stopped; people ran out of shops to see. Some laughed, others remained indifferent; some, when they saw who it was, averted their gaze to spare their eyes the painful spectacle of his madness. A gaggle of black children accompanied Rubião, some following so close they could hear what he was saying. Then more kids began to join them, and when they saw the general curiosity aroused by this spectacle, they decided to give a voice to the mob and called out in jeering tones:

"Loony! Loony!"

Their shouts attracted the attention of others, many first-story windows began to open, curious onlookers of both sexes and all ages began to appear, a photographer, an upholsterer, three or four people crammed together in a window, forming a pile of heads, craning their necks to see the man who was now grandly and graciously addressing the wall.

"Loony! Loony!" bawled the young scallywags.

One of them, by far the youngest, tagged along by grabbing hold of the trousers of one of the older boys. Rubião had now reached Rua da Ajuda. He was still unaware of the shouts, but when he did hear them, he assumed they were cries of acclamation, and bowed gratefully. The jeering grew louder. In the midst of the hubbub could be heard the voice of a woman standing at the door of a mattress-maker's shop:

"Deolindo, come home! Deolindo!"

Deolindo, the child clinging to the trousers of the older boy, ignored her; he may not even have heard her above the clamor, and he was having such fun, piping away in his childish tones:

"Loony! Loony!"

"Deolindo!"

Deolindo tried to hide away among the other children, so that his mother wouldn't see him; but she did, and she ran over and dragged him home. He really was far too young to be caught up in a rabble like that.

"Mama, I want to go see . . ."

"You're not going to see anything. Home with you!"

She ushered him into the house and remained standing at the door, watching the street. Rubião had come to a halt, and she could see and hear him clearly, his gestures and his words, as, proudly erect, he doffed his hat to all and sundry.

"Madmen can be so funny sometimes," she said to her neighbor, smiling.

The boys continued to shout and laugh, and Rubião continued on his way, followed by the same jeering chorus. Deolindo, standing at the shop door now and seeing the band moving off, pleaded tearfully with his mother to let him follow or for her to take him. Once he had lost all hope of this, though, he put every ounce of energy into uttering a single high-pitched little cry:

"Loony!"

≡ *Chapter CLXXXIII*

THE NEIGHBOR LAUGHED. The mother laughed too. She declared that her son was a very naughty boy, a little devil, who never sat still; she couldn't take her eyes off him for a minute. Give him the slightest chance and he'd be out in the street. He'd been like that since he was little; indeed, when he was two, he'd only just escaped being run down by a carriage, right there in the street; he'd come within an inch of being killed. If it hadn't been for a man who happened to be passing, a well-dressed gentleman, who risked his own life to rescue him, her Deolindo would be dead as a doornail. At this point, her husband, who was walking along on the opposite side of the street, crossed over and interrupted their conversation. Frowning deeply, he scarcely greeted the neighbor and went straight into the house. His wife followed. What was the matter? Her husband told her about the jeering crowd.

"Yes, they passed by here too," she said.

"Didn't you recognize the man?"

"No."

The husband folded his arms and looked at her hard, saying nothing. The woman asked who the man was.

"He's the man who saved Deolindo's life."

The woman shuddered.

"Are you sure?"

"Absolutely. I've seen him on other occasions since, but, poor man, how he's changed. And all those kids were yelling at him. Where are the police when you need them?"

What pained the woman wasn't so much the man's madness, or the jeering crowd, it was the part her son had played in it, the very child the man had saved from death. Although, of course, how could he possibly recognize him or know that he owed him his life? Yes, that encounter, that coincidence, really pained her. In the end, she blamed herself for everything. If she had kept a closer eye on him, the boy would never have gone out into the street or joined that mocking rabble. A shiver ran through her now and again, and she could not sit still. Her husband planted two kisses on his son's head.

"Did you see the whole thing?" he asked his wife.

"I did."

"I was tempted to take the man by the arm and bring him back here, but I was too embarrassed. Those lads might have turned on me. I looked away, afraid he might recognize me. Poor man. But you know, he didn't seem to hear any of it, and was perfectly happy, I think he was even laughing . . . There's nothing sadder than losing your mind!"

The woman was thinking about her own son's part in it, but she said nothing about this to her husband and asked her neighbor to say nothing either. It took her a long time to fall asleep that night. The idea had lodged inside her head that, years later, her son would also go mad and be the object of similar jeers and mockery, and that she would then spit angrily up at the heavens and blaspheme against them.

Chapter CLXXXIV

TWO HOURS AFTER that scene in Rua da Ajuda, Rubião arrived at Dona Fernanda's house. Little by little the horde of kids dispersed and no more came to fill the gaps; the last remaining three joined forces to give a single, terrifying howl. Rubião continued on alone, barely noticed now by the inhabitants, because he was gesticulating less wildly or conspicuously. He was no longer talking to the wall, to the imaginary Empress, but he was still the Emperor. He walked along, occasionally pausing and muttering to himself, not waving his arms about, but still dreaming, dreaming, dreaming, wrapped in that veil through which everything appears quite different, the very opposite of what it was and better; every streetlamp had the look of a valet, every corner resembled a footman. Rubião was heading straight for the throne room to receive some ambassador or other, but the palace was vast and he had to walk through endless rooms and galleries, albeit on carpeted floors, and past tall, strong halberdiers.

Of the people who saw him and stopped in the street or leaned out of windows to look, many momentarily suspended their own sad or tedious thoughts, their day-to-day anxieties, concerns, resentments, a debt perhaps, an illness, a case of unrequited love, a betrayal by a friend. All sadnesses were forgotten, which was better than merely resigning oneself to them, but they were forgotten only for a moment. Once the sick man had passed, reality closed in on them again; the streets were streets, because the sumptuous palaces departed along with Rubião. And more than one person pitied the poor wretch; comparing their two fates, more than one thanked heaven for his own travails, however harsh, for at least he had not lost his mind. They preferred their real hovel to any imaginary palace.

≡ *Chapter CLXXXV*

RUBIÃO WAS COMMITTED to a sanatorium. Palha had forgotten the obligation placed on him by Sofia, and Sofia had no memory now of the promise she had made to Dona Fernanda. They were both busy with plans for another house, a mansion in Botafogo, the rebuilding of which was nearly complete, and which they hoped to move into during the winter, when the Chamber was sitting and everyone had returned from the summer spent in Petrópolis. Now, however, the promise was kept: Rubião entered the sanatorium, where he was given special living quarters, on the recommendation of both Dr. Falcão and Palha. He put up no resistance; he happily followed them and walked into his new rooms as if he knew them of old. When Dr. Falcão and Palha left him, saying they would be back, Rubião invited them to attend a military parade on Saturday.

"Saturday will be fine," said Falcão.

"Yes, Saturday's a good day," added Rubião. "Be sure to be there, Duke of Palha."

"I will," said Palha, taking his leave.

"Look, I'll send you one of my carriages—brand-new, it is. I wouldn't want your wife to have to place her lovely body where anyone else had dared to sit. Upholstered in damask and velvet, silver harness and golden wheels; the horses are descended from the very horse that my uncle rode at the Battle of Marengo. Farewell, Duke of Palha."

≡ *Chapter CLXXXVI*

"IT'S CRYSTAL-CLEAR TO ME," Dr. Falcão was thinking as he left, "the man was the lover of that other man's wife."

≡ *Chapter CLXXXVII*

AND THERE OUR man stayed. Quincas Borba had tried to jump into the carriage that carried off his friend and he even ran alongside, trying to keep up; it took all the servant's strength to grab hold of him, restrain him, and lock him up in the house. This was exactly what had happened in Barbacena, but life, my dear reader, is made up of only four or five situations, which circumstances vary and multiply before our eyes. Rubião immediately asked them to send him his dog. Having asked the doctor's permission, Dona Fernanda took on the task of granting the patient's wish. She was about to write to Sofia, but instead went to see her in Flamengo.

Chapter CLXXXVIII

"I'LL SEND SOMEONE to fetch the dog, it's quite near," Sofia said.

"We can go ourselves, if you don't mind, that is. I had a thought. Is it worth continuing to pay rent for the house when it may take some time for the cure to work? It might be best to let it go, sell the furnishings, and get rid of whatever else is left."

They walked from Flamengo to Rua do Príncipe, which took three or four minutes. Raimundo the servant was out in the street, but on seeing people at the door, he ran to open it. The interior of the house had a neglected air about it, with none of the fixity and regularity of objects which seem to preserve some vestige of an interrupted life; yes, abandoned and neglected. On the other hand, the higgledy-piggledy nature of the furniture in the living room was a fair reflection of the tenant's madness, of his confused and distorted ideas.

"Was he very rich?" asked Dona Fernanda.

"He was fairly wealthy when he first arrived from Minas," said Sofia, "but it seems he squandered it all. You'd better lift the hem of your skirt, because it looks as if the floor hasn't been swept in ages."

It wasn't just the floor; everything had a veneer of neglect. Not that the servant offered any explanation; he watched and listened and, very softly, whistled a popular polka. Sofia didn't question him about the lack of cleanliness; she couldn't wait to escape from "that filth," as she described it to herself, and wanted merely to find out about the dog, who was the main reason for their visit, although, then again, she didn't want to show too much interest in him or indeed in anything else. The tawdriness was repellent to both her mind and heart; and the thought of the poor madman did nothing to quell her feelings of impatience. Her friend Dona Fernanda was, in her opinion, being ridiculously romantic or affected. "What nonsense!" she was thinking, while smiling the same approving smile with which she greeted all of Dona Fernanda's comments.

"Open that window," Dona Fernanda said to the servant, "everything smells so musty."

"Awful!" said Sofia, giving a snort of disgust.

Despite this, though, Dona Fernanda still did not leave. That miserable room had no memories for her, and yet she felt in the grip of a strangely profound emotion, which was not, however, provoked by the sight of all those ruined objects. The abandoned room did not prompt any general philosophical thoughts, or teach her about the fragility of the times or the sadness of the world, it spoke to her only of the sufferings of a man, a man she barely knew and to whom she had only spoken on a few occasions. And she stood there looking, without thinking or drawing any conclusions, absorbed in herself, gloomy and silent. Sofia didn't dare say a word, fearful of offending such a distinguished lady. They had both hitched up their skirts to avoid the dusty floor, but Sofia was also frantically, continuously, impatiently fluttering her fan, as if she were suffocating. She even coughed a few times.

"And what about the dog?" Dona Fernanda asked the servant.

"He's locked in the bedroom."

"Go and fetch him."

Quincas Borba appeared. Thin and glum, he stood in the doorway, wondering what those two ladies were doing there, but he didn't bark; he barely looked at them with his dull eyes. He was about to turn around and head off into the house, when Dona Fernanda clicked her fingers, and then he stopped and wagged his tail.

"What's his name?" asked Dona Fernanda.

"Quincas Borba," said the servant, adding with a sneer, "He has a human name. Hey, Quincas Borba, go and see the lady, she's calling you."

"Quincas Borba, come here! Quincas Borba!" called Dona Fernanda.

Quincas Borba did respond to her call, although he did so reluctantly and despondently. Dona Fernanda bent down and asked the dog where his friend was; was he far away? Did he want to go and see him? Still bending down, she asked the servant how the dog had been.

"He's eating again now. When my master left, he didn't want to eat or drink, I thought he was done for."

"Does he eat well?"

"No, not really."

"Does he go looking for his master?"

"Yes, it seems like it," said Raimundo, covering a smirk with his hand. "But I locked him in the bedroom so he wouldn't run away. He doesn't whine anymore. At first he whined a lot, loud enough to wake me up . . . I had to bang on the door with a stick and shout at him to get him to settle down . . ."

Dona Fernanda was scratching the dog's head. This was the first time he had been stroked after many long days of being alone and ignored. When Dona Fernanda stopped stroking him and stood up, he sat looking at her and she at him, so long and so deeply that they seemed to penetrate into each other's very soul. Universal sympathy, which was the essence of Dona Fernanda's soul, set aside all human considerations in the face of that obscure, prosaic misery, and she reached out to the dog with a part of herself, which wrapped around him, fascinating him and binding him to her. Thus, she felt the same pity for the dog as she had felt for his mad master, as if both were representatives of the same species. And, sensing that her presence brought the dog some comfort, she didn't want to deprive him of that feeling.

"You'll get covered in fleas," said Sofia.

Dona Fernanda didn't hear this remark. She was still gazing into the dog's sad, tender eyes, until, finally, he looked down and started sniffing around the room. He had smelled the scent of his master. The street door was open, and he would have escaped had Raimundo not raced after him. Dona Fernanda gave the servant some money so that he could give the dog a bath and take him to the sanatorium, recommending that he be very careful and either carry him there or put him on a leash. At this point, Sofia intervened, telling him to call at her house first.

Chapter CLXXXIX

THEY LEFT. Before stepping out into the street, Sofia looked right and left in case anyone should see her; fortunately, the street was deserted. Once she was free of that pigsty, she regained the ability to speak kindly, the sweet, delicate art of charming others, and she fondly linked arms with Dona Fernanda. She spoke to her about Rubião and what a great misfortune madness was; she also told her about their new mansion in Botafogo. Why not come with her to see the progress being made? They could have something to eat and would then leave at once.

Chapter CXC

SOMETHING HAPPENED TO distract Dona Fernanda from her concerns about Rubião: the birth of Maria Benedita's daughter. She rushed to Tijuca, showered kisses on mother and child, and offered Carlos Maria her hand to kiss.

"As exuberant as ever, I see!" cried the young father.

"And you as dour as ever!" she retorted.

Despite her cousin's protests, Dona Fernanda stayed with Maria Benedita during her convalescence, and she was so friendly, so kind, so cheerful, that it was a delight to have her in the house. The happiness there made her forget the unhappiness elsewhere; however, as soon as the new mother had recovered, Dona Fernanda went to see Rubião.

Chapter CXCI

"I HOPE TO restore him to reason within six to eight months. He's doing very well."

Dona Fernanda sent Sofia this response from the director of the sanatorium and invited her to go and visit the patient, if she didn't think it would be improper to do so. "Why would it be improper?" Sofia replied in a note. "The fact is, though, I can't face visiting him; he was such a good friend of ours, and I'm not sure I could bear to see and talk to the poor man. I showed your letter to Cristiano, who told me he had sold off all Senhor Rubião's property and it came to three *contos* two hundred."

Chapter CXCII

"SIX TO EIGHT MONTHS will pass quickly enough," thought Dona Fernanda.

And along they came, carrying various events on their back—the collapse of the government, the rise of another in March, the return of her husband, the debate over the Law of the Free Womb,* the death of Dona Tonica's fiancé, just three days before they were to marry. Dona Tonica squeezed out her last few tears, some of which were for her lost love, while others were out of despair; her eyes afterward were so red that they looked as if she had some sort of infection.

Teófilo—in whom the new cabinet had as much confidence as the previous—was a major figure in the parliamentary debates. Camacho declared in his newspaper that the Law of the Free Womb absolved the government of its impotence and most of its crimes. In October, Sofia began her salons in Botafogo with an inaugural ball, which was the most talked-about of the season. She looked dazzling. She quite nonchalantly showed off every inch of her arms and shoulders, and she wore some truly splendid jewelry, including the necklace Rubião had given her, for, as everyone knows, such

---

* The Law of the Free Womb, passed in 1871, granted freedom to all children born to slaves after that date.

elaborate pieces never go out of fashion. Everyone admired the elegance of this fresh, robust thirty-year-old; and some men spoke (with regret) of her conjugal virtue and how she clearly adored her husband.

Chapter CXCIII

THE DAY AFTER the ball, Dona Fernanda woke up late. She went straight to her husband's study, where he had already devoured five or six newspapers, written ten letters, and reorganized one of the bookshelves.

"I've just received this letter," he said.

Dona Fernanda read it; it came from the director of the sanatorium, saying that Rubião had disappeared three days earlier, and despite all their efforts and those of the police, they had been unable to find him. "His escape seems to me all the more astonishing," the letter concluded, "because he had made tremendous progress, and I believe that, in two months, he could be completely well again."

Dona Fernanda was deeply upset by this news, and persuaded her husband to write to the chief of police and the minister of justice, asking them to order the most thorough of searches. Teófilo had not the slightest interest in either finding or curing Rubião, but, knowing his wife's kind nature, he wanted to be of use to her, and, as it happened, he enjoyed corresponding with men high up in the administration.

Chapter CXCIV

HOW COULD THEY possibly find our friend Rubião or the dog when both had left for Barbacena? A week earlier, Rubião had asked Palha to come and see him, and when the latter duly came, he found him to be thinking rationally and showing not a trace of his former madness.

"I suffered a nervous breakdown," Rubião said, "but now I'm fine, absolutely fine. Could you please have me released from here? I don't think the director will object. Meanwhile, I would like to give a few gifts to the people who have helped me and Quincas Borba, and I wonder if you could see your way to lending me a hundred *mil-réis*."

Palha immediately opened his wallet and gave him the money.

"I'll try and have you released," he said, "but it will probably take a few days"—this was just before the ball—"but don't worry. In a week you'll be out and about again."

Before leaving, Palha consulted the director, who gave him a very positive report on the patient's progress. A week isn't much time, he said. To restore him to perfect health, I need another two months. Palha said that he had found Rubião to be totally rational, but bowed to the director's greater knowledge, and if it took another six or seven months, then it would be best not to rush things.

Chapter CXCV

AS SOON AS Rubião arrived in Barbacena and started walking up the street now known as Rua Tiradentes, he stopped and cried out: "To the winner, the potatoes!"

He had completely forgotten about the potatoes, both the formula and the allegory. Suddenly, as if those words had remained there intact, hanging in the air, waiting for someone to understand them and put them together, he rediscovered the formula and spoke it out loud as emphatically as he had on the day when he had embraced it as a law of life and of truth. He could not remember the whole allegory, but the formula gave him a vague sense of struggle and of victory.

He continued up the street, accompanied by his dog, until he reached the church. No one opened the door, and there was no sacristan to be seen. Quincas Borba, who had not eaten for many hours, stood pressed up against his legs, head bowed, waiting. Rubião turned around and, from the top of the street, looked down and into the distance. It was his hometown, it was Barbacena; the place where he had been born began to detach itself from the deep layers of his memory. There it was; here was the church, there the prison, over there the pharmacy where he used to buy medicine for that other Quincas Borba. He had known it was Barbacena when he arrived, but as his gaze spread wider, memories followed, whole swarms of them. He could see no one, although in a window to his left someone did seem to be peering out at him. Otherwise, the place was deserted.

"Perhaps they don't know I've arrived," thought Rubião.

Chapter CXCVI

THERE WAS A FLASH of lightning; the clouds were rapidly piling ever higher. Another blinding flash and a roll of thunder. It began to drizzle, then to rain more heavily, until the storm finally broke. Rubião had left the church as the first drops began to fall, walking back down the street, followed by his famished, faithful dog, both of them disoriented and lost in the downpour, with no hope of finding shelter or food... The rain beat down on them mercilessly. They couldn't run because Rubião was afraid he might slip and fall, and the dog was afraid he might lose him. Halfway down the street, Rubião remembered the pharmacy and turned back, walking into the wind that hit him full in the face; after a few steps, though, the idea vanished from his head; farewell, pharmacy; farewell, shelter! He could no longer remember why he had decided to turn back and so continued on down, the dog following, uncomprehending, unflinching, both of them drenched and confused, the thunderclaps becoming ever louder and more frequent.

Chapter CXCVII

THEY WANDERED AIMLESSLY. Rubião's stomach interrogated, exclaimed, hinted; fortunately, though, his madness deceived his hunger with banquets at the Tuileries Palace Quincas Borba had no such recourse, and so up and down the streets they went. Now and then Rubião would sit on the sidewalk, and the dog would climb onto his lap to sleep away his hunger; finding his master's trousers completely sodden, he would get down again, only to climb back up; the night air was so cold, for it was late at night, dead of night. Rubião stroked him and murmured a few feeble words of comfort.

If, despite everything, Quincas Borba did manage to sleep, it was not for long, because Rubião would then stand up and again start trudging up and down the steep streets. A sad wind was blowing, sharp as a knife, making the two vagabonds shiver. Rubião was walking slowly now, his weariness no longer allowing him to stride out as he had at first when the rain was pelting down. Their stops became more frequent. The dog, starving and exhausted, could not understand this odyssey, could not comprehend the motive, he had forgotten where he was and could hear nothing apart from his master's faint murmurings. He couldn't see the stars, which, free of clouds now, were once more shining brightly. Rubião saw them, though; he had again reached the door of the church; he sat down, and that was when he noticed the stars. They were so lovely, and yet, thinking they were chandeliers in a grand salon, he ordered them to be doused. He never found out if his orders had been obeyed, because he fell asleep right there, with the dog by his side. When they woke in the morning, they were lying so close it was as if they were glued together.

=== Chapter CXCVIII

"TO THE WINNER, the potatoes!" cried Rubião when he opened his eyes onto the nightless, rainless street, now kissed by the sun.

=== Chapter CXCIX

RUBIÃO'S FRIEND ANGÉLICA saw them walking past her house and took them in. Rubião recognized her and accepted both shelter and food.

"What's happened to you, my dear? How did you end up in this terrible state? Your clothes are drenched. I'll give you a pair of my nephew's trousers."

Rubião was feverish. He had no appetite and ate little. His old friend asked him about his life in Rio, to which he replied that it would take far too long to recount, and that only posterity would have the final word. Only your nephew's nephews, he concluded grandly, will see me in all my glory. He did, however, launch into a summary. After ten minutes, Angélica could understand nothing, so bewildering were the facts and ideas he came out with; after another five minutes, she began to feel afraid. When he had been talking for twenty minutes, she made her excuses and went out to spread the news. Other people arrived, in twos and threes and fours, and before an hour had elapsed, many were peering in through the front door.

"To the winner, the potatoes!" Rubião bawled at those curious onlookers. "Here, I am the emperor! To the winner, the potatoes!"

These obscure, enigmatic words were repeated and mulled over in the street, but no one could make any sense of them. Some of his old rivals barged in unceremoniously to enjoy the spectacle all the more; and they told Angélica that she really shouldn't keep a madman in her house, it was dangerous; she should send him to the prison, until the authorities dispatched him elsewhere. A more sympathetic person asked if they should call a doctor.

"Whatever for?" said one of his enemies. "The man's mad."

"It might be delirium brought on by the fever. Feel how hot he is."

Urged on by the others, Angélica took his pulse and declared that he definitely had a fever. She called for the doctor—the same one who had treated the late Quincas Borba. Rubião recognized him and said there was nothing wrong with him. He had captured the King of Prussia, but had not yet decided whether or not to have him shot; he would, though, demand an enormous ransom—five billion francs.

"To the winner, the potatoes!"

Chapter CC

HE DIED A FEW days later... He died neither a subject nor vanquished. Before his death, before the agony began, he placed a crown on his head—at least it wasn't an old hat or a basin, an illusion that the onlookers could actually touch. No, he picked up nothing, raised up nothing, and placed nothing on his head; only he could see the imperial insignia, heavy with gold, glittering with diamonds and other precious stones. The effort it took for him to sit up did not last long; his body fell back again; his face, though, wore a glorious expression.

"Keep my crown," he murmured. "To the winner..."

His face then became serious, because death is serious; two minutes of agony, a hideous grimace, and his abdication letter was signed.

Chapter CCI

I WOULD LIKE TO describe here the death of Quincas Borba, who also fell ill and whined interminably, before, quite mad with grief, running away in search of his master, only to be found three days later dead in the street. However, seeing me devote a separate chapter to the death of the dog, you might well ask if it is he or his defunct homonym who gives this book its title, and why one rather than the other—a question pregnant with still more questions that would lead us far and beyond... Enough! If you have tears, then weep for the two most recent dead. If you have only laughter, then laugh! It comes to the same thing. The Southern Cross on which the lovely Sofia refused to gaze, as Rubião asked her to, is high enough above us to notice neither the laughter nor the tears of we humans.

Biographical Note

MUCH HAS BEEN MADE of Joaquim Maria Machado de Assis's humble beginnings, and yet he, apparently, thought his own life to be of little interest and insisted that what counted was his work. Of course, in general terms, he's right, but, given his evolution from poorly educated child of impoverished parents to Brazil's greatest writer and a pillar of the establishment, a brief biographical note would not seem out of place. His paternal grandparents were mulattoes and freed slaves. His father, also a mulatto, was a painter and decorator; his mother was a washerwoman, a white Portuguese immigrant from the Azores. Both parents could read and write, which was not common among working-class people at the time.

Machado was born in 1839 and brought up for the first ten years of his life on the remnants of an old country estate perched on one of Rio's many hills, and which was owned by the widow of a senator, Maria José de Mendonça Barroso Pereira who became his godmother. He also had a sister, who passed away at four years old.

Although he did go to school, Machado was far from being a

star pupil. It seems, however, that he helped during mass at the estate's chapel, and was befriended by the priest, Father Silveira Sarmento, who may also have taught him Latin.

When he was ten years old, Machado's mother died of tuberculosis. He then moved with his father to another part of Rio, and his father remarried. Some biographers say that his stepmother, Maria Inês da Silva, looked after him, and that Machado attended classes in the girls' school where she worked as a cook. Some say that he learned French in the evenings from a French immigrant baker. Others describe Machado as showing a precocious interest in books and languages. What is certain is that he published his first sonnet in 1854, when he was fifteen, in the *Periódico dos Pobres* (the *Newspaper of the Poor*). A year later, he became a regular visitor to a rather eccentric bookshop in central Rio owned by journalist and typographer Francisco de Paula Brito, which was a popular meeting place, especially for artists and writers.

At seventeen, Machado was taken on as an apprentice typographer and proofreader at the Imprensa Nacional, where the writer Manuel Antônio de Almeida encouraged him to pursue a career in literature. Only two years later, in 1858, the poet Francisco Otaviano invited him to work as writer and editor on the *Correio Mercantil*, an important newspaper of its day. Around this time, Machado also became closely involved in Rio's theater world, writing two operas and several plays, none of which, however, met with great success.

By the time he was twenty-one, Machado was already a well-known figure in intellectual circles. He worked as a journalist on other newspapers and founded a literary circle called Arcádia Fluminense. Machado read voraciously in numerous languages—it is said that, in addition to keeping up with modern literature, he set himself the lifetime goal of reading all of the universal classics in their original language, including ancient Greek. He built up an extensive library, which he bequeathed to the Brazilian Academy of Letters (of which he was cofounder and first president). Between the ages of fifteen and thirty, he wrote prolifically: poetry, plays, librettos, short stories, and newspaper columns, as well as translations from French and Spanish, and a translation of all or most of Dickens's *Oliver Twist*. It would appear that his reported ill health, notably the epilepsy described by several of his biographers, did not in any way hold him back.

In 1867 Machado was decorated by the Emperor with the Order of the Rose, and was subsequently appointed to a position in the Ministry of Agriculture, Commerce and Public Works. He went on to become head of section, serving in that same ministry for over thirty years, until just three months before his death.

The job, although demanding, left him ample time to write, and write he did: nine novels—of which the three most celebrated are *Posthumous Memoirs of Brás Cubas* (1881), *Quincas Borba* (1891), and *Dom Casmurro* (1899)—nine plays, over two hundred stories, five collections of poems, and more than six hundred *crônicas*, or newspaper columns. He also found time to marry, his wife proving crucial both to his happiness and to the expansion of his literary knowledge. Carolina Augusta Xavier de Novais, the sister of a close friend, was five years older than Machado; they fell in love almost instantly and were soon married, in 1868, despite her family disapproving of her marrying a mulatto. Carolina was extremely well educated and introduced him to the work of many English-language writers. They did not have children but remained happily married for thirty-five years.

When Carolina died in 1904, at the age of seventy, Machado fell into a deep depression. He wrote only one novel, *Memorial de Aires*, after her death, and died in 1908. A period of official mourning was declared, and he was given a state funeral. Yet his occupation on his death certificate was given as "Civil servant," and when his final work, *Memorial de Aires*, was published later that year, it went almost unnoticed. Since then, of course, Machado has come to be seen as Brazil's greatest and most original writer, and his novels, in particular, have brought him worldwide fame.

About the Translators

Margaret Jull Costa has worked as a translator for over thirty years, translating the works of many Spanish and Portuguese writers, among them novelists Javier Marías, José Saramago, and Eça de Queirós, and poets Fernando Pessoa, Sophia de Mello Breyner Andresen, Mário de Sá-Carneiro, and Ana Luísa Amaral.

Robin Patterson has translated novels by José Luandino Vieira and José Luís Peixoto. With Margaret Jull Costa he has co-translated works by Machado de Assis, Sophia de Mello Breyner Andresen, Clarice Lispector, and Lúcio Cardoso.

More from Machado de Assis
translated by Margaret Jull Costa and Robin Patterson

"Perhaps the most hopeful book to appear in 2018. . . . [A] gorgeously designed story omnibus from the eternal optimists at Liveright Publishing. [These] stories move among a bewildering range of traditions." —Sam Sacks, *Wall Street Journal*

A *New York Times*, *Times* Critics' Top Book of the Year

A masterpiece of realism, *Dom Casmurro* probes the mind of a distrustful husband with delusions of grandeur.

"Is it possible that the most modern, most startlingly avant-garde novel to appear this year was originally published in 1881?" —Parul Sehgal, *New York Times*

Liveright Publishing Corporation
A Division of W. W. Norton & Company
Independent Publishers Since 1923